A SYMPTOM *of* Love

A novel

EMMA AISEMAN

Author of *LET IT LOVE*

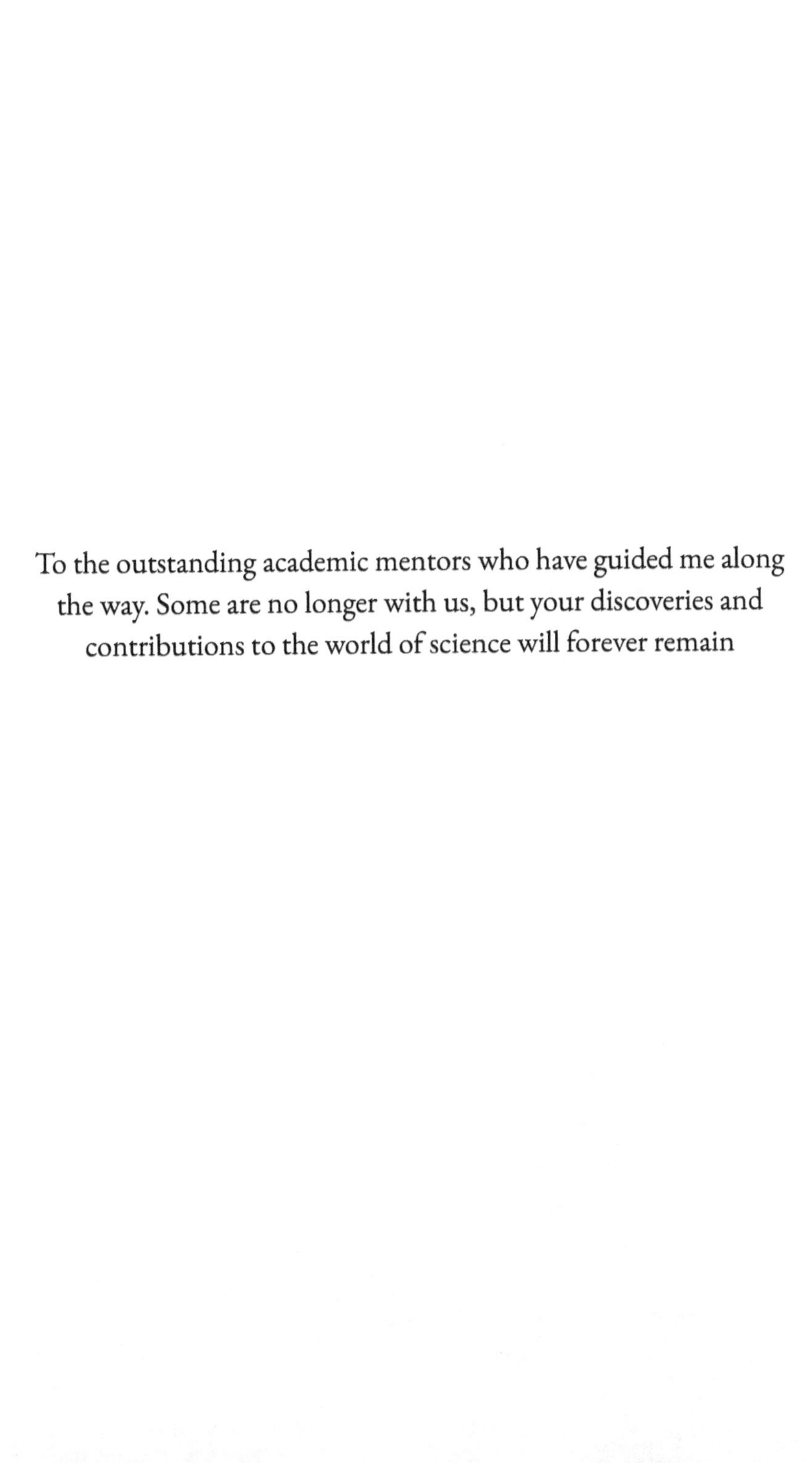

To the outstanding academic mentors who have guided me along the way. Some are no longer with us, but your discoveries and contributions to the world of science will forever remain

Contents

1
ELEANOR

Present Day

It's perfectly fitting that she finds herself in a guy's lap. A complete stranger. At an airport. Far away from home. Her bare thighs—because she just *had to* wear shorts—are resting perfectly on his jean-clad, unyielding—if she may add—quads.

Who wears shorts for a transatlantic flight in the middle of winter?

She does, apparently.

Last thing she remembers, she was sprinting to the one open seat next to the charging station. Her laptop was on its last breath before dying on her, and desperately needed charging. The terminal was already full of people blocking the hallways. But in a heroic attempt to save a battery, she decided to go for it. She recalls dismissing a *"Watch out!"* warning behind her, assuming it was someone speaking to their kid. Her way was wide open, relatively speaking, she was almost there... But her legs bumped into something. Perhaps the warning had been addressed to her after all?

Was that a suitcase? Who puts a goddamn suitcase in the middle of the path to the charging station?

Oh, and she does remember losing her balance, trying to grab on to something, anything to stop her from crashing to the floor, expecting it to hurt. Then, as if time slowed down, she had a chance to hope they'd have a reasonable first aid station nearby and that her laptop would survive the fall in one piece, as she hadn't backed up her work for... hmm... twenty-four hours. Because brilliant her had to disable the auto-save feature. Of course. Then the airport around her was spinning, or maybe *she* was spinning. Until everything came to a complete stop, quite abruptly. And it didn't feel all too bad. It felt kind of nice actually.

No pain? That's a first.

She was about to check if she was bleeding, broken, or dead when she realized she'd quite literally fallen into someone's lap.

To her defense, dropping violently onto an unsuspecting bystander who was waiting peacefully for his flight was nowhere near her intention; nor was landing with her hands on his wall-of-a-muscle-chest.

Yet... here she is. Still in his lap. Brainstorming how to fix this awkward situation. Not the fastest approach perhaps, but brainstorming is what she does, day in, day out. Albeit, usually with the company of some other scientists, not in her own vacuum, and absolutely not while indulging in thigh-to-thigh contact with a stranger. Maybe that's why it's not working very well for her this time.

Overthinking it? It's starting to feel that way.

She should just apologize. Yes, he would understand, it's a perfectly reasonable, common situation at airports... right?

"I'm sorry." Eleanor finally manages to assemble the words together and use her actual voice, trying not to turn her head to face the guy, because of the zero distance she's inflicted upon him. As awkward as it is already, it could definitely turn awkward-er if she turns her head now.

Yet, she can't resist.

And this indescribably handsome man is staring right back at her. Zero distance and all. And he smells heavenly too. At an airport. Where people like her get off a night flight and don't bother brushing their teeth. Well, had she predicted this situation in advance, she would have stopped somewhere between connecting flights and frantic terminal running, for a quick mouth rinse before storming into the terminal.

"Are you okay?" A deep voice rumbles through her. He can speak, too. Perfect English. Deep, beautiful blue eyes are looking at her, concerned.

She is surely delusional; it must be the fall. This is not real.

She shuts her eyes, letting his obviously unrealistic fresh-out-of-shower scent wash over her. She opens them again, taking a concerned peek in the direction where those blue eyes were staring at her before.

He's still there.

"Your nose is bleeding." That voice again. A tissue is delivered quickly to her nose. A hand brushes a strand of hair away from her face, setting it gently behind her ear. It feels nice.

What?

His fingers trace her forehead.

Checking for bruises?

She looks down to her legs and sees a slightly bruised knee, maybe a tiny cut. Wearing shorts on an international flight while completely ignoring her mom's warnings that airports and airplanes tend to be cold might not have been a smart decision. Eleanor did feel a little cold earlier, come to think of it—but she doesn't feel cold anymore, she actually feels warm and snug right now.

Maybe a bit too warm...

Her consciousness finally re-establishes connection with the world. "I'm okay." Eleanor's voice sounds rusty as she shakes herself from her reverie. "Sorry if I crushed you." She reluctantly untethers her body from his lap and situates herself in the seat beside him. The plastic feels cold and unwelcome on the back of her thighs, her body already protesting. She takes possession of the tissue held to her nose, her fingers grazing his and a light shiver trailing down her spine.

She must have a concussion. A severe one.

"You didn't crush me." He sounds somewhat amused.

Oh, thank God.

Judging by his thighs and arm muscles that she had just been so comfortably attached to, it would take much more than her full-falling body weight to crush him. He's not an easily crushable guy, it appears.

And thankfully not easily annoyed.

"Thank you." She realizes she hasn't expressed her gratitude yet. "For catching me."

"Careful next time." Concern is still laced on his handsome face. "Let me see your nose," he orders, and she dares look deeper into these eyes again. They're absolutely her favorite shade of blue. "I think the bleeding has stopped," he informs her, and she realizes she's left her right hand in his space bubble, still clutching his arm.

That's a hell of a concussion...

But she's made it to the charging station. The last free charging station at their gate, before her final destination.

"Are you sure you're okay?" The blue-eyed stranger asks again, this time with less concern but it does sound like he actually cares for some unknown reason.

"I think so," she responds, pulling her hand back to her side as nonchalantly as possible. An impossible move when her hand is shaking.

Cold? Hungry? Or worried about her laptop?

Yes, that must be it, her laptop!

The laptop that desperately needed charging. Which is why she was running to begin with. Did it survive the crash landing safely? She reaches for her backpack, which fell at the guy's feet, pulls out her precious laptop and opens it. It turns on... It's working! She quickly hooks it up to the charger.

"Thank goodness." Eleanor gives out a loud sigh of relief. The man who's just saved her life slowly shakes his head.

"What?" She gives him a side look. "My life's work is on this thing!"

He furrows an eyebrow at her, battling a smile. It's a gorgeous look on him.

Why is she even noticing all these details about a stranger in the airport whom she knows absolutely nothing about?!

Must be the concussion.

"Did I hit my head?" She tries for an ordinary, conversational tone.

"No," says the man beside her.

"No?" Double-checking is important, especially when the less-desired option is the one you get.

"No, you did not," he reassures her, shaking his head.

"Are you sure?"

"Pretty sure."

"Oh." She can't hide her disappointment. "It was a solid rationale." Like when a lab experiment doesn't yield the expected results and one realizes they forgot to add an essential reagent. Annoying, yes, but at least explainable, potentially salvageable and does not warrant the need to kill a perfectly good hypothesis.

Not the case now though—she's going to need to come up with another hypothesis to explain this strange collection of symptoms that her mush of a brain is experiencing. She's at a loss.

"Rationale for what?" he asks, confused.

Of course she had to say it out loud.

"Symptoms..." And better keep it at that.

"You did hit your nose with your hand when you were trying to gain your balance." Those blue eyes study her face, followed by a large, warm hand assessing the bridge of her nose. A pleasant buzz goes through her. "But it looks fine, nothing's broken."

"Yes, typical me." Must be the third time this week she's bumped into something.

Not into someone *though...*

He gives her a pointed look before he says, "And your knee. I should have a band-aid somewhere." Reaching out to his backpack, he retrieves one and gently applies it to the little cut on her knee.

Is it possible to get a concussion without hitting her head? It's the only reasonable explanation for what's happening to her right now. She should definitely Google it later.

2
GOODBYES

One Day Earlier

"Ellie, honey, are you coming? Everyone's here. Time to put this laptop down already!" her mom scolds gently in Hebrew.

"Just one last sentence, gotta finish this email," Eleanor shoots from behind her screen, not taking her eyes off it.

And some data crunching and she'll be done—maybe, possibly for the next hour or so.

> Dear Professors Harrington and Kowalski,
> I hope you are both well.
> I received the final visa approval and paperwork and will be arriving in the US on December 21st.
> I look forward to meeting you both.
> Happy holidays!
> *Eleanor Benjamin, PhD*

She types the message quickly and sends. Her laptop is resting in her lap, legs sprawled on her bed in her childhood room. At this time tomorrow, she'll be on a plane. The anticipation will most likely keep her awake all night. Her inbox pings; looks like an automatic email response from Professor Kowalski.

Dear sender, thank you for your email. I'm currently traveling to attend an international conference in Spain, returning December 21st. During this time, I'll have limited Internet access and my responses may be delayed. For urgent matters, please contact Dr. Yan Dimitrov.
Best,
Professor Andrew A. Kowalski, PhD
Genetic Disease Branch
Gene and Epigenetic Research Institute (GERI)

Followed by another ping. Wow, that was fast!

Dear Dr. Benjamin,
I'm pleased to hear it went smoothly the second time around. I do regret the initial confusion with your paperwork. Mrs. Jones sends her sincere apologies for mixing your last name with your first.
Please bear in mind that our offices will be closed from December 22nd until January 2nd. The labs will be open, but a badge is required for building entry. I am sure you are anxious to get started. Professor Kowalski is trying to find a work around so you can get started right away.
I look forward to meeting you soon.
Safe travels and happy holidays,

Professor Jim Harrington, MD, PhD
Head, Genetic Disease Branch
Gene and Epigenetic Research Institute (GERI)

And yet another ping shortly after, despite his previous automatic out of office response.

Dear Dr. Benjamin,
Glad that things are moving along.
I hope you'll find GERI a new home away from home.
Per Professor Harrington's request, I'll try to see if I can get you a visitor pass. In the meantime, please use this break for settling in and getting to know the area.
Happy holidays and I look forward to seeing you in the new year.
Professor Andrew A. Kowalski, PhD
Genetic Disease Branch
Gene and Epigenetic Research Institute (GERI)

So formal. Calling each other *'Professor.'* Eleanor hopes they will be open to moving to first-name basis once they meet in person. She's a little disappointed that she might not get to do too much until the new year, but it's just a bump in the road.

One more email. The tips of her fingers buzz in a pleasant, unfamiliar way as she types. She's excited by the realization that the plans she has been meticulously crafting for the past year are finally turning into her new reality.

Dear professors,

> Thank you for your kind welcome emails.
>
> A visitor pass would be great!
>
> In the meantime, while I patiently wait for the visitor pass or the new year, please see attached my updated research plan for my first year at GERI, with your suggestions incorporated.
>
> Thank you again for your insightful comments.
>
> *Eleanor Benjamin, PhD*

She hits *send*. There. She's done. Or not… stupid excitement.

"Sorry, forgot the attachment, here it is," she types quickly, making sure to attach the file this time. She's been writing and perfecting her research plan so much in the past several weeks she could probably recite it in her sleep. She sighs and resends.

"Eleanor!" Her mom's voice, more impatient now, brings her back to earth. She did promise to get out of the room sometime today. Moving back in with her parents at the advanced age of twenty-eight—albeit only for two weeks—has been challenging. She had to clear out her rental apartment and pack up her stuff in preparation to move across the world. She's glad she could stay with them for her last two weeks before going away, although they may have been less than excited—gently put—about her optimal times (1 a.m. to 4 a.m.) for performing data analyses or reading scientific papers. Or her typical working hours (noon to midnight) at the lab. Her parents are generally not too excited—again gently stated—about her work-life balance, or lack thereof. Saying she's not a morning person might be a gross understatement. And living alone for the past several years may have accentuated it.

Eleanor closes her laptop and jumps up to her feet. A quick glimpse in the mirror.

Gosh, she looks like a scientific mess… Which—unlike a regular mess—is a more established, hypothesis-driven kind of mess.

She runs a quick hand through her hair, fixes the hem of her shirt and changes her pajama shorts to actual jean shorts. There. Ready to tackle the day, or late afternoon, to be precise.

Has she been in her room for so long?

"There you are!" Her dad smiles warmly as she emerges and pulls her in for a side hug.

"Ellie, I can't believe you're going so far away." Her mom takes her other side for a parental cuddle collab. "Now go get yourself a plate." She nudges her toward the large island in the center of their kitchen, filled with amounts of food that could suffice for her entire postdoctoral period, times three. "You've been stuck in that room of yours for hours. You must be starving!"

Eleanor wonders how she'll feel not hearing Hebrew all around her anymore. Not being surrounded by family. Not being nudged to take a break. Or rest. Or eat. Or get a life.

"You have to try the chicken," her aunt Orly loads a pile on her plate before she has a chance to resist. "I tried a new recipe!"

"She doesn't like chicken." Her mother's see-all-know-all voice carries from the other side of the kitchen.

"Nonsense!" Orly laughs happily, unfazed. "Ellie loves my chicken."

"Eloosh!" She manages to hear before being grabbed from the back and swung in the air by her best friend in the world.

"Gillie!" she fake-scolds without turning her head, trying to balance the chicken on her plate. "Put me down, you big bear!"

"I'm going to miss you," he says, but eventually lets her feet touch the floor again.

"Here!" She hands her best friend the plate. "You have to try my aunt Orly's new chicken recipe." She's too excited to eat right now.

Gillie takes the plate willingly and disappears into the kitchen to make himself useful and load some more food on it.

Eleanor moves over to the backyard, sliding the glass doors open to join the rest of the gang that is busy chatting, chewing and generally enjoying the nice Tel Aviv weather outside. A warm, breezy evening in December is not unusual, although it is technically considered winter. She hopes the Washington D.C. winter will be as mild. She hasn't actually had a chance to check but—

"Ellie!" She's greeted with an attack of canonical voices and smiles. All heads turn toward her. Yes, they are all here for her. Her going-away party.

"I am going to miss you, kid!" Her grandpa huddles to the side of his bench to make room for her beside him. He looks at her proudly, eyes gleaming.

"I'm going to miss you too, Saba." She lets her head rest on his shoulder.

"Are you done packing?" Her grandma scurries to take her other side, sounding her usual concerned-self.

"Yes Savta," Eleanor reassures her fondly.

"But you're not eating?" Still concerned.

"I'm too excited to eat right now. I'll grab something later, don't worry."

"It's her job to worry," her grandpa says lovingly.

"Exactly," her grandma agrees, "and you need to eat something, grow some curves, if you want to be able to find a husband in America." Savta's a tease, but there's a serious tone to it too.

"I'm not going all the way to America to look for a husband, Savta," Eleanor tries to say while her brother ruffles her hair as he walks past them.

"Prince Charming may be waiting," he says mischievously.

"Har'el!" She laughs while pushing him away. Then, turning back to her grandmother, she adds, "I'm going to be focusing on my research. I don't have time for romantic fairytales." She tries to move her hair from her face after her brother's doing.

"Har'el may be right, you just never know. Prince Charming

may indeed be waiting for you there, so keep your eyes and your heart open. I know you have all these important sciencey thoughts in this smart head of yours, but don't forget to leave some room for love. I want to meet my great grandkids in this lifetime." Her grandma sends a fond smile above Eleanor's head, meeting her grandpa's eyes as he nods in agreement, reciprocating the smile. Her grandparents have been together since high school and are still deeply in love. That must be a one-in-a-million kind of love story. What are the odds? Basically impossible. Come to think of it, her own parents actually share a similar success story. Which, by all means, has to be statistically impossible. And even less likely to replicate yet again.

"Did you hear that Ha'rel?" Eleanor rolls over the responsibility to her eternal bachelor of a brother. "You better hurry up, Savta wants great grandkids soon."

"I'll consider it," Har'el says unconvincingly.

"Going to get a drink, can I bring you anything?" she asks her grandkids-hungry elders. Not a master at segueing but still a reasonable attempt.

"No, honey, thank you, go mingle with your guests," her grandmother commands, letting her off the hook.

Eleanor gets up to pour herself some grape juice, trying to wash away the topic. Romance talks give her skin rash. She doesn't even like romantic movies. Well not since Oren, her ex, that is. If given a choice, she'd probably prefer the frog over Prince Charming.

She joins Har'el, Gillie, and her cousins across the backyard. All seem to be interested in her upcoming journey. Eleanor is the first one in the family to leave their home country's embrace and move across the world for a postdoctoral fellowship. She's also the first one with a PhD. So many firsts. Exciting and terrifying.

"Gillie, can you tell my sister to stop making up words? Is *epigenetics* an actual word?" is Har'el's response to Eleanor bringing up her research plans.

"Epigenetics *is* an actual word." Gillie barks out a laugh. "People tend to overestimate what their DNA sequence can tell about them. But our DNA is only part of the story," he explains. "It tells you the *what,* but it doesn't tell you the *how.*"

"He's a revolutionist," Eleanor tries to lighten up the conversation.

"*She's* the revolutionist." Gillie smiles sheepishly, pointing at Eleanor, but nothing can stop his enthusiastic flow of words. "There are different factors, modifications, chemical markers, which can turn certain genes on or off, change the way they're expressed in our body."

"Like a switch? You can turn it on and off as you wish?" Har'el is actually taking an interest in the conversation.

"Not as you wish. Not yet, unfortunately. But yes, in many cases the body can use this mechanism to adjust based on needs and the changing environment. But there are also permanent changes or modifications that you can't reverse."

Eleanor rolls her eyes. "Don't get too attached to this theory, permanent modifications are an exception." Yes, Eleanor is a stickler for temporary changes. "Like relationships. Not everything in life is permanent."

"Your parents and grandparents might disagree here," Gillie reminds her.

"They're an exception too," Eleanor agrees. Because going by her last relationship, with Oren, these feelings don't really tend to last.

"Your genius sister," Gillie points to Eleanor, bringing them back to the science, "is studying diseases that are caused by these changes. The first thing that comes to mind is cancer—these mechanisms play a big role in cancer. But Eloosh here, is focused on rare autoimmune diseases. What makes someone's body suddenly attack its own cells or certain organs? Epigenetics may be an underlying cause."

"Look at you, Gillie, explaining chromatin modifications in normal people's terms!" Eleanor squeals.

"Still sounds like a made-up word to me. And by the way—it's *layman's terms,*" Har'el chuckles. "Now for your New Year's party plans, sis," he switches back in anticipation.

"No party plans," Eleanor snickers. "Can't wait to get into my new lab, though." She flashes a grin at the sight of her audience's disappointed, yet unsurprised, faces.

Har'el rolls his eyes, turning to Gillie. "Can epigenetics explain how this weird person is my sister?"

"Partially, yes."

"Enough science for one night. How is tomorrow looking?" Her cousin is thirsty for details.

"Flying over in the morning, have an overlay in Madrid, just a couple of hours, then USA!" Eleanor stands for a funny celebratory dance.

"Anyone picking you up from the airport?"

"Probably taxi, Lyft, Uber? Whatever they have there." Eleanor hasn't actually figured out these details yet. She'll do it as she goes.

"So no balloons and welcome signs at the airport?" Her cousin sounds disappointed.

"It's not like here," Gillie pitches in, "where the entire family waits at the welcome hall and jumps you after you pick up your luggage."

Yes, it could get sentimental, hectic, and quite vocal at Ben Gurion airport. Eleanor recalls returning home from her last trip to Greece. She had hardly been there for a week but had the full welcome-back reception. Her parents, grandparents from both sides, Har'el, Gillie and even Aunt Orly, were waiting for her at the airport welcome area with flowers, food, hugs. The greeting completely diminished the after-trip slump. It might seem embarrassing for an outsider, but it's part of tradition. It may suck for an introvert, but one can't really grow up to be an introvert in the Benjamin household.

When she wakes up the next morning, the house is full of people again. Chatting, laughing out loud, singing to the music playing in the background, cooking. A typical Friday morning at her parents' house, only it's not even a Friday.

Eleanor had planned to chart out her route from the airport to her new place in D.C. but got sidetracked by an unexpected data point, which might have sent her through a rabbit hole for a good chunk of the night. Priorities. She is exhausted, but she can make up for the lost sleep on the plane.

She rubs her eyes. This morning, uncharacteristically, she has no urge to go back for a short snooze—yes, from the way she's been abusing that snooze feature, the alarm on her phone may grow hands one day and swat her. Not today though. She is completely and utterly awake.

Today is THE day. Her mind is literally singing, despite her acquired dislike for music in the past few years. It's either the excitement or Gillie's silly song, the one he kept humming yesterday. It's still stuck in her head.

She jumps out of bed and into the shower. It's a hot, humid day, and by the time she's done dressing up she almost needs another shower. One of the downsides of living close to the beach. Although for the most part, the pros outweigh the thick soup-like humidity, especially the sound of the waves on her (not too early) morning runs, being able to go for a swim at any given moment, or just watching the sun disappear into the waves at sunset.

When was the last time she did any of those things? Uncertain. Guess the pros are not such a huge advantage in her specific case, all things considered.

She applies some sunscreen on her already too-freckled nose. Her hair looks like a frizzy beach mess, so she tucks it in a ponytail, away from her face, letting her unruly bangs hang on her forehead—she knows better than to fight that battle. She debates between leggings and jeans—both are too warm for today's weather—settling for jean shorts again, and a short-sleeve T-shirt.

"You'll be too cold on the plane," is her mom's first reaction when Eleanor enters the kitchen.

"I'll take a jacket," Eleanor dismisses reflexively, landing a small kiss on her mom's forehead. "It's just too hot right now, I'm melting."

"Don't say I didn't warn you," her mom grouches but hugs her warmly and hands her a plate already filled with eggs, chopped salad and cheese burekas. "Have some breakfast, today is a big day."

Eleanor munches on the flaky, salty burekas while still standing.

"Someone looks excited this morning!" Her aunt Orly appears behind her, smiling playfully. "Are you all packed?"

Eleanor nods enthusiastically and tries to shove one more piece of food into her mouth. But to her rumbling stomach's grave disappointment, she is way too nervous for food. And whether she does or doesn't eat won't change the loud rumbling anyway—it's a typical morning thing for her, gets quite embarrassing at morning lab meetings, even when she eats a full-blown breakfast. Hopefully it settles before she gets on the plane. The people sitting next to her don't need to be brought up to speed on her digestive system specs.

"Where's your backpack?" Her mom's always on top of things.

"I've made some snacks for you for the flight."

"Thanks Ima [1], you're the best." Eleanor offers her hand for the snacks, but it actually requires her full two hands plus Orly's hands to carry them all. "Ima, it's just fifteen hours. I'll be in the U.S. in no time, and I'm sure they have food there," she says fondly, but knows better than to resist the load.

"Whatever doesn't fit in your backpack you can store in your luggage. You might get hungry before you get a chance to run for groceries," Orly suggests.

Or find the nearest grocery store....

Eleanor did google the area once or twice, but her focus was on how long it would take to get to the metro and how long of a walk it is from the metro to the lab. Not so much groceries. Again, priorities.

She'll get the gist as she goes. It's like playing a board game for the first time, when you're too excited to read the instructions.

The ride to the airport is interesting. Unsurprisingly, her family all decide to see her off, which requires three separate loaded cars—her parents, Har'el, Aunt Orly, her cousins, her grandparents from both sides and Gillie. They all walk in with her to the luggage drop-off, then try to see her to the gate but are stopped by security. Her dad tries to talk their way through, but that doesn't work out quite well.

"Aba [2], it's okay, I've got this." Eleanor persuades him with a big hug—the only way she can—in the hope he'll abort that last mission.

"I guess that's it then," he says reluctantly, eyes glassy, but then slaps on a proud smile.

They all go through the typical group family hugs and noisy cheek kisses routine, only this time the hugs are longer and more emotional—well, she *is* going away for a while... Two years? Maybe more? She hasn't really made plans yet on when she'll come back to visit. The longest time she's ever been apart from this incredibly tight-knit gang of hers was maybe two weeks. And she was always a few hours away. Never so far.

"Don't do anything I wouldn't do," are her brother's wise-ass words. "Actually, do *everything* I wouldn't do," he smirks and gives her a hug.

"Keep your heart open for Prince Charming." From her grandma.

And a few more words of wisdom from the others that admittedly don't work quite as well in other languages as they do in Hebrew.

"Don't forget to write letters Ellie!" Her grandpa winks at her.

"Orly, will you please help him download WhatsApp and teach him how to use it, preferably today?" Eleanor pleads. Orly salutes in response.

More hugs, more kisses, tears are shed—not hers, her mind is too focused on the thrill ahead, the adventure she's about to embark on.

"I'm so coming to visit you!" Gillie smashes her in his bear hug. "Never been to America before!" He sounds as excited as she feels.

And this could go on for hours, but the security guard is getting antsy and sends her flock back on their way.

I love you guys! she mouths in their direction, and waves as their figures get small and a little blurry, and everything turns quiet. Well, metaphorically speaking, because it's an airport after all. Eleanor blinks some potential tears away and she's back in the game. She's going to start new research—her dream project—in a new lab, equipped with well-picked mentors to guide her through the different skills, tools, and techniques she's about to add to her repertoire, and funding! Actual generous research funding. Her PhD mentor had said that she would have access to all the fancy-ass-last-word equipment and tools she's ever needed.

Well, he didn't actually use the word *'ass'*, but the rest of it was word-for-word. And Eleanor can't wait to test it all out.

She breezes through the last security check and sits down for ten minutes to sip a cappuccino. Maybe a bit more than ten minutes, because at some point she has to sprint to her gate, before finally settling down in her seat on the plane. Turns out the seat next to her is not taken—which means she can spread out and spend the entire first segment of the flight reading papers, making slides and crunching more data from her last whole genome-sequencing spree. That last one experiment she did before officially graduating from the place that has been her home for the past five years: her PhD lab.

---

1. Hebrew word for mom

2. Hebrew word for dad

3

Airports

The Day Of

The flight lands in Madrid. Still deep into her latest data analysis, Eleanor does note that despite the brilliantly smooth landing, there is no clapping, no singing.

Does the "good to be home" kind of cheering after touchdown not happen in other countries? Guess not... She hasn't really noticed that before.

The flight attendant blurts something in Spanish over the speaker. Eleanor can't quite make anything out, and waits for the English translation to follow, but it doesn't. There's background chatter she can't understand, but people seem annoyed.

"What's wrong?" Eleanor turns to the family sitting behind her.

"Storm," the mom answers in a Spanish accent. "Many flights are delayed."

Great. Or actually maybe not so bad, she can find a place with WiFi and an outlet to charge her laptop and go on with her work, all she's ever needed.

As people start rising from their seats, Eleanor shoves her laptop into her backpack, throws it over her shoulder and heads toward the long corridor that leads from the plane to the airport.

Just a slight delay, she can make the most out of it.

"Arrived in Madrid," she texts her mom, who will surely spread the word through the family vine immediately. Her mom sends back hearts and kisses emojis and a photo of her dad snoring on his couch with the TV remote in his hand. Business as usual.

Eleanor breezes through the busy airport. She passes by some shops and fast-food restaurants. Her strides are wide and urgent, trying to get to her gate sooner than later—'*Any time not used for work is time wasted,*' the infamous quote from grad school. Gillie always says that this is the stupidest quote he's ever heard and that the correct one starts with '*Any time not used for sleep...*' Eleanor isn't sure if either of those are common quotes, but the thought brings a smile to her face as she passes by the flashing-red arrival and departure display boards.

People start gathering next to the screens, fussing and blocking the passageway, which makes her turn her head to look. The red writing is in Spanish but she's pretty sure it means 'delayed,' and from the flight numbers and destinations, there's no doubt that her flight to Washington D.C. is no exception. But that's a technical detail she's already assumed, so nothing new here. Eleanor shrugs and completes her journey to where her boarding pass says her gate should be.

She's relieved to see an empty row of seats next to a charging station that is somewhat secluded from the main seating area. Electricity, WiFi, and peace of mind to do her work, what else can a girl ask for? She takes a seat, pulls out her laptop and lets her brain trail back to work. Pleased that she was able to find that nice spot, the rest of the world can definitely wait.

Eleanor's not sure how long it's been. But when her laptop signals she's almost out of battery—of course she forgot to plug it into the charger, despite sitting right next to it—she lifts her eyes to realize it's already dark outside. It wasn't very sunny earlier with the storm outside and all, but now it looks as if nighttime has already taken over a while ago. She glances at her phone, which confirms she's not wrong. Has it been so long? Time does seem to fly when she's focused on her favorite hobby: work. Or rather: science. Or actually: both.

Eleanor's stomach is growling. She completely forgot about that, or maybe she's just assumed she'd eat on her next flight, which would have been a few hours ago.

She gets up, laptop still in hand, and walks to the flight info display boards, happy to see the confirmation that her flight hasn't left yet but will soon be boarding.

Good!

And that it was delayed.

Not a surprise and only a minor inconvenience as long as she has her laptop with her, and some WiFi. It doesn't even have to be high speed.

But the terminal and gate numbers that appear next to her flight are different.

Oh shit... She's been sitting at the wrong terminal this entire time?!

Eleanor packs her stuff frantically and runs to the closest area map to figure out her way to the *correct* terminal and gate. She plans her route quickly, throws her backpack straps over her shoulders and sprints. She makes it to her gate out of breath, panting. A long line of people already lined up to board the plane. She stops by the screen to double check the destination and flight number. Can't make the same mistake twice, at least not on the same day. Relieved to see she's made it to the right place, and at the right time, she sighs.

Well, barely, but that still counts.

It was a slight scare, but looking on the bright side—if her flight had to be delayed, at least she was able to find a nice quiet secluded area to do her work and even got to squeeze in some unplanned exercise.

The lady at the gate makes an announcement through the speakers and while awaiting the English translation, judging by the general disappointment in the crowd and the fact that the long line of people is starting to spread around, Eleanor gets a sense that this is not good news. Then the English message follows, announcing that the flight will be boarding—eventually—but not now. When? That's a mystery.

Oh well. Her eyes scan the area for a decent place to hook up this laptop of hers so she can go back to data crunching. Her battery is just about to die, so Eleanor must act fast. She spots the perfect place—which happens to also be the last empty seat—and makes a run for it.

Which inevitably lands her in this handsome man's lap.

4
BACK IN THE MOMENT

Present Time

"Will you watch my seat for me? I've worked hard to get it." She attempts a joke with this gorgeous blue-eyed guy, who's just saved her from a run to the ER. He gives her a bemused look. "Going to wash my face," she explains, blaming her need to leave on her messy appearance, omitting the fact that her bladder is about to explode any minute now. Got to go easy on the guy.

"Maybe try walking this time," he says, face unreadable.

Okay then...

Staring at herself in the bathroom mirror does confirm her suspicion about the mess part. Her hair would make the typical bad hair day seem good, her nose is stained with dried blood and her eyes are begging for some sleep. Miraculously—and thanks to the healthy instincts of this handsome stranger—she didn't get any blood splotches on her clothes. She washes off the dried blood, trying not to splash herself, which proves to be not very successful and just perfect when wearing a white T-shirt. Finally, in an attempt to put some order in her unruly hair, Eleanor pulls it back into a ponytail, wetting her bangs to lay them flat on her forehead. She's not sure why she cares, but so be it.

She stops to buy two water bottles—one for her and one for the lifesaving person—in case he hasn't run away screaming—and goes back to her seat next to the charger. *This time* extra slowly, which is still faster than the way reasonable people walk, but it's not running.

A small sense of joy creeps up on her when she sees he's still there. But she pushes this alarming feeling away, handing him a water bottle and chugging the other one at the speed of light. He opens his bottle and hands it back to her, clearly implying she could use that one too.

"This one was for you," she says, wiping some water off her upper lip.

"Hmmm," is his response, as he takes her hand and wraps her fingers around his bottle. A buzz.

Her pulse quickens a notch, before she complies and chugs this one too.

Then she pulls out her laptop, praying that:

1. She didn't accidentally break it while she was too busy falling.

2. The battery hasn't died yet, which would mean her precious unsaved work is not lost to the digital black hole. She should really turn on the automatic saving feature.

Eleanor presses the power button and sighs with relief when the screen wakes up, maybe a bit too loudly, as it makes the guy turn his gaze toward her with a slight eyebrow furrow. Actually, both eyebrows. He shakes his head. Again.

"I know." She beams at him. "I'm like an entire entertainment crew." And since he doesn't say anything, she adds, "Hey, at least you're not bored anymore while waiting for your flight."

"I'm certainly not bored anymore," he admits.

After drinking two whole water bottles and making sure her laptop is alive, she remembers how hungry she is. Thank goodness for mom-made sandwiches—and relentless insistence. Her mom definitely knows her well. Eleanor pulls the mighty sandwiches out of her bag and offers some to the guy, but he politely refuses.

"You sure? My mom made a ton of these. You've just saved my life, and I drank all your water too. The least I could do is give you a sandwich." She shoves it in his hand. "My mom would not take no for an answer," Eleanor warns.

"What's in it?" He hesitates.

"Don't ask, just try it."

"I think I should know—"

"Do you have any food allergies?"

"No."

"Then just try it. No questions."

The guy gives her a stupefied look but eventually gives in. "It's good!" he admits, after politely finishing his first bite.

"Told you, my mom's sandwiches are the best." She gloats while devouring her sandwich and watching him enjoying his. "It's one of these things that you shouldn't question, just trust the magic."

"You make sandwich eating sound like a philosophical activity," he says, still bearing his serious expression.

"Isn't it?" she asks, watching his lips twitch to an almost smile before he can help it.

A small win.

She considers going back to work, but noticing those blue eyes wandering to her screen—or maybe it's just her imagination—she decides to switch from her precious data mining to reading an older *Nature Review* paper about cellular barcoding. The idea of being able to track specific cells across time and space is fascinating to her, and she's been fantasizing about maybe bringing some elements of it into her own research now that budget won't be an issue. She can finally let her brain go wild. Or wilder.

Eleanor sneaks a quick peek in his direction, curious to know whether he might be staring into her screen, but he's finished her mom's sandwich and is now deep into some auto magazine, reading away about new electric car models.

Who's staring at whose reading material now?

The speakers announce that their flight will be boarding soon. Eleanor reaches to her front backpack compartment to retrieve her phone. She needs to send an update to her mom. Her fingers search but come back empty. "Shit!"

"What's wrong?" Life-saving guy looks straight at her, his blue eyes concerned, again.

Did she just say that out loud?

"My cell phone," she mumbles. "I probably dropped it when I ran here from the other terminal." She recalls glancing at it just before finding out she had been sitting in the wrong place. It must have fallen, possibly smashed somewhere along her frantic running route.

"Where were you before?" he asks with a stern look. "I can help you look for it."

What makes some stranger want to be so helpful? Is he always like this?

"Pretty much all over the place," she chuckles. "That's probably a lost cause."

His eyebrows crush together in the sweetest expression. "You don't come across as someone who would give up without a fight," he says.

"That's a pretty accurate assessment, but there's no way we could make it back in time for the flight," she says despite herself, trying to be responsible for once. "Thank you for the kind offer, though."

"Come with me." He gets up and holds out his hand.

Apparently not a quitter either.

They inform the flight attendant, who promises to let Eleanor know by email if they find anything. The woman even goes the extra mile and calls the other terminal to ask if they found an orphaned cell phone—which they haven't.

They also scan the nearby area but come back empty-handed.

"Can I ask you for a huge favor?" She looks up at him. "Hmm, another one, I mean." She rubs her forehead, smoothing her bangs to one side. He nods. "Just don't think I'm a weirdo or something. Unless you already think that, then it won't make a difference anyway," she chuckles.

"Go ahead," he says, clearly intrigued.

"Can you please text my mom?"

"Your mom?" Some degree of amusement in his voice.

"Yes, just to let her know that surprisingly I'm still fine and that we'll be boarding soon. She's probably worried. Tell her I lost my phone and not to worry. That I'll contact her when I get to... Well, hopefully they'll have a phone there. I would email her, but she never opens her email. Oh, tell her to check her email tomorrow."

"Okay." He obliges, pulling out his cell phone.

"Oh, and she doesn't do regular text messages. Do you have WhatsApp?" Eleanor continues. He gives her a confused look that probably means he doesn't. "Can you download it? I'm sorry, I know I'm asking for a lot here, but I don't want to call her in the middle of the night, that would freak her out." Eleanor takes a second to breathe. "And could you also download a Hebrew keyboard? She won't believe it's really me if I text her in English."

The guy looks speechless and somewhat stunned, but he's up for the task and follows Eleanor's directions to the best of his ability.

Then hands her his phone so she can text her mom.

Thank goodness for handsome, life-saving guys at airports.

"Let's just hope she doesn't block you," Eleanor utters, typing. The guy quietly chuckles. A sound that bears the potential to mess with her mind. She can already tell. But when she looks up at him, he's back to his serious face.

They both glance at the screen anxiously, or at least that's how she feels, until the two check marks turn blue.

"She's reading it," Eleanor announces ceremoniously. Relief. Boarding commences around them, but they stay put.

"Ellie, is that you?" her mom responds in Hebrew, which he probably can't read. "Are you okay? You weren't kidnapped or lost or anything?"

"She's double checking it's really me and ruling out some crazy scenarios that *naturally* come up in a concerned mother's mind," Eleanor summarizes for him, smiling.

"I'm OK Ima, don't worry," she writes back in Hebrew. "Going to board the plane now, so got to give this nice guy his phone back. Love you, please read your emails. I'll email you when I get there."

"Love you honey, have a safe flight and don't forget to enter your new apartment with your right foot first," her mom responds, this time in English—she doesn't like to exclude others in a conversation.

"Thank you so much!" Eleanor smiles widely at her new favorite stranger who's just saved the day. "You've helped alleviate my worried mom's concerns. Saving my life twice in one day." She hands him back the phone. Mission accomplished. Their eyes meet for a second longer than the stranger-to-stranger-in-the-airport kind of normal.

And... there's something magnetic about it.

"That's my boarding group," he finally says, gesturing to the screen. Group two, nice for him. "Are you coming?"

"Oh, I'm with the lowly group five, but you go ahead." She smiles. "It was nice meeting you."

"Likewise," he says. His manners take her by surprise. She's been nothing but a big headache. She expected something along the lines of 'good riddance.'

Thank you again for saving me, she mouths as he disappears into the line of the respectable group-two-boarding people.

Will she ever see him again? Probably not, but that's surely for the best. She came all this way for her science, for her work, and being next to this guy in the last—has it been an hour? Two? She's lost track of time—has been quite distracting. Plus, she doesn't even know his name.

5
FLYING HIGH

When group five is finally called, Eleanor walks slowly into the line of people, making sure not to leave any additional belongings behind—especially and most importantly her precious laptop.

She scans her boarding pass and the machine beeps.

Great... is it the wrong flight?

"You have a seat change," the attendant reassures her and writes down her new seat assignment. Judging by the number, it seems much better than her original back row seat neighboring the bathrooms, so no complaints here. "Enjoy your flight." The lady gives her a wink.

Hopefully the person next to her had a chance to shower at least once in the past several days and is not a sprawler. Or a violent teeth grinder. Or a loud snorer. Eleanor really doesn't ask for a lot. Oh, and if possible—someone who doesn't stare curiously into other people's laptop screens and will let her do her thing in peace. There are a few more tasks she has planned for today and not hitting them could mean a delay. Time cannot stand in the way of science. She needs to design twenty primer pairs to be able to order them once she starts her new collaboration with Professor Kowalski, and a few papers to read.

Eleanor goes over the tasks in her head while strolling down the tight plane aisle. She examines the faces she passes, wondering who her seat mate is.

"Are you stalking me?" A maybe-amused-maybe-serious-hard-to-tell warm voice fills her ears. Eleanor shifts her gaze to meet those blue eyes again. She double checks the seat number, matching it with her new assignment because—*what are the odds?* The numbers match.

"I guess I am." She can't help her smile. "Hmmm... your window seat looks very enticing, would you like to swap it for my awesome newly assigned aisle spot?" she offers playfully.

"You want my seat?" The man gives her an incredulous look. She may be imagining it, but there's a ghost of a smile bouncing on his lips before he gets up and lets her slide in, shaking his head. Yes, he may try to hide it, but Eleanor is pretty sure he's battling a tiny little grin there.

She positions herself carefully in the window seat, making sure not to bump into his wall of a body on her way there. Well, maybe just once for good measure. Or twice.

"You are very kind," she says as he takes the aisle seat next to her. She takes in more of his impossible fresh-out-of-shower scent.

How does he do it? He must be magical.

"Your mom sent back heart emojis," he says. So he hasn't deleted WhatsApp yet. "And a picture."

Uh-oh...

"Hopefully not one of me naked."

The guy smirks quietly and hands her his phone. A family selfie from the airport. Eleanor hadn't even noticed they took it, but she's in there too. "Your family?" he asks. His careful-you-might-drown blue eyes have a different shade to them. *Is it longing?*

"Yes, my grandparents from both sides." She leans into him, pointing at the little figures in the photo. "My mom, dad." She points. "My younger brother Har'el, my best friend in the entire world Gillie—"

Eleanor stops mid-sentence. She's letting a complete stranger into her life and he doesn't even know her name. How rude of her!

"I'm Ellie, by the way." There's a very small circle of carefully selected individuals who are allowed to call her that.

And this guy has just gotten a fast pass.

Is it the life-saving thing?

The fact that he wiped her bloody nose without reservation?

His almost uncrackable serious expression?

Those gorgeous blue eyes contemplate for a moment before the man attached to them finally says, "Aiden," reaching out his hand.

Eleanor takes it. Warm fingers close on hers, and they shake hands. That light buzz again. And some sort of heart palpitation. Probably part of the side effects of, let's see: not enough caffeine, barely sleeping, wearing short sleeves and shorts in a cold airport, falling, being blessed with a nosebleed, possibly a concussion, the list is endless. A typical Eleanor-mess. Minus the nosebleed, because that one is new. Must be some crazy symptom of something.

His phone beeps and he takes it back for a quick glance. "Your mom asks if I'm Jewish," he snickers. "She says you're twenty-eight and single." This time there's no doubt, he's amused.

"Oh, come on, she's already playing matchmaker! Please delete the app before she turns it into a new version of Tinder. You can block her too—"

But he's ignoring Eleanor, typing something back on his phone. "Wait, don't answer that, it will just keep her going, don't encourage her!" Eleanor protests but he turns the screen away from her and keeps typing away. He's almost chuckling now. She can tell this guy doesn't get amused often. Well, her mom does have this effect on people.

His phone beeps again. "Okay, time to put your phone on airplane mode," Eleanor tries a different approach that fails as well. "Give me that!" She attempts to grab the phone away, but he intercepts, and she lands in his arms for the second time today. Her cheek pressed against his chest.

Yeah, he works out, no doubt about it.

"Sorry," she mumbles as she straightens herself back up to a more appropriate doesn't-really-know-her-seatmate-that-well position. Which means keeping all of her body parts on her side of the seat. Not an easy task, considering the recently discovered magnetism.

The flight attendant gives them an admonishing look, as apparently, they were making too much fuss and interrupting the usual crash-landing-and-oxygen-mask safety training. Her partner in crime finally puts his cell phone on airplane mode.

Thank goodness.

Eleanor tries to dig out her sweatshirt from her backpack, since planes do tend to get cold, just like she already knows and was told, but then forgot and ignored. "Shit!" She sighs loudly. This seems to be a recurrent theme for the day.

"What now?" her favorite stranger, now known as Aiden, asks from his side of the seat.

"My sweatshirt didn't make it," she explains.

"Did you leave it with your cell phone?" The blue eyes looking at her are impossible.

"No, I'm pretty sure I forgot to pack it when I left home this morning. The weather in Tel Aviv was—" She starts to explain the soup-level humidity, but then turns to the flight attendant who's passing by. "Excuse me," she says to the lady, who is now busy giving Aiden a once-over. Eleanor can't blame her. "May I please have a blanket?" she asks in the nicest voice possible. The flight attendant mutters something in Spanish, then disappears.

Eleanor turns her eyes to Aiden, clueless. "I'm pretty sure she said they had no blankets," he explains.

"Interesting day," she huffs.

"Here." He pulls a hoodie out of his backpack and gives it to her. "Don't want you to freeze to death next to me."

"Meeting you today has proved very handy," she says. "But I can't take it, what if *you* get cold?"

"I won't," he says with an admirable degree of certainty. "Take it, you really do look cold."

And despite him being a complete stranger, going through this entire flight wearing jean shorts and a short-sleeve shirt might end up being a unique hardship. And unique hardships call for unique solutions. And since everything with Aiden has been unusual so far anyway, quite insane to be precise, this would just be one more item on the list. She might as well take it. And she can't really complain, because of all strangers' sweatshirts she could possibly borrow, this one smells amazing, like Aiden obviously. And reaches all the way to her thighs.

"Thank you," Eleanor says, feeling all shades of happy in it. Aiden just nods, as if none of what he's done for her today required any effort.

Once they're allowed to use large electronic devices again, she pulls out her laptop in an attempt to squeeze in some work. That is, until the flight attendant strolls in with their dinner and Eleanor has to stop and devour it. Everything tastes superb, or she's just starving to the point of not being able to tell the difference between a gourmet meal and bad airplane food. Probably the latter, based on the interesting look Aiden gives her at the sight of her empty food tray, offering up his dinner as well.

Then back to work. Aiden's eyes wander to her screen, as if he understands all those terms she has up there, and for some reason this makes her too conscious to focus.

Well, at least he smells good, gave her his hoodie, doesn't seem like a teeth grinder, and she wouldn't mind if he's a sprawler, so the pros definitely outweigh the cons. Eleanor decides to call it a night, stows away her laptop, cuddles herself inside Aiden's hoodie, hood on head and all, and tries to get some sleep.

When Eleanor wakes up, the lights are back on and breakfast is being served, or whatever meal it is—she completely and utterly lost track of time. Again.

"Good morning." Aiden's voice sounds closer than expected, rumbling through her. He sounds calm and... sweet, and she drifts off for a few more minutes before realizing her head is resting on his chest. Actually, her entire right side is pressed against him. She must have fallen to his side while sleeping. It was warm and comfortable, come to think of it, not typical for red-eye flights.

"Sorry." She peels herself off him again. This is really getting old, but after spending so many hours so close to her, he should be used to it by now. "You could have pushed me to the other side," she laughs.

"Didn't want to wake you, you seemed like you needed that sleep," he says nonchalantly.

"You could have lowered the arm rest between us, that would have kept me away." She smirks. "I'm such an annoying seatmate."

"Maybe a little when you snore," he offers kindly.

"I don't snore!" Eleanor scoffs. That ghost of a smile travels up his lips again, as he looks down in that way that people who don't smile too often do.

She straightens the hoodie. It has a familiar Pearl Drums logo. "Are you a musician?" She gives him a quick look—his slacks and dress shirt wouldn't have given it away, but she does recall rubbing her head into some pretty strong arm muscles while she was dozing off.

Not another drummer.

"A musician would be a stretch, but I do play. Drums."

So apparently, she has a type. Why does the second man on earth that she happens to find skin-prickling-attractive also have to be a drummer?

"Cool," she says, hiding the storm going off in her brain.

Why does it matter anyway? It's not like she's ever going to see him again after this flight.

"Do you play?" he asks.

"Nah." She shakes away some old memories of her ex, Oren. "I used to be a big Shinedown fan, but I don't even like music anymore."

This wins her a stupefied look from the man beside her. "I don't believe you."

"About being a Shinedown fan?"

"No, I like Shinedown. The other part."

"It's true." She used to like music, and mostly used to like watching *others* play. Others being Oren Hason... But that was a while ago, and she doesn't want to be held accountable for it.

"What did music do to you?"

"Broke my heart," she says simply, despite having decided she wasn't going to bring it up. Well, great job sticking to her made-on-the-fly decisions.

"*Music* broke your heart?" He arches an eyebrow again; this is becoming his signature adorable look. Although Eleanor is pretty sure he means to look serious, not adorable. But he is obviously failing at that. "How?"

"I fell for a drummer, once upon a time."

"I see." He seems to be piecing things together. "A drummer who liked to play Shinedown's songs?"

"Just for fun, not really. He writes his own songs actually."

"Got it," Aiden says, but politely enough he's not trying to fish for additional information.

Yes, Oren Hason, the legend. Her undoubtable '*mythological ex,*' Oren's favorite term. He had always spelled trouble. Her own personal bunch of trouble. Well, used to at least, until he decided he '*wasn't built for serious relationships*'—his words, not hers. And that his calling was to '*travel the world with his rock band, go on tours, explore*'—again, his words. At least he was honest enough to come up and say it. Although Eleanor wishes he had made this decision earlier, before she poured her entire heart into their relationship, before she started building all those castles in the clouds, before she let herself fly so high. And mostly before her face became smeared all over trendy social media apps attached to the ostentatious title '*Oren Hason's girlfriend*' and then '*Oren Hason's ex.*'

Maybe her crash landing in the end wouldn't have been so painful had he told her sooner. But just like that, Oren Hason ruined music for her and left her with fractured plans, a shattered heart and several years of starring unwarranted, undesired social media posts. The price paid for daring to be in a relationship with someone who happened to be locally famous. And on top of that was the hideous matching tattoo they'd gotten together after drinking a bit too much—their first-name Hebrew initials inside a heart. So freaking unnecessary. His on the inner side of his right forearm, hers on the outer side of her left butt cheek.

Stupid, revolting tattoo. Her perpetual Oren reminder. That, and a bunch of songs he played, way too many songs, that are still constantly featured on any Israeli radio station, as if she needs a reminder.

Who needs music anyway?

6
ANOTHER GOODBYE

There's a common theme in the past few days and it's called *saying goodbye*. A necessary step when one feels that it's the only way to focus on their career. There are plenty of people who can have it all and do it all. But unfortunately, Eleanor doesn't think she could ever belong to this lucky four-leaf-clover elite group. It's just one of the side effects of allowing herself to have a mythological ex, with mythological memories and a useless tattoo that serves as a daily reminder of how hard it is to focus on the task at hand with a messed-up heart.

So, no. Not happening again. The decision was made and sealed a long enough time ago. And it's non-negotiable. It's on Har'el and her cousins to each find the loves of their lives, get married, start their own families, and get those deeply desired great-grandkids for their grandparents. Eleanor can focus on building her science career, calmly and without distractions. There are plenty of scientists who have devoted their lives to science; she would love to get a spot on that shiny lonely-heart hall of fame.

But belonging up there feels unnecessarily challenging at Dulles

Airport in Virginia, when together with Aiden she walks off the plane and arrives at customs, where American citizens go one way and foreigners go another.

And it's not because of the extremely long line on the foreigners' side. Eleanor can deal with lines – especially an organized one like this. It's because of Aiden's "Where's your jacket?" concern when she tries to peel his warm drummer hoodie off her so she can give it back. And because he pulls on the hem of her T-shirt when it rides up, to cover her exposed skin.

"Uh... I don't have one yet," she admits. Aiden raises a bewildered eyebrow at her. "What?!" She goes for a defensive smile. "Do you know how hot it was in Tel Aviv when I left?"

"Jesus Ellie, it's freezing cold outside." He takes off his winter coat almost reflexively. "Wear this." And she can't help relishing the way he says her name. Or his commanding tone.

"I can't possibly accept it, it's not your fault that I came... clearly unprepared." Yes, she should have done her homework better.

"I don't recall asking." He wraps the coat over her shoulders, capturing her inside.

So controlling!

"No way," she says, shedding it off and giving it back, despite really liking the scent and feel of it.

"Then at least take the hoodie," he pleads.

Letting her head rest on his chest on an international flight was one thing, but she literally could not live with herself peacefully knowing she has some stranger's hoodie in her closet. She hates it when people borrow stuff and never return it.

"You don't have to give it back, I have plenty of clothes at home," Aiden insists, but seeing her contempt he adds, "If it makes you feel any better, I'll be playing at SigmaV on December 30th. May even throw in some Shinedown songs. You can give it back then."

She hesitates. And then hesitates some more. And not because

Shinedown is her used-to-be-favorite band. Or because she swore off music a while back.

But because the plan was to never see Aiden again.

Because she's now miles away from home, executing her well-crafted plan, and she can't afford distractions. And this is already showing the potential to become a huge one, starting with the fact that Aiden's a drummer, and a very handsome one, she should add. And then topping it off with the little bits of his personality he seems to be working hard not to reveal. Without much success.

And yep… A total swoon risk.

She knows one when she sees one. It's the kind of risk she needs to stay away from if she wants to keep her misshapenly-pieced-together-previously-shattered heart relatively (all things considered) intact.

"I am not sure how this will work with my dislike, with a passion, for music. Can I just stop by and leave it there for you?"

Yes, outsmart the system. Go ahead.

"Whatever works for you," He rolls his eyes at her and smirks. "It wasn't a pickup line."

Seriously?

"I didn't think it was, just stating a music fact here."

"Uh-huh…" That ghost of a smile there. He's so stingy with those smiles!

"I'll think about it," she says. Her potential head injury from yesterday at the airport might be giving out some signals here, total lapse in judgment.

"You should probably text your mom that you've made it safely." He hands her his phone.

"I told you to delete the app," she admonishes, but takes the phone anyway and quietly types as he suggested.

That was nice, he's nice—sparse on smiles, but nice.

"Thanks," Eleanor finally says, handing him back his phone. Their fingers touch. A lightning bolt.

Urgh…

"What did you write? She's sent back a poop emoji." Aiden bites down a smile.

Oh, saw that!

She huddles closer, trying to make sense of the little poop on his screen. "No, she's deleting it. And now she's apologizing for pressing the wrong emoji," Eleanor translates. And noticing she's invaded Aiden's personal space, yet again, she takes a step back.

"Excuse me." Someone rushes them from behind, making Eleanor jump into Aiden's bubble once more. "Are you in line?"

"Go ahead," Aiden pulls her closer to let the intruder pass.

The heart palpitation symptom is back.

"Okay, then, I guess it's a goodbye," Eleanor says when he lets go, trying to get this blood pumping organ of hers under control. "Thanks for letting me fall into your lap yesterday, and for letting me borrow your hoodie. Oh, and for allowing me to snuggle into your chest the entire flight. That was nice. Well, the list is endless really," she laughs.

"You're welcome." He releases something that sounds like a gruff laugh. It's rusty, but still a laugh! A surprisingly adorable sound, especially coming from someone who seems to have a painful relationship with letting his lips curve upwards.

Aiden holds out his hand, but this seems too cold to be appropriate, so she just leans in and gives him a hug, snaking her hands around his neck before her full-of-science brain gets a say.

Gosh, he's tall.

This takes him by surprise, his arms still hanging by his sides for a second before he recovers and reciprocates. It's a friendly hug, because he's sort of been her first-ever friend in the U.S., and that's something, even if it lasted less than twenty-four hours. But it feels good, so she's stalling.

Another lapse in judgment.

"I hope I'm not harassing you," she says into his wall of a chest. "I'm used to getting hugs in airports, and there's really no one here waiting on the other side for me with a hug. So, you will have to do."

Yes, perfectly reasonable explanation.

"Glad to be of service," he chuckles.

"You're eventually going to smile," she says, letting him go.

"We'll have to see about that. December 30th, 7 p.m."

"I never said I was coming," Eleanor protests, stepping into her side of the line.

"You never said you weren't," he says impassively, poker face back on, then disappears into his line.

Dammit. A challenge. Eleanor has trouble turning down challenges.

The airport shuttle stops at the entrance to Eleanor's new apartment building. Well, *new* would be an overstatement. She contemplates asking herself why on earth she did not come for a prep visit. But that would be a useless question, seeing that she's already here and has already signed a full-year lease agreement with a roommate. She reminds herself that it's right in the center of town, close to the metro that will efficiently deliver her to work every day, and that's all she really needs.

Plus, she's managed to go through life so far without speaking to herself, so now is probably not a good time to start.

She pushes the car door open and clambers outside, letting the chill shock her like a dive into a human-size dry-ice bucket—if that was a thing. Not the mild winter she was expecting. Thank God for Aiden and his hoodie. Maybe she should have opted for his coat after all.

The driver drives off as she struggles with her two huge suitcases. They clearly weigh more than the allowed limit; she's not sure how she managed to get away without paying the extra fees at the airport. Eleanor somehow drags them up the stairs before she finally opens the front door to the building.

So this is how it's going to be, completely anonymous. No one's holding a 'welcome home' sign for her or bringing a dish with her favorite food. No flowers, no balloons. No press preying on information on Oren Hason's long-time ex either. And that's exactly what she wanted—to get away from everything and everyone, be anonymous. Just her and her science, that was the plan.

The place looks nothing like it did online. Either the landlord had worked some Photoshop magic, or Eleanor looked at it through her imaginary optimistic sunglasses.

She must have forgotten those at the airport, along with her cell phone.

The elevator has seen better days, or perhaps smelled better at some point in the past. But it's totally worth holding her breath twice a day for the sake of science. A total bargain. The doors open into a long corridor with an interesting matching shade of dirty blue on both the walls and carpet. And despite the peeling paint decor and slight moldy smell, blue is still her favorite color.

And also seems to surround her lately.

Eleanor scans the little signs on each door in search of her apartment, rolling her gigantic suitcases behind her, one in each hand, until her eyes finally land on the anticipated 511. Ah! She's made it.

She picks up the little plant standing on a stool by the door and digs in the ground for the key. When Alannah, the roommate she hasn't met, said she was going home for Christmas, Eleanor was quite concerned about her key hiding spot of choice, but apparently it's the technique that counts.

She jiggles the key into the lock. The door makes a squeaky sound, the kind that puts WD40 on her emergency shopping list. Then she brings her right foot forward, just as her mom instructed, and makes her way into the place that from this moment on, although might require some adjustments, will be called *home*.

7
WELCOME HOME

Alannah Meyser, Eleanor's chosen roommate, apparently has a great taste in home décor, and a soft spot for pink. Once Eleanor shuts the squeaky door behind her, she takes in the soft colors, the long curtains and the extremely well-equipped—albeit small—kitchen. The living room has a bright-pink statement couch, a small white coffee table and a fluffy pink carpet. Minimalistic but cozy. Alannah, apparently, is also very fond of plants. Green is everywhere in cute little pots, and each has a popsicle stick with its name and a note attached to it with watering and sunlight exposure instructions, down to the science, in neat handwriting. There's also a welcome note on the kitchen counter, fixed to a little 'Welcome home' balloon. Looks like Eleanor has gotten her balloon after all.

Eleanor,
So sorry I am not here to welcome you in person,
Spending Christmas with my parents.
I can't wait to meet you soon,

Call if you need anything!
Have a blissful holiday season and welcome home!
Alannah

That's sweet. Eleanor gives herself a tour in search of the bathroom and her new bedroom. She guesses it's the one with the naked bed, empty desk, and ample sunlight, already exceeding her expectations. Except for maybe—no ceiling lights? Mental note, right after the WD40, a winter coat and possibly gloves, she needs to get some light source for her bedroom.

She had been so busy that it never occurred to her to check the forecast when packing for this adventure. And even if it did cross her mind for a lonely second, she's never owned a real winter coat before, and wouldn't even know what to search for. Tel Aviv winter just doesn't justify the potential space that a large fluffy coat would take in her closet. A fleece jacket was really all she ever needed, so far. And even that was, for the most part, too toasty. Well, that is until the moment she stepped out of the airport this morning. Thank goodness for her own personal handsome blue-eyed stranger.

Eleanor rolls her oversized luggage into her new empty bedroom and digs in for some much-needed long pants, boots, her beanie and her fleece jacket. Then she puts it all on, because the place is freezing. She could probably use a crash course on how to use the thermostat. Yes, December is considered winter in Israel, but the Washington D.C. winter has just provided her with a new definition for the word 'cold.' So that's what her mom meant when she used that esoteric term.

And after a brief session of familiarizing herself with the new apartment, she can finally pull out her laptop and hook it up. She did remember to get (and bring) an adapter for the American outlets.

And this is called having her priorities straight.

She lets herself crash for a second on her linen-less bed. Might be gross, but right now there's no one around to express an opinion about it. No one to tell her to put down her laptop, take a break, go eat. Complete freedom.

Finally.

Eleanor takes a deep breath, enjoying the silence. The endless possibilities and all the time in the world to read papers, write grants, hypothesize, plan her experiments, design her primers, dwell on her results. Her own scientific haven. What else could a workaholic ask for? She glances through the window next to her desk, overlooking the parking lot and partly, really just very partly, overlooking a park. That will do for her daily dose of view.

Her stomach is growling, reminding her she has one empty fridge and a rioting digestive system to fill. She steps outside, already wearing all the warmest clothes she owns. The cold, crisp air is refreshing but is definitely too cold for the clothing she brought. She needs to go shopping ASAP. Her nose and eyes start watering quickly from the chill. Her mom was absolutely not joking when she said Eleanor's jacket would be like wearing a paper bag as a bathing suit—Eleanor's not sure where she came up with this analogy, but it made her laugh then as it does now. Only now, her laughter is accompanied by teeth chattering and her lips are too frozen to properly move.

She looks around. Where does one get a winter coat in this place? And who to ask? Not having her cell phone at her disposal makes her feel almost helpless. But just *almost*, because her eyes spot a small local grocery store to the rescue.

A quick trip through the shelves, and to Eleanor's delight, it appears that their last-minute Christmas gift aisle is somehow stocked with linens too, although they only have one size (double) and one print (Disney princesses). And despite her Oren-induced dislike for all fairytales and happy ending romantic stories, she grabs it off the shelf. One can't afford to be picky these days. That is, if this specific one wants to sleep in a bed with actual bedsheets tonight.

Unfortunately, the tiny local store does not sell jackets. So she gets some groceries, as much as her hands can carry. Then sprints back to her apartment, bags in hands, before she gets hypothermia or frostbite or whatever other wondrous things could happen to the human body at twenty-six degrees Fahrenheit. Granted, these temperatures may not be too exciting for the locals, but they are for her.

How much is it even in Celsius? Isn't that the temperature in her freezer?

Back at her new still-doesn't-feel-like home, she boils some water and opens the pack of instant coffee she worked so hard finding at the grocery store. With a hot cup of coffee in one hand and a sandwich in the other, Eleanor lets herself sink into the soft pink couch in the living room, sighing loudly and contently. Her newly purchased colorful fuzzy Christmas socks look up at her happily too.

Eleanor gobbles her sandwich and grabs her laptop. She hasn't done any work for like forever. Almost since falling into Aiden's lap, that is. Was it because he seemed interested in whatever was going on her screen? Or was it she who was interested in whatever was going through his mind? Either way, she can now safely make up for the lost time. She opens her little electronic bundle of joy—thank God for free building WiFi—and clicks her inbox icon. There's an email from Professor Kowalski waiting for her.

Dear Dr. Benjamin,

Welcome to the US. I hope you had a nice flight.

I have some good news and some not so good news. I assume you'd want the latter first.

I've made an attempt to get you a temporary visitor pass for this week, but unfortunately the GERI security department is adamant on you taking orientation, on-boarding and lab safety training before gaining access to campus during the holiday shutdown. I'm sorry about that, I'm sure you wanted to get started ASAP.

But for the good news – we did manage to get your stipends to start effective today, so please enjoy some paid time off, and please feel free to contact me should you encounter any issue.

Happy holidays,

Professor Andrew A. Kowalski, PhD

Epigenetic Disease Branch

Gene and Epigenetic Research Institute

A financially responsible, reasonable person might choose to focus on the good news in Professor Kowalski's email. She's going to get paid for about ten days of doing absolutely nothing. Indeed, it's very nice of him to get her stipends started right away. But that's beside the point, because for someone like her, not very reasonable and very much not financially driven, not being able to go into the lab for so long is very disappointing. Her hands are already itching to get those microcentrifuge tubes in a row, try out her new set of pipettes, take a stab at their real-time PCR machine. Probably a newer model than the one she was using back home in her PhD lab. And mostly just comfortably sink back into her science. She was counting on it to make her feel like she belongs again. She knows nothing else in this new place, no one else.

Wait, what happened to her fun-peace-and-quiet, all-on-her-own high? She only arrived a few hours ago, and being alone is already losing its appeal?

She writes back a quick note to Professor Kowalski, acknowledging the information just received and thanking him for his generosity, both on the stipends front and for breaking the bad news first. Then, she reluctantly moves on to the next email.

This one is from Iberia airlines. She's about to press delete, never in the mood for taking a survey, when her eyes register the precious word 'phone' in the subject line.

Well, not *that* precious, actually, she's not a phone person. Aside from texting her family on WhatsApp and googling scientific topics occasionally, she rarely glances at it. Hence losing it in the airport.

But that was before. Before her family and friends were thousands of miles away.

And all it takes is the combination of *'found your phone'* with *'driver will drop it off tomorrow at the address you have provided'* to make her never-been-attached-to-her-phone self become positively cheerful again. She may have asked for some peace and quiet—but for someone growing up in the Benjamin household, a couple of hours of this is already an overdose.

Would someone make some noise around here?!

So Eleanor channels it all into work, knocking herself out with scientific papers. Literally, sort of, because at some point she loses track of time and space, and when she wakes up cold and confused, she forgets where she is for a moment. She opens her eyes into the dark and not-yet-familiar living room, feeling her way through the walls in desperate search for the light switch in this ceiling-lamp-depleted apartment. There's some noisy bumping into stuff, some potential knee and elbow bruises, until she finally manages to find her new bedroom, slides herself under her new princesses covers, curls into a ball—trying to keep warm—and dozes off again.

No, it's not as easy as it sounds. Doing absolutely nothing is considered an art, at least by some, because it takes talent to actually do it properly. And no, Eleanor doesn't appear to possess such talent. So needless to say, it's not working too well for her.

She wakes up to chirping birds and the sound of a garbage truck backing up under her bedroom window. Maybe the bird chirping was actually part of her dream, but the garbage truck sound is very realistic. She has no idea what time it is or how long she's slept. Still in yesterday's clothes, snuggled in Aiden's—yes, still hasn't reached the right state of mind to take it off—hoodie. She's not sure why his image is still haunting her mind, or why thinking of him during these confusing moments of sleep-shedding makes her feel less alone.

And more importantly, why, all of a sudden, being alone is bothering her? Like a dose of emptiness before her coffee.

When has her precious alone time—that she'd so desperately been craving—crossed the line into loneliness?

Eleanor grabs her laptop. 'Can you get a concussion without hitting your head?' Time to consult Dr. Google. She sorts through the sources, trying to find an actual scientific publication to back up some of the million findings at her fingertips. How did people even live before the Internet age?

Unthinkable.

According to her on-the-fly search, this could happen due to injury somewhere else in the body. Eleanor walks herself into the bathroom, where she recalls seeing a larger mirror, and checks for bruises. Aiden did a pretty good job catching her. Recalling it brings a smile to her face. The search comes back clean. No bruises other than her knee that's still proudly bearing Aiden's band-aid, and a few small ones she added to the collection last night while blindly searching for her bed. Surely not the culprit for her potential concussion. Clumsiness is a skill Eleanor has carried with pride since she can remember. Her dad always says it's because she's too busy thinking *smart sciencey thoughts.'* And so far, she's managed to live through it with only minor scratches and bruises. Nothing serious. She can't recall anything like her newly discovered symptoms.

She looks up 'concussion symptoms to watch out for.' The list includes 'light and sound sensitivity'—nope. 'Changes in sleep patterns'—that could be part of her jet lag, so not really. She keeps scrolling.

Hmmm... 'Changes in thinking and memory'—well... She may have a few symptoms to fit under this category. She mentally tries to list them:

1. Thinking of a guy she's just met briefly at the airport, and then on a plane. Then getting those weird excitement shivers running through her spine just from touching his fingers, and again now just thinking about it. This can't be a good sign, and very unusual for *her* specifically.

2. Having a hard time telling the difference between true fun (being alone and doing work), to what her brain somehow perceives as fun at the moment (attending a noisy family dinner party, texting her entire family in a gigantic group chat, going to that bar Aiden mentioned to watch him play...). *What? Impossible. She doesn't even like music*

anymore.

3. She's definitely experiencing short-term memory loss right now because she can't, for the life of her, remember significant details from the past 48 hours. Including where she had saved the last primer design sheet she was working on during the flight from Tel Aviv to Madrid or what she had for dinner on the plane. The only thing she can remember is... Aiden.

Definitely a concussion.

She glances back into what might be a not-too-reliable source of online information but continues reading it anyway. The list says 'emotional changes', and yep—that too, because her heart was racing when she hugged him, and that is totally not something that happens to someone coming from a very warm all-hugs-and-kisses-on-both-cheeks family. That little twist in her stomach when they said their last goodbyes. This is way out of character for her and definitely out of her comfort zone.

Therefore, and based on all of the above, her next search shifts to the recommendations on recovery from a concussion. It's mostly just rest. Then she adds her own personal recommendations—breakfast, a much-needed cup of coffee, and perhaps even a shower could be a good place to start.

A few hours later, back in her bedroom, tasks accomplished, Eleanor is trying to figure out what to wear. The weather outside looks sunny and clear, but it deceivingly looked like that yesterday too, so she's not buying it this time.

Sigh.

Her hand reaches back to Aiden's hoodie, which still possesses his scent, summoning his memory before her.

Stupid concussion.

Eleanor shoves it in the laundry machine along with the very colorful Disney linens, which smell like paint factory.

She puts on her favorite sweatpants and hoodie.

Her other favorite hoodie, not Aiden's.

She pulls her hair into a bun. Time to make this place feel like a home. *Her* home. Maybe that would make things better.

A doorbell ring startles her, as she's not expecting anyone. She doesn't even know if this neighborhood is considered safe enough to answer the door. But then, considering the fact that her apartment key was buried in the pot outside, untouched, for almost a week... She decides to take her chances.

She peeks through the peephole, getting a view of a middle-aged man. Not too threatening, but she has no idea who he is or what he's after. Eleanor didn't take the *What to do when a stranger rings your doorbell in a new country on which you know absolutely nothing about* course, and hasn't read the memo either.

"Who is it?" she reflexively asks in Hebrew through the door.

No answer.

Well of course not. Why would the guy on the other side speak Hebrew? She's definitely not in Kansas anymore. Or rather—Israel.

"Who is it?" she tries again, this time in English, considering whether she'll need to put her long forgotten krav-maga skills to use. She's been out of practice for years now, but hopefully it's like riding a bicycle.

"Iberia delivery," the guy answers. Or at least that's what she hopes he answered. And just to rest his case, he reaches for something in his side bag.

Hopefully not a gun; that would be a total waste of relocation funds. She hasn't even had a chance to see the lab, not to mention she's still working on designing those PCR primers.

But he pulls out a cell phone. *Her cell phone!* The email did say they would send it with a driver once it reached the U.S. on the next flight, but that was quite fast, plus she's already come to peace with the fact that she's suffering from some short-term memory loss.

Anything-not-Aiden-related loss.

To think she was contemplating whether or not she should answer the door, and now she can't open it fast enough.

The delivery guy is quite shocked at her joyful reaction to being reunited with her phone, and with the overly generous tip she shoves into his hand. She takes pity on him after he leaves, and patiently counts to ten behind the closed door, before unleashing her happy screams.

"Got my phone back!!!" she quickly texts to their newly created multi-participant family WhatsApp group. Feeling connected again.

Grandma: "Thank goodness, I was starting to worry."

Grandpa: "Starting?"

Grandma: "It's my job to worry." She adds a laughing emoji.

Mom: "I miss you already! And can't wait to hear all about your journey!"

Grandma: "First can you tell us who is this handsome young man?"

Eleanor: "I'm sorry, who are we talking about?"

Orly: "Give her a minute to scroll back through our chatter, she's just got her phone back. Ellie, honey, get yourself up to speed." A laughing- crying emoji.

Gillie: "I have to admit, I'm curious too!"

Yes, Gillie is the kind of friend who one can't even recall a time when he wasn't part of the family. Which of course wins him an honorable spot in Eleanor's family WhatsApp group.

Eleanor: "Gillie, I thought you were on my side. *Deeply shocked*"

Gillie: "Eloosh, I'm 100% with your savta on this one. Make it 200%."

This makes her laugh out loud.

Who thought that relinking herself with this small annoying electronic device, the one that always beeps and rings and causes perpetual distractions, a total nuisance, would bring her so much joy?

A piece of home.

Her phone rings.

"Eloosh! I miss you already!" Gillie's shiny grin covers the screen in a WhatsApp video call, bringing a big smile to her face. Gillie is the only one who still insists on using her childhood nickname, Eloosh, which is what everyone else used to call her until she decided she was too old for that, sometime around second grade, shortly after she and Gillie became BFFs. Gillie is still stuck on the Eloosh phase though.

"I miss you too!" She sighs. "Gosh, it's so quiet in here, it's driving me crazy."

"Already? I thought you wanted some alone time to focus on your work."

"I did," she admits. "But Gillie, it hasn't even been two days and I've already reached an important realization about myself."

"And what's that?"

"That I really don't like being alone."

"A shocker," Gillie chuckles. "Kind of saw that one coming." He lets his contagious laugh roll out, lighting up the mood in her lonely apartment.

"Could have warned me..."

"I think it's important to let people do their own exploration in life." He makes his signature imitation of their high school bio teacher. It's been almost ten years since they graduated. That one teacher made her mark. "Anyway, would you have listened if I had?

"Nah. You're right," she sighs. "Do you hear that?"

"Hear what?"

"The unbearable sound of complete silence. I think I might go get myself one of those white noise machines."

"Where's your roommate?" Gillie straightens his lab coat and sits down. The familiar lounge room in their cell biology department comes to view on the little screen. Not seeing Gillie in the lab every day is going to be hard. Not that they shared the same advisor, but his PhD lab always had all and every possible piece of equipment. They had quite a few generous grants to fund their research, plus ample more to spare. So for Eleanor, stopping by Gillie's lab to borrow some much needed goods was not unusual. Once-twice-a-day-at-least kind of not-unusual.

"She's spending the holidays with her parents, she won't be back before the new year. How come the lounge is so quiet?" The lounge is typically the center of activity.

"It's already pretty late here, seven hours difference, remember?"

"Right, so then I have time to give you a tour." She gets up from the couch and travels around with her phone. It doesn't take more than five minutes to walk him through the small apartment.

"Cute! I like the plants!" Gillie sums it up.

"Yeah. These are my roommate's babies."

"And for someone who dislikes fairytales, your Disney princesses bedsheets are a bold statement!"

"Shut up! That's the only set they had at the store."

"Busted!" He laughs out loud. "How was your trip there?"

"Uneventful." She's quick to summarize. Convincing oneself starts with convincing others. Right?

"Really?" Gillie smirks. "That's not what your mom said. Who's that hot guy you were sprawled over on the plane?"

"Sprawled over? Just the guy who was sitting next to me."

"Looks like you were totally invading his personal space."

"What do you mean looks like? And what was my grandma asking about a *handsome young man*?" Is Eleanor's boring life back to being smeared all over social media?

AGAIN?!

"Your mom sent that selfie to the group chat. He's HOT! Does he happen to have a handsome gay brother by any chance?"

"Hold on... What selfie?"

"The one the handsome guy you sat next to probably took for your mom. I swear, Eloosh, you're the only person in the world who doesn't notice when people take selfies with you."

"Why would he take a selfie with me? That's creepy."

"Your mom asked him to, don't judge. You know how hard it is to say no to her. The poor guy was just following orders. He knew you wouldn't notice anyway."

"How could he have known?"

"You mom told him that too."

"Gillie!"

"She literally told him—*take a selfie, she won't notice*. She shared that in the group chat too. Geez, you really don't read your text messages."

"Seriously? My own mom turns against me?" Eleanor clutches her heart in feigned shock.

"You're missing the point," Gillie says and messes with his screen before an image appears on her phone. "I mean, look at those blue eyes. The undeniable jaw line. His five o'clock shadow, the delicious biceps showing under his shirt. I bet he also owns some amazing pecs and abs." Gillie drifts off. "And look at you all lit up like a complete set of Hanukkah candles. Tell me you're going to see him again." Her best friend is smiling like the devoted matchmaker he is.

"You know me better than that!" Eleanor protests. "You know I came here to work. I need to focus." She tries to make the photo go away, pressing everywhere as quickly as possible. "Great," she sighs. "Gillie, how do you change the screen saver image? I think I accidentally replaced it with this stupid selfie."

"You mean your lock screen or your home screen?"

"Both."

"Not telling you," he chuckles. "Now you'll get to look at yourself smiling at this gorgeous man every time you reach out for your phone."

"Gillie!" she protests.

"Anyway, back to what I was saying. You'll have plenty of time to focus, leave some time for fun."

"Working in the lab is all the fun I need. Besides, he's a drummer."

"A drummer?!" His smug smile is unmistakable. "Darling, sounds like you have a type!"

"Tell me about it. And just to be clear, you'll never catch me dating a drummer again."

"Right, because all drummers are Oren Hason?" Gillie challenges. She wouldn't expect any less of him, but still.

"Yes."

"That's some next-level logic. Would you rather date a scientist?" Yet another one of Gillie's challenging questions.

"Of course not! That would be even worse. Bringing work home."

"You already bring work home. On like a champion-league level."

He has a point.

"True. Okay, then that would be sleeping with the competition, so NO," she insists.

"Doesn't have to be competition, not every single scientist in the world is interested in diseases caused by epigenetic aberrations, you know?" He attempts a serious expression.

"How is that even remotely possible?! And anyway, still a no."

8

Hypothesizing

I t's December 30th. The day Eleanor was *not* planning to go see Aiden play. *Not* see him dominating the room with his drumming skills. *Not* put her willpower to the test. And mostly *not* spend her time constantly thinking about him. But all of these plans have obviously failed, seeing as she's freezing her butt off strolling the wintery D.C streets, making her way to this SigmaV bar.

The past week had gone by slowly. Eleanor was able to dig out her misplaced file thanks to the search function on her computer—her most-used function right after the 'undo' button. Two incredible features that could have served her well had they existed in real life. Especially the latter—she would have been able to undo the frantic running in the airport to a very slow, turtle pace, maybe even snail-pace walk, on her way to that charging station. Or better yet, go find another charging station, avoid that fall and the lingering consequential concussion-like symptoms. Avoid meeting that life-changing guy.

Oh, did she say life-changing guy? A Freudian slip. Meant

to say life-saving guy... The drummer and the owner of her favorite-shade-of-blue stunning eyes who's been inhabiting her thoughts lately—also known as Aiden. So yeah, the 'undo' button. Because not meeting him in the first place would have been more in line with her original plans, where science proudly sat on its rightful throne as the one and only thing on her mind. Always and forever. Wouldn't that be nice?

Would it, though?

She's done designing twenty primer pairs and loading them into the cart of her favorite primer synthesizing vendor, ready to order once she's set up in all of the GERI systems. She's also read the entire list of papers she'd downloaded during the last month while planning for her relocation. And cleaned up the apartment—twice. Watered Alannah's plant-babies while adhering to each and every single sticky note instruction carefully. Then video chatted with the family back home—parents, grandparents, Har'el, her cousins, Gillie—multiple times. Then played catch up on some lost sleep. And last but not least, attempted to take a walk outside, which was a big mistake because it's so freaking cold, and she hasn't found the right mindset or the right place to get herself an actual winter jacket. And mostly because all the beautiful jolly holiday decorations, lights, and music made her self-inflicted *alone* feel even more lonely. The loneliest.

And this came as a surprise, because she had no idea, never having gone through it before, that loneliness feels a million times worse on holidays—especially Christmas—despite being Jewish and all.

So now that she's officially exhausted all means of occupation, she's in desperate need of getting into a lab, any lab, lining up those microcentrifuge tubes and run a few experiments. She's contemplated breaking into GERI, but decided that getting herself on their naughty list before her first day on the job might be counterproductive. Unlike her PhD department back home, there's no one she can call to let her slide through the gate, unlock a back door, leave an open window...

And although her last lapse in judgment—based on her own historical data—hadn't ended up well for her, she seriously considered allowing another. Her conclusion so far has really been based on a sample size of one. One single, annoying lapse in judgment, bearing the name of Oren Hason. And everyone in the entire state of Israel, thanks to Oren being the paparazzi's favorite, knows how that ended. But as a scientist, she knows all too well that sound conclusions cannot be based on a single data point—public as it may be. One can't even calculate a p-value for that.

No.

At the very least, three data points are needed. Which means she's allowed at least two more mistakes, two more observations before she can wholeheartedly claim that these things are true trouble. Worse comes to worse, she'll end up with another stupid tattoo. But that can probably be avoided if she limits herself to no more than one beer on nights out.

So driven by a purely scientific motive to collect evidence and add data points to her hypothesis (yes, that same one involving impulsive decisions and unfavorable outcomes), she completely ignores an important and well-established rule: that under no circumstances, should scientists test their own hypotheses on themselves.

She also ignores the fact that unlike typical experiments, this time she is actually hoping to dispute her hypothesis rather than prove it. Which would mean that following her heart... err... impulsive instinct, doesn't always lead to trouble.

Impossible.

And since Eleanor has been suffering from a severe case of boredom, jet lag, hunger, and a bunch of unexplained concussion-like symptoms—she also ignores the fact she no longer likes music. Which is how she finds herself on her way to SigmaV, clutching Aiden's washed and neatly folded hoodie, her excuse for showing up here.

According to the esteemed Dr. Google, the place is casual (attire-wise) and a short, ten-minute walk from her apartment. This time, for a change, Eleanor made sure to switch from that little car icon to the pedestrian option. She's already made that unfortunate oversight several times.

The unfavorable—gently put—outdoor conditions make the ten-minute walk feel more like thirty minutes, despite her resorting to running for the most part. When she finally pushes open the much-anticipated glass door under the SigmaV sign, she sighs with relief. Well, more like finally breathes, because her throat burns from the cold air, and her face defrosts so quickly her cheeks sting. A quick look at her watch shows it's about halfway through the show. Fashionably late. She sniffles and looks around, willing her teeth to stop chattering.

The smell of food and beer, sounds of people chatting, glasses clinking, instantly warm her up. It reminds her there's life out there—outside her desolate apartment, and mostly outside her own head. The being-alone sensation she was supposed to enjoy slowly melts away, and the music she's supposed to not like is admittedly good.

Her eyes spot Aiden, positioned behind a drum set on stage, sticks in hands. In his element. So focused, so serious, so handsome.

Wait, what?

The corners of his mouth pull up a tad as he exchanges a quick nod with the band. And before she realizes, their next song seems to sound like an upbeat version of Shinedown's "I'll Follow You." Did he plan this? He did make a threat-promise to play her used-to-be favorite band.

She wishes she'd come a few minutes later and skipped that climax in the song, that moment where the drums kick in, bringing the whole thing together, because it's making those little hairs on the back of her neck stand to attention, and undoubtedly makes this one specific handsome drummer shine. And despite her declaration about not liking music, this is a good song to display her new favorite stranger's talent. An uncalled-for excitement fills the air, and a fresh crop of goosebumps appears on her skin even before her last bout dissipates.

No, not again...

What is it with her and drummers? And this new storm inside of her, who invited these butterflies?

She shakes her invasive thoughts away and takes a seat at the bar. It might be her imagination, but Aiden's eyes seem to travel in her direction and stay there, an actual smile now playing on his handsome face.

For her?

Eleanor is that person who would wave back enthusiastically at a complete stranger waving from across the street, just in case it's meant for her. She's well-aware that she has terrible facial recognition skills. Not the case now, but from that little bit of time spent around this man up there, she is pretty certain that he doesn't smile very often. Eleanor would not want to steal that smile away from its rightful recipient. So she takes a quick glance around, expecting his plus-one to come into view, but there's no one behind her. Looks like Eleanor might be the proud beneficiary of this heart-swelling smile.

So she smiles back. And waves. Because... Why not?

Two girls on the other side of the bar are eyeing her suspiciously. She wouldn't be surprised if one of them is Aiden's girlfriend, probably the beautiful, possessive blonde with the too-short, too-tight black dress. In fact, it wouldn't be much of a shocker if there was already a lineup of future girlfriends just preying on that girl's downfall. But Aiden seems oblivious, eyes focused on his drums, or occasionally meeting Eleanor's eyes. Helping her win herself some criticizing looks from the two girls. And lose some heartbeats in the process.

Look at her, already a crowd favorite, always making new friends...

Well, at least it's not all over the gossip columns.

Yet...

The band is now playing an original song. Their lead singer is quite good, but it's hard to tell, because her eyes and ears are so focused on the drummer.

Ugh.

Music is what reminds her of Oren, the number-one reason for her no-music rule, one of several rules she abides by, which is where her strict no-romance rule lives as well. She banned these things a while ago because they bring uncalled-for gloominess with them.

And longing.

And disorientation.

And they mess up with her focus.

But interestingly enough, sitting here, at this moment, locking eyes with Aiden, watching him orchestrate the beats and control the atmosphere, doesn't make her sad.

No, not today.

In fact, there's a slew of other things she's feeling right now, and sadness is definitely not one of them.

"Anything to drink?" The bartender stops by her.

"Water please," she says, offering a smile in response to his disappointed look. Got to keep her self-control in check. But he nods kindly and moves on.

The show ends. Warm cheering and clapping from the crowd.

Some high-fives and hugs amongst the band members, and Aiden's off the stage, making his way through the crowd. His strides are confident and determined. Eleanor bets he's making his way to the two girls that are ear-to-ear smiling at him. She looks down at the menu, busying herself with the important technicalities of her next meal. After all, she's only here to return his hoodie, and she's starving. She may order to-go though. Eating alone is not her thing.

"Hey stalker, you came." A voice startles her deep debate over food options, making her drop the menu to the floor. The owner of the voice leans down to pick it up before Eleanor has a chance to process, giving her a nice glimpse of his back and shoulder muscles through the thin fabric of his shirt. Not that she was planning on looking, but now that she has...

Damn.

"Hey stranger, nice job out there! I came to return your hoodie." She jumps off the stool and stands, shoving the hoodie into his arms to fill up the space between them. Before she uses her own body to close that gap, that is.

"Despite your strong aversion to music?" A content expression on his face.

"Despite that. But you should have warned me you were going to play Shinedown songs."

"I keep my promises."

Apparently so.

And it's the way he says this last statement that's doing all kinds of things to her.

"Yeah, well, anyway, thanks for letting me borrow your hoodie. And again, for letting me fall into your lap, that was a real face-saver, literally. And for letting me sleep on your chest on the plane, that was fun," she prattles on. She can't ignore the piercing stares from those two girls on the other side of the bar. His girlfriend might not be too excited to hear the details surrounding that flight. And although they're too far away to hear anything, she decides to stop there and let him go back to his life.

Or wife?

"You're welcome," he says.

"Hey A!" The bartender approaches for a fist bump with the star drummer, then smirks at Eleanor from behind the bar. "More water for you, hon?"

"Sure, thanks." She takes a last sip and pushes the glass toward him.

"Can I get you an actual drink?" Aiden asks.

"I was actually about to leave anyway."

Yes, leave. Better safe than sorry—it's a brilliant quote she needs to start taking more seriously.

"Leave? You were looking at the menu a second ago." Aiden studies her.

"Nah, just doing my due diligence on types of foods served at bars in America." Her stomach growls in disagreement and she crosses her arms around it in a lame attempt to make it stop. The background music ends exactly at that one quiet moment her stomach decides to rumble yet again.

"Uh-huh," Aiden says, looking at her crossed arms.

Busted. Another proof that music is just never on her side.

"No, really."

"Very convincing," he quips. "Can I get you anything to eat?"

"Hmmm." She means to say no, but some parts in her brain seem to have fallen asleep on the watch.

"Burger and fries? Or you have something against junk food too?"

"I don't have anything against any food. Well maybe against Brussels sprouts, but I doubt that they serve those here."

"Two burgers, no Brussels sprouts," he says to the bartender, amused. "Beer? Wine?" His blue eyes turn back to her, and she shakes her head a bit too vigorously. Can't trust this mouth of hers to adhere to her strict rules. "So water for me too," he says. The bartender nods and disappears from sight.

"Avoiding alcohol?" Aiden asks matter-of-factly. He takes the seat closest to Eleanor, motioning for her to sit as well.

"Yes, but not for the reason you might think."

"How do you know what I think?"

Yeah, how does she know what he thinks?

She shrugs and sits down. "I tend to do stupid things when I drink. Last time it ended with…" Eleanor stops to rethink that last statement. She may want to skip the part that describes the tattoo on the left side of her butt. "You don't want to know. Let's just say my alcohol dehydrogenase is probably on the lower side."

"Now I'm curious. Does it have anything to do with your dislike for music?" He looks intrigued.

"In a way. Just a guy I don't particularly want to recall." Well, since she's already walked herself into it, she might as well. "Oren, my mythological ex."

"Your what?" His eyebrow furrows. A gorgeously sexy gesture. "Is that even a thing?"

"My *mythological ex*, is that not a term in English?" And since Aiden looks a bit clueless, she goes on "You know, THE ex… It's a mythical status."

"I would love to know what prospects upgrade an ex to a mythical level." Even dubious looks adorable on him.

"Again, not what you think."

"Again, how do you know what I think?" A small smile playing under his breath. And she wants more of it.

"I can imagine you were thinking about the sex. Yes, it *was* legendary, that's how drummers are, I guess, but that's not why."

"I wasn't thinking about sex," he says in feigned offense. "I hope you are aware that guys are capable of forming complex thoughts that are beyond sex."

"I'm aware."

"But back to your fun fact about drummers—" He moves to the second part of her statement.

Oh shit. The things she does and says around this guy are just incredible.

"Oh, I was joking. I've only been with one drummer, so I can't really provide any statistics about it yet."

"*Yet?*"

"Did I just say *yet*? Sorry, I meant *regret*."

So lame.

"Uh-huh." His lips twitch to a real smile now.

"See? And I haven't even taken one sip of alcohol." She takes a sniff of her glass. "What are the chances the bartender spiked my water? You don't want to know what happens when I let alcohol into my system." This makes him chuckle. A marvelous sound. "So anyway, mythological means this stupid ex of mine has been elevated to a legendary rank in my brain, and that's where he's been stuck since we broke up five years ago. And unfortunately for me, that's probably where he'll stay."

"Sounds like a myth. Mythological exes," he shrugs, "they don't exist."

"Not 'they,' just one, and he exists in my head."

"Because that's what you decided you want to believe in." He touches her hand while he speaks, obviously passionate about this topic. The girls from that other side of the bar take notice.

Her swarming butterflies take notice too.

"Maybe you're right but I'm not planning on testing this hypothesis. There are too many hypotheses I'm already working on as it is."

Including the current one. The kind that will hopefully not put her heart on the line again.

"Noted," he says, filing away that information.

"By the way, I think your girlfriend there is not enjoying our conversation." Eleanor takes the opportunity to divert from her slippage.

"What girlfriend?" Aiden looks confused.

No girlfriend? Or she's not here?

"That one." She gestures with her eyes, and he turns his head slightly, really just for a second.

"Why do you think she's my girlfriend?" He frowns, returning his gaze to Eleanor.

"She's been giving me these angry looks since I walked in. And the way she looks at you, I can tell."

"I don't even know who she is," Aiden says, stupefied.

"Seriously? Well, maybe she's a fan then."

"I don't have fans," he chuckles.

"Aiden, you're a drummer." Her hand gravitates to his arm. Her fingers haven't completely regained their normal temperature from being outside earlier and his warm skin feels like a welcomed fix. He doesn't seem to object, so she leaves her hand right there for a few more seconds, just until she defrosts a bit. That ghost of a smile plays on his lips again, as if he's battling whether to let it show or not. And she realizes that for the first time in forever, her mind didn't wander back to Oren when she said the word *drummer*.

"I play the drums, I'm not really a *drummer*," Aiden says bashfully as the bartender comes back with their food. It smells delicious.

Humble. She likes that in him.

"This is good," she says after taking a giant bite of her burger. "I am famished!"

"I can tell." He takes a bite as well, a little more reserved than her ravenous eating at the moment, but hey—it's not like she's planning on seeing him again anyway.

"So I take that you don't have a mythological ex?" She tries to shift the conversation from her complex relationship issues to possibly his.

"No, I've never even heard that term until now."

"Ah, interesting," she says without taking a break from chewing.

"Not really."

"Oren used to say that everyone has a mythological ex."

"And what do *you* think?"

"I don't know. But it seems you have a solid opinion you'd like to share."

"I think it's a load of crap. I think he liked the idea of keeping a piece of your heart to himself even after you two broke up."

"Ah." She considers it. "It does sound like something Oren might enjoy." Then she steals a French fry off Aiden's plate for good measure.

Maybe he has a point.

"Help yourself," he says, pushing his plate closer to her.

"Just checking if yours taste the same," Eleanor laughs, feeling much better now that her stomach is busy digesting.

"And?"

"And what?"

"Do they taste the same?"

"Uh, no, yours are better," she says in a serious tone, feeding him one of her fries. He seems surprised by her possible boldness but cooperates.

What is she doing?

She'll do anything for another one of these smiles...

What? NO.

"Yeah, you're right, mine *are* better." He chuckles as their eyes meet. "So how are you finding the US so far?" He takes a sip from his water.

"Interesting." She tries to put the last few days' worth of adjusting into words. "No ceiling lamps, and it's so cold here, even in my apartment. I think I need to get another blanket."

"Is your apartment's heating system not working?" A small dose of concern crosses his expression.

Eleanor shrugs. "Also, it's so quiet here, lonely almost," she adds. And as the words leave her mouth, she wants to take them back. It sounds way too desperate, and forlorn is not her thing. "I'm just waiting for this holiday season to end so I can finally go to work."

Aiden smiles. "What do you do for work?"

"Science. I'm a scientist."

"That I could definitely guess."

"What gave it away?"

"The *Nature Review* paper you were so eager to read at the airport. The data you were mining on the plane."

Does she want to talk about work? No, not really.

"What's your favorite band to play?" She quickly changes the subject; Oren hated science talk. Also, avoiding technical details about her work will make it easier to steer clear of getting too personal or anywhere near the term that scares her the most... *Relationship.*

She came here to return a hoodie.

Stick to the plan.

Aiden cocks his head to the side, clearly aware of her tactic, but plays along. "The Beatles are my absolute all-time favorite. Their songs are constantly in my head. There's something uplifting about their music." His eyes shine when he says it.

"But they have some sad songs too, no?" And she's heard quite a few of those. Her dad used to sing "Eleanor Rigby" to her until she was old enough to understand the words and asked him to switch to something less depressing.

"That's true. And I like their sad songs too," he says, studying her expression intently.

What is he thinking?

"What do you like to do for fun?" he asks, accepting her attempts to keep the conversation light. And she's grateful for that. Serious conversation, in her mind, runs the risk of bringing peoples' hearts closer. Eleanor has no plans going there. Not with anyone. Not ever.

"I don't do fun," she says.

"Why not?"

"I mean besides work," she admits.

"So no mountain climbing? Cliff jumping? Skydiving?"

"Nope. *Science* is my hobby," she admits. At least for the past few years.

"Mine too," he says in earnest. Strange statement coming from a drummer, but hey—who is she to judge. She looks around. The bar has emptied by now. Even those two girls left. How long have they been sitting there?

Aiden tries to pay for the food, but the bartender insists it's on the house. They step out, back to the cold.

And no, she is definitely not prepared for the outside breeze. More like arctic freeze, especially with the drop in temperature once the sun—which is deceiving anyway—is no longer visible. After-hours December coolness is apparently much worse than during the day, that much is obvious. She better start getting used to it.

"Where's your jacket?" Aiden demands.

"This *is* my jacket." Eleanor points to the fleece layer she's trying to zip up, her hands already shivering from the temperature drop.

"That's not a jacket." Being the helpful guy that he is, he steps closer and helps her with the zipper like it's the most natural thing to do.

Hmmm, he smells so good.

"Yes, I can see why you would think that now," she tries to say through her teeth chattering.

Aiden shakes his head in disapproval and takes off his jacket, handing it to her, but she refuses.

"No, no, we've been there with your hoodie already, I can't keep borrowing your clothes." She hands it back.

"Right," is his response before he wraps his winter jacket around her and zips it up with her arms trapped inside.

"Hey!" she giggles, pushing her hands through the sleeves.

"Can I give you a ride home? I don't want you to freeze to death."

"No need, it's a ten-minute walk, and now I'm not cold anymore and you don't have a jacket." She grins.

Aiden shakes his head again, then puts on the hoodie she's just returned, layering over the sleeveless T-shirt he was wearing. "I'll walk with you then."

"You'll be cold!" is her lame attempt to protest, but really, she doesn't mind the company, and there's nothing that would convince her to take this toasty jacket off her right now. So instead, she opens one side of the coat and tries to partly cover Aiden's side with it, huddling close to him, squeezing herself against him. It barely covers his lats, but the proximity to him feels unexpectedly uplifting.

There's a quizzical look on Aiden's face, perhaps even a pent-up breath, but he plays along. He keeps her warm. And he smells heavenly. That's why she lets herself remain exactly where she is as they stride in unison to her apartment building, enjoying the holiday decorations and lights all around. And when Aiden asks if she wants him to take a look at the faulty air conditioning, she lets him in. She attributes her current lapse in judgment and the erratic beating of her heart to the fact that he too is, as was her one mythological ex, a drummer.

"You can't set it to sixty degrees and expect the place to be warm," Aiden says after a complete assessment of her thermostat.

"I don't," she huffs, affronted. "I keep bumping it up to eighty every time I walk by, and it always goes back to sixty." She takes a step closer to demonstrate how she's been operating the old console on the wall, feeling an incredible pull surrounding them.

"Mad looks cute on you," Aiden smirks. "Just press this button after you set the temperature you want." He points to the little circle in the middle of the panel that's labeled 'hold.'

"That simple? Ha."

Annoying air conditioning.

"You're welcome." He runs a hand through his hair. "Nice plants by the way," he says, observing the colorful little notes still attached to each one of the pots.

"Thanks. I guess my roommate really likes plants."

"Seems quite particular about their care protocols."

"Very," she says. "I had to put a reminder on my phone, so I don't forget to water them. Don't want to ruin my first impression."

"You got your phone back!" He makes the observation.

"Yes! Now you can officially remove WhatsApp from your phone if you haven't already."

He pulls out his phone.

Wow, can't do it fast enough.

"Sorry, I have to take this one," he says, and she realizes it's buzzing. "Kim, everything okay?" Aiden says into that annoying little device. Concern fills up his already serious face. Eleanor can hear a woman's voice fussing on the other side of the line but can't make out what she's saying. "I'll be there shortly," he says, then hangs up the call.

The jealous girlfriend? Worried wife?

"Is everything okay?" she asks.

"I have to go, I'm sorry," Aiden says, grabbing his coat from the sofa. He gives her a curt, maybe pained look before turning to leave.

"Thanks for fixing my air—" she calls after him, but he's already gone.

Despite the fact that most hypotheses in the history of science have failed miserably (or at least more often than not), the one personal hypothesis that Eleanor was hoping to disprove for a change is kind of showing signs of being indisputable.

What would Murphy have to say about that?

Her PhD advisor says that failed hypotheses improve creativity.

Eleanor can only say—*Drummers...* She really should have known better by now.

This was her one chance to break free. Her little experiment is clearly not going in the direction she... Wait, was she hoping it wouldn't work? She's not sure anymore, but Aiden is clearly busy tonight, and not with her, and that doesn't make her feel good. So she puts on her plaid pajama pants and an old comfy T-shirt, brushes her teeth and bickers with her reflection in the mirror—can she finally refocus her mind on her mission? That one mission that doesn't have Aiden in it. The one she came all the way to the U.S. for?

Well, of course not. Because Aiden has to do this silly, adorable thing and text her. To her cell phone. Even though she never actually gave him her number.

"It's me," he writes, as if he's the only 'me' on her mind right now.

Which is painfully true.

"Who's me?" She can't help herself. If he has a girl waiting for him at home, he can't possibly be Eleanor's me.

"Don't get mad, your mom gave me your number." He ignores the question.

Moms... Urgh!

"Is she awake right now? I'm going to have a word with her." Midnight... that means 7 a.m. Most likely awake.

"She is."

"Why are you texting my mom for?!"

"Actually, she texted me."

"What?! Why?"

"To ask if I could take you winter jacket shopping."

"I don't know, can you?" she snaps. But of course he can't see that over text.

"If you want."

"I don't believe you!" she writes back. This guy has the nerve—doing these endearing things when he has a girlfriend.

Aiden sends a screenshot of his recent chat with her mom.

That's not the part she didn't believe. It really does sound like her mom.

"I meant the other part."

"What part?"

But then again—maybe he's just being nice? Following her mom's orders without any girlfriend disloyalty plans. She always jumps to conclusions so quickly. It's not like he tried anything.

And he did fix her air conditioning.

"You should have deleted the app by now."

Really, it's for his own good.

"I like this app, I think I'm going to use it regularly."

"No, you shouldn't..."

"Why not?"

"Shouldn't be texting my mom."

"Why not?"

"Because you don't know her."

Because this is exactly the situation they should avoid.

"I am sorry I had to run earlier."

Well, it was for the best. Can't trust her with this gorgeous man alone in her apartment.

"No worries, thanks for fixing my air conditioning."

"Is it starting to get warmer there?"

"It is."

For multiple reasons.

"Good. I'll pick you up tomorrow around noon."

"What for?" She's still feeling spiteful.

"We'll go find you a coat."

"Can't, I'm busy."

"Doing what?"

"Things."

"Take a break. Noon."

"Don't you have other things to do? It's New Year's Eve."

"I could spare a few hours to make sure you won't keep walking around in your fleece jacket. January is typically colder than December."

"Seriously? It's going to get worse?!"

"Depends on how you look at it," he types. "With a good jacket you'll be fine."

Why does he have to be nice and listen to her mom?

"You are pretty convincing," she writes back, ignoring orange lights, red lights, stop signs, speed limit signs.

"I know."

9
Happy New Year

"Are you always this serious?" Eleanor asks as they drive quietly. The urban views are gradually replaced by countryside.

Since Aiden picked her up from her apartment, they've been in the same idle status; Eleanor—mostly stealing glances at Aiden from the passenger seat of his SUV, still wondering whether last night's phone call was his girlfriend or his wife, or someone else altogether, and why on earth he's choosing to spend the last day of the year with her instead of whoever was calling him. Aiden—busying himself driving and doing imaginary sexy drumming moves with his hands to the rhythm of the music playing on the radio. Looking handsome in jeans and a sweater, wearing shoes that look slightly too elegant to align with the local bar's drummer look he had last night. His dark hair is slightly tousled, his deep blue eyes alluring as ever, his jawline displaying traces of I-don't-shave-on-weekends-or-holidays stubble. His expression serious. Looking—

Damn, she can't avoid admitting—hot.

"Serious?" he returns the question she almost forgot she asked before her mind started drifting away.

"Yes, serious."

"Haven't thought about it. Probably my resting face," he answers. "Just thinking. That's what I do." His last night's almost-playful mood is gone. Her last night's spite has also dissolved.

Focus. No flirting with a guy that may be taken.

"What about?"

Just making conversation.

"Work mostly. Are you always so talkative?" His tone is slightly amused. He doesn't seem to mind the mini interrogation.

"In my family, I'm considered the quiet one." She smirks.

"Hmmm," he says, and his lips may be battling an urge to curve up.

"I see you trying to smile there, no need to fight it," she says, poking his arm gently with her finger. "You can think and smile simultaneously. I do it all the time. I can imagine it might be hard to smile while controlling your beats. Maybe you should consider science as a career instead."

"Maybe." He steals a quick look in her direction. And now it finally appears, that gorgeous shy smile that was so worth waiting for.

"There you go!" she says. A rare, hard-to-resist smile. It makes something flutter inside her.

Maybe she shouldn't encourage it.

Her phone buzzes in her bag and she pulls it out. "I hope you're on your way to get an actual winter coat," is her mom's WhatsApp message in Hebrew. Something catches Aiden's eye as he glances at her phone while stopping at a red light.

"Yes, Ima, thanks to you," Eleanor texts back in Hebrew. "And please stop texting Aiden, I came here to work, despite Savta's plot to get me a husband."

"You can find a husband and work at the same time," her mom responds. "Have fun sweetheart!"

"Urgh," Eleanor grunts and puts her phone back in her bag. "My mom, just making sure her plans are being executed." Her gaze carries itself to the blue in his eyes, another smile. Subtle perhaps, but there is no mistaking here.

"What?" she asks, because he seems overly content.

"I like your wallpaper," Aiden says, gesturing to her phone. "Secretly looking at our photo together?"

Shit. She wasn't supposed to see him again, and he certainly wasn't supposed to see that.

"I wouldn't call it *secretly*," she says boldly. "Besides, you're the one who secretly took it." That's it, offense is the best form of defense.

"I was just trying to alleviate your mom's concerns. And it's a selfie, how secret can selfies be?"

"Apparently I have a special talent for appearing in selfies without noticing," she explains what he probably already knows. "And I have to admit, it's a good picture, and you're almost smiling in it, so it's worth keeping."

"Almost smiling?" He curves one eyebrow at her.

"Don't worry, we'll work on it, I might even get to hear you laugh."

Aiden laughing—why does that feel so desirable?

"Okay," he just says. And of course her brain decides to take on the challenge.

"So where are we going?"

"An outlet mall in Maryland, they have several stores that sell good winter coats. Are you looking for something more on the fancy side or practical?"

"Practical of course. Not that I have much experience with coats, but fancy is not really my thing."

"I'm with you on this," he says as he pulls into a huge parking lot.

"What kind of coat are you looking for?" a salesperson with a cute name tag asks. After getting overwhelmed with clothing possibilities and heat terms Eleanor never knew existed, she decides to ask for help.

"Something for extreme sports," she explains.

"Exciting!" What kind of extreme sport do you do?" Janna with the name tag asks, eyes quickly scanning Eleanor's appearance, trying to guesstimate whether it's snowboarding or glacier climbing they're talking about.

"Walking outside," Eleanor answers, trying to smother her laughter as Aiden snorts quietly beside her. "What?" She smiles over her shoulder, meeting his blue eyes. "You have no idea how adventurous walking in this weather is for me!"

"I got you," Janna offers, somewhat disappointed, but handing Eleanor a coat that looks pretty darn fit for the task. She then gives Aiden a once-over and a flirty smile, which he—very obliviously—doesn't reciprocate.

"I think it's love at first sight," Eleanor says, trying on the jacket. Aiden gives her a quizzical look.

"The coat. I love it! Never taking it off," she clarifies.

"This should keep you warm," he approves. "How about gloves? Snow boots?"

"Snow boots?" She can't hide her excitement. "Does it snow here during winter?" She hasn't really had the chance to experience fresh snow before. Not in Tel Aviv. And traffic to Jerusalem gets so bad when, and if, it starts to snow, that the chances of seeing anything but ice, coming from Tel Aviv, are usually pretty low.

"Looks like you haven't done much homework on your new location." Another smirk.

"I've done the important part of the homework—choosing my mentors. But snow is a very nice bonus."

"What size are you in boots?" He leads them to the back of the store.

"How would I know? Is it the same as normal shoes? Probably thirty-nine, which is what here—eight?"

"Possibly, take off your shoes," he commands, handing her a box.

She does as she's told, liking the controlling tone, and helps herself into the most comfortable, fuzzy pair of boots.

"How do you even tie these things up?" She wrestles with the laces.

Aiden shakes his head and kneels before her, lacing up her boots.

Tying shoes never felt this sensual before.

"Wow! These are majestic. My very own snow boots!" Eleanor perks up, but really is just trying to hide this unexpected tingling. "Ready for the snow!" she says, striding over to the register with her new treasures. Aiden grabs snow gloves and a warmer winter hat than the one she already owns. Then he pulls out his wallet.

"Uh-uh," Eleanor pushes his hand back. "You're not paying for my stuff!"

"Why not?" Aiden looks surprised, hurt even.

"Is that another one of my mom's ideas? I can afford to pay for my own shopping. You can buy me lunch." She shoves her credit card into the hands of the helplessly confused Janna behind the counter.

"I really like this new coat, and the boots!" Eleanor says happily, a couple hours later, as they walk out of the pizza restaurant that was conveniently located just outside the coat store. A full stomach, a nice toasty coat, snow boots, gloves. And this handsome guy by her side. He might seem serious two-hundred percent of the time, but she can already tell the difference between his serious-serious to his almost-smiling-serious and his on-the-verge-of-almost-laughing-serious. They stride lazily between shops. Holiday music is playing through the outdoor speakers, and colorful decorations are all around.

And it could be the fact that she's experiencing this kind of holiday spirit for the first time in her life—maybe it's like this for everyone—or maybe because Aiden is walking by her side. But the atmosphere feels enchanting, almost magical.

That is, until a ringtone sound breaks the spell and Aiden pulls out his phone from the back pocket, apologizing and taking the call. She can hear the same female voice from last night, Kim, his potential girlfriend. Calling. That's what girlfriends do. But Aiden not taking his eyes off Eleanor while chatting on the phone with the girl—that's *not* what boyfriends do. So Eleanor steps aside to give him some privacy, and busies herself looking through the window of the closest store she can find. Which happens to be a jewelry store, with a giant engagement ring at the very front.

No, not her intention.

She quickly moves to the next window. A flower shop.

Urg...

"I'm sorry," Aiden says when he reappears behind her after a short moment that somehow felt like forever. His hand gently touches her back and despite the layers of clothes, she feels this pleasant buzz taking over again.

No, where is the reset button?

"You need to go," she concludes, trying to will her misfiring neurons to calm down. "No worries, mission was successfully accomplished." Plus, it's time to say an actual goodbye and let him go back to his pre-Eleanor life. And for Eleanor to go back to whatever. In a couple of days, GERI will reopen and she'll finally be able to get into the lab. Her new lab. And dive back into her science. And then life will be good again.

But instead of executing this much-anticipated goodbye or putting that much-needed distance between them, he asks, "Would you mind if we make a stop on our way back?"

And instead of the polite, *'No need, I'll Uber home, you're free to go,'* that should have come out of Eleanor's mouth, all she manages is a dazed "Sure."

Seriously? This enchanting holiday spirit is really messing up with her head. Either that, or she can blame it on the mysterious concussion she hasn't really recovered from, apparently.

So now they're in his car again, driving to God knows where.

"I'll wait here," Eleanor offers when Aiden finally pulls over by a small single house in a nice neighborhood.

"Oh, no you're not," he says, stepping out and opening her door to make sure he's made his point.

"O-kay," she says, reluctantly peeling herself off the passenger seat. He *wants* her to meet his girlfriend? Is that one of those open relationship kinds of arrangements? Eleanor doesn't do relationships, not closed and definitely not open. But Aiden looks certain, and mostly just... pleading. Which somehow comes across to her as endearing, therefore, for a change, she decides to follow.

They walk slowly down the little path leading to the house and up three stairs. The front yard has a little herb garden with—judging by the unmistakable childhood-memories-provoking scent—mint. A lot of mint. Fresh mint! She should take some home for tea. If Aiden's girlfriend lets her back out with her head intact, that is.

Aiden pushes the front door and gestures for her to go in. She takes a deep breath, trying to decide how to introduce herself, what to say, what not to say.

"Aiden! Thanks for coming so quickly." A woman, maybe slightly older than Aiden, walks toward them, "I have to run back to work. There's something about heart attacks and holidays," she murmurs but stops when she spots Eleanor.

"Hello, I'm Kim," she says, holding her hand out to Eleanor. A wide grin appears on her face.

Could this get any more awkward?

"This is Ellie," Aiden says. She expected he'd sound apprehensive, but he doesn't. "Ellie, this is my sister, Kim."

Sister. Not girlfriend. Sister.

Relief. And then a sudden flood of something entirely different. Hope? Anticipation?

What? Where did that come from?

"Nice to meet you." Eleanor takes her hand.

"Very nice to meet you! Finally, my little brother brings a girl home!" Kim's smile broadens. Aiden tries to say something, but Kim moves on quickly. "Sorry I have to run, I have patients waiting. The nurse will be here in about an hour. Dad is in the living room—he's having a good day, but he refuses to eat his lunch, says he doesn't like my cooking." Kim throws her hands in the air. "Don't let him tempt you into adding salt." She gives her brother a warning look, then pats him on the shoulder, sends a friendly wink to Eleanor, and leaves.

"For the record, I'm thirty-five years old, not that little," Aiden huffs, still lingering on his sister's comment.

"And you've *never* brought a girl home?" She takes the opportunity, seeing as they're still huddled by the door, and taps her hand on his chest, surprised, yet again, by the unyielding feel of his muscles.

"Haven't in a while." He rubs the back of his neck. "Not since my last relationship mistake."

As the master of relationship mistakes, Eleanor can definitely relate.

"Don't date much?"

"Just no one significant enough to bring home."

"Oh, I'm flattered! First you let me land in your lap, you clean my bloody nose, you fix my heating system, take me coat shopping, and then I get to meet the fam!" Eleanor chuckles. "That's what I call *significant*."

This makes him smile. An actual smile.

Whoa!

"Now I'd like to meet your dad please," she says, and walks herself into the direction of what she hopes is the living room. Aiden follows slowly.

His dad is an older version of Aiden, same eyes, almost the same facial features. He's seated on the sofa by the television, wearing one of those old-fashioned tweed jackets with a white linen shirt and a tie underneath. There's something in the air about him that reminds her of one of her late professors from graduate school, a brilliant scientist and mentor who sadly passed away about a year ago.

"Hello," he says formally when he sees Eleanor, getting up from his seat to shake her hand.

"Nice to meet you, professor," she guesses. "I'm Ellie."

"A pleasure to meet you Ellie, I'm Gordon." His handshake is firm, just like Aiden's.

"Hi Dad." Aiden closes in, lowering his head to kiss his dad's forehead, his arm gently brushing her shoulder.

"Good to see you, son," Gordon says. Then turns back to Eleanor. "Are you one of my students?" A flash of confusion crosses his face as he speaks.

Eleanor gently shakes her head. "No. But I *am* a student."

"Finally, some academic company," Gordon says warmly and gestures for her to sit. "And you make my son happy," he adds on a whisper.

Looks like her guess may have been spot on.

"Dad, I'm going to get you something to eat." Aiden's voice sounds worried. "Ellie?" he says in a half question, unsure whether she'd want to join him. She gives him a happy nod in response, staying right where she is. She misses her family so much right now, and the thought of spending some time with Aiden's dad is comforting.

"Ellie is fine here with me." Gordon waves Aiden out. "My kids think I'm a four-year-old. I might be old, but I can still read scientific papers, you know? Instead of these shallow TV shows."

"What do you like to read?" Eleanor starts to mentally go through potential reading material options. "What field of science?"

"I'm a biochemist," he says, smiling modestly,

"Really? Me too! I might have some good stuff for you to read." She opens her backpack and pulls out the pile of papers she's finished reading but still takes everywhere with her. "Here," she says, handing a few to him.

Gordon pushes his glasses up his nose and looks through them, skimming the headers of the manuscripts.

"They are not all new, but should keep you busy for a few hours," she offers.

"Kowalski." He points to the last author of the first paper in the stack.

Yes, most of these papers are either the latest publications of Professor Andrew Kowalski, her newly chosen collaborator and unofficial mentor, or the latest publications of Professor Jim Harrington, her newly chosen mentor. Reading all their papers in detail, familiarizing herself with their data and theories inside and out, is good practice before selecting mentors. She's definitely done her homework.

"Already highlighted for you." She points to her colorful highlights throughout the text.

"Thank you for these!" Gordon says, bringing the papers close to his heart to show his gratitude. "Are you a scientist?"

"Yes, a biochemist," she says, and he nods, but when Aiden steps back into the room, Gordon puts down the papers and covers them with a large photography book. "He doesn't like it when I read his paper," Gordon half-whispers.

What does he mean by 'his papers?'

"Dad, I warmed up some soup for you, you have to eat." Aiden interrupts their discussion. "Do you want to come to the kitchen, or would you like to eat here?"

"This no-salt diet is ridiculous. Everything tastes bland—the curse of high blood pressure, torturing old people," Gordon huffs, looking to Eleanor for rescue.

"I got you," she says. Then gets up and walks into the kitchen.

"We have to watch his salt intake," Aiden warns, blocking her way to the stove.

"We will." She moves forward, letting herself bump into him. He doesn't back up. "Spoon?" she asks.

"Here." He reaches behind her, pulling out a spoon from one of the drawers and handing it to her. As he lowers his head, his lips hover over hers almost accidentally, but neither of them moves or takes a step back. The only hint of the insane electricity that seems to surround them is his accelerating breathing. Or is it hers?

Without breaking eye contact, she takes the spoon, dips it in the bowl of soup and brings it to her mouth.

"Uh... No wonder he doesn't want to eat, have you tried it?" Her voice is a rough whisper. And without waiting for a response, she dips the spoon into the soup again, blows on it softly and feeds it to Aiden.

Who thought salt-less, taste-less soup could up her blood pressure so quickly?

His eyes hold hers before he says, "You're right, it's missing a lot of salt."

"No, it's missing flavor. Salt just helps cover lack of flavor." She empties the bowl back into the pot. "Now, where does your dad keep the spices?"

"I can't believe you made my dad eat. And like it too!" Aiden says in admiration when they're back in his car. As if she's just single-handedly run a year's worth of successful experiments and gotten a paper accepted into *Nature*, or *Science*, or both.

"It was a good soup, just needed some spices, and some more cooking, and a bit more ingredients. But once we got that out of the way..." Another smile. A third, maybe even a fourth real smile from Aiden for the day—and she cannot be blamed for counting. One in the kitchen, when she almost kissed him, one when Aiden's dad complimented the improved soup, one when he told Aiden he would not let him in again without Eleanor. And counting.

"Also," she tries to tread carefully, "I may be overstepping here but I think your dad needs some more stimulation—he told me he's a biochemist? I gave him some papers to read, and he was SO grateful. He's frustrated, watching too much TV."

"Ellie, my dad has Alzheimer's. Today was a good day. He's on an experimental treatment, as part of a clinical trial, which has been giving us a lot of these good days." He sighs. "But for the most part, he doesn't remember much of his science anymore and he gets frustrated when he realizes it." That may explain why he thought these were Aiden's papers. "We have nurses around him almost 24/7. Kim and I split the rest of the time between us. I'm sorry, I should have said something earlier."

"I'm so sorry," is the first thing she can think of, taking his hand and giving it a squeeze. "I didn't know."

She thinks back to the framed photos around the house. They only starred the three of them—Kim, Aiden and their dad, at various places and ages.

"Do you have other family members that could help?" It must be so hard, so much responsibility.

"It's always been just the three of us. My mom died giving birth to me," he says matter-of-factly.

Eleanor reaches out with her free hand to gently stroke his face. He leans his head into her touch, making her heart squeeze. She can't imagine growing up without a big family tightly surrounding her ten-minute perimeter. Her massive support system.

"That's okay." He shakes off the heavy beat, but leaves their hands connected. "I had a happy childhood. I can't complain. My dad's a good man." His expression is soulful. "Kim and I almost literally grew up in his lab. That's what made me fall in love with science."

Falling in love with science. Another relatable fact about him. Yet he chose to become a musician and not a scientist?

There's so much more she wants to know about him. But she doesn't ask, because the more she learns, the harder it gets to stay away from this man.

"I like your dad! Would it bother you if I came to visit him once in a while?"

It's an outlet. A way to soften the blow of letting Aiden go. Or is it?

"Bother me?" He looks pleased with the proposition. "I'd love that. But you don't have to do this for me, we have nurses coming every day, and Kim and I have the rest of it covered."

"It's not for you, it's for me. I really miss my family."

"And here I thought you were starting to like me." He smirks, but his eyes are grateful. "And maybe we should find a way to keep him connected to science. He did appear happier than usual after I left him with you alone for five minutes."

"Ha, he said the same about you." Eleanor can't help herself.

"Said what?" Aiden raises one eyebrow in what may as well be his signature look.

"That I make you happy." And there it is, another smile. *Wow!*

And there's that incredible pull again. She shouldn't let the intrusive thoughts in, but since they'll be saying goodbye soon anyway, she allows herself to bask in them, just for a bit.

"Can I be completely open with you?" Eleanor asks as they stroll lazily toward her doorstep. It's New Year's Eve. The lab will open in a couple of days, and she can finally go back to work. But there's this warm sensation building up in her core that is in total contradiction to her staying-apart plan. Her mind already brewing a brand-new hypothesis, in which unrealistic expectations may be harder to deal with than just a small kiss to chase away this... whatever this *is* exactly. Then they can go their separate ways.

Aiden nods severely. So she continues. "I'm not looking for anything serious. Not looking for anything period, actually. I came here to focus on my science. And I want to make sure I don't lose sight of that," she explains, unsolicited-ly.

Plus, this heart of hers can't take any more beating. That is, if she wants these smooth muscle cells to keep her blood pumping.

"O-kay." Aiden draws out, giving her an apprehensive look. "I appreciate you sharing this information with me."

"I would have done it sooner, only I didn't think it was relevant info with the girlfriend and all." And when he returns a puzzled look she adds—"You know, with Kim calling you last night and today..."

"Kim, my sister?"

"Yeah, well, I didn't think she was your sister until today." Her eyes hold his gaze. "Anyway, that being said..." She takes a step closer. "I just find you so hard to resist. Maybe it's the drumming thing, or your eyes, or this smile that you don't let show. I'm not sure. And I'm not the one-time-fling-thing type either, so I'd better say goodnight now," she continues but despite her narrative (and rationale, *where did it go anyway?*) her feet carry her another step closer. She can now feel his body heat. His serious blue eyes from up close are so darn stunning.

"Yeah, you'd better." Aiden reaches out and gently tucks a strand of hair behind her ear, awakening that giant magnetic force.

And the butterflies, a brand-new wild swarm.

Gosh, his touch is mesmerizing.

"Would it be really terrible of me to do *this*?" she asks, pulling on the collar of his coat so he has to lower his head to her level. From there all she has to do is close that last bit of gap between them and taste his lips. And it doesn't take too long before he opens his mouth and lets her tongue explore, devour him.

"Not terrible at all," he rasps between her little assaults. His hands slide beneath her jacket, reaching her back, pulling her into him, breathing her in. Her heart beats so insanely fast. Or is it his? She can't tell anymore, already breathless, on the verge of needing an oxygen mask.

It was supposed to be a New Year's Eve goodbye kiss, exploratory at best. It wasn't supposed to feel this good.

Certainly wasn't supposed to be sooo HOT.

In fact, Eleanor doesn't recall kissing being such a heated activity, not even with Oren, and he was a legendary kisser.

Or so she thought.

This is quite... unusual. Unexpected. And just impossible to let go. And the fact that Aiden is a drummer doesn't seem to cut it as a plausible explanation anymore.

She stops for a second to catch her breath and admire the damage. "You look a little shocked," she pants. Perhaps projecting, because shocked only begins to describe how *she* feels.

"I've just never met anyone like you before," he says, breathing as erratically as she is.

"Never met anyone with such a unique combination of awkward and quirky you mean? I bet you haven't," she giggles, and her mouth finds his lips again before he has a chance to respond. Her hands slide under his shirt, across his chest. She pulls him into her apartment, anxious for more of him.

This brings out a much welcome side of Aiden she hasn't quite met yet. A ravenous side.

And... wow...

He kisses her fiercely, backing her up to the wall, trapping her tight against his body. His hands travel under her shirt, awakening thousands of goose bumps in their trail. His scent is her new drug, and she's already addicted.

"Hmmm," is her response to his growing hard-on.

"That's your fault," he chuckles, lifting her up, letting her thighs pull him in closer.

Science. She tries to remind herself. That's why she's here in the first place.

Why can't she think of science right now? No, not that kind of science… It's been so long.

An unexpected noise from the direction of the door makes their heads turn abruptly.

"Oh, was I interrupting anything? I'm Alannah, your roommate." The person attached to the very cute voice holds out her hand as Aiden lets Eleanor lower her feet to the floor and stretches her shirt back to where it was before he had a say in it. Then turns away to adjust himself, looking somewhat… confused? "You must be Ellie. You go by Ellie, right?" Alannah asks, battling some awkwardness.

"Uh, right." Eleanor smiles broadly—might as well. "Nice to finally meet you," she says, shaking Alannah's hand, trying to quiet her breathing. Her lips still burn from those hungry kisses. Five more minutes and this scene would have looked a whole lot different.

Talk about timing. Well, Alannah did mention she'd be back around New Year's…

"This is Aiden," Eleanor says, gesturing her hand to the guy she would have loved to undress, currently putting his coat back on.

"Aiden." Her roommate repeats the name as if it's the most unexpected scientific discovery of the year. Her face looks like she's just simultaneously read through a long review paper on the science of sexual attraction and the logic behind conspiracy theories, if there was such a thing. Or trying to live down the heated scene she's just walked herself into. "I'm Ellie's roommate," she says once she recovers.

"I see," Aiden says in a weird formal tone, still transmitting a great degree of confusion. Or is it an expected reaction to the sudden drop of oxygen inflicted by the kiss? He contemplates for a moment and then adds in that same formality. "I'll let you two get to know each other. Have a happy New Year."

10
ALANNAH

"Sorry for interrupting your... steamy moment, with—" Alannah cuts her sentence short to clear her throat.

"Probably for the best," Eleanor snorts. "You saved the poor guy from inevitable harassment."

"He didn't seem like he needed saving." Alannah's cheeks redden.

"Oh, he couldn't get out of here fast enough, didn't you see?" Eleanor's eyes trail to the door where Aiden stood just seconds before.

"No, I'm pretty sure you weren't the reason he left," her new roommate says, giving her a knowing look. And there's something else in that look, like there's an entire backstory. But since she's known Alannah for about a minute, there can be so many plausible explanations. "Okay, I need a shower urgently." Alannah shakes away the awkwardness. "I've been in airports for way too long. Give me ten minutes and I promise a proper introduction, and some food to celebrate the New Year!"

"Sounds awesome," Eleanor agrees eagerly, mostly because she needs a few moments to breathe properly. And a cold shower. Then some food wouldn't hurt. A cup of mint tea would be nice, but of course she forgot to ask Aiden for some fresh mint from his dad's garden.

Eleanor washes her flushed face. Then walks back into her room. Her cell phone beeps with a reminder to submit one of the grants she's been working on, awakening that silly lock screen image of her and Aiden.

Gosh, she can't keep having his image surround her all the time. But she can't help it either.

"You got lucky," is her exploratory text to Aiden at the same number he messaged her from yesterday. Compliments of her mom. None of this would have happened if it weren't for her mom giving him the number. He'd probably deleted his WhatsApp by now, so shouldn't be getting this message anyway.

"Lucky?" he responds instantaneously.

Hmmm. He hasn't deleted the app...

"Yes, lucky. You got spared," she explains quickly. "From a voracious assault."

"*You* got spared," he rebuttals.

"It wouldn't have been an assault. Very much consensual," is her response.

Very, very much. But she shouldn't be flirting with the guy...

"Same here."

Yet this makes her all kinds of happy inside.

"You're probably driving right now, so no sexting and driving."

Oh no...

"Sorry, I swear I meant to write texting," she corrects.

"I am not driving," he writes back. "Your sexts are too distracting, I had to pull over."

"You're funny!" She can't help herself, laughing out loud over a text message.

"I'm really not."

"Serious as always. Okay, I'll stop distracting you. Going to do some bonding over New Year's dinner with my new roommate. Drive safely."

Alannah's cheeks remain quite flushed even hours later. She must be extremely shy. Or maybe just not used to seeing people making out in public. Although this would be hardly considered *public*.

Nevertheless, it turns out this new roommate loves to cook, which would have been amazing since Eleanor loves to eat and barely ever has time to spend in the kitchen, but unfortunately for all meat lovers out there—and this leads to a follow-up discovery—Alannah is vegan. Which is unfortunate, since her superb dish-crafting skills will never include an avid carnivore's favorite ingredient. But one can't really complain when it comes to home-cooked meals prepped and served to her.

And then there's the meat smell issue— apparently Alannah finds it repulsive. Yes, they've talked about all the important stuff. Eleanor will limit her meat cooking—which she rarely does anyway—to when Alannah's not home. In return, Alannah promises to cook fresh vegan food for the two of them every day *"until you see the amazing benefits of going vegan,"* were her exact words. The least Eleanor can do is give it a try.

The initial rationale behind choosing one another as roommates was based on one big thing they have in common—Alannah is a postdoc at Professor Kowalski's lab, Eleanor's newly chosen main collaborator, and unofficial mentor—so having a lab and a commute buddy was a winning argument. But aside from their shared love for epigenetics and their superb mentor selection skills, it appears that there are a few small differences in their approach to life, other than veganism.

Alannah is an early riser—she wakes up at dawn and is in bed by 9:30 p.m., which might be a bigger challenge than her nutritional predilections, given Eleanor's a night owl. She also does not believe in sex before marriage—which may explain the amount of time it took Alannah to recuperate from the X-rated scene she walked into—but she goes by the *live and let live* approach, so this part should be fine, as long as *"you don't leave men's boxers around the house or let them walk into the kitchen naked when I'm here. And please close the door."*

She must have had some interesting roommates in the past...

They'll have to see about that part.

"So is he... your boyfriend?" Alannah, after what seems like painful contemplation, finally decides to address the elephant that unfortunately is no longer in the room. They're sitting in the living room on the pink couch, sharing Alannah's homemade vegan coconut ice cream. Which is hands-down incredible.

"Aiden? No, not my boyfriend, and not mine. I really shouldn't be starting a relationship right now," Eleanor says, but seeing Alannah's surprised look she adds, "I came here for my research. And he's really distracting."

Can't-get-him-out-of-her-head kind of distracting.

The kind that has the potential to obliterate her heart.

"Oh, it looked more serious to me," Alannah says, going crimson.

"I just..." Eleanor tries to explain this one simple fact she's still struggling with, "find him hard to resist, if you know what I—"

No, of course she wouldn't know. Alannah believes in forever love, and happily ever after, like Eleanor's grandparents. And mostly chastity before marriage.

"But doesn't that mean something?"

"Huh?" Eleanor tries to buy some time.

"That you find him irresistible? That you can't stop thinking about him?"

"It means he's sexy as hell and that I want him badly. Sorry, just stop me if I'm being too much."

"You're fine."

"Anyway, that's why it's a bad idea for me to see him again."

"A bad idea?" Alannah gives her an astounded look. "Good luck with that."

"Yes, because I might not be able to control myself. And I don't want to get emotionally involved. I also don't want to hurt him."

Just thinking out loud.

"And you're not already?"

"Hurting him?"

"No, emotionally involved, silly."

Is she?

"Hmmm... I hope not."

11

THE HARRINGTON LAB

The big day is finally here. Eleanor spent the first day of the new year bonding with her new roommate, eating some of Alannah's homemade—and surprisingly delicious for a carnivore like herself—vegan cooking, hearing the backstories of her plant babies, and chatting with family over video, all of whom wanted to wish her good luck on her first day at her new scientific home. The place where she's planning to spend every possible minute of her time—GERI, which stands for Gene and Epigenetic Research Institute—the prestigious spot where scientists gather from all over the world to engage in cutting edge, well-funded, scientific research.

Eleanor wakes up before her alarm clock for a change, extremely rare for her night-owl, totally-not-a-morning-person self. Excitement is running through her veins.

"Good luck on your first day!" is the first text message that welcomes her when she glances at her phone.

Aiden... Yes, he's still in her head, still on her lock screen. Still the one to blame for that pleasant stir in the pit of her stomach. And he remembered it's her first day, even though she probably only mentioned it once, several days ago. What is she going to do with him?

Or rather—to him?

It might be her wishful thinking, but maybe things will sort themselves out once she can finally put on a lab coat and gloves, align her microcentrifuge tubes in a row, shove a pipette into her hand—hopefully made by Gilson, her PhD lab was never able to afford that kind of luxury—and get back to her science in its totality.

But for now, she sends Aiden back a *thank you* with a smiley face, showers, gets dressed, annihilates Alannah's homemade nutritious breakfast—not because she likes scrambled tofu but because she is grateful for this roommate. And also wants to make a good impression on her first day at work—a grumbling stomach could be counterproductive. And yeah, alright, it actually tastes good.

It's a short walk to the metro alongside Alannah. The wintery morning is still freezing. But now that she's equipped with the winter gear Aiden picked out for her, walking outside becomes bearable, maybe even fun. Full disclosure though—it does bring uncalled for memories of this man. And unfortunately for her, as she's trying for a nonchalant façade, these memories now include all five senses.

Sigh.

"Excited?" Alannah asks, warm foggy clouds coming from her mouth as she exhales into the cool air.

"VERY! Ecstatic! Can't wait to meet people face to face, see my new spot at the lab. I wonder if they'll want me to sit in Professor Harrington's lab or Professor Kowalski's."

They remain quiet on the packed train, separated by the crowd, each in her own head.

"That's our stop." Alannah gestures toward the door of their metro car after a pretty short ride. A vast mass of people quickly walks out. Looks like the GERI stop is quite popular. "Sorry, you were saying?" Alannah reminds her of their earlier conversation, but as the GERI front gate comes into view, Eleanor loses her train of thought.

"Wow, this place is huge!" she observes. Larger than she expected.

"That's just the entry, wait until we get in," Alannah laughs. "You'll need to enter from there." She points to a small building by the gate. "Get a temporary daily pass until you're done with the paperwork. Once you have your permanent badge, you'll just scan it and go through the gate," she explains.

"Sounds good! Don't wait for me, see you at the lab later." Eleanor waves and then turns back to face the serious-looking security guy by the front door. She does a little happy dance, then chirps "Hello," in his direction.

"Good morning," he answers politely, looking a little overwhelmed by Eleanor's energy level at this early time of morning on the second day of the new year. "ID please."

"Thank goodness for my roommate!" Eleanor says excitedly and digs it out from her backpack. Alannah made her go back to their apartment when they were already by the elevator to grab her passport and GERI acceptance letter, *just in case.*

"First day?" The security guy eyes her suspiciously.

"Yes!" she confirms. Even his party-pooper expression can't wipe that big smile off her face.

"Can I see your invitation?"

"Here you go." She shoves the printed paper with Professor Kowalski's signature on it into his hand.

"Professor Kowalski's lab?" he asks warily. Gosh, people must find this guy's attitude so intimidating. "Let me just confirm this with him," he mutters, stepping aside to an old fashioned-looking phone and dials the number that's printed next to Professor Kowalski's signature.

Is all this formality really necessary?

"Professor Kowalski?" she hears the guy say. "I have Dr. Eleanor Benjamin here at the gate, are you expecting someone by this name?" Then he turns quiet, listening attentively. "Yes, very well professor. No it's just that..." He lowers his voice, turning his back to her. "It's just my impression, but she may have had a drink or two before showing up here today, I..."

Wow... Can't a girl be happy on her first day of work?

"No, of course not, I do apologize Professor Kowalski, I didn't mean to—" the security guy says, then looks into the phone, contrite. *Go Professor Kowalski!* Then turns back to face the gloating Eleanor. "You may enter through this gate now, Professor Kowalski is expecting you," he finally says, gesturing for her to proceed.

"Thank you!" she says. Then with a big smile spread across her face she adds, "I am not drunk, just high on life." Then turns and walks away.

The best place to have meaningful work conversations, learn important details about future coworkers and bosses, and make new friends is of course—drum-roll—the lunch room.

It takes Eleanor about ten minutes to find her new building—building twenty-three, which sensibly enough is located just next to building two (the cafeteria building). The rationale behind GERI's numbering convention is top-notch. Another big 'thank you' goes to Alannah, who gave Eleanor a much-needed heads up that getting through security and around campus for the first time might take a while.

Eleanor stops by the coffee machine to send her a quick *thank you* text. "The security guy at the entrance thought I was drunk."

This wins her a laughing-crying emoji from Alannah. "Do you think it's the mouth wash or the kombucha?"

"You must be Dr. Benjamin!" a pleasant, jolly voice attacks her ears.

Eleanor looks up from her phone to see a colorfully dressed woman, possibly in her sixties. "Please call me Eleanor," she says, happy to finally see someone who can match her energy level.

The woman looks back at her, as if completing an in-depth assessment of her qualities. "I'm Mrs. Jones," she finally says, and her smile indicates that Eleanor has passed a character test of sorts. "And although Professor Kowalski insists everyone here stays on last-name basis, you can call me Tara, but that's just because I can already say—I like you."

"Nice to meet you, Tara." Eleanor shakes her hand. "I'm so happy to see a smiling face here. The security guard thought I was drunk," she laughs. Something about Mrs. Tara Jones' now-friendly face reminds her how much she misses home.

"Oh, of course, they can't see why people should be happy on the first day back to work after the break. Please forgive him, post-holiday blues." Tara smiles broadly. "And I should apologize to you," she says, patting her arm gently.

"Apologize, why?"

"For mistaking your last name with your first, which inevitably made Professor Harrington believe you were a male scientist."

"No harm done, it happens to me a lot, actually. In middle school I was put in an all-boy classroom because my counselor thought I was a boy named Benjamin Eleanor."

Which was actually kind of fun, so no complaints there...

"Well, I feel bad now. Had I known I would like you so much I wouldn't..." She trails off. "Well, I would have double-checked your name. But this may very well be the first and last chance to get a female postdoc into the old man's lab. And it was so easy for him to assume you're a guy named Benjamin, you know? People tend to hear what they want to hear, see what they want to see, believe what they want to believe."

Hmmm... Sounds like this was a calculated mistake.

"It's time for Professor Harrington to realize that women can do everything just as well as—if not better than—men," Tara adds with conviction.

"Why do you think he's not aware?" Eleanor's curiosity gets the better of her.

"Honey, I've been working as Professor Harrington's admin for forty years. Believe me when I tell you—he isn't."

"But there are rules against gender discrimination at GERI, I'm sure."

"Of course, he's just been able to somehow avoid hiring females. He's quite... evasive. The esteemed Professor Harrington goes by the motto that to be successful you must be willing to sacrifice everything, including nights, weekends, holidays, family... Life, pretty much." Tara rolls her eyes, hands vividly making her point. "And he had been practicing what he preaches to an extensive amount. Until he turned seventy-five and his doctor ordered him to slow down. It just never occurred to him that women can do it too."

"Well then, intended or not, I'm proud to be his first female postdoc. I'll be more than happy to take an active part in the re-education efforts and help guide him through his journey from the eighteenth century to our modern-day times," Eleanor says, and the two of them shake on their newly formed alliance. "Now, what can you tell me about Professor Kowalski? Does he also share these dinosaur-age opinions?"

"Oh, Professor Grumpy? Nah, he's broody but he doesn't discriminate; he's his same crabby self toward everyone. He is very much in support of women's rights. In fact, he was quite pleased when he found out about the inevitable... mistake that led Professor Harrington to hire—the unthinkable—a woman. He is a brilliant young man. Just recently received his tenure. Handsome too. Just too serious and always deep in thoughts. And he likes formality for some reason, go figure." Tara scratches her head. "But believe me when I tell you, he has a heart of gold. And he could really use a significant other to brighten up his life a little, you know? I tell him that all the time, but of course he wouldn't listen. Although I must say," Tara halts for a second, then lowers her voice, "he's been smiling all morning today. I don't think I've ever seen his beautiful teeth before, so it might just be your lucky day."

"Thanks for the insider information." Eleanor grins, although not as broadly as earlier. Maybe she should have opted for a video interview before accepting her postdoc appointment.

She only had to choose one or two mentors for her postdoctoral fellowship. And apparently, one is a well-known chauvinist, the other a broody grump. Oh well, too late to beat herself up now.

"You are very welcome honey. Professor Kowalski's office is inside the last lab on the right." Tara points her out of the lunch room and into a long corridor. "And Harrington's office is in the same direction, two floors up. Good luck and stay blessed." She gives her a jovial smile. "I'm sure you'll get along with those two gentlemen just fine."

Hoping her very first in-person meeting with Professor Harrington will go a bit better than her current state of lowered expectations (hashtag optimism-forever), Eleanor takes the stairs to the fifth floor and down the hall to Professor Harrington's office, following Mrs. Tara Jones' instructions. It's kind of convenient to have both of her mentors in the same building, just a couple floors and a long hallway away from each other.

"You're our new postdoc?" A voice catches up to her as she's about to knock on the door.

"I am!" She turns around.

"I'm Mano!" An outwardly friendly guy with a suspicion-laced smile—a very disappointing combination—stands before her. She is not the tallest of girls, but this guy is at least a head shorter. Yet he stretches his neck like a peacock, inflates his broad chest as if to demonstrate superiority, and gives her an unfocused look that turns into a slow uncomfortable once-over. It takes a special talent to do all that in a span of a second, and he's certainly nailed the move. A dubious achievement. "I'm *the* Professor Harrington's right-hand person." He holds out his hand.

Creepy is the potential definition for the vibe he's exuding.

Is that the result of working too long in an all-male-no-female-ever lab?

And why would he be presenting himself as *the* Professor Harrington's sidekick? Shouldn't he have a role of his own?

"Nice to meet you, Mano," she says and takes his hand, manners getting the best of her. Wrongful first impression? *Hopefully, though unlikely.*

"*Very* nice to meet you, Dr. Benjamin." He has an arrogant vibe about him, yet he considers himself someone's sidekick.

"Please call me Eleanor."

What is it with the formality in this place?

"Okay, Eleanor. Have you seen the lab yet?" A cocky smile.

"No, actually I haven't." Despite the creepiness, someone is finally willing to give her a tour. "I'll just pop in to say hello to Professor Harrington," she says, about to knock on the door.

"You might want to email him first," Mano says apprehensively. "He doesn't like to be disturbed when his office door is closed."

Seriously? Even on her first day?

"Does he ever leave his door open?"

"Nope."

"Ah. So what do you do when you need to speak with him?"

"I email him, or call," Mano smiles contently.

An unapproachable professor—that's nothing to smile about.

"But he's right here..."

"Yes, that's the way he prefers." Mano shrugs.

"What if it's urgent?"

"Still the way he prefers."

"Got it," she says, taking a step closer to the door. "But it's not the way *I* prefer."

"Oh... If you want, I can show you where your new office is and help you set up your computer and you could email him."

"That's very kind of you, Mano. I'd love to do it later, but first I'll go in and introduce myself." And with that she knocks once, and without waiting for a response, opens the door and peeks in. Call it fearless, call it cultural differences, call it Eleanor Benjamin. Mano winces in the background.

"Good morning, Professor Harrington! I'm Eleanor Benjamin," she announces in a celebratory tone. Because yeah, it's an exciting day.

"Oh, Dr. Benjamin, come on in." A friendly old guy, with tousled white hair and heavy framed glasses gets up from his chair slowly and walks toward her to shake her hand. He's dressed formally, in an old-fashioned style, under an open lab coat. His high levels of energy make up for his slight, frail appearance, and his smile is warm. He doesn't at all seem to mind the interruption. And despite some potential prejudice she expects to uncover, and certain future disagreements, he's surprisingly a very likable person.

"I'm sorry Professor Harrington," Mano interrupts from the doorframe as Eleanor lets herself into the office. "I tried to warn her that you do not like to be disturbed."

"Thank you, Mano, that will be all," Professor Harrington says, signaling for Mano to leave and shut the door. Mano's face screams disappointment. This is going to be interesting.

"I'm very pleased to finally meet you Dr. Benjamin," Professor Harrington says as he steps back slowly into his chair.

"The feeling is mutual," she says. "Please call me Eleanor."

"Very well, Eleanor. Please," He gestures to a chair facing his desk. "I trust that you'll meet Professor Kowalski later?"

"Yes." She nods. "That's my next destination."

"I have to be honest, when I first read your CV, I thought you were a male scientist."

"Because of my last name, that's totally fine, I'm used to that." She smiles politely.

"Not just your last name," he admits openly. "The caliber. Your resume is impressive; first in your class, your publications, military service." Professor Harrington may have been better off omitting the additional information. She's not sure whether she should be flattered or offended for the sake of all the female scientists out there. This is so high on the scale of non-politically correct. But his eyes are bright, almost naive, his voice so enthusiastic. And it occurs to Eleanor that Professor Harrington is not trying to be hurtful or make a sexist comment. It's just the voice of someone who unfortunately got stuck some few centuries behind. So she decides to take it as a compliment.

"You know, army service is compulsory in Israel," she says calmly. "Luckily women don't need to wear corsets anymore, would have made that part quite uncomfortable."

This makes him smile fondly. "I like your sense of humor," he says. "You may not know it, but in the fifty years I've worked at GERI, I've never had a female work in my lab. Aside, of course, for my administrative team."

"I gathered that," she says, not wanting to throw Tara under the bus. "May I ask why not?"

"I thought they might not have what it takes to become good scientists," he says. "Not because they're not smart enough, just because they have so many other things on their minds—relationships, starting a family, raising children. They are inherently bound to being distracted."

Hah!

Despite the content of his striking little speech there, she's surprised by his honesty. This gives her something to work with.

"You are surely aware of the multiple women who've made incredible scientific discoveries throughout the years?" She treads carefully, wanting to keep the conversation to a friendly level. Raising antagonism would not be the ideal approach to get through to him. And as long as he's smiling—she has a chance to open his mind a bit.

"Of course," is his simple response.

"And nowadays, men have all of those things on their minds as well," she grins.

"Some of them, of course, which is why not everyone succeeds," the old professor says. Somehow, to her surprise, his thoughts and statements don't provoke her. There's something immature and adorable in the way he sees the world, despite having been in it for like eighty years.

"And yet you decided to bring me on," she says triumphantly.

"Yes. Well, first, as I said, I thought you were a man. But then when I realized you were not, I looked again at your accomplishments, which are remarkable. A woman who has achieved all that—I realized you must be extraordinary. And with your military training, I figured you must have been trained to eliminate distractions and focus on your target."

She might want to skip the part where she tells him she had an office job in her military service.

He stops for a short second to assess her reaction. Seeing as his words did not cause perturbation, he smiles contently and proudly adds, "So I decided that if the world is progressing, perhaps it's time for me to join the revolution."

He may be a few years late for that revolution, but she'll go with it.

"I'm glad you chose me for the task," she decides to say. Proudly—because along with Tara, she may be the catalyst that will make Professor Harrington join the twenty-first century. Now it's her job to show him that she can do better than many of the male scientists that came through his lab over the years, maybe even make him regret he waited fifty years to hire a female scientist.

"So am I." He smiles. Something in this surprising naivety he possesses makes him so likable. At least in her eyes. "How do you like GERI so far?" He leans back in his chair.

"I haven't seen much of it yet, but so far I like it a lot."

"Perhaps we could start with a tour then," he offers and slowly rises.

"Mano promised a tour later." She tries to save him the trouble but he waves the idea off and opens the door for her. "It would be my pleasure to show you around." He smiles fondly.

They walk down the hallway. The Harrington lab is split into several smaller rooms across the entire corridor. Each has a space for maybe one or two fellows and hosts both their benches and desks, but most are loaded with instruments. Not ideal for cross-contamination and certainly not for coffee-while-reading habits like hers, but certainly ideal for the loud-music-when-pipetting. Once upon a time, this used to be her thing. Although the past few days may have been part of a new—Aiden no-idea-what's-his-last-name era, so she'll have to see about that.

"You've met Mano already," Professor Harrington gestures to the lab closest to his office. "And this is Dr. Antoine Martin." He points to a guy who shuffles through the hallway with a large gel apparatus, "he is a postdoc here, from France. And Dr. Benjamin is from Israel." Origins seem to be very important to Professor Harrington, apparently. Or maybe he's trying to emphasize the diversity? Now having added a female to his staff—he's certainly on a roll.

"Very nice to meet you Dr. Benjamin," Antoine says in a cute French accent and gives her a friendly wink. "I'll put this thing in the cold room and come back to shake your hand," he says apologetically.

"It's Eleanor, and take your time," she grins.

They proceed to the last room in the hallway. "And this is your very own lab," Professor Harrington cordially announces, opening the heavy metal door to a tiny old lab with no windows, letting her in first. Eleanor lets her eyes adjust while taking in the small, stuffy space. It has two lab benches, two desks and a chemical hood.

Her own hood is undoubtedly a positive part, if one insists on looking at the bright side. And she does. But, on the other hand, if one isn't particularly keen on positivity, the place looks like a small, disorganized warehouse, probably used to store anything and everything that no one needs, with reagent bottles and kit boxes that may have expired some years ago, ten at a minimum. It doesn't look like anyone has worked in this room since... ummm... the sixties maybe. A dungeon might be a more suitable description for the place. She's going to need a moving company to help clear out the amount of boxes. Some of them could even be blocking a potential window, hopefully. Or a secret passageway. She also might need a biohazard suit for the clean-up task.

But hey, positive thinking, right?

"Did you say my 'very own lab?' No lab-mates?" She points to the desk opposite them that houses stacks of old dusty science books and a computer from the time when monochrome screens existed.

"I wanted to give you peace and quiet to focus, and avoid... interruptions," Professor Harrington says uncomfortably. "Up until today, this has always been an-all boys' lab, the boys here get distracted easily."

He talks about these highly-educated scientists as if it's a kindergarten group...

"Might get a little lonely in here," she says. "Is there another space I could use? I saw Mano has a spare desk."

"I had a very large lab with many students, but unfortunately, over the last few years parts of it have been re-allocated, in favor of other, younger professors," he says wistfully. "There are several rooms with various instruments, and you can use any of them when you run your experiments. But as far as a dedicated space with your own lab bench and desk—it's really just this room. It's a little... unorganized... but I'm positive that with some magic touch it will be very nice."

Thank God he didn't say 'female touch' because there's only so much patience her feminist mind can muster.

Okay then. Looks like she'll just venture out of her dungeon whenever she wants company. Or spend extra time at the Kowalski lab. Hopefully there's a nicer spot there for her.

They walk back to the door, where Mano is caught snooping. "Mano," Professor Harrington gives him a stern—albeit unsurprised—look. "Can you please show Dr. Benjamin our break room?"

"Of course!" Mano gives her a part-suspicious, part-sleazy smile. *Fabulous.*

"After you," he gestures to Eleanor as their professor retreats back into his cave. "It's a great room, me and *the guys* like to have lunch there, or just hang out sometimes."

Did he put an emphasize on the word 'guys' just now? Or was she imagining?

And while Professor Harrington can get away with these things in his cute, old-school, graceful way, Mano definitely can't. He's also not old enough to enjoy the benefit of the doubt.

12
REALIZATIONS

Eleanor opens Professor Kowalski's lab door and lets herself in, marveling at the sight of his lab equipment—an incredible abundance of machines and kit boxes she could only dream of, coming from her tightly budgeted PhD lab.

Wow, her PhD adviser was not joking when he said GERI labs enjoy ample funding.

Unlike The Harrington lab that is split into multiple rooms across a long hallway, Professor Kowalski's lab is a one spacious open-concept unit, with his office strategically located inside it. And while her formal mentor and sponsor is Professor Harrington, most of her work will be done with Professor Kowalski—her main chosen collaborator. Which in a way makes him her informal, yet pretty important, second mentor. And seeing his impressively equipped lab, Eleanor hopes to be able to conduct as much of her research as possible in this space.

"Good morning," she says to a girl sitting at a central lab bench, who's messing with one of those infinitesimal 384-well plates. Eleanor's PhD lab only used 96-well plates, thank goodness. Trying to pipette anything into these tiny wells make her feel old and like she potentially needs glasses.

"Morning," the girl responds bleakly without turning her head. Remembering which well to pipette into is a confusing enough task, Eleanor can definitely relate. So without further ado, she continues her stroll through the lab benches and amazingly organized reagent shelves. And yes, looks like each bench has its own set of Gilson pipettes. There are surely more expensive brands, but for Eleanor it's a dream come true.

Her very own scientific heaven!

There's a door leading to a computer lab, where she spots the enthusiastically waving Alannah with a few other fellows crunching data. She waves back at her, matching the energy. Eleanor will make sure to bother them and introduce herself later, but first she has a meeting with her new professor, and she's already VERY fashionably late.

The door to Professor Kowalski's office is labeled clearly with his name and title on it and a 'by appointment only' sign, referring any unsolicited incomers to Mrs. Tara Jones, her new ally.

Since Eleanor technically has a meeting with him—although looking at her watch it would be more accurate to say *had* a meeting with him—and mostly since scary warning signs on office entryways don't intimidate her, she knocks on the door. Professor Kowalski will have to get used to her. She doesn't do appointments. A risk he's taken on himself once he took on the collaborator role and co-signed some of her paperwork.

"Come in," she hears a voice from inside, her imagination willing itself to believe it's a familiar one, for an obscure reason.

Eleanor opens the door to find it weirdly occupied by—

"Aiden?!"

He's sitting at Professor Kowalski's desk as if he's taken over the throne, wearing a light blue button-down shirt layered under a gray sweater and topped with a lab coat. His hair is combed back, and he looks serious and important and stunning as ever.

What is he doing here?

Seeing Aiden's handsome face chases away all traces of first day and new place anxieties, which Eleanor typically never has, but started experiencing this morning, after her little chat with Mrs. Tara Jones.

Aiden looks up, his serious blue eyes brightening as he sees her. His lips curl to this beautiful, rare, lop-sided smile. "Hey!" he says and rises from Professor Kowalski's chair, looping his arm around her waist, pulling her in for a kiss.

He looks surprised, pleasantly surprised. And admittedly—putting aside her plan to keep him out of her life and mind—it feels good to be wrapped in his arms again. And despite planning that kiss at her doorstep to be a one-time thing, she can't help but claim this handsome guy to herself again. Aiden does not complain, just pulls her closer, annihilating her with another kiss. Whatever force was wrapping them together on that New Year's Eve night, it's very much still here, growing stronger by the second, taking on a life of its own, consuming everything in their surroundings.

So much for a *small kiss to chase away unrealistic expectations.*

Another one of her failed hypotheses. But hey, good science has to come with a wide repertoire of failed experiments.

"So you couldn't get away from me after all?" he asks, quite pleased with himself.

"Well, actually I'm supposed to meet my collaborator here, I'm a little late," she says, stunned by her refusing-to-subside sensations. "What are *you* doing here?"

"I work here," he says, confused.

"You're a scientist? Why didn't you say anything?"

Yeah, why didn't he mention it?

"You pretty much insisted on changing the subject every time I tried to mention science. Not everyone likes to talk science outside of work, I respect that."

"I assumed you were a... drummer." She tries to piece the information together. "My ex hated it when I talked science with him, I was trying to spare—"

"You *assumed* I was a drummer?" He gives her an amused look. "A scientist making assumptions without collecting data?"

"I *was* collecting data! Still am, obviously. You were playing the drums, at a club, quite well actually..."

And doing these sexy drumming moves with his hands occasionally, and some additional things that kind of sent her mind into... other places.

"Thanks," he says bashfully, rubbing the back of his neck.

Now that she thinks of it, he may have given out some hints—*'that's what made me fall in love with science'* for instance, should have been quite obvious. But she had systematically dismissed every single one of them.

"And you know, after sharing that steamy moment," Eleanor decides to deflect, watching Aiden's mouth curve up in that sexy way of his into a beam, "I now realize, I don't even know your last name."

"Interestingly, I've come to realize the same thing," he chuckles.

"Okay, you go first."

"Nice to officially introduce myself." He lets go of her waist and takes her hand in feigned formality. "I am Aiden Ko—"

The door opens in his mid-sentence attempt and Mrs. Jones's head peeks in.

"Oh, Dr. Benjamin," Tara says into the room. "I see you've found Professor Kowalski. Excellent choice by the way, Professor Kowalski, I really like our new postdoc." She gestures with her head to Eleanor, giving her a broad smile, then pulls her head back out and closes the door. Leaving the two of them gaping, shocked.

Aiden coughs and appears to be choking. Reaching for a water bottle on his desk, he takes a sip, then takes a deep breath, then another sip, then resorts back to being shocked.

Well, the term 'shocked' wouldn't do it justice. On the verge of losing his mind may very well be an understatement.

Realizations are important moments, of course. Eleanor can't say they aren't, it's always better to know all the facts over... what's the alternative? Not knowing? Relatively speaking of course, because there will always be new facts to uncover, that's how science works.

Yeah, well, maybe just for this one instance, they would have been better off not knowing all the currently available facts. This specific realization is just too groundbreaking. Quite profound really.

Aiden looks dumbfounded. Or rather... horrified. Which is a pretty accurate depiction of how she probably looks too.

Her jaw drops, as more comprehensive realization hits her. She might need to pick it up from the floor sometime after the shock dissipates and once she regains control over her body. But right now, she's not sure when that would be.

Perhaps not today.

"Tell me you have a twin brother," is her potential breakthrough resolution.

"Why?"

"So I know I didn't just kiss my professor," she mumbles.

"You did just kiss your professor. Regardless of whether or not I have a twin brother, which I don't."

And here she'd thought that him being a drummer could pose a potential issue. Why hadn't she done the video interview thing before committing to this collaboration? Why didn't she google-image Professor Kowalski while she'd frantically downloaded every single one of his papers?

How had this small yet significant detail escaped them?

Perhaps PubMed should start adding author photos next to each publication...

"Okay, breathe Ellie." Aiden's voice shakes her out of wherever she was. Now he just looks concerned, a little like the way he looked at her in the airport.

She feels a drop on her hand and that metal taste in her mouth. Blood.

No, not again.

Before she has a chance to think, Aiden—or actually Professor Kowalski, she should start getting herself used to it—pulls a pack of tissues from his desk drawer and puts a bunch against her nose.

Might as well make it a habit.

"Sit," he orders in a hot, commanding voice as his arms help her to a chair. "Does that happen often?"

She shakes her head. "It only happened once, at the airport, when I fell into your—"

"It's the dry air. Winters here are dry." Aiden... Urgh... Professor Kowalski's voice is meant to be soothing, but right now she's anything but soothed.

They sit there like that—Eleanor, helpless on the chair, Aiden, kneeling on the floor between her knees, his one hand holding the tissue against her nose, his other hand supporting her head. They were so close together just a couple of days ago that this level of intimacy still feels legit.

And sexy as ever.

And with every slight move of his arm to grab another tissue, her breath hitches. And if it wasn't for her bloody nose, professor or not, she would reach out and kiss him. Because in light of this new information, God knows if she'll ever get another chance to be this close to him again.

"Looks like it stopped," Aiden says eventually. "Are you okay?" He brushes a hair strand off her face and gently tucks it behind her ear. She presses her cheek to his palm and lets it linger, enjoying the touch of his skin for what might be the last time.

"How can you seriously ask if I'm okay?" Eleanor's voice comes out a little rusty. "In the last ninety minutes I found out that one of my professors is a dinosaur who probably doesn't think women should have the right to vote, much less have an academic career. Definitely not in his lab. And then I find out that my other professor is the hot sex-God I badly wanted to bang..."

"Fuck." He gets up and starts pacing across his office. Looking exasperated and flattered and... helpless, all at once. As if this new revelation is resurfacing for the first time, again.

Looks like it might be coming in waves, for both of them.

"Okay, you prefer fuck over bang, fine. But I guess now I need to store my smutty fantasies about you for like... forever."

"I—No, I meant it as..." He rubs the back of his neck, "well, this goes for the both of us." He stops behind his desk, attempting to put some distance between them. His eyes lower. "You have blood on your blouse."

"So much for first-day impressions," she jokes dismissively. Among her list of current concerns, walking around with a few blood stains on her shirt seems insignificant. But Aiden has taken off his lab coat and is now pulling his sweater off his head in a swift motion. His dress shirt underneath hikes up, exposing a set of enticing abs.

Goodness gracious. Undressing this guy is still a prominent thought.

She should look away, but hey...

"Take it off." He pulls at the hem of her blood-stained shirt. His commanding tone throws her back into that lustful moment against the wall in her apartment.

Damn.

"You'll be cold with just your shirt. And I'm not taking your clothes again," she tries to resist the temptation.

"Not an option. I'm not letting you walk around campus like this. You can return my sweater tomorrow, at 8 a.m. when you come to our first 1:1. And be on time."

"Yes sir, Professor Kowalski," She smiles mischievously, stripping off her blouse in front of this hot guy. Slowly. The tortured look on his face as his darkening eyes linger on her naked torso is irresistible.

"Don't call me that. And please put my goddamn sweater on already, I'm having a hard time controlling myself as it is," he grumbles.

"You're the one who told me to take mine off," she chuckles and puts on his sweater. It's warm—still possessing his body heat. And his core-melting scent.

Smile-sigh...

It does look like she's wearing her man's sweater, but it's stylish. Worn over her skinny jeans and boots, she might be able to pull it off.

Her man's sweater. Gosh, she has to start getting these intrusive mind-slipups under control.

"Happy?" she asks. His content look at the sight of her wearing his clothes again is tempting.

"I'd be happier not having unethical thoughts right now," he huffs, then deflects. "You should go wash the blood off while it's still fresh. Cold water, if you don't want it to leave stains."

"Thanks for the tip," she says. "And the sweater." She's about to turn toward the door but there's a nagging technicality on her mind. "By the way." She takes a confrontational step closer. "Why did you introduce yourself as Aiden if your name is Andrew?"

"I go by my middle name. Andrew is just used formally," he

answers, clearly not startled by the proximity. Or the question. "According to my dad, Andrew was what he and my mom agreed on. But Aiden was my mom's favorite name. And apparently, as a little kid, I was more inclined to respond to it." By the tone of the last few beats, she can tell this is not a piece of data he lets out easily.

Little kid Aiden. Big, beautiful, inquiring blue eyes. She can picture it.

"Oh."

And now that she's managed to take her eyes off his lips, she does notice that his lab coat has 'Kowalski' embroidered above the left pocket. Something she completely missed when she walked into the office and let her tongue invade his mouth.

Tara's words—'people see what they want to see'—the woman was spot on!

Eleanor sighs deeply because it's been a while since she's taken an actual breath. "I can't believe I almost fucked my collaborating professor. If it weren't for Alannah walking in on us—" And as he shakes his head in response, another piece clicks into place. "That's why she looked so stunned when she caught us making out!"

Aiden gives her a scolding look, wordlessly begging for a change of topic, the recollection making him look deliciously hungry.

Awkward silence. Eleanor doesn't do silence.

"Can you show me around?" she decides to ask. Because staying away from this man is impossible. "Professor Harrington gave me a tour in his lab, introduced me to all the lab members—"

"You mean Mano gave you a tour, on behalf of Professor Harrington?"

"No, I mean what I say—Professor Harrington, in the flesh, gave me a walk-through. Despite his biased opinions on the entire female gender, he was surprisingly and unexpectedly kind."

Aiden makes some kind of a coughing sound to that.

"Okay, now for your tour professor, I expect it to be no less enjoyable than Professor Harrington's."

"Don't call me professor," Aiden warns. Rising from his seat. "Now, shall we?" He moves past her and opens the door. "Welcome to the Kowalski lab."

Aiden shows her around the lab. The benches, the instruments, the perfectly organized shelves of reagents, the freezers, tissue culture room—yes, his lab has its very own tissue culture room!

"Gone are the days of signing up for a time slot at the hood!" She can't hide her excitement.

They stop by the bathroom for her to wash the blood off her shirt, then spread it over the vents in his office to dry. Then continue the tour.

"Your own dark room?! No fucking way!" She can't hide her surprise as they step into the revolving door. "This is heaven." A cushioned budget is a superb thing! She spins twice before jumping in the dark room, spreading her limbs, and losing her balance, landing in Aiden's arms again.

This time on purpose.

"I may have found a possible bypass to what's considered appropriate lab behavior," she whispers.

Aiden just looks at her from up close, trying to bite down an impending smile but failing miserably.

"Despite all the complications," he says quietly after making sure they're alone, "I think I'm going to enjoy having you around." She can feel his warm breath on her face before he releases her from his embrace.

"You will, I promise." She grins.

"We have lab meetings every Wednesday at 7:30 a.m. And journal clubs on the first Thursday of each month at 2 p.m."

"Seven-thirty a.m.?!" she chokes.

"Bright and early."

"A morning person. Should have known." And then, bringing her head closer to his ear she adds, "Hmmm. Didn't take you for the tormenting bossy type."

"You have no idea."

They walk back to the open space. "This is going to be your bench for when you run experiments in my lab." He points to the spot closest to his office. How fitting. "And here is the computer room." He opens the door to where all of the other fellows are bunched at the moment. All seem pretty focused on typing or reading papers or staring at data points.

"Hello!" Eleanor says loudly. Four heads turn toward her, Alannah amongst them, attempting a neutral I've-never-er-seen-these-guys-making-out-in-my-hallway expression. And then trying to hide another knowing look as her eyes narrow on Aiden's sweater. Eleanor smiles broadly at her, willing her to park these thoughts away, then waves at the others. "I'm Eleanor."

"This is Dr. Benjamin, the new postdoc at the Harrington lab, and our new collaborator for the autoimmunity project," Aiden announces formally. "This is Dr. Yan Dimitrov, our staff scientist." He points to a tall guy in the farthest corner. "Ms. Zoe Holland is a PhD candidate." That's the one who was focused on pipetting earlier. Even when idling she seems unfriendly. "Dr. Finn Anderson, who will soon be finishing his postdoc and leave us for greener pastures." Aiden gestures to the guy standing to his right. "And you know Dr. Alannah Meyser already," Aiden tenses, giving Alannah an apprehensive look, not sure how this is going to go. Alannah nods with a your-secret-is-safe-with-me reassurance.

Wow, Aiden is really into this last name thing.

"Very nice to meet you all." Eleanor smiles brightly.

"Nice to meet you too." Yan shakes her hand. Zoe doesn't look too pleased, might be a resting face thing, but nods politely.

"Very nice to meet you," says Finn. He shakes her hand warmly, holding her gaze slightly longer.

"Same here." She smiles.

He's tall, although not as tall as Aiden, and looks more like a surfer than a scientist really, with dirty blond tousled hair, green eyes, and a nice tan despite the D.C. winter. Not her bad-boy drummer type, but undoubtedly someone who'd normally make her heart thump a little harder, head turn a little longer. Except not today. It does absolutely nothing to her. No bristling, not even a single goose bump out of place. Stable heart rate.

Is she broken or something?

And instead of wanting to stare at Finn, she has to battle an urge to steal a glimpse at Aiden.

Shit.

Aiden clears his throat, sending a minuscule warning glare at Finn. "This is your work station." He gestures to Eleanor, conveniently picking out the farthest computer from Finn, next to the unfriendliest Zoe. Then summons his commanding tone. "Let's continue your tour."

Hmmm...

The tour ends at the coffee machine in the lunch room. Aiden's still lost in thoughts, while Eleanor's wishing she had a glimpse into said thoughts and also trying to process the new information and form some sort of a plan. But plans don't typically form themselves. One of them will have to eventually take the lead on this incredibly complex crafting task. And not that this will get them any further in this activity, but another realization comes to mind.

"OH MY GOD!" Eleanor unintentionally lets out her best excitement scream, covering her mouth with her hand.

From the way Aiden winces, he's not sure this was a happy scream.

"Are you okay?" Mrs. Jones, who's just entered the room with her empty mug turns her head in concern. "Professor Kowalski, what did you do to her?!"

Oh, he could have done wonderful, wonderful things, if not for Alannah's interruption.

"I wish I had something to do with it, but I can't take credit," he grunts.

"Your dad is Professor Gordon Kowalski?!" Eleanor finally lets them in on her unique association process.

"Obviously."

"*THE* Professor Gordon Kowalski?! I think I probably own every single one of the biochemistry textbooks he's written, memorized his theories... I'm a fan!"

"Oh yes, his father is a big-shot scientist," Mrs. Jones explains. "Well, the apple didn't fall too far from the tree." She gives Eleanor a wink, then fills up her mug and retreats, leaving them alone again.

Alone to ponder over the original realization.

Yeah, that one...

"Perhaps I should have googled you before accepting that collaboration offer," Eleanor says playfully.

"You *never* googled me? So much for doing your homework beforehand."

"Clearly, I was looking for a collaborator, not a husband. I read every single one of your papers inside and out. I already knew you are a brilliant scientist, why would I care about how you look? And it also appears you hadn't done much googling either."

"Well, I guess you have a point."

Despite the overly healthy vegan breakfast made and served to her by Alannah, but mostly because of not being able to eat anything since, Eleanor's stomach starts giving out the usual hunger signals.

"You need to eat something," Aiden says in a tone that sounds more like a command than anything else. Yes, the loud rumbling has officially made its way to his ears.

"I do. And then I have a bunch of orientation and lab safety trainings to partake in at Professor Harrington's lab. So yeah, have a great day!" She slaps on the best smile she can gather and turns to leave.

"Not so fast." He grabs her by the hand. "We need to have an actual conversation."

"O-kay," she says, enjoying his touch-induced sparks. "I'll be here tomorrow for the early morning 1:1 you've planned for us. After I'm well-fed from Alannah's fabulous breakfast, and possibly fed up with my newly discovered prejudiced Professor Harrington. Note to self—it's not enough to know someone's science out and in to determine whether they should be one's boss."

"You'll be fine. I trust that you'll successfully rebut all of his biases. If there's anyone on earth capable of doing that, it would be you," he says with impressive certainty.

Hopefully he's right.

"Eight a.m. tomorrow. Don't be late."

13
Roommates

"I thought you knew," Alannah says incredulously as they meet for dinner back at their apartment.

"Why would I want to make out with the professor I'm supposed to collaborate with?" Eleanor says, bewildered. "I know this may sound like someone's fantasy but that was never on my list. At least now I know why you were looking at me funny when you walked in on us... But why didn't you say anything?"

"Already told you. I go by live and let live, you do you, and I couldn't have possibly known you guys had no idea you'd be working together." She smiles awkwardly. "I mean, you knew he was a professor, with the last name of Kowalski, it's just putting together a few simple facts." She gives Eleanor an amused look. "Where did you say you got your PhD from? YouTube?"

"Hey, don't hate on YouTube," Eleanor laughs. "I didn't know he was a professor, let alone *my* collaborating professor. I didn't even know he was a scientist, I thought he was a drummer. And I never actually asked for his last name." So many seemingly unrelated details leading up to one big mess.

"Wow girl, not gonna lie, getting naked with a guy before even asking for his last name, you're quite the adventurous one," Alannah smirks. "There's probably not even a single girl on campus who doesn't know who Professor Kowalski is, except for you, apparently."

"Really?" Eleanor's curiosity is officially piqued. "Tell me more."

"I don't think I need to explain that to you—I am sure you are very well aware of his handsome face and... very nicely built body."

"Says the celibate member of his lab," she chuckles.

"I may be celibate, but I'm not blind."

"Oh, so he's a player?"

"Definitely not. Never mixes his professional life with... pleasure. And anyway, he doesn't seem to be into the women at GERI, and believe me—many have tried to flirt with him, come into the lab, walked up to him after class. He's completely immune. Keeps his personal life very private and separate, like science is the only thing for him, as far as we lowly postdocs know. I had this theory that he might be asexual or something. Until I saw how he looked at you."

"Oh, believe me, he's very much not asexual," Eleanor chuckles.

"It's gonna take me a while to unsee your spicy scene," Alannah blushes. "So, yeah, I believe you."

Eleanor's mind drifts off somewhere else. "That's why his dad said these were *Aiden's papers*," she mumbles, thinking back.

"What? You've met his dad? How serious are you guys?"

"No, not serious," Eleanor tries. "I was planning on not seeing him again, ever. But that obviously didn't work out very well for me."

"Not seeing him again, why? You guys looked very much... into each other," Alannah points her head to that wall Eleanor was pressed against just the other night.

"Yeah…" The annoying uninvited butterflies in her belly make their comeback. "I'm really not looking for a relationship right now. I came here to focus on my science."

"Well, life sometimes has other plans for us, you know? Besides, no reason why you can't focus on your science and be in a relationship. Lots of people do it."

"I am not very good with multi-tasking. And even more terrible with juggling."

Especially when hearts are involved.

"I still don't get how you didn't recognize him from the interview." Alannah's questions keep on coming.

"I never actually met him before coming here. Same with Professor Harrington," Eleanor admits. It seemed reasonable at the time, but it does sound silly now when she says it out loud.

"You didn't come for an in-person interview?" Alannah's mouth forms into a big, wondering O. It appears to be the one technical detail that strikes her the most.

"No, at that time GERI had their no-visitor policy…"

"But there's Zoom, Teams, Google Meet, you didn't even have a video interview?"

"Professor Harrington is old-school. We exchanged some emails. Enough to know it was a good match—strictly scientifically speaking—so that was it, I didn't need to see how he looks to know. And same with Professor Kowalski."

"But face-to-face interaction is so important when choosing your collaborator. What if you didn't have chemistry?" Alannah shoves Eleanor's plate closer, reminding her to eat. "Well never mind, you two are clearly not lacking any chemistry."

"Yes, maybe a bit too much chemistry…"

Mind-blowing, sparks flying everywhere, can't-get-him-out-of-her-head kind of chemistry.

"So wait, you said a drummer. Why did you think he was a

drummer?" Alannah asks, taking the first bite from her gluten-free, vegan, nutrient-rich, meat-deficient, home-cooked dinner. There's an identical clone just like this waiting on Eleanor's plate. But since finding out her GERI collaborator is the handsome hot guy who pinned her against the wall and kissed her senseless, she hasn't been able to breathe long enough to manage with the mechanics of eati ng.

"Because he *is* a drummer. He invited me to watch him play and I came with the excuse of returning his hoodie. I really was only testing the hypothesis that—"

"Babe, you're not making any sense, I'm missing some crucial details. How did you have his hoodie?" Alannah looks overwhelmed, and mostly just overwhelmingly confused.

"Okay, you might want to sit back for this story," Eleanor chuckles.

"Oh. Wow," Alannah says after sitting quietly, holding off chewing her dinner, for over twenty minutes. Learning about accidental meetings at airports, nosebleeds, airplane seat buddies to snuggle on, selfies, mom texting, drummers, coat shopping, family introductions, soup improving, making out, interruptions and lab meetings. A full memoir.

But now she's speechless.

"I hope I didn't break you," is Eleanor's story wrap up.

"No, just a little surprised is all. It takes much more to break me," Alannah says, her face flushed.

"Good, because I like you."

"I like you too. But Ellie, you *need* to drop the idea of having him as a mentor. Give Cupid a chance."

"Professor Harrington is my official mentor. Aiden is not really my mentor, he's my collaborator, and I was hoping he could also mentor me, unofficially. This—" she gestures to that same wall— "makes it a bit more challenging. But hey—I'm not one to shy away from a good challenge. And I wasn't looking for a relationship anyway. Besides, Cupid is deceitful and was not invited to *this* party."

"Okay, the fact that Professor Harrington is over eighty years old tells me he might not be the safest long-term bet, but for now—can you just drop the collaboration so you can go back to dating Professor Kowalski?"

"Why would I do that?"

"Are you for real? You know, I've been working at the Kowalski lab for over three years now. Never seen this guy smile once. That is, until I saw him with you. You should have seen how he walked in this morning! Or how his eyes beamed when he said your name at the introduction. I know my math. And the way you two look at each other... Man! You shouldn't dismiss that, it might be your once-in-a-lifetime forever opportunity." Alannah speaks with so much passion it's almost contagious.

"No, no, you've got it all wrong," Eleanor insists. "This thing here—this amazing collaborator I've picked for myself—is the once-in-a-lifetime opportunity to get my science to places I'd never be able to achieve alone."

"Okay, but science is science. True love is not something you just throw away."

"Yes, science is science, only the most important thing in my life. And true love—what are you even talking about? Love is a distraction. And I wouldn't even know true love if it landed in my dinner right now. It's just not on my list of capabilities, and I'd like to keep it this way." Eleanor gives her a determined look, topping it off with a smile. "Where did you even get this hideous L word from? You've seen us interact for no more than a few minutes, and most of it was against this wall."

"You are funny. One glance at you together is all I needed. You two are so infatuated with each other. Yet it might require an entire peer-review process for you to understand." Alannah picks up Eleanor's fork that's now resting next to her plate and shoves it into her hands. "You have to eat. Starving is not compatible with thinking," she says.

"Not infatuated," Eleanor says, finally taking a bite. "It's called lust. And how do you tell the difference, you might ask? By the very apparent fact that I shouldn't be left alone with him because," she says, mouth full, "well, the because part is X-rated... But that's all it is. Anyway, please don't tell anyone," Eleanor pleads. "This could kill his career."

"Don't worry babe, your secret is safe with me," Alannah gives her a cute wink. "Incidentally, his sweater looked good on you," she chuckles.

"Oh, that's because I had a nosebleed and he insisted I change my shirt. By the way—your cooking is superb."

"Thanks. And no need to explain." Alannah makes a heart with her fingers. "So how are you planning to handle it?"

"Still struggling with that part."

"The way I see it, you have three options," Alannah offers. "The first option you obviously didn't like—switch the collaboration so you guys can ride hand-in-hand into the sunset."

"No way I'm switching a collaborator. I told you, I specifically chose him for his provocative hypotheses. I came all the way here for—"

"Yeah yeah, heard you the first time, I was just listing the options. So fast forward to option two—you dial it back to a strictly professional relationship. Each of you go back to your boring pre-love state of mind, where getting your clean PCR results or the right band size on your gel is the highlight of your day."

"Hey, those *are* the highlights of my day!" Eleanor jumps in defensively. "And it's not boring, science is life!" Then takes another bite. "Mmm! This is good." She helplessly tries to divert the conversation.

"Thanks babe. And I agree, science is life, but there's more to life than science."

"Not for me."

"Good luck with that." Alannah pats her arm emphatically, then continues. "It wouldn't be complete if I didn't mention option three—you guys can embark on a secret undercover love affair. Strict mentor-student relationship during the day, lovers during the night."

"Sounds like the perfect script for a Netflix series, if you ask me," Eleanor chuckles.

"I know, right?"

"And a major distraction... and ethically wrong, if not illegal?"

"Well, if you drop the unofficial mentor idea, there's nothing unethical or illegal here. I don't think there's any written rule regarding what GERI employees do with other GERI employees in their spare time, outside of GERI. Except for students. But luckily postdocs are not considered students, so you're probably exempt."

"I hope you're right."

"So which option did you like the most?" Alannah bats her eyelashes at her.

"None of them stood out. I think I'll just have to mix and match. And improvise."

14
Rules

"This is going to require some adjustment," Eleanor says as she enters Aiden's office, still overwhelmed by how her heart skips a beat at the sight of her... errr... collaborating professor. "Early mornings are not my thing." She blows her bangs off her forehead with a huff.

Aiden studies her intently, still looking every ounce as shocked as yesterday. "It's your second day and you're already five minutes late."

"Five minutes after is not considered late." She lets herself drop into the seat in front of him, kicks off her sneakers, leans back with a sigh and stretches her legs on her side of his desk.

"What is it considered then?" He frowns handsomely, staring at her socks.

"It's considered right on time," she explains.

"Right on time is right at the time scheduled. Or even a few minutes before."

"No, you've got it all wrong. A few minutes before is being too anxious."

"No, that's being punctilious. What's wrong with being exactly on time?" His general expression appears troubled more than anything else, but there's also a ghost of a smile hidden in there.

"I didn't want to appear anxious," she chuckles. "Jeez, I'm trying to make a good impression here. But okay, I'll take that into consideration the next time I debate between hitting the snooze button a few more times or rolling myself out of bed."

"You shouldn't be hitting your snooze button when you're supposed to be meeting with me."

"Well, I can do whatever I want in my own bed. Unless you're in there too... then I might consider you in my plans." Her mischievous comment seems to spark a lightning storm in that beautiful blue of his eyes.

He clears his throat. "I think I should report myself to the office of ethics and workplace miscon—"

So that's what's eating him this morning...

"Report yourself for doing what?" Eleanor cocks her head to one side, trying to appear serious. Feet still wiggling on his desk.

"Misconduct obviously. Unethical behavior and intrusive disruptive thoughts. Exploiting my position of power for—"

"Pffftt!" is the sophisticated vocabulary Eleanor chooses in response, snorting. "Professor Kowalski!" she says flirtatiously before a vocal burst of laughter escapes her. "If anything, I'd be exploiting *you*. And I bet my thoughts about you are a thousand times more intrusive." Aiden looks simultaneously intrigued and concerned. "Hey," she continues, "you didn't even know who I was. And believe me, it was very much consensual." She tries for serious. "And the thoughts part—maybe one day I'll tell you mine."

Or better yet, show him.

His eyes grow darker as he shakes his head slowly. "So what do we do now?"

"We follow our plan, our original plan that is. The one I came here for. I'll peacefully and enjoyably do my research, you do your professory stuff, you know."

"My professory stuff?" He furrows a brow at her.

"Yeah, do the things you normally do. Sit here, brood, look handsome."

"I don't brood."

"That's not what I heard," she chirps. Still no smile. "Okay, don't brood, just do your deep thinking. A common feature between scientists and musicians. Maybe that's why it was so easy for me to assume you were a full-time drummer," she mumbles.

"And what about us?" Aiden asks cautiously.

"Us? As in the one-night-stand no-strings-attached-we-al-most-embarked-on us?"

"Jesus Ellie," he sighs.

"What?" Gosh, this man is confusing.

And she's really loving the way her name sounds when he says it.

"I'm being serious here."

"I can tell." Eleanor lowers her feet from his desk and sits up straighter. "Are you the kind of person who has to plan everything in advance?" she asks, and he nods slightly, as if trying to decide whether this is a trick question. "Just leave some room for spontaneity. You might find that it's actually the things we don't plan that turn out to be the best."

Yes, she feels much more philosophical on a full stomach. Alannah's vegan breakfast was spot-on.

"I'd feel more comfortable if we set some ground rules between us, so we know what to expect and how to handle certain situations."

"Oh, we can have our own code of conduct! Or would you prefer a standard operating procedure?"

"You're impossible," he sighs.

"I'll take that as a compliment!" Eleanor puts her shoes back on, stands up and takes a brand-new notepad from what looks like Aiden's—very organized—supply shelf. "I actually think it's not a bad idea, Professor Kowalski." She pulls the chair to Aiden's side of the desk and sits beside him.

"Okay, rule number one—you can't call me Professor Kowalski."

"It does sound kind of kinky." She rubs her chin. "Okay, what should I call you?"

"Aiden would do."

"Well, my sources tell me that you go by Professor Kowalski in your lab. Wouldn't that seem suspicious if I'm the only one exempt?"

"No."

"Might be a little challenging to explain how I've made it into this prestigious circle."

"They'll have to live with it."

"Okay, rule one is settled. You'll just need to figure out a convincing public explanation for this discrepancy in naming conventions, but I trust you."

"Thank god."

Eleanor reaches under him for a pen. His breath hitches.

He smells good.

But she already knew that. There have been multiple times that she's taken a breath-full since falling into him at the airport. But still.

"Rule number two," he says. "No seduction until we figure this thing out."

"Oh, come on, that's the best part. Are you serious right now?" This man is a real party pooper.

"Ellie, we could get ourselves kicked out of GERI, ruin our

reputations."

"Listen, I don't know what the rules are here at GERI, but I'm a postdoc, I've completed my studies. I'm here as a scientist doing research." She stops for better impact and a breather. "Yes, you are my main collaborator and, in a way, I hope you'll serve as an unofficial mentor. And yes, your budget is partly funding my research. But it's not like I'm your student. I'm not even *your* postdoc. I'm not a kid looking up to their professor. I'm twenty-eight years old, and perfectly capable of making my own adult decisions."

Well, for the most part. There may have been some outliers.

"I don't see why my 'no seduction' rule would make much of a difference to you. If I recall correctly, you said you weren't looking for a relationship. '*Not looking for anything period,*' I believe were your exact words," he challenges.

"That was before."

"Before what?"

This guy is persistent. Dammit.

"Before I knew that I'd be seeing you every day."

"I see." His gaze disappears into some imaginary void. "So seeing me every day has the potential to change your pre-made decision?"

"It will surely make it harder to resist." She bites her lip. "Okay, I'll do my best. Now for *my* rules," she deflects, handing him the pen.

"I wasn't done," he says sharply.

"I'm sure you weren't. We'll come back to your rules later. Now mine." She gestures to the pen she shoved into his hand. "My one and only rule is honesty. This is not going to work if we don't tell each other what goes on in our heads. And I mean it. As harsh or as smutty or as wonderful as it may be. I am a terrible guesser, and an even more terrible liar."

"*Smutty?*" Aiden deadpans.

"Yes, write it down." Eleanor points to the paper.

"Any other rules?"

"Just this one. And I think we should just take it easy and figure things out as we go. Not everything has to be predetermined. This can be a living document, just like a real SOP—every time you feel the urge to add a rule, just do it, with my permission of course, and up the version number." She chuckles. "We can't think of every possible scenario right now. And mostly—you should really just relax, don't worry, everything will be fine." She slaps on her best smile.

It feels good to say it even if she doesn't one-hundred percent believe it. And it mostly just feels good to hear it, even if it's coming out of her own mouth. Ah, the power of positive thinking.

"Why do I get a bad feeling when I hear—*don't worry?*" Aiden sighs, running a resigned hand through his hair.

"It's not just a regular 'don't worry,' it's *my* 'don't worry.' And don't listen to that voice in your head, it's just your—how do you call someone who isn't spontaneous?"

"Planned? Calculated? Responsible?" he offers.

"I believe uptight is the word I was looking for."

"I'm not uptight."

"Yeah? So are hugs allowed?" she challenges.

"No, that's against the 'no seduction' rule."

"I meant friendly hugs, you know there's a wide spectrum—"

"You want honesty? I don't think I should put my self-control to the test when it comes to you."

"That's a very nice, candid response Professor Kowalski!"

"You're already breaking the rules."

After an interesting 1:1 with Aiden that included a lot of discussion around drafting their three rules—yes, Eleanor never actually let Aiden get through the rest of it, admitting she's terrible with rules and having too many would just render most of them useless—and Aiden conceding. Eleanor walks up to the fifth floor, stopping by the boss's office. "Good morning, Professor Harrington!" she says, knocking gently and opening the door simultaneously.

"Good morning, Dr. Benjamin." The old professor looks surprised by her audacity. Well, he'll need to adjust. "Can I help you?" he asks politely, probably wondering if a meeting had been scheduled for them first thing this morning and he somehow missed the memo.

"No, just came to say good morning." She beams.

"Oh?" he says in a graceful half-question.

Is that such an unusual habit in this lab?

"Well—that's how I usually am, I say good morning when I come into the lab, that is. I hope you don't mind." She smiles broadly, not really seeking permission. Even if he does mind, she's still planning on doing it every single day. He'll get habituated to it eventually.

"Oh," Professor Harrington says, this time without a question. "I don't mind at all."

"Just came to warn you, I might do it every day from now on. And I might also barge in unannounced during the day if I get some groundbreaking results on my experiments."

"Please do," he approves.

"You bet!" she says, then pulls her head back and closes the door, feeling a small sense of victory over Mano's warning-advice.

Now it's time for the inevitable—cleaning up the dungeon. She steps into her new—yet very old and messy—lab, puts on her crisp new lab coat that bears the abbreviated 'Dr.' Followed by her last name embroidered neatly right next to it in a fancy blue font, then some gloves and even goggles, not really knowing what old chemicals may be lurking in those big piles of chaos in front of her. And digs in.

It takes a while until she's able to see the actual lab bench hidden underneath, but when she finally does, a minuscule sense of accomplishment takes over, making her smile.

"What the hell is this?" A familiar growl echoes through the room, blowing warmth into her.

She turns her head to face Aiden. "My new lab." She grins. Seeing him here, basking in his presence, has an unexpected effect of broadening her smile, which makes her cheeks bump into the edges of her goggles. He's taken off his lab coat and his button-down's sleeves are rolled up, exposing an attractive set of forearms.

Aiden's eyebrows crush together. "I'm not letting you work in this shithole," he decrees. "I'm going to speak with Professor Harrington right now!" He tries to storm out of the room, but Eleanor slides off her dirty gloves quickly and catches him by the forearm. His skin feels warm and unyielding under her fingers.

Damn, why does touching him feel so enticing?

"Aiden, you can't be acting like a protective boyfriend around here, it's going to look suspicious. Don't worry, I can handle—"

"I don't like it," he huffs. "You have a perfectly good space in my lab, why do you even bother with this?"

"I need to spend some of my time here too," she reminds him.

"Don't worry, it's going to look great when I'm done. Eventually."

"At least let me help you." It sounds more like a command rather than an offer.

"That's very nice of you, but you have to treat me like you would everyone else," Eleanor says calmly. And at the slight chance of getting him all worked up she adds, "You can get your postdoc Finn to help me."

"No fucking way!" he snaps. "You're off limits and I'll make sure Finn knows it."

"Why Professor Kowalski, I didn't take you for the jealous type." She gives him a mischievous smile. "I was just teasing you."

Aiden sighs, his other hand closes on her fingers that are apparently still clutching his forearm, thumb gently stroking the back of her hand in an unspoken longing moment. "I'll help you clean this place up. End of discussion."

"I see you don't waste any time," says Professor Harrington, amazed, when he stops by her room on his way out. "This place hasn't looked so nice in years," he admits.

Was this whole thing a test? Well, he ain't seen nothing yet.

"She had some special help," Mano has to interject. He seems to have eyes and ears everywhere. Eleanor might need to watch her back.

"Oh?" is Professor Harrington's half-question-half-statement.

"Yes, you'll fall over your feet if I tell you!" Mano grins from ear to ear.

"Mano, this form of speech does not sit well with someone my age." Professor Harrington gives him a cynical look.

"Good point, Professor," Mano says, still excited by the prospect of sharing his piece of gossip. "It was Professor Kowalski!"

"Professor Kowalski...?" His curiosity on the rise. This piece of news seems to be almost as exciting for the old professor as it is for Mano. "How interesting." His face forms into a surprised smile. Eleanor doesn't quite know what to make of it.

"I love what you did to the place!" Antoine chimes in, squeezing himself into her small room, warmly patting her shoulder.

"Thank you, Antoine, that's the reaction I was looking for." She beams at him.

"You're welcome!" He grins, then sends quizzical looks to the other gentlemen in the room, realizing he's missed an essential part.

"Guess who her secret helper was?"

"Not secret, obviously."

"Professor Kowalski!"

"Mano, that's not how guessing games work," Eleanor quips. "You didn't even give him a chance to make a single guess."

Professor Harrington chuckles at that last comment and leaves them to their fascinating discussion.

"Why is that so exciting? Sorry, I didn't get the joke, maybe my French?" Antoine looks clueless, sharing Eleanor's sentiment.

"Antoine, have you been living under a rock? I've never seen Professor Kowalski help anyone or interact with anyone if it's not part of a scientific discussion. He's not really known for his superior small-talk abilities, in case you haven't noticed." Mano throws his hands in the air to help make his point. "But apparently he has a soft spot for Eleanor here."

She wouldn't exactly call it a soft spot.

"Professor Kowalski is hot!" Antoine says in a cute French accent, "And he is a brilliant scientist. His contributions to the world of science are *superb*." He says that last word with a French emphasis and gives Eleanor a wink. "He doesn't have to hold small talks if he doesn't want to."

"I swear, Antoine, I don't know how I'm even friends with you." Mano sighs, shaking his head.

"Is that a coffee cup you're holding there, Antoine?" Eleanor can't help herself. "Not trying to change the topic but I could really use some caffeine. Where can one get a decent cappuccino in this place?" She takes off her lab coat and puts on her jacket. Her caffeine withdrawal symptoms are starting to show.

"My very own coffee buddy!" Antoine's face glows. "Come with me, I'll show you," he says happily, adjusting his scarf and linking arms with her. "Ciao," he waves at Mano.

"Wait, can I join too?" Mano asks petulantly.

"You're up for the good coffee, Mano?" Antoine gives him a dubious look.

"I am today," he says and trails behind them.

They walk out of the building, down a narrow path between a few smaller buildings until they finally emerge into a large grassy area, albeit grayish-yellow in color due to the freezing weather, with a volleyball court, some benches, and—drumroll—a real coffee shop!

It has no sign or name attached to it, but the pleasant aroma of freshly ground coffee beans carries itself through Eleanor's olfactory system before they even open the front door. Inside, there are just a few tables with chairs and a barista who greets them warmly.

They get some GOOD coffee, finally, and sit down by one of the empty spots.

"So, when do you usually have lab meetings?" Eleanor realizes she's missing some crucial info.

Antoine and Mano exchange looks. Crickets.

Okay...

"Journal clubs?" she tries again.

Still crickets.

"Other meetings?"

They both shake their heads.

"Okay guys, this is like the weirdest conversation ever. No lab meetings whatsoever?"

"Professor Harrington used to hold them once a month, but we lost track a few years ago, and... I guess forgot about them," Mano finally chimes in. "These were no good anyway, very boring."

"Boring? Why?"

Mano just shrugs.

Eleanor chugs the rest of her coffee before it has a chance to get cold. Looks like she has some work to do and some status quos to change.

So this is how it's going to be from now on, given Aiden's 'no seduction' rule. A new-old routine. A scientist during the day and a scientist during the night. That's all she's known in the past five years, that's how she had it planned out, that's what she came all this way here for. Eleanor is sprawled on her bed, waiting patiently for midnight, which will be a reasonable morning time back home. Last night Eleanor was too exhausted and too confused to speak with anyone, family included, after her sensational discovery.

Tonight, she finds herself battling with her phone, looking at the funny selfie with Aiden that's still etched to her home screen.

"Hey." She shoots him an exploratory text. A whole minute goes by before her phone beeps in response. It feels like forever.

"Hey."

"Looks like you haven't deleted WhatsApp yet."

"I've decided to keep it," is his response after a few seconds of hesitation.

"Did I wake you?"

"No, can't sleep."

"Me neither. Is it crazy that I feel excited?"

"No, it's not crazy," he texts back. "You've just started a new postdoc fellowship in a new country, would be crazy not to be excited."

"These are good reasons, but I don't think these are the only reasons." Another exploratory text.

"Understandable."

"Enlighten me please," she teases. Adding a smiley face.

"Can't."

"Why not?"

"Rule number two," he writes back.

Ah. She sighs deeply. What is she going to do with this man?

"How was your second day at GERI?" Her mom's text message arrives right on time.

"Looks like my mom is awake, I promised to call her. Good night for now, hope you dream of me," she writes, then regrets the last part a second too late. She considers deleting the message, but another text from Aiden beats her to it.

"I hope you do too."

More messages start to trickle in as her family back home is waking up for the day.

"Ima!" Eleanor says into the screen when her mom appears on the other side of the WhatsApp video call, spreading love into Eleanor's empty and oh-so-far-away room.

"Ellie! How were your first two days? Tell me everything!"

"Exciting," Eleanor answers, knowing her tone might start an entire conundrum but she can't bring herself to lie.

"What's wrong honey?" The famous mom's sixth sense kicks in, her mother's laser mom-eyes scanning Eleanor's face for any and all unspoken subtexts.

"Remember that guy from the plane?"

"Aiden, of course, he has a thing for you, I can tell you that... Wait, did he do something wrong?"

"No Ima, but I found he's a professor, Professor Kowalski." Eleanor pulls on the string of her hoodie and starts rolling it on her finger nervously.

"Oh, he's a professor? Honey, that's not a bad thing. He's also a nice Jewish boy, I asked him—"

"No, Ima, THE Professor Kowalski, my collaborator."

"Oh..."

"Yeah, and we've been kind of hanging out before we knew."

"Honey, you can be collaborators and lovers, I don't see any problem with that." Her mom's smile broadens.

"I had been hoping he would serve as my unofficial mentor..."

"Oh, just keep the second one, what's his name?"

"Professor Harrington."

"Yes, just keep Professor Harrington as your mentor, you don't need two. Then you can keep hanging out with Aiden."

So simple, yet...

"I'm not sure I can do that, Ima. I chose both because each of them specializes in different fields and techniques. I need both of them. You know how long I've worked on finding the right mentors for my project."

"It's also not easy to find the right guy," her mom interjects, still smiling. Relentless romanticism must have genetic roots in her family. Although Eleanor's generation may have been skipped.

"Ima! I am not looking for a boyfriend, I didn't come all the way here for *that*."

"I'm sure you two will figure it out. But if you want to take your Ima's unsolicited advice," her mom cackles, "science is important, no doubt, and I know how much it is important to you, honey. But love is important too, and finding your one might only happen once in a lifetime. So while you're busy formulating your hypotheses and testing them with sophisticated science experiments, make sure you also listen to your heart."

15

Just Another Day

Hard-to-solve issues tend to feel slightly more solvable after a good night's sleep and a big cup of coffee. Unfortunately, Eleanor hasn't been able to enjoy the benefit of either this morning after spending an entire night wide awake, thinking about Aiden, who just had to have the last word, wishing she'd dream of him. And regardless of who said it first, for Eleanor it still sparked a night full of... him. She also can't put a checkmark on the coffee thing, because once her swollen, sleepless eyes came into her roommate's view, Alannah insisted that caffeine is the last thing she needed and made her a green-purplish-brown rejuvenating juice made out of fruits and some unidentified greens. Eleanor was afraid to ask what else was in it, but it did the trick. Rejuvenated she is.

"Have a peachy day today, babe!" Alannah hugs her when they part ways at the GERI security booth.

Eleanor reciprocates the hug. "Thanks Al. Same to you!" she says to the best roommate a girl could ask for.

Trying not to freeze, she goes straight through the security stop to retrieve her temporary daily pass—somehow, she hasn't earned a permanent one yet—then stops at the blessed little coffee place Antoine showed her yesterday.

Happy and caffeinated, she approaches Professor Harrington's office.

"Good morning," she greets him through half-opened door. "Do you have a minute?"

"Good morning, please come on in." The old man smiles widely at her and gestures for her to sit. That's progress.

"Thank you," she says and takes a seat. He gives her a conspiratorial 'what's on your mind' look, as if he knows her already. Well, he's absolutely moving in the right direction.

"I was meaning to ask you," she takes the golden opportunity, "what are your thoughts about having regular lab meetings?"

"From what I gather," he smiles, obviously suspecting she has some idea, "young scientists find these meetings boring and un-necessary."

"Well, I can help make them *un-boring*. And I'm sure you'd disagree with the unnecessary part."

"What did you have in mind?" He gives her his signature intrigued look. That's her cue.

"I'll let you in on my trade secrets." She gives him a content smile. "So, here's what I'm thinking. We're going to have a signup sheet; we can make it a weekly series. Everyone will sign up to present—we can have one or two people presenting every time."

"I'm not sure they'll be able to keep up with this pace of generating data…"

"That's fine. Some weeks they'll be presenting data, on others they'll be presenting their plans or hypotheses, or their interpretations," she explains, already unstoppable. "Then to make it more engaging—each speaker needs to bring some food for the group to share."

"Food? That's your trade secret?" He smirks.

"Yes, and the trick is that they have to make it. To get them more invested. You want people to brainstorm, and bring up ideas, and share their thinking. And also criticize when needed. The food makes the conversation flow and adds the fun component into it."

"I don't know about criticizing, I am not looking for fights in my lab." The look on his face indicates she may be pulling on a sensitive nerve here.

"Constructive criticism. Better get that from your labmates than a harsh reviewer who might kill your paper later. It's also a good habit to discuss your science with peers, especially when stuck. It helps get you out of your own rabbit hole."

"I like the way you think, Dr. Benjamin." He leans back in his large office chair.

"Thank you, Professor Harrington. So do I have your blessing?"

"Blessing? This sounds awfully religious, I don't give blessings. But you have my unwavering support. Make it an early-morning meeting series so they're fresh and not in the middle of any experiment."

She winces at the thought of chalking up another early morning every week. "How about we make it a lunch meeting? Every Tuesday," she offers. "Speaker's in charge of the food, whatever they choose, hopefully nobody gets food poisoning. Would you be willing to put aside some budget for it?"

"Budget for food?" he coughs.

"For ingredients. Postdocs are typically broke," she chuckles. "The food aspect would be a major upgrade. Just give it a try."

Professor Harrington's lips twitch before he lets out a laugh. Then nods. And then it's settled.

After her successful pitch, she decides to stop by at the Kowalski lab. Because her last night's dreams are still fresh in her imagination and also because early-morning tormenting is apparently her thing.

"Morning," she says as her eyes land on Aiden's handsome face. He's sitting at his desk, staring into his computer screen, engaged in one of his deep-thinking sessions. He does look broody, exactly like Tara said.

"Ellie." He looks up, blue eyes shining at the sound of her voice, spreading warmth and some other sensations through her core.

Goddamn his no-hugging rule.

"Thanks for helping me turn my dungeon into an actual lab yesterday. It looks awesome now. I can't believe you found there was a window hiding in there behind all these old boxes."

"You're welcome," he says, gesturing for her to sit down.

Eleanor looks around. She had been so dumbstruck in the past few days that she didn't even notice he had a couch in his office. And some plants along the windowsill. And lots of science books and journals. All neatly organized. Dare she say alphabetically? She wouldn't expect any less of him.

"Nice couch!" she says and lets herself sprawl on it, kicking off her shoes. "Almost like a therapy session," she sighs, resting her head on the arm rest.

"Make yourself comfortable." Aiden smirks.

"By the way, I'm keeping your sweater. Need something to make up for your no-hugging allowance."

"All yours."

"Do you have any food in here? I'm starving."

"I have some energy bars and a banana," he offers.

"I need meat. Alannah's vegan food is surprisingly delicious—I'll give her that—but I've been dreaming of that burger you and I had at SigmaV."

"So you're dreaming about food while wishing me sleepless nights full of dreams about you?"

"No, I daydream about food. My night dreams are slightly different, and all about you, I promise," she says teasingly. "And incidentally, the sleepless part—that was your choice with your 'no seduction' rule."

"Smartass," he mutters, glancing at his calendar. "Lunch in my office tomorrow, I'll get the burgers." He doesn't ask, it's more of a notification.

"Can't say no to that!"

"And then after lunch we'll talk science." Aiden switches to a more business-like tone.

"Can't say no to that either!"

Science, food and Aiden. This has the potential to fulfill most items on Eleanor's hierarchy of needs.

"Good." He seals the topic. "So how do you like GERI so far?"

"It's decent."

"Elaborate, please." His blue eyes studying her intently.

"Am I really the first female scientist to ever worked at the Harrington lab?"

"Yes, you really are the first."

"That's insane. I mean, I like the old guy but... this trick he just pulled on me with the dungeon clean up—" The handsome guy beside her releases a gruff sound at the word *dungeon*, which makes her smile. "He's definitely testing me."

"So far, you're acing his tests. And look at the bright side—you are making a major dent in his biased way of thinking, paving the way."

"A debatable achievement, but I guess I could look at it this way."

"You are always welcome to make your spot in my lab permanent."

Somehow the combination of the words 'my' and 'permanent' sends her mind somewhere completely different.

"Surprisingly, I actually enjoy the old man's company," she chuckles.

"And how is your collaborator?" he asks, a tentative smile playing on his lips.

"He's way too hot to be my collaborator, I'll need to figure out what to do about it." She smirks, then stands up and grabs the banana he offered earlier. "I'm starving."

"Ellie," he reaches out and rests his hand on hers, sparking pleasant tingling all around. "I know we're still figuring things out." His tone is serious again. "Putting that aside for a second—you chose me as one of your mentors. Unofficial as it may be, I want to make sure I live up to your expectations and give you what you need."

"I have high needs and even higher expectations." She grins impishly at him.

"As you should," he says, eyes darkening. "I meant it on a professional level."

"Me too," she says. "But I have high needs and even higher expectations on all levels."

16
SHOPPING

The next few weeks go by quickly. Eleanor splits her time between lab safety training, waste disposal training, online cybersecurity training, and finally some lab experiments in her new dungeon. Which doesn't really look like a dungeon anymore, thanks to some intensive clean up, a horrendous task she has committed to memory as a fun activity. And it might have had something to do with the handsome blue-eyed professor being involved.

Aiden, the person she was planning to never see again, is now an integral part of her weekly calendar—1:1 mentorship meetings, lab meetings, or just around when running experiments. Inhabiting her thoughts, colonizing her dreams.

But it's not even remotely enough...

Eleanor's not sure why she had these unrealistic expectations that Aiden would continue their newly formed nighttime texting tradition. She's been hoping for more of those short-flirty end-of-day message exchanges. Which is a ridiculous expectation, since she's the one who had told him she wasn't looking for a relationship. She's the one who had said she wasn't interested in *'anything period.'* And now that they're supposed to keep whatever this is to a strict professional level... she definitely shouldn't be expecting late-night texts from him. Yet when her phone chirps around midnight, for a brief second, she's always hoping it will be him, despite it being the usual time that her family back home wakes up.

And then before falling asleep, she just has to take a quick glimpse at her lock screen—their selfie. She should really put an end to this habit. And mostly change her lock screen already, someone might see it and get the wrong idea.

Or actually the right idea. Whichever is it?

But she pushes through. Busying herself with science is her best medicine. Results are trickling in, and things are looking up.

"Heard you're already making an impact at the Harrington lab." Tara Jones's big smile comes into view as Eleanor passes by the lunch room.

"I hope so." Eleanor grins at her.

"I know so." Tara winks in her own special way, stepping into the hallway, gesturing toward Aiden's lab. "And there too."

Hmmm, that's a different kind of... impact.

"And that's where I'm headed to now," Eleanor says cheerfully, opening the heavy lab door.

"Hello," she says into the large open space as she enters. Looks like the time-for-lunch memo hasn't reached the Kowalski lab yet.

Zoe gives Eleanor what seems to be her best fake smile. How she has managed to get on Zoe's bad side so quickly is a mystery. Or perhaps that's her default side.

"Hey," says Finn, aka Dr. Surfer, looking up from his very large collection of colorful microcentrifuge tubes.

Where does he get his tan from? She needs to know.

"Hey Finn." She smiles.

"Want to catch lunch later?" he asks, switching the dial on his pipette.

"Have a meeting with the boss, maybe another time," is her polite evasion. She keeps walking and sighs inwardly for having turned down a lunch invitation—this is now the third time—from a perfectly nice and good-looking guy she would normally spend at least a few seconds ogling. Yet she only has eyes for one man. And it goes against every single part of her short and long-term plans.

She lets her feet carry her the last few steps to Aiden's office, gently knocking on his door for the sake of formality, but then she lets herself in, of course, without waiting for a response.

"What's up?" she says to the handsome man peering at her from his desk.

How long will it take before she's able to walk into his office without experiencing this swarm of butterflies swirling inside her? The insanely fast heartbeat?

"Hey!" Aiden's face lights up, almost as if his expression has a before and after-Eleanor-comes-into-view.

And she likes that immensely.

In fact, it makes this treacherous blood pumping organ of hers switch from beating to thumping and hmmm ... a whole list of symptoms she can't quite decipher.

Good thing she's not capable of falling in love anymore. Not being able to touch this man is already giving her a heartache.

She does, however, need to find a way to dial down the heat if she wants to be able to do any kind of professional work in his lab.

"Hey," she says back. "Do you still have that WhatsApp app?"

"Yes, why?" he asks, giving her his complete and undivided attention.

"I don't know, you haven't been using it much." Assuming he's not texting anyone else on it.

"Did you want me too?" His face is either confused or hopeful, she's not quite sure. But yeah, she kind of did.

Does. Would. Will.

"I wouldn't mind that," she says, feeling like a sixteen-year-old girl all over again. "If you want. It was your turn to write. Has been your turn for a while."

"I didn't know we had a rule for that," he says, almost apologetically.

"We make these up as we go, remember?" She plops into the chair closest to him, kicks off her shoes and draws her feet up to a cross-legged position. "You can add it to the list, 'nighttime texting,' right under my 'honesty' rule.

"Duly noted," he says and pushes a takeout bag in her direction. "I hope you're hungry."

"SigmaV burgers?" She beams. "I've been craving that! How did you know?"

"That's what you were craving last week," he says. "And the week before."

And the week before too. SigmaV burger lunch is becoming their tradition.

"What can I say? I'm nostalgic." She pulls a burger out of the pink paper bag and unwraps it.

"I share your nostalgia." Aiden pulls the other burger from the bag, two bottles of water and a big box of fries.

"Hmmm... the taste of a load of B12!" Eleanor devours her burger in large bites. "It has the taste of that night at SigmaV, when I was certain that you were a drummer. And a distraction."

"And now I'm not a drummer anymore or not a distraction?" That tentative smile is challenging his lips.

"You're still both, but now you're also... other things."

"Good things or a bad things?"

"A load of good things," Eleanor says playfully and grabs a few fries from the pile.

"Heard you already have some exciting data."

"Where did you hear that?"

"On my weekly meeting with Professor Harrington. He couldn't stop bragging about his new female postdoc."

"Well then, since you asked." She puts down her burger and slides her lab notebook to his side of the table, leaning over and opening it on her latest data summary. "Let me know if you want me to walk you through my analysis, once I'm done enjoying this burger." She smiles proudly.

"This is awesome!" he says, admiring that fine little image of her latest lab results. "What were your controls?"

"It's on the previous page." She leans over again and turns the page.

"A very creative, flawlessly designed and executed experiment, I'm impressed," he concludes contently, after reading through her extensively descriptive notes and results. His blue eyes lift from the lab notebook to her face. "Although I have to say, I'm not surprised."

"Why, thank you, Professor Kowalski!" She feels her cheeks heating up. "Now for part two, which will need to take place here. There are a few techniques I'll need to learn."

"You have my entire lab at your disposal. And you can start ordering reagents, I'll email you my lab's payment info."

"Oh good, I've already made a long list of stuff I need."

"Brilliant. If you need anything sooner, you can try the on-campus self-service store."

"A *what* now?" Did she hear correctly? "What is that?"

"Exactly what I said. A self-service store, it has some basic reagents and kits, restriction enzymes, antibodies, tissue culture media—"

"Professor Kowalski, I can't believe I'm only hearing about this magical place for the first time now! You're so taking me there after lunch!" Eleanor can't hide her excitement.

"You got it, Dr. Benjamin."

"This is unbelievable," Eleanor chirps.

Aiden is pushing the cart while she's busy dancing and spinning around the aisles of shelves filled with research-grade equipment and lab supplies, exactly like he promised. "It's like taking a kid to a giant toy store and telling her she can choose whatever she wants, all expenses paid." Eleanor has to share her thoughts out loud. Maybe a bit too loud.

A few smiling heads turn toward her.

"I have a feeling you are talking about yourself as a kid?"

"Probably not just as a kid..."

"Still have a thing for toy stores?" There's a mix of amusement and fondness in his expression that could make the frozen-est of hearts melt.

"Of course! I was heartbroken when I heard Toys "R" Us closed their stores," she says, pouting.

"I think they've reopened in some capacity. And I think Target has a decent toy section."

"Well, then you'll know where to take me on a date if you... um... if that ever comes up."

Why on earth is she talking about dating?

"I'll keep that in mind," he says, regardless of the big elephant that should be lodging itself between them.

Some reagent shoppers give them curious looks, including a few stares from several girls as they spot Aiden. One of them looks exactly like that blonde who was ogling him at SigmaV.

Why does this make Eleanor jealous?

"You have a fan club here, and we're making waves," she half-whispers when they turn into an empty aisle.

"Don't be ridiculous," he protests. It's actually endearing to see how oblivious he is to that.

"Look there." She turns his head toward some of the surprised faces.

"I don't usually hang out at the self-service store," Aiden explains. "Or hang out with people."

"Hmmm... I'm not just *people*!" Eleanor says in feigned disapproval.

"Correct, therefore I'm here."

She has to resist the urge to hug him, because that last statement was awfully cute. Especially said with his all-serious face. "Can we add an amendment to the 'no hugging' rule under special circumstances?" she hears her voice asking before running it by her common sense. Aiden looks contemplative, but she doesn't stick around for his response, because her eyes spot the marvelous restriction enzyme freezer, and she has to check it out.

Back at the Kowalski lab, Eleanor is busy unpacking her latest shopping spree items on her newly assigned part-time shelves and lab bench, admiring her shiny Gilson pipettes and organizing her new and expansive collection of restriction enzymes in her *very own* freezer.

"Have you decided how you're going to split the time between your two labs?" Aiden appears beside her.

"I'll probably spend three or four days here and three days at the Harrington lab, depending on which experiments I need to run. I think real-time PCR and Western blots I'll probably do here because you have it all in one place. I also like your dark room," she says. "I mean for developing Western blot films, not on the sexual innuendo side." She chuckles because both came to mind. At least to her mind. And then chuckles some more because Aiden gives her a hungry look.

"So according to your plan, if I counted correctly," he changes to a safer topic, "you're planning to work between six and seven days a week?"

"That's correct, your counting skills are superb, Professor Kowalski," Eleanor says, organizing her new lab notebooks on the lower shelf. Keeping records the old fashion way—pen and paper—draws out inspiration.

"I don't let my students work during the weekends," Aiden says, his face turning serious. Well, serious-er.

"What? No, I have to. Plus, I'm not really your student. I guess I'll spend Saturdays and Sundays at the Harrington lab then."

"You know," he says, leaning on the wall beside her, their elbows almost touching. "My PhD advisor had a strict rule against working on weekends. He also had this phrase he used to say when he saw me working long stretches or pulling overnighters—*I can tell you're working too much and thinking too little.*' He believed that to be a good scientist one has to be able to take a step back to process and look at the big picture," Aiden's tone is passionate and determined. "Every time I had gotten stuck, a day or two away helped me get the right perspective or wrap my head around data that didn't make sense." His eyes hold her gaze, "I can't tell you what to do, Ellie, especially when you're at the Harrington lab, but at least give it a try."

"It's an interesting theory, but if I don't work on weekends—what the hell am I going to do with all my spare time? Is reading papers allowed?"

Aiden shakes his head. "Just give it a try."

After a long but fulfilling day at both labs, having gone shopping for her favorite supplies twice in a span of one afternoon—once with Aiden and his lab budget, then later with Antoine, equipped with Professor Harrington's budget, and then squeezing in a few more experiments—things are on the up and up. Stocking up on supplies for two different labs almost feels like living in two different homes. She'll have to keep track of what's needed where, what's running low where. Two separate shopping lists. This might get tricky for someone who can barely remember what she had for breakfast. No, actually that was before Alannah... Those brownish wheat-grass hulk juices, with whatever goes inside them, are undoubtedly unforgettable. Although she has to admit, she's warmed up to them, and they do the trick. Her coffee dependency, in this span of a few-ish weeks, is already becoming more bearable. She now can go an entire morning before storming into Antoine's room and dragging him to the little sign-less coffee shop.

Eleanor takes off her shoes at the entrance to her little apartment and heads straight to the shower, trying to scrub off whatever DNA fragments or reagents she may have carried over from her afternoon extraction. She was wearing a lab coat and gloves, but after taking all these GERI mandatory lab safety training courses, she almost feels paranoid. Despite having worked in a lab for the past eight years, being very well-aware of the risks of working with different reagents and practicing all the rules of reducing the risks of cross-contamination, hazardous exposures and all the other sophisticated names that come with it, she's been thinking about this shower ever since she walked out of the lab.

"I'm traumatized." She shares the vivid images from her latest safety training with Aiden when he texts her, exactly as she instructed him to do. "That lab safety video makes me question every single move I make, every single thing I touch. My brain is possessed by that poor scientist from the video now."

"That's the point of the training," he writes back.

"Traumatize poor postdocs? Deter them from doing lab work?"

"No, creating this thought process. Take off their gloves before they reach for their phone or their water bottle, or the door handle."

"Oh gosh, I've waisted so many good glove pairs along the years, taking them off to answer phone calls."

"Good, because I once fired a staff scientist for chatting over the lab phone with his dirty gloves on."

"Fired?" No wonder people look wary around the man.

Well, the phone in Aiden's lab does have a bold sign with the words 'clean phone, no gloves, offenders will not be tolerated' warning on it.

"Yes, and that's why you got yourself five boxes of these fancy purple no-powder gloves you asked for. Use them generously."

This guy writes text messages like he's speaking them out loud.

"Thanks for taking me to the store today, I had a great time."

"You're welcome," Aiden writes back, and then there's silence. Text silence, that is.

So from talking about everything *but* work, they've shifted to talking about *nothing* but work... Is this how it's going to be now?

A slosh of disappointment settles in her stomach as she lays her phone quietly on her nightstand and walks out to the kitchen.

The trouble with expectations...

"What do you miss the most being far away from home?" is Aiden's text message waiting for her as she walks back into her bedroom. She is showered, well-fed (thanks to Alannah) and tired, but this sparks a new streak of anticipation. A small glow settles in.

Oh, come on... Happiness governed by someone else's doing. She did not sign up for that. Well, not knowingly.

"I miss the food. Not that Alannah's isn't good, but I miss my mom's cooking," she writes back.

"I thought you were ignoring my message."

"Just playing hard to get," she writes, smiling, even though he can't see it. "And I miss my family." Her mind is still unwrapping her thoughts about his question. "And hugs," she adds. "And feeling like I belong."

"You don't feel like you belong?"

"No, I think belonging takes time." If that's even a word... "But it was only when that feeling was taken away that I realized what I had in the first place," she admits, also to herself, for the first time. "And I also think belonging takes action. I have a feeling it's not going to happen by itself."

"Anything I can do?" he writes, which is sweet, all things considered.

"Hmmm," she responds, stalling, even though the rules of texting may not require it. "You diplomatically omitted the *hugs* part."

"Well, considering the circumstances," is his unwavering response, "I might consider appealing for a temporary reversal of the 'no hugging' rule."

"I fully support your petition."

17
ROUTINES

"Going home soon?" Eleanor's favorite voice prompts her to lift her head from her notebook to see Aiden leaning on the doorframe to her lab, holding his coat over his shoulder. Just another one of these late nights at the Harrington lab.

"No, I'm trying to make sense of today's experiment. Can't wrap my head around it. I'm not going anywhere until I do."

"It's pretty late. Walking out to the metro here at night is probably not the—"

"Oh, I do this all the time, don't worry," she dismisses.

"This makes me even more worried." His eyes fill with concern. "Take a break, go home. Things will make more sense tomorrow, after you let yourself take a step back."

"I know you're right, but I mentally can't. I'm going to run one last experiment for the day, don't wait up."

"Well, you might want to reconsider," he says, pointing to the window. She lets her gaze follow, noticing large white flakes dancing around the sky, slowly covering the grass outside.

"It's snowing?!"

"Yes, that's why I came up here. I had this suspicion that I might find you still working. And now that it's confirmed, I'm going to make sure to drag you out of here every night."

"And that's how a girl gets herself a regular ride home," Eleanor quips.

"Smartass. Now let's get out of here before they close the roads."

"My first real snow!" Eleanor squeals, closing her notebook and putting on her winter gear. "And you're so going to play snow fight with me right now!" It doesn't take her more than five minutes to pull Aiden by the sleeve, shut the door behind them, run down five flights of stairs and into the beautiful white world that's waiting for them outside.

It's probably been snowing for a while, as everything is covered with a soft, feathery powder. It's a whole new dimension under the GERI campus lights. Eleanor can't help herself, jumping up and down, spinning around and landing in the snow.

"I've always wanted to know how it feels to make snow angels!" she exclaims. "Don't just stand there," she shouts, making snowballs and throwing them at the handsome, serious man looking at her.

"Don't challenge me," he warns before he gives in and starts chasing her around the backyard of their GERI building. Their footsteps fill the entire area within minutes.

"Hey, you're cheating!" she says at the sight of him making snowball stashes.

"How is this cheating?"

"You obviously grew up with snow. I can't even make a decent snowba—" She laughs as some of the snowballs come flying at her. "Show off!" When he bends down for another batch, she leaps forward and knocks him down, wrestling him for that last snowball.

"You're crazy," he laughs as they both roll down on the ground together. A rare, pure, carefree laugh, from Aiden. A glorious, magical moment. And she's utterly dumbfounded. Dazzled. A complete goner.

"I warned you," she says quietly as their eyes meet. Their legs and thighs are intertwined, boots and jackets tangled and covered in snow. "Sorry, I'm breaking all the rules," she laughs. But she lets her lips hover over his for a few more moments, basking in his warmth and scent, letting that lightning sensation travel through her before she forces herself to disconnect and gets up. "I'm ready for my ride home now."

"How are the withdrawal symptoms?" Aiden texts her on Saturday morning.

"From not working?" A big smile spreads across Eleanor's face. Night texting is becoming a habit, but weekend texting—this is a pleasant and an unexpected surprise. "I don't even know how to not work on weekends, I'm getting jittery. I have no idea what to do with all the spare time and energy."

"I'm sure you can think of something. Based on your experimental designs and your first author publications, I don't think creativity is an issue for you."

"In the lab, yeah."

"Well, I can think of a few things outside the lab too, but that might go against rule number two," he writes. And she wishes she could see his face right now.

Actually...

She presses the little camera icon on the screen, prompting him for a WhatsApp video call.

"You can't just throw out statements like that while depriving me of your facial expressions!" she protests playfully as his handsome face comes into view. His hair is unruly and there are signs of a stubble that give him a ruggedly sexy look.

"I deeply apologize," he says, allowing a slight, lopsided smile to escape.

"I made a list of things I could do, but nothing comes close to running a real-time PCR or engaging in DNA and RNA extractions," she says. "What are you planning to do today?"

"Going to visit my dad, taking a double shift. Kim was on-call last night, so I'm giving her a pass. My dad has been asking for you, you know?"

"Really? He remembers me?"

"You're unforgettable, even for an old man with Alzheimer's. He says he won't eat until you make him that soup again," Aiden deadpans.

"Your dad knows what he's talking about." She smiles to herself, remembering his old biochemistry books. "Okay, I think I've just made plans for the day," she says, her mind set up.

"It doesn't involve hanging out at your postdoc lab, I hope."

"No, but it does involve hanging out with my unofficial postdoc mentor. And his dad."

It doesn't require any convincing. Or debating whether it goes against any of their rules. Although seeing Aiden in his ripped jeans and hoodie thirty minutes later, with this weekend stubble that looks so much better in real life, surely and undeniably defies their 'no seduction' rule.

Eleanor climbs into his car, planting a small kiss on his cheek and stealing that hug he said he'd appeal for the other night. It's reflexive, like friends do when they meet. But his scent, the feel of his embrace, the touch of his bristles on her face, are nothing short of electrifying. And as she takes her body back to settle in the seat, it feels like the world moves in slow motion.

Whoa...

Aiden's eyes darken and linger on her for a moment, as if he's debating whether to ravish her mouth or casually turn the car on and start driving. Unfortunately, he decides to go with the more conventional option and puts on his seatbelt. Driving it is.

They spend the day having pleasant conversations with his dad, who is excited to see them show up together. It's another one of his good days according to Aiden. Eleanor has come equipped with a new batch of scientific papers for Gordon to read. Now that she knows that he is THE Professor Gordon Kowalski, she is able to tailor these papers to his specific scientific field and present one of his biochemistry books for his autograph. This almost brings Gordon to tears. Excited tears. Eleanor is surprised at how humble the man is.

She also cooks up some new favorite salt-free foods for him, making sure to gently bump or rub into Aiden at any chance she gets while they are in the kitchen, just because she can, enjoying his little feigned admonishing grunts. Gordon happily eats her creations, and just like that, visiting Aiden's dad becomes her new weekend routine. Maybe not working on weekends is not such a bad idea after all?

Time goes by quickly, her life taking on a sort of rhythm. A disorganized rhythm at times, because no one day for a scientist looks like another. Even running the same experiment has the potential to yield slightly different results. Never boring is definitely a life motto for her.

Days turn into weeks, weeks turn into months. Eleanor's mornings before she gets to the lab are pretty much the same. She wakes up, usually with her cell phone still laced between her fingers or nearby—a product of late-night texting with Aiden that typically ends with one of them, at some point, usually Eleanor, falling asleep. Or staring at her phone's lock screen, remembering the moment when letting her body sprawl all over Aiden was uncomplicated and allowed. Or at least considered—based on the collection of facts known to society at that point in time—as ethical.

The days at both labs are uneventful. That is if heart palpitations and deep-core butterfly swarms are considered typical. This new reality—where Aiden is her collaborator, and she can't do anything about this nonsensical growing list of manifestations—what is the culprit exactly? Excitement? Frustration? Whatever it is she's been nurturing inside is disconcerting. So in light of all that, and since there's nothing else she can do about it, Eleanor just has to accept that this entire collection of symptoms should now be regarded as normal. Her new normal.

Her own list of Aiden-induced symptoms.

She is also acquiring new expertise—polishing her fine motor skills by pipetting tiny 384-wells plates or generally staying focused in the face of her racing heartbeat or her occasional hair-bristling attacks that seem to appear randomly, whenever... Aiden. He doesn't need to look at her, or even be in her vicinity. Heck, not even in the same room. The mere thought of him, a fraction of a memory, a brief sniff of his scent, one syllable or a gruff sound of his voice when he's talking to the other members of the lab or on the phone, can send her mind on a field trip.

Is it the same way for him?

Aiden has also embarked on a brand-new habit of keeping his office door open, a thing that, based on Tara Jones' crucial fact-sharing during hallway conversations with Eleanor, had apparently been unheard of prior to Eleanor's joining his lab. The other lab members are still undecided as to whether they are in favor of this new habit or not, but it sure gives Eleanor free range to observe Aiden at all times, so no complaints there.

Throughout the weeks, Eleanor makes her best effort to show up on time to the way-too-early lab meetings and the journal clubs at the Kowalski lab—and being on time, especially as defined by Aiden, is no easy task for a last minut-er like Eleanor. It's a different case with the newly revived lab meetings and journal clubs at the Harrington lab. Since Eleanor is their sole initiator and organizer, they are governed by her own rules, which also include her own individual time management preferences with regards to their start time, typically meaning on-*timish* plus five to ten minutes buffer, or rather—after. After all, one has to stay loyal to her principles. And, importantly, adding food adventures to these meetings has been proving to be a tremendous success.

In between all these meetings, she runs her experiments, keeping herself busy, hypothesizing, designing, planning, dreaming up theories, crunching data, creating graphs, presenting, brainstorming, writing papers, sending abstracts to conferences, meeting with her mentors, re-educating Professor Harrington, going on short coffee breaks with Antoine, coaxing her lab members into having lunches together. It's all fine, and engaging, and interesting. But there's still something missing that she can't quite pinpoint.

Once in a while her mind drifts again to this strange collection of Aiden-induced symptoms. Yeah, the ones she keeps dismissing. She's tried really hard, very unsuccessfully, to find a scientific rationale for them.

Other than lust of course. And potential feelings she would deny if asked about.

But when the symptoms start becoming more and more frequent, she starts charting them in one of her lab notebooks. A little heart for the fast heartbeats that should not be compatible with breathing or living. A triangle for the occasional nosebleeds; thankfully these don't happen often, but when they do it's always when Aiden is around. A star for the insane flock of butterflies in her stomach. And a circle for every time her mind summons uncalled for thoughts. Thoughts that invade her personal brainstorming bubble, her scientific daydreaming and her nighttime.

Which up until the distraction known as *Aiden* crashed into her life, this was unheard of. Impossible. But unfortunately, despite devoting a great chunk of her career to gathering and mining data, she cannot make any sense of the odd collection of these observations or find any patterns.

None.

Nada.

Other than... Aiden.

Frustrating.

"What are these little marks on your lab notebook?" is Aiden's observant response as she shows him her weekly results.

"It's just me charting. I'm having this strange collection of symptoms."

Along with an unexplained urge to share this info with him.

"What symptoms? Are you okay? Is there anything I can do?" His beautiful blue eyes fill with worry as he studies her.

Yes, there is something he can do in fact, but that might go against most of his rules...

"Don't worry, it's just symptoms." She offers a smile.

"What do you mean just symptoms?" His eyebrows crash together.

"Fast heartbeats, butterflies, maybe some erotic thoughts..."

"Okay smartass," he says, a small smile playing on his lips.

"What's the root cause? Come up with a diagnosis yet?"

Yes, she's suffering from an incurable disease called "infatuated with this marvelous man who also happens to be her unofficial mentor."

"No, but I know the prognosis."

Hopeless. Doomed.

"Symptoms have underlying reasons. You don't just deal with symptoms, you need to deal with the culprit." Aiden gets up and approaches her.

"Not in the modern healthcare system you don't. That's what keeps drug companies in business. Wouldn't it be better to solve what's causing high cholesterol levels instead of taking statins? Cure type 1 diabetes instead of taking insulin?" She gets up as well, meeting him halfway. "Yet you don't see that happening, do you?"

"Ellie, are you seriously comparing feelings to chronic diseases?"

"Yes Professor Kowalski, and if there was a cure, I would gladly take it."

Her evenings have settled into routines as well—she goes home, spends some time with Alannah, some much-needed WhatsApp video time with Gillie or her mom, and mostly chats along on her family's giant group chat—they always make her laugh and make sure to give and get full and complete updates. So needless to say, there's never a dull moment. And she's grateful for that, because it really helps alleviate that strange homesickness she never thought she'd experience, but she too often does. Especially when things don't work out the way she wants them to. And that happens because that's life. And although it seems sometimes that dropping everything and just going home—her real actual home, thousands of miles away—is the magical solution for literally everything, even if it really isn't, it's not always easy to push through.

But then the good, the bad, the everything, it all gets sucked into that black hole of one single moment. The moment she and Aiden reconnect. Not the professional mentor – postdoc, scientific brainstorming and data relationship. The personal one. The longing for his texts—now almost like gasping for air—can only be resolved with that much anticipated chirp of her phone, announcing an incoming WhatsApp text from Aiden.

This is how she knows she has it bad.

Really bad.

"Your turn to ask a question," she writes one night.

There are millions of questions circling through her mind. So many things she wants to know about him. So many things she wants him to know about her.

"Do you regret not meeting me for a face-to-face interview before committing to this collaboration?" he asks.

"Regret? No. No regrets," she writes. "And full disclosure, I probably won't ever be able to reverse the memory of our kiss, or the feel of your hands on my skin. And even though it would make my life easier, I'm not sure I want to forget."

This feeling was supposed to wane over time, like memories often do. But it doesn't. If anything, her longing for this man keeps getting stronger by the day.

"I don't want you to forget."

"Good," Eleanor writes back. She wants to ask if *he* has any regrets, but she's not sure she'd be able to live with his response, either way. The impact of knowing he has regrets could be crashing. And if he has no regrets—well, it might present a much greater challenge to her already pretty challenged self-control.

So instead, she considers letting him in on a more intimate detail. "Would you ever consider getting a tattoo?"

"What kind of question is that?" he answers so quickly. "No, I don't like tattoos. Why?"

Well, abort then...

"Just wanted to know," she writes back. Her mind trails to the stupid tattoo on the left side of her butt. The one that bears her and Oren's initials. Aiden, apparently, is not a fan of tattoos... Retrospectively thinking, she doesn't like them either. And despite her best efforts, there's a pretty high likelihood that Aiden will never see her naked, so he might never know. Therefore, she deflects and writes "Okay, your turn," hoping he'll let that one go.

"Okay, a tough one," he writes. "How do you define success?"

"Uh, isn't that a question you should ask me during our mentorship 1:1 in your office?"

"Is this your idea of evasion?" he insists.

Looks like the professor wants an answer.

"Success to me would be publishing several high-impact manuscripts, getting my own lab in a few years, becoming a full professor before I'm 35 and doing all that with minimal distractions. Not a tough question at all." She finishes typing and sighs, realizing she is already failing on the minimal distraction front. "How about you?"

"Success to me would be to achieve my goals while they're still my goals, and to do that without having to sacrifice the things that are important to me."

"Why Professor Kowalski! Well said!" she writes in response, feeling those goosebumps awaken on her skin. "Very inspirational!" But then she considers it. "Hold on, wait, is that your way of emphasizing your no-work-on-weekend rule?"

"No, but not working on weekends is one of the things I do to achieve it."

"Sounds like you're on the right track then."

"I used to think this way, but I'm not so sure anymore," is his response.

"What do you mean?" Interesting coming from a guy like him. Already a professor at the age of thirty-five, an incredible track record of extremely high-impact publications, a very well-funded research at a prestigious research institute, a following of students who respect and look up to him. What else is he missing? "Is it about the sacrifice?"

"Possibly. Potentially," he writes.

"Really? What is it?"

"It's this one big thing that I hope *would not* become a sacrifice. It's my new daily struggle, I just need to find a way."

"You're being very elusive, Professor Kowalski."

"I know, Dr. Benjamin. It's deliberate."

18
EXPERIMENTS

S he has several sleepless nights in a row, due to lustful dreams related to a certain professor and some thought-provoking text messages—some science-focused, some focused on other types of science—also related to a certain professor. Combine that with Eleanor's already clumsy demeanor, and she's about to show up to work with an ugly bruise on her left cheek. No, not a result of a violent fight—just the unfortunate battle with her load of laundry. Shaking the wrinkles off a wet hoodie that has strings decorated with metal beads, and doing it too close to her face—it's only a matter of time until one gets whipped by it. One being Eleanor, of course.

"Oh, my god! Who's the asshole who did this to you? Are you okay? Should I call the police?" is her roommate's supportive response when Eleanor finishes loading the drier and emerges into the living room. "How haven't I noticed it before?! Why didn't you say anything?" Alannah runs into the kitchen to grab a bag of frozen peas.

"It's self-inflicted, don't worry." Eleanor tries to calm her down, taking the frozen bag and pressing it against her cheek.

"Eleanor, that's even worse!"

"No, not what you think." She laughs and takes traumatized Alannah by the hand into the laundry room to experience her art firsthand. It's not the first time Eleanor has shaken wet laundry too close to her face, but typically it doesn't end with more than a red mark—this one might turn blue by morning.

"That's a very special talent you have there, babe," Alannah laughs finally. "Luckily it missed your eye."

And it doesn't look too good by the next morning. It's a small bruise with colorful streaks of red and blue. Eleanor considers covering it with a band-aid to avoid questions but then decides it might make matters worse. Her colleagues should familiarize themselves with her special talent. Then thirty minutes into her day at the lab she forgets about it completely.

"What's all this? Starting your own microcentrifuge tube army?" Aiden appears at her dungeon lab, leaning on the doorframe as he typically does, absorbing all the oxygen in the room and blocking any route of escape, not that she was planning to make a run for it.

Just a typical day at GERI.

"I have a massive protein extraction planned for today. Mano was supposed to help," she huffs in desperation. "We went over the plans yesterday, I even tested his pipetting skills and timed him so we could be perfectly coordinated. But he bailed on me. I had a feeling he was going to ditch when I told him how many samples we'll be doing."

"That's ridiculous," Aiden growls. "He needs to learn he can't just change his mind last minute when other people rely on him. There are too many samples for one person to do simultaneously," he assesses with accuracy.

"Well, my cells are ready, I can't wait until tomorrow—they'll get overcrowded." Eleanor pulls out one of the plates from the incubator as proof. "Have any better ideas?" she ventures, but he's already out of the lab, the heavy door closes behind him.

Jeez, thanks.

Then he's back with a lab coat, a box of XL gloves and an ice bucket.

"Make some room," he commands, and as she scooches to the left, he settles himself to her right, putting down the ice bucket and pulling one of the two pipette stands to his side.

"Huh, what are you doing?"

"Filling in for Mano," he says matter-of-factly, as if extracting samples or generally working on the bench is something he does first thing every day before his morning coffee.

"When was the last time you've done bench work?" She eyes him suspiciously. Not even once has she seen his hands-on skills in action since coming to GERI. And that's okay since he now runs his own lab and a crew of very capable scientists.

"Been a while, but I can assure you, my protein extraction skills are impeccable. I've done enough of these to last me a lifetime." He smirks, then grabs a pipette in one hand and gets to work. Doesn't seem like he's lost his bench touch. "Plus, you don't have too many options here." A gorgeous smug expression appears on his face and Eleanor has to inwardly kick herself to stay focused.

"These are precious samples, and I have a Western blot planned right after, in your lab, Professor Kowalski. So I'm expecting some quality work here," she warns.

"You bet, Dr. Benjamin," he chuckles.

They work side-by-side in harmony; it's almost like playing a four-hand piano piece. Maybe it's his drummer skills or the hours he's logged playing with a rock band. She's worked with other scientists before, but typically each of them did their part on their own bench, and there was never this level of coordination. As if he's effortlessly matching her rhythm, anticipating her steps and movements.

She turns to the pre-cooled microcentrifuge to load the tubes, noticing Aiden's eyes narrowing as they lock in on her left cheek.

"What?" She gives him a puzzled look before her recollection of last night's unsuccessful clothes washing activities come back to her.

"What the hell happened to your face?" he demands. A handsome, protective expression takes over, followed by a jaw clench and a, "Ellie, if someone hurt you I swear to God—"

"Hold your horses," she laughs but allows a few more seconds of suspense, setting the time on the centrifuge and starting it. "It's my own doing. I did the laundry."

"I am going to need a little more information to understand this one," he growls, still wearing his pissed-off going-to-beat-up-the-shit-out-of-whoever-did-this-to-you look.

His overprotectiveness is equal parts flattering and sexy.

Aiden takes off his gloves, then washes and dries his hands before closing the distance and letting his fingers skim her cheek, turning her head to examine the damage from up close. His gentle touch is a striking contradiction to his mad expression.

"I was trying to shake my hoodie to get rid of wrinkles and the tip of the string slapped me on the cheek." She smiles, struggling to hide her erratic heartbeat inflicted by his touch. And when his expression doesn't soften, she adds, "Ask my mom, it happens to me all the time, I'm that kind of clumsy," she laughs again, "as you may have noticed at the airport." Eleanor takes her gloves off and covers his hand with hers, letting her fingers brush over his knuckles, leaning into his palm. She watches as his eyes darken, his protective expression turning hungry. Feral. But neither of them moves. Or speak. Or breath.

Well... they obviously breathe, but it sure doesn't feel that way.

They stay like this, surrounded by flames and fireworks, and air of opportunity, until the noise of the slowing down centrifuge shakes them out of their reverie, reminding them it's time to let go of each other, put on their gloves and go back to reality.

"Laundry is a dangerous, *dangerous* thing." Aiden shakes his head, his face visibly more relaxed now. "Can I talk you out of doing it again?" A faint lopsided smile is starting to pull from the sides of his mouth. If she keeps her eyes fixed on him, she might forget her protein extraction protocol. Not recommended.

"You may not like the consequences," she giggles and turns to collect the tubes from the centrifuge. They resume their coordinated four-hand masterpiece as the door opens. Professor Harrington walks in, his eyes running between Eleanor and Aiden, and a content smile slowly stretches across his face. The kind that points to him thinking he knows something they haven't yet figured out.

He turns on his hearing aid. "What a pleasant surprise, Professor Kowalski. I see I'm getting two at the price of one," he quips.

"Yes, I have a big experiment today, massive really," Eleanor says coolly before Aiden has a chance to tear apart Mano's career for ditching her. "And Aid— Professor Kowalski has graciously offered to help me." She tops it off with a bright grin.

"What a wonderful and unusual idea." Professor Harrington clasps his hands together. "Very well, please proceed," he says cheerfully and then turns on his heels, turns off his hearing aid and leaves.

Eleanor can already sense Aiden's presence as he enters the dark room through the revolving door, bringing in a breeze of his scent, sending a pleasant quiver into her core. "How does it look?" he asks, completely unaware of what his voice does to her. Or maybe he is.

"Pushing your luck, that's bold," she teases. Aiden typically doesn't enter the dark room when the lights are off and the red light is on. And more specifically—not when he knows Eleanor is alone in there, peacefully developing her Western blot films.

"I'm a grown man, I can handle myself." His gruff voice carries through the dimmed red light.

"You sure you can trust me in the dark?" she asks playfully. That moment in the lab earlier may have loosened a few of her self-restraint screws.

He really shouldn't.

"The key is self-control, now show me the film." He comes to stand next to her.

Eleanor picks up the film to face the light. "It looks good, but there's a faint band there I'm not sure about."

"There's definitely a band there," he says, his face so close she can almost feel him breathing.

"I'll do a longer exposure," she says and Aiden nods in agreement.

The door turns again, and a guy comes in. "Oh, Professor Kowalski," he says, surprised, sounding tense to the point of an imminent cardiac arrest. "Would you mind if I use your machine?

Ours broke, I just have one film to develop in thirty seconds," he pleads nervously.

"Go ahead," Aiden says, giving him a curt nod and walks back to clear the table.

The guy thanks him profusely as his timer beeps.

"Go ahead before me," Eleanor says, "I need a longer exposure."

Barely visible in the dark, the guy quickly opens his cassette and feeds the film into the machine. "Thanks." He gives her a quick grateful look.

She opens her cassette and slides in a new film, then closes it and sets her timer. The room is dark, lit only by the small red lamp shining faintly above the table. The corners of the space are just big patches of darkness.

Eleanor takes a few steps back, very much aware of Aiden leaning against the wall behind her, her shoulders almost touching his chest. She can sense his body heat. "Don't lean back," is Aiden's warning whisper, already anticipating her mischievous plan. His words are muffled by the attempt to not draw too much attention toward them.

The noise from the machine takes over the room. The guy anxiously shifts in front of it, counting the seconds to visualize his results. Or get out of there.

Eleanor smiles to herself and takes another step back, her butt just barely grazing Aiden's front. She can feel his body reacting instantly, welcoming her. It's been so long since that kiss. Yet at this moment, it feels as if not even a second had gone by.

"I warned you," he growls quietly, sounding out of breath. "Don't you dare move." His order somehow sounds more like a challenge. So she does just that, closing the last bit of gap between them, pressing herself tight against him, his hard-on threatening to lash at her through his slacks. "So cruel," he grunts quietly into her hair, his lips gently brushing her ear, sending enticing electrical currents through her bones, his hands slowly reaching for her hips on their own account.

The film appears on the other side of the machine. Eleanor quickly sidesteps before the intruder collects the film and turns back.

"All yours," the guy says into the darkness, oblivious to the storm that's been forming behind him. "Thanks for letting me use the machine." Then he walks through the revolving door and leaves.

"Jesus Ellie! Have some mercy!" Aiden releases a pent-up breath, then turns to adjust his lab coat.

"The key is self-control," she says flippantly, using his own words against him. "And for a nice Jewish boy, you sure call Jesus a lot."

"It's an interesting observation, but you have a few incorrect underlying assumptions there."

"Oh?" Eleanor steals the Harrington's signature-in-trigued-phrase. "You're not really Jewish?" Not that it matters, but he's the one who brought this up.

"I am, but you are probably the only person on earth to mistakenly define me as 'nice,' and at my age I don't think I qualify as a 'boy' anymore." He stifles a smile.

Yeah, this man is definitely not a boy anymore.

"Wow, you like your facts, don't you?" She chuckles.

"And that completely goes against the 'no seduction' rule," he scolds as the timer goes off.

"Well, you challenged me." She gives him a sly smile. "I have a soft spot for your challenges."

19
HAPPY BIRTHDAY

Eleanor starts her morning at the Harrington lab, with what has now become her signature morning activity for the past few months since she came to GERI; A brief knock on Professor Harrington's office door, followed by his part questioning—part expecting, *"Yes?"*

Next, a *"Good morning"* chirp from her and then his welcoming, *"Dr. Benjamin, please, come on in."*

Not that she had any doubts that he would eventually adapt to her interruptive morning greetings, but he also seems to have developed a soft spot for it, and a daily space on his calendar. Furthermore, Eleanor didn't expect it to morph into their daily thought-provoking scientific brainstorming ritual, but it has, pretty quickly actually. And she likes it a lot. Professor Harrington has the most unconventional, provocative ideas when it comes to science, and, as it turns out, will take any side in a debate for the sake of debating. And so needless to say, this is now one of her favorite parts of her mornings at GERI. Right after watching Aiden step into the hallway, with his fresh-out-of-shower scent, wearing his signature light blue or white button-down shirt, and charcoal or navy suit pants or slacks. And depending on whether he's teaching a class that day or not—a tie.

"I have some interesting data to show you," Eleanor says, opening her beloved lab notebook and lays it neatly on Professor Harrington's desk.

"Data, my favorite." The old professor clasps his hands in anticipation.

"That's my latest real-time quantitative PCR." She points to the graph of changes in gene expression in her cell lines, explaining in detail each and every aspect of it, topping it off with her interpretation.

"Outstanding," he says, after listening intently.

"But then I ran another experiment, after transfecting the cells with my new plasmid. Something must have gone wrong here." She turns the page to the second graph. "This doesn't make sense." Her finger resting on one of the data points on her carefully calculated and drawn graph.

"Have you tried to repeat?" he asks.

"Of course. Several times. Threw away the cells and started from scratch, made a new plasmid, repeated the transfection with brand new reagents. Still the same. Must be an artifact."

"Or an actual observation."

"An artifact," she insists.

"Just because we can't understand it with our current knowledge and tools doesn't make it an artifact," says Professor Harrington, closing her lab notebook and handing it back. "Eleanor, you must know that when running experiments, one might come across a once-in-a-lifetime observation they might not be able to understand. This one may turn out to be an artifact in the end, but make sure to explore it fully before you throw it away. The history of outstanding science is built upon exactly those unique and unusual observations that someone was either smart enough or naive enough to explore."

"Can I join your discussion too?" Mano shoves his head through the door to Professor Harrington's office, interrupting their inspirational moment, using his best suck-up tone and a smile that only brings about suspicion.

"No," Professor Harrington says dryly.

"You can come in," Eleanor offers, "I was actually on my way out. Need to further explore something here." She smiles to herself, watching the old professor reaching out for his hearing aid, sending her off with a conspiratorial look. He does that whenever they are done debating, and especially around Mano, the hearing aid thing. She asked him about it once. *"Background noises disturb my deep thinking,"* was his vague response. If Mano is aware, he's not showing any signs of it.

A thought crosses Professor Harrington's face as he reaches to his ear again. "Mano, I am not pleased with the way you left Dr. Benjamin all on her own with her experiment the other day," he chastises. *All* on *her own* makes her sound so incapable. Would he have said it the same way if she was a male scientist? And how does he know Mano ditched? She never mentioned it.

Mano gives her an incredulous look. "You had to tattle-tale to the boss?" He looks hurt.

"She didn't," Professor Harrington jumps in to her defense. Not that she needs it. "I walked in to find her dealing with a very large number of samples, an experiment you signed up for. Luckily Professor Kowalski was there to help."

"Professor Kowalski?!" Mano looks terrified. "Fucking asshole..." he mumbles to himself. His face twisted to an expression she can't quite decipher. Mad and... evil almost. Talk about over-reacting.

"Manners, Mano. Let me remind you that's a full professor

you're talking about," Professor Harrington reprimands.

Eleanor grabs her notebook, leaves the two men to it, and takes the stairs down to the Kowalski lab.

"Good morning," Eleanor sings into the open space as she lets the heavy metal door close behind her. The lab is busier than usual. Surfer Finn and unfriendly Zoe are working hard on wrapping up the last bit of Finn's five years' worth of hard work. Based on the news he shared on their last lab meeting, he has managed to secure a shiny and well-deserved tenure track position at Johns Hopkins and will soon be leaving GERI for greener pastures. Aiden is extremely proud of Finn and is also two-fold happy; one—because this is a dream come true for Finn. And then the second, less-disclosed reason—less competition for Eleanor's attention. Imaginary competition that is, because—and it is unfortunate—as much as she would have loved to swoon over this blond-surfer-nice-guy, a few attempts to see whether her heart might beat slightly faster around Finn have so far yielded nothing. Unless Aiden happens to walk by them at the same moment. But then again, that has nothing to do with Finn, and everything to do with her Aiden-induced spectrum of symptoms.

Strange, strange heart of hers.

Aiden's office door is closed. Perhaps he's in a meeting? Since her first day at GERI, she hasn't seen this door closed, with the exception of when Aiden is in meetings.

Eleanor drops her stuff off, puts on her lab coat and gloves, and settles into her experiment. She's been thinking about those samples on her way to work this morning, envisioning the little wells, deciding on her experimental design, the primers, the controls, the conditions. Since discovering true science, sometime into graduate school, her hobbies, her day-job, and her career have all merged into one. Mind-blowing. And mostly just pure fun.

She wipes down her work area and organizes her tubes and

pipettes, feeling the buzz of excitement that accompanies a brand-new project. A series of experiments that will test a pristine hypothesis of hers. Something she's dreamed up and polished for a while now, has discussed in detail with both Professors Harrington and Kowalski and received a unanimous raving green light.

A noise from Aiden's office startles her. A loud slam of something. A heavy book? Maybe he dropped something? Then his door opens, and he murmurs something to Yan about a grant deadline.

"Good morning," Eleanor says from behind her tubes, making sure not to take her eyes off her 384-well plate—yes, Aiden's lab uses those vicious little things—and if she looks away, despite the urge to see her favorite-blue of his eyes, she might get her entire pipetting order messed up.

"Morning," he murmurs under his breath, omitting the *good*, prowling. He exits the lab, letting the heavy door slam loudly behind him.

"Uh-oh, better stay away from Professor Kowalski today." Zoe releases a general warning into the room once he's out of earshot.

"No shit. What's the deal with him?" Yan asks. "Been a while since he looked this grumpy."

"No idea, maybe got his period," Zoe says wryly.

So that's the grumpy side Tara Jones was talking about? A side of him Eleanor hasn't seen despite being there for several months already—that is, until now.

Eleanor tries to keep her mind focused on her tasks. Aiden goes in and out of his office once, twice, and by the time she's done he's out again. She seals her 384-well plate and snugs it safely into the machine. Now it's a waiting game, until results start trickling in.

"You okay?" she texts Aiden but it looks like her message is not being delivered. Has he turned off his cell phone?

"Eleanor." Finn steps closer to her bench, raking back his

dirty-blond curls. "A few of us are going to SigmaV tonight to celebrate my new position," he says, his eyes gleaming. "It would be great if you could join us." He puts his hand on the back of her chair, lightly grazing her shoulder.

Still not a beat out of order... Dammit.

The lab door opens and Aiden walks in again. His eyes narrow at the sight of Finn's hand on the back of Eleanor's chair. He passes by them but doesn't let his glare meet her eyes.

"So will you come?" Finn's voice snaps her back into focus. A boyish grin on his face.

"Uh, sure," Eleanor answers, not completely certain what they were talking about but it sounded like a goodbye party, so as a supportive colleague—

Aiden's office door slams shut again.

What's going on?

"Great, so I'll see you there at 7 p.m.?" Finn again.

"Wouldn't miss it!" She slaps on a smile. Then she gets up and steps toward Aiden's office, knocking gently on his door.

"Not now." His voice is muffled by the closed door. She pretends not to hear it and lets herself in, closing the door behind her.

"What the hell is going on?" she asks, trying to catch his gaze. Or glare. Or whatever is going on across his storming face.

"Nothing. You?" he answers tersely, his eyes focused on an imaginary dot on the floor.

"I don't know, you tell me."

"Nothing to tell," he says, exuding some obvious *stay away* vibes.

It will take a little more than that to deter her.

"Right," she says, taking a step closer. Aiden stands up and turns toward the window, as if trying to find solace in the expansive view of spring on GERI campus. Cherry blossoms have been filling up the trees, and Eleanor has been marveling at it every single day in the past week, her phone bursting with images she's taken on the way to and back from work. But right now, it feels like they've been thrown into an arctic backdrop.

"It's not working." Aiden's voice and body language a thousand miles away.

"What's not working?"

"This." His hand gestures to the distance he's put between them. "We never talked about dating other people, we missed a point."

A tiny, insignificant point.

"There's no rule to that, you can do whatever you want." Something twists inside her as she says it. Her heart feels like a ton of bricks, threatening a pericardium rupture at any second. Aiden just nods, still focused on the damn window. And it makes everything a million times worse.

There's someone else in his life now.

Eleanor was NOT prepared for the way this makes her feel. A new symptom entirely. An unbearable one. She can deal with the nosebleeds and the erratic heartbeats. But not with this.

And his silence is killing her.

"Why are you mad?" she asks. Her mind quickly scans through the last few nights worth of text messages—there wasn't anything unusual, was it? He was asking about what made her happy, she said *science,* and *family.* Then returned the question. He said he was *still figuring it out.*

"Life." His voice is pained.

"Did I do something wrong?" Because whatever *'life'* means in this specific context, and whether it's her sole unintended doing or a twisted combination of unfavorable events, Aiden seems upset with *her.*

"No. You didn't do anything wrong. It's me I'm angry at. We need to keep our personal life separate, I need to stay objective. I deleted the app." His tone bites more than the actual nonsensical words coming out of his mouth.

He deleted WhatsApp. Their solitary means of communication outside of GERI.

This—whatever it was, is over.

"O-kay," she says, considering how to tread in this brand-new territory. "If that's what you want."

It's not what *she* wants, but he seems pretty damn determined. And after all—*she's* the one who told him she wasn't looking for a relationship. *Not looking for anything* is what she said. But besides, with his 'no seduction' rule, she's still holding on to that one single kiss at her apartment, the one Alannah so gracefully interrupted. Before the rules of ethics had to apply.

He rolls his eyes.

What's that supposed to mean?

"Are you coming to Finn's farewell party?"

"Party?" He gives her an incredulous look, "I'm not in the mood for partying," he says, bereft.

If he has someone new in his life right now, embarking on a new relationship, shouldn't he look a tiny bit excited? Because, really, he looks more like someone who's been run over by a truck. Several times.

"You're not making much sense, Aiden. It feels like I'm expected to take part in a conversation you're having on your own. But about tonight, Finn is your postdoc, you should come, show him how much you're proud of him."

And hopefully he won't bring his new date, whoever she is, because Eleanor doesn't think she'll be able to handle it.

"You're right, I should come." He pushes an irritated hand through his hair. Then gets up, resigned. "See you there at 7," he grouches, throws his messenger bag over his shoulder, and he's gone.

Going to SigmaV brings about fun little memories. How she shivered her way through the cold night, going in with the simple goal of returning Aiden's hoodie, then leaving with perhaps a different—not so simple anymore—goal. Her stupid failed hypothesis.

This time she walks in with Alannah, equipped with a whole new set of goals. These include: Bid Finn farewell, hopefully not meet Aiden's potential new plus-one (and if she does—try to keep her already taped-together heart in one piece), and try not to drink more than one beer. Her one tattoo is more than enough. Then go back home. Uncomplicated. She has matched her simple plan with a simple outfit as well—skinny black jeans, boots, and an open-back sweater.

SigmaV is exactly as she remembered, warm and cozy. Shinedown's *'A symptom of Being Human'* is playing gently in the background, as if someone is purposely pulling on her strings.

The smell of garlic fries makes her stomach grumble, reminding her she hasn't eaten much today since Aiden's strange temper tantrum. And then also reminding her of lunch in Aiden's office every so often. The almost-smile that starts forming on her face is quickly sliced by the memory of Aiden's freezing cold eyes today, making her heart squeeze too tight in her chest.

"Eleanor!" She hears Finn's warm voice from the far side of the bar. He's all smiles and cheerfulness, waiving at her. She strolls over to him, and he pulls her in for a hug, planting a small kiss on her cheek. "So glad you made it!" he says when his mouth is still close to her ear. He really is adorable.

Unfortunately, her mind is helplessly set on the grumpy guy under the gray cloud who's sitting not too far away, eying them intently and ragefully, looking broodier and more soulful than ever, and mostly glaring at Finn. No plus-one in sight.

Thank goodness. Eleanor's heart has been spared, at least for tonight.

Although Eleanor and music, coupled with this handsome drummer-professor, is really not the best idea.

"Hey," she throws a nonchalant greeting at him.

"Hey," Aiden responds, unsmiling, a beer in hand. His other hand is nervously playing with a colorful cardboard coaster. Then he turns to the other side and starts a conversation with Yan.

It doesn't take a genius to know when she's not welcome, so she goes back to the sunny side, where Finn, Alannah and Zoe are already chugging a round of beers.

"Can I get you a drink?" Finn asks softly.

"Corona would be awesome," she says and a cold bottle with a wedge of lime hanging off the top is delivered to her hand within seconds.

"So what is the first thing you'll do in your very own lab?" Eleanor tries to shake off the broody vibes and, at least outwardly, sound excited.

"Make hot chocolate on a Bunsen burner for my students," he says, a playful look in his eyes.

"Trying to get the safety squad to shut down your lab on the first day?" Eleanor chuckles, making Alannah snort.

"I'll come work for you if you throw in some marshmallows!" says Zoe, Finn's biggest fan.

"I see you're making careful considerations in your career choices," he teases Zoe. "But seriously speaking, I want to excite them, spark their imagination and enthusiasm, like Professor Kowalski has been doing for us." His eyes are beaming as he talks. "There are some days he calls me to his office with a new idea, and it gets me all pumped up with theories and hypotheses, and then I go back to the lab and pull on an all-nighter because I just can't wait to see the results," he says. "But don't tell that to Professor Kowalski, he doesn't like it when people work in the lab at night."

Yeah, Eleanor is very well-aware.

"Completely agree," Alannah nods. "I don't know how he does it. He seems all grouchy and intimidating, insisting on his formality, but really, he's always supportive, always willing to brainstorm ideas and solutions, always available for troubleshooting, despite this 'by appointment only' shit sign he has on his door. And lately even that has come off. Now he leaves his door open."

"Yeah," Zoe says, "he's been smiling lately! Well, if you take out today."

"I'm going to miss having him as my mentor," Finn concludes. "I hope he's not mad that I'm leaving, he seemed mad when we chatted this morning."

"I don't think it has anything to do with you," Eleanor jumps in. Because obviously it has something to do with her. "He's really proud of you." She pats his shoulder.

"Thanks, Eleanor," Finn says, touching her arm gently.

Still nothing. Despite Aiden's new point about dating other people.

Zoe and Alannah embark on a football discussion. Finn somehow takes it as a cue. "And now that we won't be working together," he says, pulling her aside, "Do you want to go out to dinner with me sometime?"

"Dinner?" is Eleanor's best attempt at stalling.

"As in a date," he clarifies, clearing his throat. She wishes she could say yes, *she wishes she* wanted *to say yes.* But it's already a known fact. The findings are already well documented in her lab notebook. Saying yes to this man won't be compatible with her long list of Aiden symptoms.

And mostly just not right.

"I'm sorry," she says and Finn's face falls, "if I gave you the wrong message," she continues. "You are extremely smart, and kind, and handsome." She offers an honest smile.

"But?" he asks.

"My heart is set on someone else. Heavily set." And hearing these words come out of her mouth surprises her even more than the feelings behind them.

"You have a boyfriend... I'm sorry, I didn't know."

"Not exactly. It's complicated. But it wouldn't be fair to go out with you when—"

"When you're in love with someone else. That's okay, I understand. And I appreciate your honesty. Maybe give me a call sometime if anything changes."

In love with somebody else. In love?

From an angle, she can see Aiden's eyes burning a hole through both of them.

What's his problem anyway?

"Whoever he is, he's a lucky guy," Finn says finally, oblivious to the scene.

Well, this particular guy might disagree...

"Thanks." Eleanor smiles and the two of them join the football conversation.

An hour goes by, maybe two. Yan has left for the night. Aiden is not in a talkative mood, still sitting under his own personal gray cloud, chugging another beer. Eleanor tried to keep tabs on his bottles but has already lost count. Is it his third? Fourth? Would the bartender stop him at some point? Where exactly is he going with that? But then he gets up, rolling his car keys between his fingers, looking... wobbly.

Oh no…

"Congrats Dr. Anderson," he says to Finn. "Well deserved, I'm proud of you," he adds, his words sound slurred.

"Thank you, Professor Kowalski. For everything," Finn says earnestly.

"Going home now." Aiden nods and heads toward the door.

"This guy is an accident waiting to happen," Zoe pitches.

"I don't like this," Alannah agrees, giving Eleanor a concerned look. No one is really doing anything to stop him. Do they not care? Too intimidated to dare get into his business?

"Later people. Going to try to drive our professor home," Eleanor jumps in. "And you, keep in touch." She gives Finn a friendly hug, pulls her raincoat on and runs outside into the cold, wet spring night, catching up to Aiden, who's zig-zagging along the street.

"Where is your car?" she asks, "I'm driving you home." Thankfully she didn't even finish half of her one beer.

"I'm fine," he stammers, "go back to the party." He tries to pick up the pace but he's way too drunk to be able to muster speed walking at this point.

"Not happening." She grabs his car keys, stretching his arm over her shoulder to enforce walking in a straight line.

"I'm okay," he insists but doesn't resist. They walk quietly in the direction he's headed, hopefully to where his car is.

"Do you remember where you parked?" Eleanor asks. And when he doesn't answer she presses that thank-God-for-the-person-who-invented-car-remote-panic-button, and to her relief she hears his car alarm goes off near them. She finds the car and helps him into the passenger seat. Aiden is not really in a high-functioning state at this point, so she leans over to buckle his seat belt. His warm alcohol breath is on her face.

He's drunk, she tries to remind herself before her heart starts speeding again and her skin responds with a fresh set of goose-bumps.

"Where do you live?" she asks once the car is on and the warm air from the vents starts bringing back the sensation to her fingers.

Shouldn't spring in D.C. feel warmer?

"Huh?" Aiden helpfully answers.

"Your address?"

Now he doesn't answer. Perfect.

Driver's license, this should have his address on it.

"Going to search you up for your wallet, okay?" She gives him a heads up. Her hands dig into his pockets, making her heart risk a speeding ticket. Aiden releases a dazed smile. At least his grumpiness is gone.

"Got it!" she says finally, pulling the little plastic card from his wallet.

Even in his driving license photo he's handsome. God help her.

The address is in Maryland. Eleanor types it into Waze. Then she peeks at his license again, a double take, taken aback by the little line labeled *Date of birth.*

It's today.

"Why didn't you say it was your birthday today?" Eleanor asks while closely following Waze's driving directions. It's her first driving experience in the U.S, in the middle of the night, on unfamiliar roads, with this drunk, handsome man beside her.

Aiden is beyond the point of communication. Her mind drifts back to his matter-of-fact words *'My mom died giving birth to me.'*

His birthday also happens to be his mourning day. An incredible load of guilt fills her mind, making her heart squeeze so hard she has to struggle for a breath. She pressured him into coming to Finn's farewell party instead of being there for him, supporting him on this one day he really needed someone in his corner.

But then, that doesn't really explain why he threw the '*dating other people*' bullshit into the mix. And why separating their personal and professional lives had to be done so urgently today, of all days?

"Arrived," the Waze app announces after the longest thirty minutes. Eleanor lets out a sigh of relief. Well, partial relief—they are there, but they're still inside the car.

It's a single house, on a nice quiet cul de sac, surrounded by trees and grass and a white fence. She pulls into his driveway. There are only two steps leading to his front door; at least she doesn't have to drag him through elevators and long hallways.

"Let's go," she sighs, releasing his seat belt. Drowsy but cooperative, Aiden clambers out of the passenger seat and backs into a side hug position, leaning against her. They walk up a cobblestone path decorated with tiny solar lanterns and up those couple stairs. He's not saying much, but at least can carry his own weight.

"Keys?" she asks, without much success, so she turns to face him, resorting to searching his pockets again. Aiden puts his arms around her, mumbling something unintelligible, turning her key-digging attempt into a hug.

And despite knowing he's helplessly drunk, has no idea of what's going on, and will probably not remember any of it, it feels good to be so close to him again. She had no idea how much she missed it.

Sigh...

She finds the keys. A turn of a lock and they're inside.

Aiden's home is as neatly and efficiently organized as his lab and his office. Not a single thing is out of place, not a single unneeded object or piece of furniture. The place smells nice too, and squeaky clean. Hardwood floors, large open kitchen, a small fireplace in the living room. Some photos of his family of three on the mantel. And a few colorful abstract photos on the walls—but a closer look confirms that these are images of cells captured using fluorescent microscope. Eleanor can definitely appreciate the creativity and the science behind it, and can't help the smile creeping up on her face as she recognizes some of these cells.

"Where's your bedroom?" she asks, not expecting much response as they walk slowly through the hallway. Aiden makes a quick stop to the bathroom before finally finding his bed. He collapses into it while she struggles with his shoes, then helps him out of his clothes, leaving him in his boxers, shirtless, already half-asleep. She hasn't really had a chance to take a good look at him until this moment. Stripped down to his boxer briefs, that is.

And yep, maybe it was a good thing that she hasn't seen him half-naked before, because now, after taking a good uninterrupted glimpse of this sleeping handsome man, it's going to be harder to get a grip on herself throughout those long days at the lab, trying to live up to his impossible 'no seduction' rule.

This insufferable man with his impossible, ethical values.

She allows herself a moment of self-torture, letting her fingers just briefly trace his ab muscles, drawing goosebumps on his warm skin. Then pulls the comforter over him gently. "Good night." She ruffles his hair.

"Don't go..." His voice sounds far away. Probably drifting off to a dream about that other girl he's planning to date or is already dating.

The sheer thought of it is dismantling.

"Please stay." His voice is pleading now.

She can't leave him like this, on the anniversary of his mom's death, on his birthday. Too broken and drunk to be alone.

"Do you want me to call someone? Your girlfriend?"

"There's no one," he mumbles. "Just you..." His voice is muffled by his pillow. "You're everything."

Yeah... He must be confusing her with someone else. Plus his grammar makes no sense.

"Ellie, please stay."

He is asking for... her.

He needs her.

Eleanor takes a deep breath. "Okay, I'll stay," she says softly. She may have spent the last few months breaking all of his written rules. But now she's breaking all of her unwritten rules at once. "I need something more comfortable to wear," is all she manages.

"Clo...set," is his sophisticated response.

"Right." She opens his closet and helps herself to a neatly folded gray T-shirt and a pair of his boxers. "Be right back," she says, making a quick stop at the bathroom, ditching her outfit for the comfort of his fresh-laundry-scented clothes and some Aiden-owned-toothbrush teeth brushing.

When she emerges, Aiden is sprawled on his bed, partly covered. She can't resist and bends over for a small kiss on his forehead.

Gosh, this man smells good even after God knows how many beers.

He opens his eyes partly, and a relieved expression spreads across his face.

"You're staying," he sighs. Looking so vulnerable. And grateful.

"Where's your guest room?" she whispers, but he picks up his blanket and in one swift motion pulls her in beside him. She considers bailing, but he snuggles tightly into her, knotting their legs together. His skin is so warm on hers. It would take an impossible amount of will and torture to make her move. Aiden's muscles relax instantly, his breathing slows, and within seconds he falls asleep.

And yeah, she's fully aware he is overly drunk. Fully aware he has no idea what he's doing and will probably not remember any of it tomorrow. But in this very moment, tangled and cuddled deep in his arms, his slow, sweet breaths in her ear, she feels like she belongs again.

20
Early Morning Lab Meetings

Eleanor has no idea what time it is. She opens her eyes into a bright sun-lit bedroom. From up close, eyes—bearing her favorite blue—are slowly opening, looking at her.

Aiden.

Their legs and arms are still tangled together. She has no particular desire to move or go anywhere. And that's when realization strikes them both.

Shit.

"I'm sorry," Aiden rasps beside her. Then winces at what must be his hangover headache. "I think I had way too many beers yesterday." He rubs his eyes. "Did we...?" He looks under the blanket, finding himself in his boxers and her in his T-shirt and boxers too. Another pair of boxers, but still his.

"You think I'd take advantage of my drunk professor?" she says in mock shock. "I wouldn't dare! Besides, if we did, I sure hope you would remember."

He releases a low, scratchy laugh. Then takes a deep breath. "Thank you," he says. Turning his face toward her. His eyes sincere. "For being there for me. For staying." He sighs. "For holding on to me and not letting me break."

And she would do it again. And again. And again. If he let her. Or pretty much anything else if he asked.

"Break? I don't think you're so easily breakable." She runs her hand through his hair, and he closes his eyes. This unplanned proximity is like playing with fire.

"Last night was a special case." He lets out a rough sigh.

"Why didn't you tell me?" she prods softly, "that it was your birthday yesterday?"

"I didn't want to drag you into my own mud." His voice is sad, regretful. "Ended up doing it anyway. I'm sorry."

"Stop apologizing!" She holds a hand to his lips, indulging in the prickly sensation as she slides the tips of her fingers across the newly formed stubble on his jawline. "I am here for you because I want to be. But I can't do much if you don't talk to me." A glimpse into the life of this broody handsome man. Aiden tries to untangle himself from her, but she's not willing to let go. "Honesty. Remember?"

"It's the one day a year I allow the guilt to sink in." Solitary, disconsolate blue eyes are all she sees. "You'd think that after thirty-six years I'd be able to handle it better," he sighs.

"You're allowed to feel." Her voice is a whisper. "To grieve." Her hand doesn't leave his face.

"I went to see my dad the other night. Some people call it 'time-shifting,' which sounds like a scene from a science fiction movie. More like a nightmare if you ask me. He was stuck in the past, some thirty-six years ago, re-living that day he had lost my mom. Losing her all over again. Fucking Alzheimer's."

"I'm sorry," Eleanor says, squeezing in closer to him, trying to hug away his sadness. Unload some of the pain. Her head is resting on his bare chest, eyes turned up to look at him. His heart beating insanely fast.

"Then Dr. Anderson... Finn," Aiden grunts, raking his fingers nervously through his dark hair. "He was planning to ask you out yesterday. Just an unfortunate collection of events tightly packed into one special day," he sighs sardonically.

"That's where the *'seeing other people'* bullshit came from?" Ideally her body language would be taking an active role in this discussion. She would be putting her hands on her waist and frown at him right now. But despite the words coming out of her mouth, her voice is soft, and not a single bone in her body is willing to move away.

He needs her.

"Did he?" Aiden demands, ignoring her question.

"He did," she admits carefully, clearly aware that the storm hasn't passed.

"And?" His face impassive.

"I said no. What did you think I'd say?"

Aiden sighs. "I was afraid he'd sweep you away." He looks as if he's just come up for air after keeping his head underwater for almost too long.

"Sweep me away? From what?"

Aiden swallows hard before he lets last night's alcohol speak for him and says, "From me." His face unreadable again.

"I'm not that easily sweepable. And unfortunately—although I wish it wasn't the case because it would have made my life easier—being around Finn does absolutely nothing to me, Aiden." She pauses to look at him.

He shuts his eyes, then opens them back up, then sighs deeply before he finally says, "Thank God."

"Thank God?" she repeats, a little puzzled or just not letting the

interpretation sink in yet.

"Despite what I said, I don't think I can handle seeing you with someone else." He runs a gentle hand along her cheek, tucking a strand of hair behind her ear. This strange buzz hits her like a lightning bolt.

"You really shouldn't be saying things if you don't mean them. It's confusing. Also, I think the alcohol is not out of your system yet." She rolls her eyes.

Because otherwise why would he cross into the feelings territory?

"And as I told you before," she continues, aware of her already reduced conviction. "I'm not looking for a relationship. It's a distraction, so you have nothing to worry about."

"How can it be a distraction if we care about each other?" he asks, bringing her knuckles to his lips.

Oh sweet electricity.

"Well Professor Kowalski," she teases, trying to lighten up the load of the conversation. "Correct me if I'm wrong, but isn't that how distractions work?"

"You're such a smartass." His eyes finally brighten.

"And you don't have to worry about me being with other people, because clearly..." She's about to say before her brain catches up with her.

"Clearly what?"

"Well I haven't been much into other people since... yeah." End of sentence. Articulation is an important skill to have. And she's officially lost it.

"Since—*yeah*?" He furrows an eyebrow at her. A sexy look on him. The sparks that constantly surround them are now turning into fireworks.

"Since—yeah." She nods.

Is she blushing? Seriously? Blushing is totally not her thing. Not ever.

"Say what you really think, remember your honesty rule?" he chides.

"*This is* what I really think."

"*Yeah?* Said by the brightest postdoc in my lab?" Is that a ghost of a smile on his face?

And a compliment!

"Yes, it's part of my complex thought process," she squeals.

A smothered burst of laughter comes out of him, summoning rainbows all around her. What she'd do to be able to hear this laugh over and over again. On repeat. "That's not even a thought," he determines.

"Since you..." she tries again, can't bring herself to admit it.

"That's progress, but I'm pretty sure your sentence is still missing a verb."

"Since that day you took me shopping."

"Took you long enough." His entire handsome face is smiling.

"Well maybe when I saw you play at sigmaV." She tries to date it back.

"Still, a while," he says, his tone playful. One hundred and eighty degrees from how he is anywhere else, with everyone else. And she doesn't want that to go away.

Ever.

"Okay, maybe when you wiped my bloody nose at the airport while snuggling me in your lap. A complete stranger. Most men would have probably run for their lives at that point."

"Good. Because since that moment I haven't been able to think of anyone else either," he admits, that handsome smile still on his face.

Surely that's the alcohol talking. Part of the hangover effect?

"But that was before you found out you're my collaborator, and sort of my mentor," she challenges.

"Ellie, with your exceptional biology knowledge, you should

have, by now, come to the conclusion that not everything in life is reversible. It's not something I can just switch on and off as I choose," he says.

And somehow, distracting him with something else feels a million times safer than delving into feelings he might change his mind about later. And now that he's still a bit loopy but not really drunk anymore...

She stretches her thigh around his waist, bringing her body to straddle him, feeling his morning wood pushing through their two sets of boxers, the only thing separating them now.

"Ellie, I'm not sure it's a good idea," he tries to reason, but his strained words end on a pent-up breath.

"I'm sure it isn't," she breaths, grinding her way along the warmth of his body.

"We shouldn't," he groans. "I don't want you to do something you might regret later."

"I don't do regret," she says, already addicted to his touch. She guides his hands under her shirt, bringing them to cup her breasts, letting his fingers take charge and stroke her nipples.

"You mean..." his breath hitches as he tries to get the words out, "you don't do things that you might regret?"

"No, I just don't regret doing the things I want," she moans, her body already aflame. She lets herself disappear under the blanket, her lips lightly brushing the ridges of his ab muscles.

"Ellie ... what are you doing?"

"Something I've been wanting to do for a long time," she mumbles, pulling on the waistband of his boxers.

"Baby—" he tries to protest, but his voice changes into a raspy grunt when she lets this incredibly hard throbbing length of him loose, stroking gently. "Fuck." He groans audibly. "The things I want to do to you..." His loud breathing mixes with the sound of a phone alarm.

Her phone alarm...

Shit.

"Aiden," she whispers, finding her way upward from under the blanket, until her mouth reaches his ear. Trying to suppress the impossible electrical currents running through her.

"Ellie," he rasps into her ear, fingers tightening around her hips, keeping her close. "What's the alarm for?" His voice a whisper.

"Hmmm," she mumbles, "you might want to send out a cancellation email. Let your poor students get another hour of sleep." She stops her beeping phone to show him the reminder. *'My handsome mentor's crazy early weekly lab meeting,'* it says. "Then come back here."

"Ellie," he grunts, painfully rolling himself off the bed, wincing. "I've been dreaming up this moment since the day you fell into my lap. I'm not going to ruin our first time with a hangover."

"Saved by the bell," she smirks, rolling her eyes at him. "You're insufferable, you know that? Handsome, yes, but insufferable."

"Oh, *you* are breaking all my rules and I make *you* suffer?" Aiden chuckles. A beautiful sound.

"Well, I guess you have a point. Just you wait."

And did he just say 'first time' as in one of many?

21
Conferencing

Less than an hour later, they're sitting in the Kowalski lab meeting at the GERI conference room. The problem with deflecting distracting conversations with potentially steamy solutions is that leaving things unfinished may be an even greater distraction. She rushed out of bed without even a second to shower, shared Aiden's toothbrush, and borrowed one of his hoodies—because showing up to work wearing the same clothes as she did last night after taking her drunk professor home under her lab colleagues' watchful eyes could really only mean one thing, which—thanks to the 'no seduction' rule and mostly an annoying phone alarm—did not happen.

But now, every time her knee grazes his, or her eyes just briefly travel to that gorgeous blue in his—yes, she has been engaging in her own kind of self-torture—a rush of electricity runs down her spine and a pleasant shiver courses through her core.

Urgh...

"Now go pack up for your trip," Aiden reminds her after they all come out of the conference room. She's been excitedly counting the days, waiting for this moment, but the last twenty-four hours were distracting enough to almost make her forget about the CONFERENCE!

"Word is out that Professor Kowalski has confirmed his attendance at the conference," is the news from Alannah as she appears beside Eleanor, who's busy throwing, then folding, her most presentable clothes and shoes into her suitcase, and double-checking the volume of her not-small-enough shampoo bottle.

When her abstract had been accepted for a poster presentation at her dream conference, which happens to be taking place in sunny San Diego this year, Eleanor was ecstatic, jumping to the ceiling in Professor Harrington's office. He looked like the epitome of a proud father, despite the fact that he never actually had kids himself. And yes, it was just one poster out of many, not a big deal for the experienced scientist, but who said you couldn't celebrate the small wins? And her excitement was contagious.

Aiden was sitting right across from Professor Harrington in what looked like their regular, thought-provoking scientific discussion. And while it's not unusual for Eleanor to burst into Professor Harrington's office with news—usually with some exciting data, or new world-rattling results—it was Aiden's first time witnessing it. He looked amazed. Eleanor didn't think it was her poster acceptance news—he had been very confident that it would get accepted. Maybe it had to do with how naturally Professor Harrington reacted to her barging into his office. Indeed, the old man was adjusting to Eleanor's style. He had even expressed his regrets for not hiring women scientists throughout his entire career because Eleanor was his *'most productive postdoc.'* Professor Harrington's words, not hers.

Ha!

She'd been working extra hard to prove her point, and it was working. She had mentally patted herself on the back.

So between the two professors, a plan quickly formed—Eleanor's travel budget to the San Diego conference would come from both the Harrington and the Kowalski lab funds, split fifty-fifty. Harmony. Professor Harrington had said he was too old to travel and Aiden too busy, so it was just her and Alannah, who was also presenting a poster—and they were to share a room at the designated conference hotel. Bliss. Oh, and Mano, who'd somehow gotten onto the attendee list last minute, pulling the *'I never get to go'* and the *'She's only been here for a few months and she's already going'* cards on Professor Harrington. So him too, rooming with another postdoc from their building.

"Ground control to Ellie," Alannah's voice brings her back to the moment.

"He said he was too busy to attend," Eleanor protests, because running into Aiden in a hotel in romantic San Diego is not exactly ideal after her almost *hit-and-run* or whatever it was she was doing in his bed last night. And this morning.

"Maybe last night changed his mind?" Alannah gives her a knowing look.

"Nothing happened last night. He was so drunk."

"Says the girl who stayed over," her roommate teases.

"I just didn't want to leave him alone."

"Uh-huh," is Alannah's articulated response.

"I'm serious. Sex with an unconscious man is even less ethical than getting in bed with my professor."

And technically, she did get into his bed. Even helped herself for a pair of his boxers.

"It didn't look like nothing to me this morning," Alannah giggles.

Yes, and then there's this morning.

"Well... almost nothing."

"Almost nothing, except you two are infatuated with each other.

Peanut butter and jelly, hot chocolate and marshmallow. All vegan ingredients of course, we don't like dairy," Alannah says brightly, despite being fully aware that Eleanor and Aiden are trying very hard to keep things on a professional level.

"Oh, please." Eleanor blows a breath upward, trying to move her bangs off her now-sweaty forehead. Their last discussion still echoes in her head, Aiden's helplessly trying to claim that his feelings for her were... *are* irreversible. But that's too scary. And on the other side of the spectrum is the fact that Aiden deleted his WhatsApp, which means no more late-night texts and outside of work communications. And taking that away bothers her more than she cares to admit.

Another big URRRGH.

"I'm pretty sure he marked himself OOO on the lab calendar and asked Mrs. Jones to book him a room at the same hotel we're staying at. I heard her telling him she called the hotel and miraculously they had a cancellation, so he was able to get a room. Those hotels usually book up faster than light."

"Man..." Eleanor sighs. Somehow going to the conference doesn't feel like an escape trip anymore.

"Ellie, he's coming to support you, like the good boyfriend—" Alannah gives out a vocal cough before amending to— "mentor, that he is."

"He's coming to support *us*, he has two postdocs presenting in this conference. The end." Eleanor sighs again and returns to packing.

"You may want to ditch the old underwear for these!" Alannah pulls out a few presentable pairs from Eleanor's drawer and neatly shoves them in the suitcase.

"Are you with me or against me?"

"Both," Alannah laughs.

"I thought you believed in abstinence until marriage."

"Well, when it comes to you and Professor Kowalski, there are some rules worth breaking," Alannah gives her a wink. "You need a dress." She disappears into her bedroom and instantly comes back with a black cocktail dress. "Dress to impress!" she announces, a jovial grin stretched on her face. Eleanor just sighs.

The Uber ride to the airport and the flight to San Diego go smoothly, that is—no sign of Aiden. Maybe it was just Alannah's creative idea of a prank.

Eleanor is proudly carrying her poster—rolled inside a plastic tube—in one hand, pulling her suitcase with the other. They check in at the hotel and go for a walk down the San Diego streets, try out that beer tasting place everyone talks about and get some next-level Mexican food. Things are still looking bright when they put on their business attire and appear at the registration desk to pick up the fancy conference lanyards with their badges and a printed program booklet, or rather—giant book. People are starting to trickle in, get reacquainted with old friends and colleagues, and introduce themselves to new ones. The air is buzzing with excitement; A few days of lectures, presentations, and discoveries. Scientific heaven.

When they break into sessions—Alannah to her cancer epigenetics session of choice, Eleanor to a session on epigenetic components in autoimmune processes—there's still no sign of Aiden. But that's okay, because as far as she knows, his attendance at this conference is an urban legend, and not experiencing potential tempting situations is probably the best avoidance strategy.

And it works, at least for the night. Well partly, because she can barely sleep, but she blames it on the excitement of tomorrow's poster presentation and braving her way through a WhatsApp withdrawal syndrome—somehow she resists testing whether Aiden truly removed that mighty app from his phone. At some point she falls asleep, grateful to see light shining through the curtains when she opens her eyes again. A new day.

There's no sign of Aiden at breakfast either.

"You look disappointed," says her observant roommate, enlightening her with thoughts she had no intention of considering. But now that this seed has been planted, Eleanor has to admit... despite the fact that they're both better off not seeing each other here, at a hotel overlooking the sunny San Diego beaches, she *is* disappointed.

"Disappointed? No I'm not!" And of course denial is her best bet right now as she nonchalantly stretches the napkin across her pencil skirt, making sure her business attire stays clean for the poster presentation.

"Who's disappointed?" They hear Mano's voice carrying itself to their table. He's holding two platefuls of breakfast meats and situates himself between Eleanor and Alannah, creating a pleasant breakfast atmosphere for vegan-can't-stand-the-smell-of-meat Alannah. Then he tops it off with giving each of them a slow, unpleasant once over and filling the air with sexist jokes and anecdotes. Until they *finally* break into their morning sessions.

Around noon, they all join forces at the largest hall. The poster session has officially started. Both Alannah's and Eleanor's posters are already on display, one next to the other, awaiting the large crowd that will soon fill up the space. A Stanford professor is already by Eleanor's side, introducing himself politely, complimenting her on her work and asking for a poster walk-through. Her favorite topic. A few students and postdocs join in on her on-the-fly presentation. Another professor from UCLA, a few students, and some industry scientists all ask her to walk them through her poster, offering fresh perspectives and ideas.

Then life comes to a sudden halt because... Aiden. He's casually traveling the aisles of posters, chatting, asking questions, listening to presentations. He looks so handsome in a suit and tie, freshly shaved, his dark hair arranged in that perfect way that somehow looks elegant and tousled at the same time. A conference lanyard and badge rest on his expansive chest.

Damn...

She can see his eyes searching until they meet hers. His serious gaze brightens and the slightest of smiles rides up his face. One blink and she'd miss it.

Good luck! he mouths before letting himself blend in with the crowd.

Eleanor keeps her focus, eagerly discussing her research with a group of postdocs from the National Cancer Institute, and then with a bunch of other professors who stop by with thought-provoking questions, a challenge she gladly takes on. Alannah is also doing her fair share of presenting next to her own poster.

A couple hours go by in a matter of seconds.

In between visitors, Eleanor reins in her desire to let her eyes drift to Aiden, for the most part. Until the session is done and Aiden is back at their side, praising her and Alannah, looking proud as ever. He takes a few pictures of them by their posters, keeping everything on a professional level.

"Man! You girls looked *hot* in your business attire." Mano's voice sounds behind them before his sly smile makes its appearance, gracing them with his unsolicited opinion. "All fancy and serious, speaking to all these important people!" Of course, he doesn't skip a repeat of the morning once-over. This time it's somehow even slower, almost excruciating.

"Thanks Mano," Eleanor chooses to say, watching Aiden turns his head toward him, eyes narrowing.

"I can see why professors would want to hire women to work in their labs. I could spend my entire day just watching your sexy figures walk around the—"

"That's enough!" comes Aiden's irritated voice, taking a protective step closer to Eleanor. "You're out of line."

"Oh, *I'm* out of line?" Mano's face morphs into some sort of a vicious expression. Or maybe it's just Eleanor's imagination.

"What's that supposed to mean?" Aiden growls,

But Mano just turns around and leaves, chanting "Fucking asshole," behind him.

"Well, that was awkward." Alannah decides to be the first to break the new ice layer that's quickly spreading.

"Just when I was beginning to think that the Harrington lab was making progress." Eleanor's voice is a bit scratchy from the constant speaking, her legs a bit tired from standing on her high heels. But despite Mano's interesting remarks, call it jealousy? Call it being stuck in the Stone Age? She still feels elated, filled with a sense of accomplishment. High on science, that's what she is. And there's nothing Mano can say or do that could ruin this moment for her.

It takes a couple more hours until the low caffeine in her blood-stream starts giving out desperate signals. That, combined with the post-presentation drop in adrenaline equals a unique emergency of sorts. So when Aiden is off for a meeting and Alannah goes to check out the freebies at the vendor show, Eleanor embarks on a caffeine hunt across the road from the conference. Only instead of caffeine, she finds something else.

Someone else, to be precise.

Spoiler—it's the last person she wants to see.

Re-spoiler—she only has one name on her people-she-doesn't-want-to-see list.

Re-re-spoiler—despite the interesting night and yesterday morning at Aiden's bed, the drunk confessions and way too many unfulfilled needs, Aiden is not on this to-be-avoided list.

The unmistakable voice strikes her ears first, along with the Hebrew that takes her by surprise because it's been a while since she's heard Hebrew outside of long-distance conversations with her family and Gillie. And even longer since she's heard this particular voice. At first Eleanor slaps herself inwardly, trying to will her wild imagination to stop the psychedelic hallucinations. But when this attempt fails, she resorts to making herself as invisible as possible, which fails as well, because she's already been spotted.

Bamba, her childhood Labrador retriever, may he rest in peace, used to think that freezing on the spot made him invisible, acutely unaware that a seventy-pound dog can't just disappear into thin air. But at this moment, she understands this desperate instinct, which he'd deploy when caught with a helpless bird that he found in the backyard in his mouth, or spotted happily feasting on a piece of chicken he stole from the dinner table. Not that Eleanor stole any food, she hasn't even found a decent coffee place, but she's definitely caught off-guard when the person on her didn't-want-to-see-list pulls her into his all-too-familiar hug.

Oren Hason. *The* Oren Hason. The drummer. The same guy who regards himself as her *mythological ex*. Is here, in San Diego, at the one coffee place she was about to try. Doing God knows what.

"Ellie!" He is as surprised to see her as she is him, only he looks extremely pleased with the prospect, as if he's into saving birds and a wounded one has just landed in his hand. While Eleanor is...

Whatever would be a complete opposite of that. A fallen bird with human PTSD?

Why is she thinking about birds? She has no idea. Perhaps a result of severe caffeine deficiency combined with memories of her late, beloved dog Bamba.

Oren keeps his hand on her shoulder for old times' sake, staring into her eyes as if trying to retrieve all the information he's missed in the past five years.

"I've been thinking about you a lot lately, and here you are!" He says in Hebrew. One would think that hearing Hebrew again would bring the warm feeling of home back to her, but surprisingly—when it's packed in Oren Hason's voice—it doesn't. It just makes her feel distant. And lonely. Lonelier. "Join me for coffee," he offers in Hebrew, "let's catch up."

So many hours and days had been wasted on willing such a moment to happen. On thinking about running into Oren accidentally, just like this. Analyzing how it would make her feel, what they'd talk about, the way they'd look at each other again, touch each other again. How her heart would race again, how everything would go back to feeling warm and fuzzy inside. But nothing prepared her for the way she feels right now, which is—

Nothing. Not the slightest excitement. No nostalgic feelings. Not a single heartbeat out of place.

That is, until a short moment later, when her heart starts thumping and her legs feel wobbly, and an arm loops around her waist, pulling her tightly and possessively into the strong body attached to it. That's when she knows Aiden has summoned himself to her rescue, once again. A different kind of rescue this time.

"There you are, baby." Aiden smiles widely at her, yet with some slight apprehension in his beautiful blue eyes.

And she loves the sentiment.

He's still wearing his on-brand light-blue button-down, now without the jacket, dousing her in his impossible fresh-out-of-shower scent and bearing that conference lanyard with his name and affiliation on his hard, impressive chest.

The novelty of this man will never get old.

Her eyes thank him wordlessly and her body melts into his proximity. That little wounded bird, if one insists on using the same analogy, at least until she gets her caffeine fix, is drawn to safety. Although, really, Eleanor doesn't feel little, or wounded.

Not anymore.

Hmmm. The effects of a phenomenon called—Aiden.

She tries for an introduction. "Aiden, this is Oren, my ex—"

"Ellie's mythological ex," Oren interrupts her proudly, as if this is an Olympic achievement, eloquently switching back to English.

Heck, can he gloat any further? There were times in her life she actually thought a mythological ex was a real thing, or at least her reality, but that was before Aiden stormed into it and stirred the whole thing completely.

"That's debatable." She can't help herself. "Oren, this is my ad—" She's about to say *advisor*, just because it might sound morally better than mentor or professor, but Aiden beats her to it, leaving her mentally gaping with his—

"Aiden, her actual boyfriend, and myth-buster." The words seem to casually slip out of him with such an impressive amount of certainty, she almost believes it herself. He has a content smile on his face for nailing this pissing contest, and Eleanor resists the urge to raise her eyebrow at him. One—because of the rarity of his smile. She'd give everything to make sure it stays on. And two—because the stunned-disappointed look on Oren's face is worth every bit of potential trouble this slippage might cost them or their careers.

The two men vigorously shake hands. Miraculously, next to Aiden, Oren looks less like the cloned version of Thor she remembered and more like... a regular person. He still looks good, still the badass drummer that he is, Eleanor can give him that, but that's about it. He doesn't at all match the idealized memories that her brain had skillfully nurtured. And certainly no more butterflies.

Not for him, that is.

"Funny, Ellie never mentioned you," Aiden says brazenly.

What a bold lie.

Oren rolls his sleeve up his heavily inked forearm, exposing his replica of his and Eleanor's Hebrew initials inside a heart, the same ludicrous tattoo as the one living on the left side of her butt. "I'm the proud inspiration behind her sexy ass tattoo," Oren smirks.

Great. Round two of their pissing contest.

And HOLY SHIT, this round is rigged, because:

1. Aiden despises tattoos, that's a known fact, at least to her.

2. She hasn't really gotten around to tell him that she has one, and that it's on her butt, and mostly—

3. She hasn't made it known that the aforementioned tattoo bears her and her ex's initials.

Her fake-boyfriend for the past few minutes—*busted*.

Aiden gives her an inquisitive *'What fucking ass tattoo is this idiot talking about?'* look. And when she doesn't deny it, he leans in and plants a small kiss on Eleanor's neck, sending a delectable shiver through her. "Remind me to deal with you later," he whispers in a domineering tone that sounds more like a promise than a threat.

Hmmm...

"Can I steal your girlfriend for a coffee?" Oren continues, unperturbed.

"I'm sure you know Ellie makes her own decisions," Aiden responds, giving her butt a squeeze. "Come find me when you're done, baby," he says before he leaves, taking the last bit of air in her lungs away with him.

What's just happened?

"I see you've moved on," Oren says after taking a long sip of his cappuccino, comfortably switching back into Hebrew. "You look good."

And here she is, finding herself sitting across the table from Oren Hason, after swearing she'd never do it again. Then day-dreaming about it for years. Then making the promise all over again.

There are two guys sitting at a table behind them, both wearing ear pieces, seemingly drinking coffee casually—Oren's bodyguards. Having spent three years with this guy, she's become a master at spotting them. Looks like his success has reached an international level. At least in his eyes.

"Oh my god! It's Oren Hason!" Two teenage girls whisper to each other—not very quietly—as they approach. "Could we take a selfie with you?" one asks sweetly, looking like her heart would split in half if he said no.

Apparently not just in his eyes.

"Of course, sweetheart," Oren answers adorably and lets the excited girls do their thing. He's always had a soft spot for his fans. It's one of the things Eleanor liked about him.

"Sorry." He gives Eleanor a half-apologetic, half-smug smile once he's back into their conversation. "So tell me about your new—"

"What are you doing here?" Eleanor is not interested in digging into this topic too much, hoping to avoid detailed questions on her brand-new fake relationship with her pretend boyfriend for several legitimate reasons. Yes, she likes to have her rationale organized:

1. She has zero understanding of relationships, let alone fake ones.

2. It's a known fact that uncoordinated stories are key to exposing any kind of hoax. She's seen these things go down in so many crime shows.

3. It may have been a while since they broke up, but Oren was known for his ability to read her like an open book, so better to avoid the topic altogether.

4. Last one, for now, and probably the biggest reason: She's still trying to wrap her head around the underlying reason that compelled Aiden to pretend he's her boyfriend. Especially after they've worked so hard on pretending they weren't unbelievably, irresistibly, uncontrollably drawn to each other.

Which throws her into a rabbit hole. This pull between them, the Eleanor-Aiden-magnet, is insane. Unmatched. Impossible. Stupefying. So under this new state of affairs, do they need to pretend they're faking it in the opposite direction? Or do they just stop pretending altogether?

Gosh, this hurts her brain.

No, scratch that, her brain is on the verge of exploding...

"I'm here on a tour. Staying at this hotel," he points to the one she's staying at.

"Oh," Eleanor croaks, realizing her fake relationship may need to extend further.

I live in Los Angeles now." Oren's words snap her back. "I followed the band and somehow made it to California. Fell in love with this place, fell in love with a girl, ended up staying."

"You? Fell in love? Wow." She had no idea he was capable. It stings a bit, but not as much as she thought it would.

"Yeah, well, I thought I did, but it didn't last long."

Nothing's new under the sun.

"And now I see you, of all people. Might be fate." He grins, taking another sip of his coffee.

"Not really, I'm here for a scientific conference."

"With this guy."

"Aiden, my boyfriend." She can't believe these words are coming out of her mouth. Dr. Eleanor no-serious-relation-ship-ever-again-science-foreva Benjamin.

"I don't buy it," Oren cackles.

Who asked?

She doesn't say it out loud, but her eyes possibly do.

"The face he made when I mentioned your ass tattoo—he clearly hasn't seen it." He makes a sly face.

It's one of those moments where the person drinking the coffee on the other side of the table spits it right back into their cup. Only in Eleanor's case, it goes up her nose.

"It's really none of your business," she answers after drying her face with a napkin. "Besides, maybe I'm shy and I prefer getting naked in the dark."

Why is she even going there? Why does she feel like she owes him an explanation? Lack of caffeine can't be the excuse anymore.

"You? Shy?!" He laughs out loud. "But I'll let you go back to your guy. I bet he can't wait to see your tattoo." Then he gets up and signals his two bodyguards that the party is over. They both get up quickly.

"For what it's worth, Ellie," Oren leans in closer, "I regret that moment I broke up with you," he says earnestly. "I was still a kid, didn't know better."

Yeah? Well...

"I don't," she says honestly. "Not anymore."

And it feels liberating, having her heart no longer belong to Oren.

Problem is, this beating little organ of hers now belongs to someone else.

22
RELATIONSHIPPING

"If anyone asks, Aiden is my boyfriend," Eleanor notifies Alannah when they meet again.

"Oh, so now it's finally official?" Alannah muses, trying to balance several tote bags and a handful of colorful tubes, brochures, a double-helix-shaped squishy and a stuffed animal that looks more like a... chromosome maybe? The results of her latest freebie-hunting at the vendor show.

"Yes... I mean, not exactly. My fake boyfriend, kind of. Unless someone from GERI asks—then no."

"Ah, and who exactly are you faking it for?" Alannah stifles a laugh.

"My ex, apparently. Of all people in all places, I had to run into him here. What are the odds?" Eleanor stops to take a breath. "And Aiden, I don't know what's gotten into him... He appeared out of nowhere and introduced himself as my boyfriend, and now—"

"Professor Kowalski did what now?!" Alannah raises an eyebrow.

"Well, Oren, my ex was kind of asking for it."

"So Professor Kowalski got jealous and decided to claim you." Alannah is clearly enjoying this soap opera episode.

"Claim me?"

Why is the thought of it making her all warm and tingly inside?

"Yes! Wow, I'm impressed! Didn't know he had it in—" Alannah's gaze shifts abruptly.

"There you are, *baby.*" Aiden's voice appears in her ear before his arm loops around her, creating all kinds of new sensations.

Did he just purposefully put an emphasize on her new pet name?

He sweeps Eleanor away from smiling-winking Alannah, who's telepathically transmitting *'your kinky games are safe with me'* vibes.

"We need to talk." His voice has an edge to it.

"Oh, do we?" Eleanor chuckles. "Which of the gazillion items that come to mind should we discuss first?"

"Your goddamn tattoo," he growls. "Now."

"As my fake boyfriend," Eleanor says mischievously, resting a hand on his tightening chest, "You might want to find a more private spot to get me naked." He's so close she could just reach out and seize those lips that are busy pouting at the moment.

But Aiden remains motionless, studying her intently with his beautiful blue eyes, which are now wild and hungry. And puzzling.

Eleanor takes his hand and pulls him back to where they left Alannah. "I'll take your stuff back to the room," Eleanor offers, jumping on the excuse to relocate this heated conversation to a more private location. Alannah, perfectly reading the room, nods in agreement and hands Eleanor her collection of sweepstakes and freebies.

"So now you're my fake boyfriend?" Eleanor asks incredulously as the two of them are alone in the elevator.

"I'm asking the questions now," Aiden orders, provoked.

"Hmmm... A commanding, out-of-control version of you. I like it when my fake boyfriend gets all domineering like that." She smiles teasingly.

"Jesus, Ellie, how many fake boyfriends have you had?"

Is that a new vein in his forehead?

"Aiden, I was just joking with you, you're my very first one." She laughs as he grunts. "Gosh, what's gotten into you?"

But he remains quiet, tightly clenching his jaw, until they get to the room. Eleanor swipes the keycard and opens the door, laying Alannah's treasures next to her friend's bed.

Aiden walks in after her, so tall and broad he takes up the whole space. The last bit of oxygen is now gone too. She takes her high heels off, deepening their height difference. But it feels good to be standing on stable ground again. She can feel the tension level rising, if that's even possible. He's so close that she can't help but rest her hand on his chest again, tracing the ridges and grooves of his muscles through his pressed shirt. His breath hitches.

"Don't," he commands, grabbing her palm. "Before I lose control."

"Oh, believe me, there's nothing I want more right now than see you lose control—"

"What fucking *ass tattoo* was this guy talking about?" Aiden backs her against the wall. His eyes are so dark she can barely see the blue in them.

"You don't get to pull the possessive boyfriend card on me," she warns. "Although it is kind of sexy." Seeing him all worked up, for her, makes her want to pull him by his shirt and kiss him hard. "You're just *pretending* to be my boyfriend. We aren't even dating. Remember? Your very smart brain somehow decided to come up with this hoax less than an hour ago. It's not like I was hiding crucial information from you."

"Show me." His eyes are furious, voice is low and... still commanding. He's clearly not thinking this through.

Why does it turn her on so much? She could easily jump him right now.

"I need to see it," he says. Something in his tone shifts, sounding pained. "Please."

"I'd love to show you." Eleanor can't help the smile creeping up on her face, despite his desperation. "If you're willing to waive your 'no seduction' rule."

"The one that you've been ignoring completely," he admonishes.

"Yes, that one." She tugs on his conference badge. "*Ass tattoo,* remember?" And before he has a chance to take it back, she slides her pencil skirt up her thighs, turning to her side, giving him a front-row view of her past connection with Oren Hason.

Aiden drops to his knees. His composed self is all at once broken, his eyes glassy, breath heavy. "Fuck," he says, his hand gently tracing the two little identical Hebrew letters.

"Why?" he just mumbles.

Why is he taking it so hard?

"I... I can't see why you'd want to walk around with some guy's name on your body for the rest of your life."

Is he ... jealous?

"Scientists are not expected to be smart one hundred percent of the time," she offers.

"Why the hell not?"

"In my defense, Aiden, I was young and stupid. And naive. And in love. And I thought Oren was my forever."

This idea seems so distant now. Aiden has taken up every ounce of that sentiment so quickly and so profoundly.

"What am I going to do with you?" He shakes his head, and his eyes gradually soften. "I wish I'd met you first. Maybe you'd have a different letter up there." He removes his hand, taking the warmth away.

Eleanor straightens her skirt and joins him on the floor, taking his handsome face in her hands. "You know, Oren is not the only name that starts with the Hebrew letter Aleph. Aiden does too. You clearly hadn't been paying attention in Hebrew school."

"Are you trying to make me feel better? Aiden starts with an A, Oren with an O. I never went to Hebrew school, but I can tell the two sound completely different," he says, but there's a spark of hope in his eyes.

"Well, lucky for you, my jealous fake-boyfriend, Hebrew doesn't work this way." She gets up, grabs the hotel's notepad and pen from her nightstand and goes back to the floor next to him. She writes his name on one side of the paper, in Hebrew. Oren's name on the other side and then her name at the bottom.

No, she didn't mean it to look like a triangle.

Then she circles the first letter—which is incidentally the same for all three. "See? My name starts with aleph too."

This seems to make him feel so much better.

Wow...

Never in her wildest dreams did she imagine a guy getting so worked up over her stupid tattoo.

But Aiden is not just any guy.

So she gives him a hug, resting her head on his chest, letting her mind drift off to the loud thrumming of his heart. He reciprocates her hold with his own embrace. And it feels good. Too good, not like pretending should feel. His heart thumps go from a nuclear bombing intensity to maybe a spacecraft take-off. Whatever's calmer on an explosive power index. She waits for the beats to calm down further, maybe to a grenade level, but that might take some time.

"Let's go get you something to drink, and work on our backstory," she offers finally, before she does something she will definitely not regret, but Aiden might. He nods, contrite, and follows her outside the room, back to the elevator.

"Now do you want to tell me what this whole thing is about?" she asks after Aiden's usual composure is back, at least on the surface level. "Why, after keeping our relationship professional for so long, trying so hard to keep your impossible rules, did you decide to introduce yourself as my fake boyfriend? This would be hilarious if it didn't make my brain hurt so much," she chuckles. She's completely ignoring that one confession on his birthday. Drunk Aiden didn't know what he was saying.

"Now, this might shock you, but there wasn't a well-thought-out science experiment behind it. No protocol, no control samples." He rubs the back of his neck.

"Wow, Professor Kowalski, you never cease to amaze me," she laughs.

"You looked like you were trying to save face in front of your ex," he says simply. So there was no master plan, no plan whatsoever.

"Oh, did I now?"

"You're welcome by the way." He sighs, running a desperate hand through his hair. Desperate or not, he still looks handsome.

"And what about the complications? You're not worried about us wrecking our careers anymore?"

"He was gloating about being your mythological ex." Aiden pinches the bridge of his nose. "This guy broke your heart, made you forever appalled by the word 'relationship.' I just snapped. I wasn't thinking."

"Not thinking... That's uncharacteristic of you," she teases him. Again.

He was being protective. Of her.

"Ellie, nothing I do is characteristic of me when I'm with you." Those blue eyes look deep into hers, desperately trying to find something.

What is it?

At a loss for any better words he might be hoping to hear, she says, "You're going to need to up your game, because Oren is staying in this exact hotel, and he wasn't buying it."

"He clearly had the upper hand. I was missing some essential data to defend my dissertation," Aiden says, eyes trailing lower toward where her scandalous tattoo is.

"I just didn't think my butt tattoo would ever become relevant information," she says, leading them to a quiet sitting area in the hotel lobby.

"Cherry-picking data, are we?" His tone is a tad more relaxed now.

"It's not cherry picking!" She chuckles. "I should warn you though, Oren being Oren," she gives Aiden a serious look. "I'm not sure how good you are at pretending or how long you were planning to carry this through, but my guess is that the show is not over yet."

Why does her voice sound so excited?

"Good."

"Good?" Is he for real?! "What if someone from GERI sees us? Mano is here, as you know. And I've seen a few others."

"Alannah has been pretty good at keeping a poker face. We'll figure out the rest, like you had suggested a while ago."

"Okay, who are you and what have you done with Professor Kowalski?"

"What can I get you?" A waiter approaches them. A beer would probably be fitting, but they have to stay focused, in case Oren shows up again.

"Do you like chocolate milkshakes?" she asks Aiden. He shrugs. "Good, it's my favorite. So a large one for me and my boyfriend to share," is her order. Because sharing a large milkshake sounds like something a good fake couple might do. But mostly because it's been a while since she's had a chocolate milkshake.

"I see you're starting to like the idea of our fake relationship." A ghost of a smile, finally.

"Don't mind if I do."

The milkshake arrives quickly and she moves closer to be able to share their giant serving, which has whipped cream and a cherry on top. "I love milkshakes!" Eleanor says after her first vocal sip, winning herself another almost-smile from her handsome fake boyfriend. "So, how did we meet?" she asks, resting one hand on his thigh. Might as well take advantage of the situation.

"At the airport, you fell into my lap. Quite unforgettable," he says. "There's no need to make up a new backstory, just stick to the facts."

"Okay, that's easy. And how long have we been together?"

"Since that pivotal day we met at the airport, love at first sight." His eyes say so much, yet she can't uncover a single thing.

"I thought you wanted to stick to the facts?" She laughs but he remains unreadable.

"Hey you two!" Oren's voice, this time in English, sounds from a distance. They turn their heads toward him. Oren is clutching a beautiful brunette in a mini-dress beside him. The two body-guards from earlier are close by. "This is Tiffany, my girlfriend," he says. Funny he never mentioned her earlier.

"Nice to meet you both," Tiffany says brightly. She has an incredible charm and an obvious knack for people, like Oren's perfect girl would. She might actually enjoy the press's attention, the fans screaming, and paparazzi sightings. Something Eleanor was not quite successful at. Not that she ever intended to be.

"Nice to meet you, Tiffany, I'm Eleanor," Eleanor gets up and shakes Tiffany's manicured hand. She has beautifully painted nails, the kind that would most definitely be peeling under the constant wear of latex gloves and one-handed tube-opening at the lab. "And this is Aiden, my boyfriend," she adds. She can't believe how this new title glides out of her mouth so effortlessly.

Aiden gets up to shake Tiffany's hand politely and then sits back down, pulling Eleanor with him, wrapping a protective arm around her. Then, playing his part as the dotting fake-boyfriend, he shifts Eleanor's hair gently off her face and plants a small kiss on her cheek.

The gesture feels exhilarating. And real. And Eleanor is grateful for that, because it makes this whole situation of meeting her ex's new girlfriend surprisingly easy.

"We're going to catch a movie later, would you guys like to join us? A double date?" Tiffany suggests, either oblivious to Oren and Eleanor's history or just confident enough to not care.

"We actually have plans." Eleanor makes her best attempt to avoid a potential pressure-cooker, but comes up short on the specifying-the-actual-details part.

"Yes," Aiden takes over, giving her a very not-typical mischievous smile. "I'm taking Ellie to Toys "R" Us. She loves toy stores."

Such an Eleanor-tailored plan! He remembered. Can a heart literately swell?

"Oh, that's so cute!" Tiffany says. "So maybe join us for dinner afterward?"

"Hmmm, I promised my boyfriend my undivided attention tonight..." Eleanor lifts her eyes to Aiden, resting her hand again on his thigh, suggestively. He plays along, fingers grazing her rib cage.

Gosh... What a small motion of this man's hand can do to her.

"Come on, it will be fun, and you'll have each other all to yourself later. Tonight is just one night of many, right?" Tiffany retorts cutely. "I barely know any of Oren's Israeli friends."

Friends? Does Tiffany have any knowledge of the past romantic nature of this specific friendship? It was all over the Israeli gossip magazines and social media, but probably didn't make it outside of their small country.

Eleanor shoots a *'you better come clean'* warning glance at Oren. But he seems unbothered. Or doesn't own those mind-reading skills any longer.

"Yeah, guys, dinner on me tonight," Oren says. "I insist." He shoots a meaningful look between her and Aiden.

Aiden's eyes lock on hers. He has an adorable, playful look about him, an unspoken reassurance that whatever decision she makes—he's game.

"Okay then," Eleanor says finally. She can't resist the temptation of testing Aiden's limits. "Dinner. After our toy store date." She turns to Aiden again, to make sure this dinner doesn't stretch for too long. "Then you'll have my undivided attention."

"So, what did you have in mind?" Aiden asks after the royal couple and entourage finally leave. His fingers are still sprawled across her ribs from their make-believe just minutes ago, the playful look still on his face.

"What?" She's having a hard time keeping track of any piece of conversation under these conditions.

"Your plan, to give me your undivided attention," he smile-chuckles.

Since when does this man smile and chuckle at the same time?

"Oh, it depends," she lets her hand climb up his thigh by the slightest. "As my fake boyfriend, do you still adhere to this impossible book of rules?"

Aiden clears his throat. "No more rules."

23
Double Date

Once the lectures and scientific sessions end for the day, Eleanor goes up to her and Alannah's room to shower and get ready. What does one wear for a date that includes a trip to a toy store (her favorite activity outside of science) and a double date with her ex and his girlfriend (least favorite would be an understatement)?

"You guys are like an entire Netflix series," Alannah chortles after hearing the story of Eleanor's day.

"Sounds like a compliment," Eleanor laughs as she walks out of the shower, wrapped in one of the hotel's giant towels.

"I can see why you'd think that." Her roommate grins. "Are you going to a fancy restaurant?"

"I think so, it's an Italian place. Google has three-dollar signs next to it."

"Then you need a dress."

"Need?"

"Yes," Alannah determines with certainty.

"Black jeans and a blouse are fine and are most suitable for a fake date at Toys "R" Us, don't you think? I'm not really looking to make an impression."

"Suit yourself." Alannah gives her a disappointed look and turns on the TV. "You might want to get dressed, your date should be here any—"

A knock on the door. "Gosh, this guy runs like a Swiss watch," Eleanor says. "Stall him," she orders and goes back into the bathroom for a few more minutes.

"I thought you'd be on time for our first official date," Aiden teases when she finally emerges from her hotel room. He's leaning on the wall in the long hallway, just outside the door, taking her in. He looks handsome as always, wearing a black button-down that accentuates his chest muscles and suit pants that hang from his waist in the sexiest way.

Fake boyfriend or not, she better stop checking him out.

"You know me better than that," she chuckles.

"Yes, I do, you're right. Five minutes late is on time." He makes use of her famous quote.

"Exactly." She grins.

"You look good," he says, holding out his hand to her.

"Thanks," she says, taking his hand. "Not too bad yourself." *Pretty hot actually...* "I think I should go change to something a bit more fancy." She turns around.

Should have listened to Alannah.

"No, you don't." He pulls her hand, spinning her back into him. "I like what you're wearing. Reminds me of the night you came to watch me play at SigmaV." His face is gleaming.

"You're right," she realizes. "I wore the exact same thing. You remembered." This brings a big smile to her face.

"Of course," he says, leading her into the elevator. "How could I ever forget?" His blue eyes are so bright.

This is just purely adorable and very hug-worthy. And since he's now her fake boyfriend, a hug feels like an appropriate thing to do. So she wraps her hands around his neck, climbs to her tippy toes and rests her head under his chin for a bit. She's blown away by the harsh mutual thumping going on between their chest walls, but as the elevator doors open into the lobby, Eleanor breaks the hug.

"This is so much fun!" is Eleanor's gleeful remark as they walk hand in hand—even though no one's watching—down the long aisles of her favorite toy store chain. A celebration of games, and shapes, and colors, it gets her every time, as if she's still a kid looking for that perfect toy that will spark her imagination and carry her into a world of fantasy.

"What's your favorite?" Aiden asks, looking around, his hand warmly wrapping around hers, a sensation she hadn't realized she was craving. Until now.

"Used to be action figures," she says, "as a kid, I mean."

"Not barbies?" he teases.

"Nah, that's for girly-girls. I wasn't that."

"Because you like to be different." His look is almost ... admiring.

"Exactly," she says proudly. "You're probably the first guy I've gone on a date with who appreciates it."

She forgot to say fake. Fake-date.

"I do," he says, battling a smile, completely ignoring that missing word. "How many guys have you dated?" That little jealous streak crosses his face for a short moment, making her smile.

"What a smooth transition. Not too many," she says. And when he insists on holding her gaze, she clarifies, "Like on a date-date? Only two-ish."

Including this one fake date.

There have been men, but none serious. Not to the point of calling it a date. Summing things up like this, makes her realize that her no-relationship rule may have gone on for slightly too long.

"How about you?" Deflection is her best strategy for avoiding self-reflection.

"I've dated," he says and she feels like there may have been too many to count.

"Anyone serious?" Her curiosity takes the lead, despite the sense that her heart might take a blow in the process.

"Not nearly as serious as your past relationship with your ex. No Greek mythology here."

"And yet?"

Seriously, why is she doing it to herself?

The corners of her vision are starting to blur as he considers her question. The thought of him having feelings for another woman, being with another woman, are making her stomach flip.

She might be starting to understand his tattoo reaction.

"There was Riley," Aiden says quietly. Their fingers tangle between them as they continue to stride through the toy aisles.

Her favorite-blue comes into view as his eyes look into hers. "It's not a pretty story, though." He scrunches his nose.

"I'm not looking for pretty." She squeezes his hand. "Otherwise, I assume she wouldn't be your ex."

So she's kind of glad it's not pretty.

"We were together for a couple years. Even considered moving in together. Then one day she confessed she had a thing for my best friend, Elliott." He throws the information out there, then takes a long second to shake it off and recover his composure. Their linked hands are now a lifeline. "I cut them both from my life on the same day." His face is impassive as he says it. "They had secretly been screwing around behind my back for God knows how long. I had no idea."

"Aiden, I'm so sorry," she says. Her heart squeezes hard, feeling his pain. Mostly for losing his best friend. Not so much for losing the slutty girlfriend. "Did you love her?"

"I thought I did, but obviously I didn't really know who she was, so not sure I can say I truly loved *her*." His voice is soft and quiet. "Losing Elliott was harder."

"Do you miss your best friend?"

"I can't think of him as a best friend anymore, by definition. I was mostly mad for a long time, now it's just a distant memory. Anyway, in case you wondered where I got my trust issues from."

"I didn't know you had trust issues."

"Oh trust me," he quips. "I do."

"But you trust me," Eleanor points out.

"How do you know?" He still keeps that serious outlook but his eyebrow creases in that way that goes along with his signature almost-smile.

"I just do," she answers. It's as simple as that. "You let me into your life. Let me meet your family, even when you barely knew me." She sends a gentle hand to his face. "You let me in, here," her fingers reach for his forehead. "And here," she slides her hand to his chest, pressing against those harsh thumps, that ease and quicken all at the same time, into her touch.

"It's because you're honest. You've made that a rule. You're always honest. Even when it doesn't play out in your favor," he says with conviction.

"When has that happened?" Now it's Eleanor's turn to trench an eyebrow.

"You've had your moments," he chuckles, letting amusement burst into the conversation.

"I like it when you smile." She lets her fingers trace the sides of his mouth.

"You know, since we're talking about exes, I've been told I was too grumpy, and that I never smiled."

The mere mentioning of his ex again makes her stomach churn.

"Maybe she-who-shall-not-be-named didn't give you enough reasons to?"

Aiden considers it. "Do you think I'm grumpy?"

"Do I think you're grumpy?" she stalls, trying to decide how to break it to him gently. "You *are* grumpy, but I think it's cute. And it makes your occasional smiles feel so much more special, like little victories." His blue eyes give her a dazzling look. "And besides, there's no such thing as too grumpy, there's just not enough sex."

"There's zero sex."

"Why is that? Not dating much?" Eleanor asks, despite already concluding that the thought of him with other women hurts so much it feels like physical pain.

"You really don't get it, do you?"

"Don't get what?"

"The only one I want is the one I can't have."

"That's usually the case, right?" she says flippantly.

"Ellie, I wasn't generalizing." He sounds frustrated with her pretend inability to read between the lines.

"Oh?" Stealing professor Harrington's highly verbal phrase is allowed in special situations, and this might just qualify as one. "Sounds like a special person," Eleanor says. "Why can't you?"

"Because I'm not going to let her risk her career for there to be an us." That wistful, longing look reappears on his face before he shakes it away, slaps on a fresh expression and says, "Now let's get you some action figures."

"I'm not into action figures anymore." She allows the mood switch. "It's puzzles now."

"Okay, then let's get you a puzzle." He turns to the nearest sales rep. "Where do you keep your more challenging puzzles?" he asks.

"Right here." The guy points to an aisle to their left, and they follow the path.

"I won't be able to fit it in my suitcase," Eleanor protests.

"We'll finish it before the conference is over." Aiden slides a thousand-piece puzzle box of a colorful beach town off the shelf. "Puzzles happen to be my favorite too."

"I see you have big plans for tonight." Eleanor accepts the box happily.

"I do."

"My turn to ask a question," Aiden says as they walk out of the store, holding the Toys "R" Us bag with their brand new puzzle.

"Ask away," Eleanor says, bringing her fingers back in between his.

"How did you and Oren meet?"

That's what he wants to know?

"Oren is kind of a big shot in Israel. We met at a concert, his band's concert. Gillie, my best friend, had this humongous crash on their lead guitarist and he knew someone who knew someone and managed to get a VIP pass for a meet and greet, and had to drag me with him. Oren took one look at me, and almost overnight it turned into a very public, high-profile relationship."

"I can't really picture you as someone who would enjoy being in the spotlight. And I mean that in a positive way."

"You're quite correct. Fame was never my thing, still isn't—very much the opposite, actually. It's something I had to reluctantly live with in order to be with Oren." She stops by a candy store, letting her eyes absorb the colors. "Waking up to images of the two of us all over the internet, news reporters following our every move—even *my* very uninteresting moves. Fans crying out his name." She scrunches her nose, pulling Aiden after her into the colorful sweets store. "And then having it all in my face, rubbing and picking at my wounds after we broke up. Bleh..." She tries to blink away the memories.

"Sounds like the perfect rock star fantasy," Aiden says sardonically, obviously knowing enough of her by now to understand this whole situation had never been on her wishlist.

"Someone else's fantasy for sure," she sighs, picking up a small bag and filling it with cherry and cola gummies. "These are my favorite!"

"And what happened? Why did you break up?" He reaches out for the bag and hands it to the guy at the register, as if buying her gummies at a candy store is their usual habit. "What did Oren do to you that made you think you're incapable of falling in love again?"

Wow, a heavy one.

Eleanor gives it a few thoughtful moments while Aiden hands the guy a few dollar bills. She's been avoiding this kind of reflection for a few years. And now, for the first time, it seems that her insights have shifted.

"He didn't choose me," she says finally. "Well, he did at first, but then he stopped."

"Stopped choosing you?" Aiden's hand wraps around her, providing some much-needed assurance, and the bag of gummies.

"Yes, life is something dynamic, things change all the time. If you want to be with someone, you need to keep choosing them. And he chose not to choose me anymore."

"Why?" Aiden asks, as if not choosing her is in total contradiction to all laws of nature. Every single one of them. All at once.

"He said he wanted to be free. Free to travel the world with his rock band and his celeb buddies, free to be with other women, free to not need to think about anyone but himself."

"Sounds like an immature asshole to me," Aiden says. And all at once, as if he waved some sort of a magic wand, it chases away the typical burn in her stomach and makes the lump in her throat go away.

"That he was." She opens the bag of candy, pops one in her mouth and one in his. Aiden doesn't refuse, although he doesn't seem too crazy about candy.

He chews the little gummy before asking quietly, "What about you? Your choice?" This is an aspect she hadn't actually considered. "Did you want to keep choosing him?"

"I... don't know. I guess?" Had she been so busy dealing with Oren's choices she forgot to ask herself what she wanted?

"It sounds more like a question to me." Aiden gives her a quizzical look.

"I wish someone had asked me that question back then. Maybe things would have been different. Too late for me."

"Oh baby, it's never too late." He pulls her into his chest, and she almost believes him.

"Ah, trust me, it is. These useless romantic fragments left in me are probably beyond repair," she says dismissively. "But I like that you call me that. Baby. It's sexy." It's a two in one really—attempting to lighten up the atmosphere and making sure he keeps using that new nickname. "And as you know, I've been trying to stay away from relationships since, because when that breakup had happened, it completely ruined my ability to focus, threw me off balance. I don't need these kinds of distractions, it's bad for my science."

"But it's part of science," he refutes.

"I figured you'd say that."

Although she isn't at all sure what he means.

"Do you still believe in this dumbass's mythological ex idea?" Aiden looks like he's holding his breath while waiting for what comes next.

"Not so sure anymore," she admits, realizing it for the first time now. And loving that it makes him look relieved.

The truth is that at some point in time between her epic fall into Aiden's lap at the airport and now, she completely stopped thinking about Oren. And seeing Oren again doesn't hold the power to reverse this new development, not even by one bit. Every single cell of her body has Aiden etched all over it. Every trace of Oren had been wiped clean and completely replaced. Except for that hideous tattoo. So she adds, "Maybe it's just a primitive way to put a space holder until my Mr. Right comes along."

Or in her case, probably Professor Right....

"So how did you guys meet?" is Tiffany's inquiry as they munch on appetizers in a private room at what Oren coined *Tiffany's favorite Italian restaurant.* So far, judging by the bread, the burrata salad and the wine, Eleanor is definitely an eager supporter of this choice.

"Ellie just fell into my lap. Literally," Aiden answers.

"Oooh, I want to hear the whole story!" Tiffany's intrigued. Oren looks less so.

"I was on my way back from a scientific conference, sitting at the airport, reading, and this beautiful woman was running."

Aiden takes on the challenge as promised, while Eleanor lets herself indulge in chewing the delicious bread, too afraid to ruin the flow. "I believe she was trying to catch the last available charging station. She was wearing shorts and a T-shirt in the middle of winter," he says fondly. "And as she stumbled on a bag along her trail, my world just switched to slow motion. And I caught her." He takes Eleanor's free hand and brings it close to his chest. "I just remember thinking how beautiful she was, and when she turned her head to look at me, sitting in my lap, I just knew."

Knew? Knew what? What is he talking about?

"Wow!" Tiffany clutches her hands together, a dreamy look on her face. "Love at first sight!" She looks at Oren, who doesn't seem as excited as she is, so she moves on to Eleanor. "Did you feel the same at that moment?"

Maybe...? She remembers looking into his eyes, overwhelmed by the blue. Then thinking about the fact that she hadn't brushed her teeth since leaving home that morning.

"She was confused from the fall," Aiden jumps in to her rescue. Again. "And her nose was bleeding."

"Oh, no!" Tiffany looks horrified.

"I would have pushed her away at that point," Oren jokes, trying to lighten up the intense romantic notes of the story. But he's not lying.

"You would, wouldn't you?" Eleanor jabs. "But not Aiden." She picks up another piece of bread. "He kept his calm, held a tissue up my nose until the bleeding stopped."

"This is like next-level romantic!" Tiffany squeals.

"Then we were called to board the plane, and I asked the attendant to switch our spots so we could sit together. I couldn't bear the thought of not seeing her again."

"*You* did that?" Eleanor can't hide her surprise. Aiden nods, a small, content smile on his face.

"So, Aiden, what do you do?" Oren asks. He's never been a fan of romance. Especially not the one that involves his ex and another man.

"I'm a scientist," he says, "Like Ellie."

"Really? Ellie, you said you'd never go out with a scientist!" Oren snickers.

"I also said I'd never go out with a drummer again. And Aiden's also a drummer."

"For real?" Oren doubles up on the surprise. Eleanor just nods.

"Well, drummer in my spare time, it's more of a hobby," Aiden says.

"That's awesome man," Oren says.

"So you guys were..." Tiffany is starting to catch up.

"Five years ago," Oren explains. "I'm her mythological ex," he adds proudly, at least omitting the info about the shared tattoo.

"Was," Eleanor corrects him, feeling Aiden's arm wrapping around her protectively, his body tenses.

"I've lost my status?" Oren pouts.

And before Eleanor has a chance to consider her response, Aiden leans in and kisses her. It's a small kiss, to show his support, or conviction. Or just to spare her from having to think about this question. "If you don't mind, I'm going to punch him now," he whispers into her lips.

And maybe because she thinks Aiden is adorable for getting all worked up about it, or because she wants to avoid needing to bail her fake boyfriend out of jail tonight, she pulls him by the collar for another one. A full-blown kiss this time, with bells and whistles and butterflies and fireworks, and she's so breathless that she has to pull away.

Wow...

And from the look on her drummer ex and his girlfriend's faces, whatever doubts they might have had about her and Aiden's relationship have been obliterated. Completely.

24
Wild Fires

"What kind of event is it?" Eleanor asks when they enter the fancy nightclub, stretching her shortish tight cocktail dress—which Alannah insisted she wear—over her thighs. Aiden is holding her hand, like the flawless protective fake boyfriend he's proving himself to be. And despite knowing it's part of the show, Eleanor is secretly enjoying it.

After dinner with Oren and Tiffany, they managed to escape back to the hotel and spend a good chunk of the evening eating ice cream in the lobby and working on the puzzle Aiden picked out during their Toys "R" Us date.

"I have no idea. A fancy banquet-style dance party?" Aiden makes his assessment, bringing her back to the moment. His voice and scent are her fix, sending a small shiver down her spine. "You look beautiful!" he admires, even though he doesn't have to—fake relationship and all.

"Thanks." She smiles. "And you look handsome!" She gives her man a quick once-over, for the thousandth time tonight, trying to not visibly bite her lip. He's wearing the same button-down as earlier, with an added black tie, his dark hair combed back. The invitation did say it was a black-tie event.

Damn. This is even better than his drummer looks.

"There's a high likelihood dancing might be involved," she concludes, spotting Tiffany chatting away with a few people near one of the side tables.

"I don't dance," Aiden says, gaze following hers. "But since your ex-boyfriend is here, I might make an exception." His eyes carry the conversation to the large, busy dance floor.

When Oren and Tiffany walked in on their puzzle and ice cream moment at the lobby, they just had to ruin it with a will-not-take-no-for-an-answer invitation to join them at this party.

"The night is young," were Tiffany's words. And Oren shoved a VIP invitation to Aiden's hand and whispered something in his ear, which made Aiden say that they'd be there, and prompted Eleanor to pull them both upstairs and change to a more black-tie appropriate attire. That's how she ended wearing Alannah's black cocktail dress.

"What did Oren whisper to you earlier that made you want to come here?" Eleanor is curious, shouting over the music.

"That these are your favorite kinds of events. It got me intrigued."

Eleanor laughs. "That's a straight-up lie!"

"I'm realizing it now," Aiden deadpans.

"Well, then, my fake boyfriend, would you like to ask me to dance?"

"As promised. But I have to warn you, I don't do dancing." He rubs the back of his neck, face unreadable.

"Even if your fake girlfriend wants to dance with you?" she asks playfully. "And you can't use any off-rhythm excuses, seeing as I've already observed your superb drumming skills."

"Well, if my fake girlfriend wants to dance, then dancing it is." An adorable, bashful smile appears on his face. One that Eleanor hasn't seen before.

Eleanor stands up and tugs his hand. "Come on, it won't be painful, I promise." She snakes an arm around his waist, making him follow her into the dancing crowd.

"I thought you said you didn't like music." His lips touch her ear when he says it, sending another one of those pleasant shivers through her.

"Correct. And I don't care too much for dancing either, usually," she says loudly through the beats. "But for you I'm willing to make an exception." Eleanor turns to face him, pulling his other hand around her, bringing them tight together, exactly where she wants him to be.

The problem is, the impact of the proximity to this man, coupled with their bodies moving in perfect sync to the rhythm of the music, equals trouble. On like a major scale.

"What floor are you on?" she asks as they enter the elevator together after some dancing and some stolen hot kisses, mostly when Oren or Tiffany were looking, but also when they weren't. Aiden is on his way to his room, Eleanor to hers. She scans her room key and presses the big circle with the number five on it.

"Fifteen," he says, scanning his room key as well and pressing the number, their eyes locking.

"That was fun!" she says, noticing the atmosphere is growing tense and heated. Might be her pounding heart—a regular symptom since she met Aiden, but now it's getting harder to breathe.

"It was," he agrees. His voice takes on a raspier shade than usual.

"You know," she dares say, "it's not really against the rules. *Us.*" She motions to the space between them as the elevator lights indicate they're nearing the fifth floor. "Well, that's my floor," she says, before Aiden has a chance to process that last statement, yet hoping he'll stop her. But since he doesn't, she just adds, "Goodnight, fake boyfriend," and gives him a hug. His embrace feels so good she takes a little longer to break it off, secretly enjoying his cologne.

"It *is* against the rules," he growls as the elevator doors open.

"*Your* rules maybe, not GERI rules. And besides, you said *no more rules.*" She pulls him by the tie, studying his expression as his eyes grow darker.

"Don't test me. I've been holding back for so long," he rasps.

"Maybe you shouldn't have. Maybe you shouldn't anymore."

"Maybe I shouldn't," he echoes the sentiment. All it takes is a light touch of his lips on hers, a small kiss. Something she has to repay with her own kind of kiss, a fiercer one. This is no longer part of their pretend show for her ex and his girlfriend. And by the time she's done with her little attack, the doors close again with her still inside. The elevator is now in full swing—relatively speaking, for an old elevator—climbing to the fifteenth floor.

"I think you missed your stop," he says, his gruff voice vibrating through her.

"Yeah, might have been intentional," she admits, sliding her hands across his chest. "This saying goodbye thing hasn't worked so well for us."

At the airport, at SigmaV, after going coat shopping and visiting his dad. At her doorstep. She was planning to never see him again, but life sometimes has its own plan.

"No, it hasn't," he agrees. "Maybe we should stop trying to say goodbye?" His husky tone almost pleading.

"Maybe."

"Maybe remind me what you were doing in my bed just before your alarm went off?" Hands pull her tight against him.

Vivid memories will themselves into her mind, flooding warmth through her core.

"Oh, you need a reminder?" she laughs. He nods expectantly. "Right after you remind me of what you were doing while poor Alannah walked in on us," she challenges.

Hmmm... that moment she pulled him into her apartment. Back when she had no idea who he was. And he had no idea who she was. When things were still simple.

"This," he says, backing her up against the elevator wall, kissing her deeply, rendering them both to a level of breathlessness most likely not compatible with life. Again. "This moment..." His arms pull her up effortlessly, letting her thighs wrap tightly around his waist. "I've been thinking about it... Every—" He grunts in between their kisses. "Fucking. Day."

"Yeah?" she breathes. "You and me both."

"And your little breaches of our 'no seduction' rule were not helping." His voice a rough whisper as he gently rubs his newly formed stubble over her neck.

And as the elevator doors open onto his floor, Aiden lets her back to her feet.

"I thought you said you had self-control." She pulls him into the hallway by his tie.

"*Had* is the correct term," he agrees, struggling with his room card, not taking his eyes off her, then pulls her in with him, closing the door behind them. "I can put out a small flame," he gruffs, biting gently on her bottom lip. "But with you it's a whole fucking wildfire."

"Maybe we should investigate the root cause of the fire," she says playfully between ravishing his mouth and gasping for air.

"Root cause analysis is very important," he agrees.

"Very important," she groans. And at the risk of being a turn-off, she adds, "I should warn you again… I suck at relationships." Her hands are loosening his tie, peeling his collared shirt off him, marveling at his exposed chest, now all hers to take.

"Seeing as you excel as a fake girlfriend, I'll take my chances," he grunts, stepping out of his shoes, sliding his hands beneath her dress, pulling her up against him. His touch is driving her insane.

What is it about him? She just can't hold back.

When their bodies start moving of their own accord, swaying to a beat only the two of them seem to know, still with their clothes on, she lets herself drift into that sweet cloud of sensations, just for a moment. Until that one second before her wants and needs take over her common sense. Before rational decisions and grown-up responsibilities and ethics have a chance to weigh in. And then she lets those go too, along with his tie and shirt, unbuckling his belt next. Her hands push him onto the hotel bed, ridding him off his pants and boxers, watching him in his full naked glory as he crosses his arms behind his head and lets her do as she pleases. She plants soft kisses on his chest, enjoying the trail of goosebumps she's provoking in her wake. Excited by the prospect that this bossy man has no problem giving her full control.

She lets herself explore his sensitive spots, pacing herself downward until she reaches that part that makes him groan. "You wanted a reminder?" She smiles widely, slowly circling his shaft with her tongue, letting his hard length sink into her mouth. Sucking, then pulling away before ravishing him again. Matching the pace to his breathing, driving him insane.

"Baby… Not yet," he strains, pulling her back up, unzipping the dress and deftly stripping her of her last bit of clothes. "My turn now," he says, turning them in a swift motion so he's on top. His hands slide up to her breasts, his mouth travels to her nipples, soft bites that make her body squirm with pleasure.

"I can do this all day." He smiles, letting his kisses trail down her body, slowly reaching that drenched spot between her legs.

"Hmmm..." is all she manages.

"Tell me if you want me to stop," he teases, letting their eyes connect.

"Don't mess with me!" she warns.

He spreads her thighs wider, admiring her naked body, letting his tongue explore every inch before reaching her folds, sinking two fingers into her, his tongue relentless, flicking and pressing. Until her body writhes helplessly and her moans get so loud, he has to resume the kissing. "I love the way your body reacts to me," he husks.

"I don't know what it is about you," she says breathless. "I want you inside of me so bad... *now*." She can barely recognize the rusty sound of her voice. Hebrew words mix into English. She can't tell the difference anymore. But Aiden seems to understand this universal language.

"Are you sure?" His gaze meets hers again, and he's not joking. He must know there's no way back from here.

"*Now*," she urges him, possibly in Hebrew. "Please..." Her body's on fire, on the verge of convulsing. And even if there was a way back from this, she would never choose to take it. Not anymore.

"Wait here," he says, pulling himself away for a quick second, grabbing a little wrapper from his luggage, tearing it with his teeth.

"I'll do it." She snatches the little thing off his hand, rolling it over his glorious self. "Mine," she smirks as she pulls him in between her thighs, pushing herself up to meet him halfway.

"I think about you every fucking moment," he rasps as he circles through her opening, slowly sinking into her. "The way your little ass moves when you walk around my lab." He pulls out torturously, then pushes his way back in, whispering his sentences in between each delicious thrust. "The way you scrunch your nose when you have something provocative to say. The little crinkles by your eyes when you laugh." His motions and words are driving her wild. "Your cute Israeli accent... The Hebrew words that come out when you're mad, or excited." He grunts loudly as she circles her hips. "The way you casually rub into me in the hallway. In my office." His voice shakes as he sinks deeper. "That stunt you pulled in the darkroom... The way you challenge me. Ellie, you drive me fucking crazy." He slams into her, finally flush against her. Finally giving her his whole.

"You feel so good," she whispers, writhing under him, pulsing and pushing and spinning out of control.

"I've been wanting to lose myself in you for so long, baby. Lose control with you," he whispers as he picks up the pace, thrusting and pinning at the most heavenly rhythm, groaning almost as loudly as she does. His hands reach her bottom, angling her to the perfect spot, pressing her tightly against him, his fingers circling around that little spot of pleasure, sending her to what possibly, maybe, is a different dimension.

"I can't hold it anymore," she gasps, her nails digging into his skin.

"Then let go baby. Come for me," he whispers, sensing her sweet point of no return. Commanding her body.

It's like a domino effect, as if on cue—her body clenches fiercely around him, again and again until he lets go and rides that one heck of explosion with her, wild and feral. Until they collapse, gasping for air, possibly blacking out.

"Mind blowing," she mumbles into his chest when her ability to use words return to her. "What was that?! This was..."

She's had good sex before, even great sex, but never THIS incredible, out-of-this-world, fireworks-and-stars and... Well, this makes the entire thing a whole lot more complicated.

"Baby, this was the appetizer. I'm just getting started." His voice is still hoarse.

"Good, because I'm already addicted," she says softly, tracing his chest muscles and abs with her fingers.

This makes the marvelous man beside her smile. A big, full-on grin, maybe even a hint of a dimple on his left cheek.

"So that's what I have to do to get you to smile," Eleanor says. "But you know, you've gotten yourself into a bigger problem," she warns, winning herself an amused eyebrow curve from him. "I'm ready for my main course now," she teases.

"Insatiable, are we?" His grin broadens.

"Well, now that I've seen the other side." Her hand slides down his body, feeling him wakening back up for her.

It appears that fake-relationshipping with this guy is her new favorite thing.

"I'm not going anywhere, baby."

It's during those early hours of morning, after what may have been the best night of her life, cuddled into this irresistible man beside her, enjoying that post all-night-long-mind-blowing-sex exhaustion, that her brain starts crafting potential ways she could make it work, have it all, science and him. For both to coexist in her life. And when her heart starts to randomly name their unborn children, she decides it may be time to freak out. So she reluctantly slides herself from under the warmth of the sleeping Aiden, gets dressed quietly and grabs a note and a pen. "Sorry I split," she writes quickly, hoping Aiden will see it when he wakes up and not hold a grudge for her disappearing from his life after their should-be-illegal-to-have-so-many-orgasms night. "I promised Alannah we'll have breakfast together." Then she puts the little note on the nightstand closest to Aiden and sneaks out.

She tiptoes into her and Alannah's room and drags herself to the free bed, careful not to wake up her roommate. Then she stares at that selfie on her phone screen for what seems like forever. Or at least a long, torturous time, before eventually falling asleep. She's out for probably no longer than ten minutes, because soon Alannah's voice is all over her head, pulling her back from her sweet-troubled drifting. "Wake up sleepyhead." She shakes her shoulder gently. "I'm starving."

"What time is it?" Eleanor's drowsy voice carries from under the blankets.

"It's eight-thirty. The breakfast buffet ends in thirty minutes and I'm sure you don't want to miss the ten o'clock keynote session."

"Shit," Eleanor mutters as cognition hits, trying to sit up. Her body is sore, reminding her of their all-night-long extracurricular activities, and she tries to bite down her impending smile.

"I see someone was partying last night," Alannah says smugly. Eleanor gives her a wary look.

"Don't worry, whatever happens in Vegas..." Alannah laughs.

"We're in San Diego," Eleanor groans.

"Come on, your boyfriend will probably be at the keynote session too."

"I was actually planning on not seeing him again."

"That's going to be challenging." Alannah rolls her eyes at that ridiculous aspiration. "Seeing as you still work in his lab."

"Yeah." Eleanor rubs her eyes sleepily. "I clearly wasn't thinking it through."

"Right," Alannah snorts. "More like overthinking it for months."

"I better not hang out at the dining room. Maybe we can order room service?"

Yes, avoidance, the best way to evade the consequences of her latest actions.

"Well, from the way you guys were looking at each other last night when you came up to change into the dress, I would never guess you'd want to avoid him." Alannah's smile turns serious. "Has he done something wrong?"

Something really really right actually...

"No, that's not the problem, I just—"

This confusing response bumps up Alannah's concerns. "Ellie, what has he done to you?"

"Oh, wonderful, incredible things, which you might not want to hear about..." Eleanor can't help herself.

All traces of panic on Alannah's face are quickly replaced by a chastising smile. "Okay, you can tell me the PG-13 version over breakfast." She pulls Eleanor off the bed. It's decided.

"Please don't look at me like this." Eleanor covers her face with her hands when Aiden's beautiful eyes come into view, right as she was trying to load some scrambled eggs onto her plate. Most people have already finished breakfast. Alannah is waiting patiently at their table. But of course, Eleanor has to find herself at the buffet alone with the one man she was trying to avoid.

"Sex hair looks hot on you," is his greeting, a teasing smile etched on his face. He looks... happy. Happier than she's ever seen him. And it's endearing in a way she didn't know possible.

"Alannah dragged me out of my bed just now, I haven't had a chance to—"

"I was hoping to find you in *my* bed this morning," he whispers, gently removing her hands from her face, planting a small kiss on her cheek.

"I've warned you, me and relationships, a terrible combo," she says, despite the way his body looks in his button-down that stretches on his chest and those suit pants hang from his waist. Despite the butterflies swarming in her stomach.

Butterflies. All kinds of new species of butterflies. She never signed up for that...

"I disagree," he says, still smiling. "You're the best pretend girlfriend I've ever had."

This is exactly it—and it scares the hell out of her—she wasn't pretending.

"Maybe we should make it a one-time thing," she offers desperately, loading up her plate distractedly, not even noticing the food items she picks. "I did warn you."

"A one-time thing?" An eyebrow arch. "Funny," he says quietly so only she can hear. "I counted more than three before I lost count. You made me go down to the drugstore for supplies, remember?" A ghost of a smile reappears on his lips.

"Yeah, I remember that." She can't help the content smile that must be smeared all over her face now. "I don't recall you objecting." Unsolicited dreamy thoughts fill her head before she has a chance to chase them away.

"I definitely did not object." His face turns serious. "My point is—I think we're passed the one-time thing. And your warning was about you and relationships."

"Same thing."

"It's not the same thing. I didn't think you were planning on avoiding me later." He slides a strand of hair off her face and tucks it behind her ear, awakening all of her Aiden symptoms at once.

"Well, that's part of making sure I don't fall—" She stops herself, a bit surprised by whatever it is that's taking over her common sense.

Yeah… Last night was not even close to being enough but will have to do.

"Guys, keep the smut for later, I'm starving." Alannah walks over and grabs Eleanor's arm, filling the space with rainbows and sprinkles.

25
SPACING

After that breakfast encounter, Eleanor manages to go the rest of the day without bumping into Aiden. Or maybe it's his sophisticated way of giving her space. Probably the latter, because due to their shared scientific interests, they both attend the same exact lectures throughout the entire day. And luckily there's no sign of Tiffany or Oren, so they don't have to pretend they're a couple. Not anymore.

Eleanor tries to keep her heart in check and the butterflies in her stomach to fold their goddamn wings and stay muted.

An impossible task, but she has the rest of her life to master it.

In the evening, back in their hotel room, Alannah is busy packing, preparing for her red-eye flight back to DC. She has a big experiment she couldn't postpone—the price of collaborating with other groups and the challenge of finding that ever-perfect timing that works for everybody.

"So you broke up with your fake boyfriend?" She can't hide her not-fake disappointment.

"No, just taking a break after the most amazing night of my

life..."

"I can't really speak from experience, as you know," Alannah says, stupefied, "but do normal people usually need to take a break after," she air-quotes, "the *most amazing night of their life*? It just sounds counter-intuitive."

"Normal people—maybe not," Eleanor explains patiently. "But let me remind you, I'm not *'normal people.'* And I must do it—to guard my heart," And from the way her words roll out of her, it sounds as if this is the most reasonable thing to do.

"Oh, because falling in love with a guy who's already desperately fallen for you would be so terrible?"

"Desperately fallen for me?" Eleanor snorts. "None of it matters if he takes it back."

"Why would he take it back?"

"Love is a slippery thing. There's no guarantee of forever."

"No, there isn't, there's never a guarantee." Alannah agrees. "But it's worth the shot, don't you think? Why do you bother running scientific experiments? You already know most fail. Yet you show up, and you bring your best foot forward. And you don't give up. Because you believe."

"Well said, Al! Only this one experiment is not one I can afford to fail at. I wouldn't be able to deal with the potential conse-quences. Too painful. Too distracting. Not for me." And with that, Eleanor locks up the topic.

Alannah just sighs, resigned, and goes along with it. And then she's off to the airport. And Eleanor, she shifts back to actual science, her safest and most reliable aspect of life, even though common knowledge is something that tends to change too.

When Eleanor wakes up the next morning after a not-very-restful night, she tries to count the long list of her new symptoms. She's gotten used to the impossibly fast heartbeats, the vivid dreams at night, the daydreaming, the butterflies, the uncontrollable bouts of excitement. All Aiden induced. Initially in his proximity, then even when he's not around. And after their night together—it's a constant—a very-not-steady steady-state. But this—this is new. She can barely drag her head off the pillow. Her body aches all over. Her eyes are burning. And her roommate is long gone, probably back in DC by now.

Eleanor struggles out of bed, dragging herself to the bathroom. Her reflection in the large mirror confirms that she looks even worse than she feels. And she's pretty sure this is outside of any Aiden-induced symptom. So she stumble-crawls to her suitcase for that little self-test kit she still insists on carrying around with her, even though most people don't carry these anymore, and face masks came off a while ago. Her favorite online custom-made mask store converted its website to other, non-medically related products. And people don't even use the term *pandemic* in conversation anymore.

She runs through the motions, performing the test almost by muscle memory. Then she waits, staring at that little stick that within seconds already displays two lines. Once upon a time, two lines on a stick would have likely been associated with a positive pregnancy test, and oh God—that would have been so much more complicated, although unlikely for such test to come out positive overnight. But, she reminds herself, this is not a pregnancy test. And in this case, and generally nowadays, two lines on a stick are more commonly associated with a positive viral load. So all things considered—that's a much simpler outcome. Yet—the timing sucks. And what also sucks is that she's far away from home and has a flight to catch in less than twenty-four hours. And there's no mistaking here, the line is bright enough to announce she's positive, which means that she can't go on her flight tomorrow, since she's a responsible person that doesn't want to get others sick. But even if she wanted to get on that flight, she probably wouldn't be able to, because putting values aside for a minute—and that's a strong enough argument—she also feels like... shit. Which is a massive understatement.

Eleanor slams her head back into the pillow, pulling her blanket over her throbbing head, letting her eyes—which are about to burst into flames any minute—rest. She feels lightheaded, although heavy-headed sounds more accurate... She'll just sleep it through for a bit, then take care of everything else, like calling reception to extend her stay, postponing her flight, God knows what else. Every task seems like an immense effort.

When Eleanor opens her eyes again, she feels even worse. So much worse. And the room is dark now. How long has it been? Her phone buzzes, reminding her she might need to let someone know. She has like thousand unanswered calls, most of them from Aiden... "Booked us an Uber to the airport," is one of many text messages he sent her while she was busy snoozing or passing out.

"You'll have to go without me," she types. Or at least tries to; different, unrelated letters jump onto her screen. Luckily auto-correct is helping out, hopefully guesstimating the correct verbiage, because re-reading is too much effort right now. She just hits send. So of course what comes next is an incoming WhatsApp video call. *Seriously, video?*

And despite her current dubious state, her brain decides to delve into the fact that someone re-downloaded WhatsApp. She tries to decline the call but accidentally presses—

"Ellie?" Aiden's face appears on the screen, his eyes worried. "What's going on? Are you in your room? Hold on, I'm coming over."

Does he have like a sixth sense to know it's not some sophisticated way to avoid him?

"No, don't come over here. I have—" A loud cough escapes her. Great, another symptom to add to the list. "I'm positive." Her voice sounds froggish. "There was a violent cougher at the evening session yesterday, I bet that's where I got it from."

"Your voice is so cute," is what her fake boyfriend has to say. "But, man, I'm sorry. How are you feeling?"

"Had better days."

"I'll be over shortly with some soup and Tylenol. Anything else I can get you?"

"No, I don't want you to get sick too! Planning to quarantine here until I can—" another cough— "safely travel home without spreading it into the world."

"You're going to need some supplies if you're planning to quarantine yourself. And some company."

And since it might take several days before she can lift her head off the pillow, she says, "I'll say yes to the supplies if you promise to leave them outside my door." Another cough gets the better of her.

"Whatever you say, baby." He looks worried, yet amused, by her tired insistence, and it makes her smile.

"Already feeling better," she says.

Because yeah, his voice has that effect on her. Should she add that to her long list of symptoms?

She crawls into the bathroom to pee and wash her face, painfully chugging the last bottle of water in the minibar. She feels too tired, legs too heavy, to pick herself up from the carpet. Her head is spinning and pounding, her throat feels like a giant thorny lump has settled in it and will not, under any circumstance, consider relocating. She tries to cough, but her muscles hurt so much it's an extreme effort. Getting back to bed feels like an impossible marathon she hasn't trained for. She decides that a change of scenery can't be a bad idea and possibly falls asleep right there and then, or maybe it's a version of passing out.

Aiden seems to appear in all of her hallucinations, which is not surprising given he's been starring her dreams since that night at the airport. In those dreams, she is always breaking their rules, especially her rules—the *no relationship, not falling in love* rules. Her dreams are the one place where her subconscious can break free and take over, where her rationale and concerns are not accounted for and very simply ignored.

But these dreams now are different, more like prolonged, fever-induced delusions. It feels nice, being carried back into bed, and tucked in. And having her bangs smoothed off her forehead with a wet, cold towel. Even if none of it is real. Imagining Aiden next to her, helping her up, trying to feed her soup, supporting her head, bringing water to her lips. And mostly making sure she knows he's there for her. That she's not alone. Not anymore.

When Eleanor wakes up in the hotel bed, not on the carpet anymore, she has to rub her eyes. Because this gorgeous, incredible man is asleep on the couch next to her. Which instantly makes that sweet delusional world and reality collide, or rather merge. She has no idea what time it is, but judging by the bright light shining through the blinds, it has to be morning.

"Your flight!" Her froggish voice comes out as a low, scratchy sound with zero volume. "You're going to miss your flight."

Aiden opens his eyes and appears by her side instantaneously. "How are you feeling, baby?" he asks softly. There's that same motion of his hand, smoothing her bangs off her forehead, like the one she thought was part of a dream.

"Better, thank you," she says weakly. "You'll miss your flight."

"I had Mrs. Jones book us new flights. Our previous flights left a couple days ago." He gives her a fond smile.

"I've slept for two days?" Not possible.

"On and off," he says quietly. Now that she strolls through the depths of her memory, she does recall some assisted trips to the bathroom. And some more attempts to get her to eat and drink. Gosh, she's been so drowsy. And he's been taking care of her this entire time, never leaving her side. "And we'll finally have a chance to finish that puzzle." A boyish smile on his face.

"Why do you care so much?" is what her brain demands to know.

"I just do. And I promised your mom I would take care of you."

"When did you do that exactly?"

Was it after their first kiss? After that incredible night they shared?

"When you fell asleep on my chest, on the plane."

Really? Why?

And it could be the fever, but she's at a complete loss for words. A very uncharacteristic event, and very uncomfortable by all Eleanor's means.

"So you're one of these people who pay for WiFi on flights?" She brings them back to a safer territory.

"From everything we've just talked about, that's what piqued your interest?"

"Well..." She gives it some thought. "Yes."

A white lie, white lies are allowed.

"It's expense-able, under WiFi fees during business travel."

A smile creeps up across her face. It hurts her head. "I told you to stay away," she mumbles with lost conviction. "I didn't want you to get sick."

"Ellie, I could care less about getting sick right now," he says, "be it the latest pandemic or Ebola or whatever. You thought I'd leave you all alone, sick, in some hotel room in San Diego?"

"Wow, my pretend boyfriend was willing to risk getting ebola for me?" She tries to laugh but what comes out feels more like the consistency of dust.

"Ellie, I'm not pretending. I was never pretending," she thinks she hears him say. "And I hope it's not going to scare the shit out of you, but I want more than a fake relationship."

Her brain and all other possible parts of her body that would normally partake in proper thinking, speech and reaction, all betray her. Including her heart, which just beats happily and stupidly, as if she hasn't been running a fever and fainting on the carpet. They're all willing her to say yes.

Except... no.

It must all be her mind playing tricks on her. A figment of her imagination. And her cough medicine. Even if her heart will be playing it on repeat forever.

And Aiden is right—it scares the shit out of her. So she just blames it on the fever, because there's no way he's putting down what her heart thinks it's picking up. So in between her loud coughs she noncommittally says, "Even as a fake boyfriend you're still the best boyfriend I've ever had."

26
UNPRETENDING

"Ellie, we don't have to pretend to be together anymore," Aiden says as they reach the GERI parking lot, studying her carefully. Since leaving the airport he's been quiet, reserved, deep in thought. They are back. Back to DC. Back to work. Back to reality. And his voice sounds like they've reached the end of the road. "Maybe it's for the best."

"Right," Eleanor says, trying to hide the disappointment in her voice with a cough. She's spent her career studying temporary epigenetics modifications: methylation, acetylation, on- and off-switches. And despite what Aiden might think, his feelings have a switch too, because it certainly sounds like he's changing his mind.

And maybe this can all be blamed on the San Diego air. Or her fever, and the cough medicine, and dehydration, or all of these combined, that made her believe there was something more.

That they were more.

But when Aiden lets go of her hand and puts a distance between them instead of pulling her close, and the beautiful blue in his eyes travels thousands of miles away, it feels like the world might be falling apart. And maybe it's her imagination, but he hesitates before he enters the lab and lets her in first, long before he does, as if making it seem like they hadn't just spent the night tangled in each other's arms. Hadn't just had their hearts close together, pulsing and pounding out of control. Hadn't just arrived there together, holding hands on a flight from San Diego.

The end of their pretend fairytale. Prince Charming has just willingly turned into a frog. And it's time to go back to real life. Only nothing about it feels right, or real, or compatible with life.

Yet, instead of protesting or telling him her side—which is obviously pointless, plus he waived all rules, which could possibly include the 'honesty' one—she pulls back.

There once were two people who had been pretending there wasn't an unbelievably incredible pull drawing them together—because they couldn't be together. The pull grew so strong that they decided it would be a good idea to pretend they *were* together. A fake-relationship—the perfect excuse. But now they're back to pretending they *are not*. And *were not*. And *will not*. This is not how fairytales work. And despite Eleanor's dislike for fairytales, this is way too anti-climatic. Next level confusing. And mostly just... sad.

But it's also Aiden's lab meeting time and she has to pretend, yet again, that life is back to normal. A new kind of unwanted normal. And it's Eleanor's turn to present her latest data. So she tapes this bleeding heart of hers sort of together, picks up her head high, and goes into the conference room.

"I want you to treat me like everyone else tomorrow." She had made Aiden promise on their flight back. He was holding her hand and gently rubbing her knuckles in that special way that made her heart beat a little stronger. *"No favoritism at the lab meeting, judge my data as harsh as you would anyone else's."* And as the perfect

mentor and her perfect pretend boyfriend, he reluctantly agreed.

And he does. Maybe he's a bit too harsh. And when feeling under attack, even if she's not really being attacked, Eleanor's survival instincts kick in and she attacks back. Harsher. And Aiden raises his voice, and she does the same. It's not personal, or maybe it's too personal, but their scripts adhere closely to everything science, despite really meaning everything else.

"Outside of germline and pathologic processes, genomic imprinting in somatic cells is irreversible," he insists.

"As far as we know," Eleanor argues. "But our conclusion is only as good as the current knowledge we base it on." And she means it, but the passion in her voice has very little to do with methylation, or genomic imprinting, and everything to do with *them*. Her past relationship with a guy with reversible feelings, and Aiden—who has so insistently claimed his own feelings for her are irreversible, yet he's just fake-broken up with her in his car. And that's a perfect example of how romantic distractions can interfere with careers, especially for people with Eleanor's temperament. Because Aiden is correct—until proven otherwise, genomic imprinting in somatic cells is still considered very much stable. But this knowledge doesn't stop her from snapping at him. In full force.

"Obviously you have no understanding whatsoever of what irreversible means," she shouts. Because he promised to keep choosing her. Promised that what he had for her had no off-switch. Yet it feels like he's pulling away. And even if he isn't, her defense mechanisms are already kicking in, reminding her why she had swore off relationships to begin with. "You're teaching theories that you know deep inside can't be true," she argues. "That's irresponsible."

"Dr. Benjamin," Aiden says, his voice a warning. "It's not the place—"

"So now I'm Dr. Benjamin, Professor Kowalski? I'm so sick of your formality. Do you think your students would have less respect for you if you addressed them by their first names? Or God forbid let them call you by yours? Or have a chance to sleep in on Wednesdays instead of making your goddamn seven-thirty meetings on time?"

"Eleanor, that's enough," he says between clenched teeth. And it may be the first time he calls her that.

"Enough? You're the one talking about permanent modifications, while hiding—"

"I said enough!" he seethes.

Alannah gives her a *'Babe—you better shut up'* look, because she knows her roommate well enough by now to tell she's about to lose all filters. Yeah, she's just warming up. Eleanor hates it when people give in to an argument and in the heat of the moment say things they'll never be able to take back. Yet she can't help herself this time around and does exactly that. And even Zoe, who is known to enjoy a good fight, is caught off-guard by Eleanor and Aiden's fiery exchange. Or rather—Eleanor's fire.

But luckily for Eleanor, Aiden decides to be the mature person in the room, and instead of dragging her out by her hair, he finds a scientific compromise that allows her to get off that anti-permanent genomic imprinting tree she's single-handedly climbed on and stay silent about the rest of the stuff—the personal stuff. The lab meeting ends with confused expressions on her peers' faces.

"My office," Aiden says in a low voice under his breath. She follows behind him as he spreads a furious commanding whirlwind across the open space.

"Jesus Christ. What was that all about?!" he grunts, slamming the door behind them. His face raging, but his voice is measured and impressively controlled. "Were you talking about science or about *us*?"

"Both," she admits, head still held high.

"I'm sorry I went a little rough on you in there," he says, "it just took me a while to realize you weren't talking about your data anymore," he sighs. "Or rather, you were talking about our own personal life worth of data, not the data coming out of your lab experiments." He takes a strained breath. "Our own private stuff shouldn't be discussed at a lab meeting."

"Our own private stuff? The way you said we could *stop pretending*? Your distance? Your hesitation? Your formality? You acted like *us* never even existed."

He hesitates again. Then says, "I guess I have to figure out how to just be your mentor. It caught me off-guard."

"So first we pretend we're not, then we pretend we are, and now you want to pretend none of it ever happened?"

With confused expression, he says, "I thought that's what you wanted."

"Well, things change. I wanted you to treat me like you treat everybody else, but that was a ridiculous request." That's what she had asked, and he'd done exactly that. Maybe a little too well. Because it felt like a blow to the stomach. And she just can't bear the thought of him not looking at her through soft, admiring blue eyes, not touching her passionately, not holding her possessively, not kissing her like every kiss was their first and their last.

"Maybe you need to treat everyone the way you treat me."

His eyebrows crush together, as he's trying to follow her impossible logic.

She gives it some more thought, "No, actually I take that back. That won't work for me either. I just... I think you were forgetting who I was in there." She tries to stay composed but can't help the rising volume of her voice.

"I think you were forgetting your place in there." He matches her enraged tone. This anger about him is a look she can hardly recognize.

"Excuse me?"

"It's one thing when we're alone. But around my students—you can't fucking talk to me like that!" His glare is a warning. He looks furious, and mad, and hurt, and... she can't stop thinking that whatever it was, pretend or not, whatever feelings he might have had for her—those are all gone. Left in San Diego.

"Like what? Like your fake girlfriend?" That angry inferno is growing stronger. All those pretty words Aiden had said back at the hotel, they must have been her high fever and exhaustion talking. He couldn't have seriously said those words she's committed to memory and played on an endless repeat since.

"No, that's not what I meant—" he tries to say, but she's too mad now to listen.

"You know, you really didn't have to say all those cute pretty words and be this most amazing pretend boyfriend to get me into your bed. I would have happily opted in for this mind-blowing sex with you months ago, if it weren't for your stupid 'no seduction' rule. All you had to do was *not stop me.*"

"These weren't pretty words. I meant everything I said."

"Meant. As in past tense. You were the most amazing pretend boyfriend. But looks like now you'd rather pretend that part never happened. Hide whatever happened." And despite how painful the thought is, she says, "I guess it's time to let things go back to the way they were."

"Ellie, that's not—" he tries to plead, but she's crashing so fast she can't stop.

"No, you know what? Maybe you're right—not everything is reversible."

Because there's no way she can go back to how things were before. No way she can go back to work like this. No way she can look at him every day without... shattering.

"Let me spare us both the trouble—you don't have to be my fake boyfriend nor my mentor. I have no intention of being your secret fake girlfriend in a past hidden relationship you don't want anybody to know about. I fucking quit!" Her own words take her by surprise as the look on Aiden's face.

A new symptom appears on her already too-long-to-keep-track-of list. But this one is different. And it overshadows everything preceding it, thousands of needles piercing her chest, pressing, and twisting. And it doesn't stop even when she turns on her heels and opens his office door.

"Ellie, don't... Ellie—" His voice tries to pull her back in, hand reaching out to stop her. But she steps out quickly and runs away from him, her sobs bursting out uncontrollably. Had she known a breakup from this pretend boyfriend could feel this way, she would have avoided it at all costs.

Her mind drifts to the last few months, reeling through her shared moments with this infuriating man. Well, she couldn't have avoided it even if she'd wanted to. This thing between them—it's way beyond her willpower. Especially after their incredible week of fake relationshipping in San Diego. Of having this spectacular man by her side, all to herself. A whole week of fearlessly calling him her boyfriend and allowing him to take care of her until she was well enough to travel back. Because fake relationshipping sounded safe. Safe from involving feelings. Right?

The thing is, at some point in this fake relationship, Eleanor forgot she was pretending, and worse—she forgot she had a rule against falling in love. Or maybe she had already forgotten about that rule a while back, when she fell into Aiden's lap, and then again, every single day after. It all felt so real. And having a fake boyfriend was easy, and safe, because it didn't go against her 'no relationship' rule. And if anything, it showed her how stupid she was for thinking she didn't want anything more from Aiden. Because she wanted everything from him. She doesn't want to sit in lab meetings and pretend there's nothing going on between them.

She doesn't want a fake relationship. She wants a real one. The real fucking deal.

27
THE HARRINGTON HYPOTHESIS REDEFINED

Eleanor: "I'm so done with love."

Grandma: "Oh honey, you're just getting started."

Eleanor: "No Savta, I'm serious, my heart is just not cut out for this kind of stuff. Har'el, it's all up to you now."

Har'el: "Uh-oh... Way too much pressure. Gillie, please chime in here."

Mom: "Ellie, what's wrong? Do I need to get involved? Let me text Aiden."

Eleanor: "No Ima, don't text Aiden!"

Gillie: "On my way."

Grandma: "Gillie, honey, I think you texted your message to the wrong group chat. Do we need to go over texting etiquette?"

Har'el: "No need Savta, Gillie was just, unsuccessfully, trying to create a distraction. I owe you one man!"

Eleanor spends the next couple of days in her own personal dungeon at the Harrington lab, dedicating herself to science, but mostly trying to avoid everyone and everything else. She even avoids Gillie and family calls, pretty much trying her very best to avoid anyone asking her the bold question of "What the hell happened?" Or maybe they'll go about it in a more polite manner, like "What's wrong?" or "Do you want to talk about it?" Variations she's avoiding at all costs, because this might require her to reflect, or worse—put the past few months into words. But even just inwardly, even without trying to arrive at a conclusion or some sort of internal understanding, all she can come up with is a big hot mess. Mostly hot, and then a complete mess.

Aiden tries to call, and text, and show up at the Harrington lab. But she's doing an expert job avoiding him too. And he gets the hint and gives her space. Although she's not sure space is what she needs either.

And on top of it all there's this issue—a small, tiny issue—the thing she did while in the midst of going into overdrive—she quit. Quit her unofficial part of her fellowship in his lab, killed their collaboration. She could get Professor Harrington to be her sole mentor, do all of her experiments in his lab. She could let someone else manage the scientific collaboration part with Aiden, it doesn't have to be her. They can still share a paper together—he still owns half of the work, they're adults, it can be reasonable, and civilized. But it's time to discuss business with Professor Harrington. Even if that means letting him down. Yes, the dinosaur who wouldn't hire women because he spent too many years under the impression that the entire female gender was either too busy with life or created too many distractions. Eleanor was supposed to convince him otherwise. And heck, she was doing a damn good job for a while. But this—this is a major 'I told you so' moment. Like on an Academy Award level, only she won't be collecting any trophies. Because instead of being the professional that she was supposed to be, for the sake of women in science, she was too busy breaking Aide n's *'no seduction'* rule. And getting into a fake relationship with him.

And falling in love... with him.

"Professor Harrington?" Eleanor knocks quietly on his office door, knowing all too well that he might have his hearing aid turned off for his daily uninterrupted deep-thinking mode and therefore might not answer her knocking. But she doesn't peep in like she normally would every morning, because stalling right now feels more comfortable.

Yet she hears his welcoming "Come on in." As if he was expecting her.

"Good morning, Professor Harrington," she says as she opens the door. Her voice is a squeak.

"It's so good to see you," he says with a warm smile, alluding to the fact she hasn't popped into his office for a couple of days, breaking her own habit she had so eagerly enforced. "Please." He gestures for her to sit, as he's done every day for the past few months.

She takes a seat. Despite practicing her lines repeatedly ahead of time, there's no easy way to say it. It's never easy to admit one's failure. Especially when stakes and expectations are so high.

"I can tell you're battling with something," he says softly. His tone is encouraging. But of course, he has no idea what he's about to hear.

She clears her throat. Here goes nothing. "Professor Harrington, you were right." Even just admitting it, is incredibly difficult.

"Right about me, I mean, not about the entire female gender."

"Oh?" He gives her his signature wondering-almost-fascinated look. If she had his undivided attention before, now he's in heightened-mega-focus mode.

"I am a terrible distraction. I am the epitome of distraction. And I did exactly what I shouldn't have. Exactly what you were so afraid of."

"I am intrigued." Professor Harrington gives her a curious look, albeit somewhat amused. "Would you care to elaborate?"

There's no going back now. "I let my feelings come between me and my science. Got side-tracked, created a distraction that impacted not just me but also Aide—" She catches herself and quickly amends— "I mean Professor Kowalski. I fell in love. And now... now it's a whole mess." She quickly blinks some tears away and takes a deep breath.

Be strong.

"And that's exactly what you were afraid of," she continues. "And I failed you, and I let you down. I let myself down." She's practiced these lines almost all of last night, but what comes out feels more like a disastrous word vomit. So she tops it off with, "I was wrong to think that I could somehow have it all."

Professor Harrington studies her intently for a long moment until he finally says, "No, *I* was wrong. I had made a mistake many years ago, thinking love was incompatible with science. That a good scientist couldn't possibly be productive when love or family was in the way. I avoided it at all costs, for so many years. Even at the cost of my own happiness. Don't repeat my mistakes."

"I think it might be too late for that. I already quit my unofficial fellowship in his lab."

She expects no less than a look of disapproval from him. Expects the old professor to show his obvious disappointment. Maybe even shout or at least sound angry. But his voice is even as he says,

"Seeing you and Aiden—there was a special bond between you two from day one. I thought it would only be an interruption, yet the two of you together were more productive than the sum of each of you alone. Exponentially better. More than anyone I've seen. Fearless, unstoppable. And believe me—at my age, I've seen a lot." He stops for added impact. "You are an extremely bright, talented, and hardworking scientist. And in as little as—how long have you been here? Four months? You've managed to completely transform my ways of thinking. Both in epigenetics but also in life."

Eleanor shifts in her chair. This new revelation is quite striking.

"Don't make the same mistake I made—choosing one over the other," he continues. "If there's one thing you've taught me, dear Eleanor, is that you *can* have both. And actually do better. Don't give up on Kowalski, he can be a real pain in the behind at times, I agree, but... You make him smile." He halts, deep in thought, as if digging up memories. "I've known Aiden since he was a young child, playing around his father's lab. Never once heard the sound of his laughter. I've never seen him as happy before as he's been with you. And I can tell by the way you look at him."

"Can tell what?" This conversation has taken a very unexpected turn.

"That you are forgetting something very important."

"Forgetting?" She tilts her head, having a hard time following.

"Eleanor, you've been in my lab long enough to be able to cite it in your sleep." The old man shakes his head. "What you two have is special, remarkable. And as I've said before, you must never ignore a once-in-a-lifetime observation, even if you can't understand it fully. It's those unique and unusual discoveries that hold the potential to transform everything." He pauses to observe the impact of his little pep talk.

"Oh," is all she manages.

"And Eleanor," he says, a mischievous smile on his face.

"Yes, Professor Harrington?"

"This, of course, was a strictly scientific inspirational talk, and if anyone claims otherwise, I will surely deny it."

28
Apology Crafting

I t's definitely a craft of sorts. Harder than any scientific manuscript she's ever written. Delivering a proper apology to a righteous recipient requires a great deal of talent and humility, and a pinch of boldness, especially when it involves prideful, never-admit-being-wrong Eleanor. Because as far as she's concerned—she's never wrong.

Lashing out at Aiden? In her mind, that wasn't wrong.

Expecting him to want to shout she's his girlfriend from the rooftops instead of fake-breaking up with her in the car and taking the time to figure things out or hiding it altogether? Sure. He was the one who started this whole relationship stuff, faking it until they were actually making it, and then changing his mind. No, she wasn't wrong to be mad about it. Not after he had promised that some things were permanent and irreversible. And yes, maybe she was wrong to expect Aiden to read between the lines and follow her subtext, because she'd never actually confessed her feelings out loud. But rationalizing when upset is not always an available option, and defense mechanisms, as they are, can sometimes kick in too soon or spin out of control.

But it was Alannah who made her see things in a different light. *"I think you broke Professor Kowalski,"* she said, in that special half-joking-yet-dead-serious way of hers. *"He stopped shaving, stopped talking. He doesn't even lift his head from his computer, except for emptily staring out the window. And when he started calling us by our first names and permanently moved our Wednesday lab meetings from 7:30 a.m. to 10:30 a.m., that's when we all got really worried. The man is absolutely falling apart. You have to do something."*

Alannah, of course, made sure her observations were not limited to one side only. *"And look at you, you're in no better state than he is. Don't take it the wrong way, but when was the last time you showered? Or put on some regular people's clothes? Or had anything to eat other than candy and coffee? Your dentist will commit suicide at your next appointment if you keep going at this pace."*

And her roommate didn't stop there…

"I'm not saying the man is perfect, and of course I don't know the whole story," Alannah kept at it. *"But you, at the very least, owe him an apology for executing your attack during his lab meeting and hanging out your dirty laundry in front of his students. You crossed a line."*

Yes, Eleanor crossed that sacred line between personal and professional…

So she sits down on her bed, a notepad and pen in hand, in the dead of night—because that's when her inspiration peaks, and she can't sleep, and anyway, sleeping is overrated. And starts drafting what she will say when she walks into Aiden's office again, closes the door behind her and delivers that much overdue apology.

Her phone buzzes from somewhere under her covers. Yes, despite the fight with her fake boyfriend, she still lulls herself to sleep by staring at their selfie from that flight from Spain. A treacherous spark of hope rises inside her. A hope that maybe it's Aiden.

He tried to contact her several times after she stormed out of his office, but she was too angry, too hurt, too prideful to let him in. And now—now he's stopped trying. Giving her space? Or just distancing himself? Letting himself forget her? She quit their collab, so now he can safely and efficiently remove her from his life. Leave that page behind him and move on. And she hasn't done much to stop him.

She digs out her phone from between the folds of her Disney sheets. Maybe it's these princesses that have been messing with her head, blinding her with all these happy-ending fairytales. Why couldn't they have had superhero designs at that store instead? That would have been more Eleanor-suitable, and for sure safer.

"Eloosh, this is some next-level-deep shit," is a wild, toned down, English translation of Gillie's message in Hebrew. "And I mean that nicely. Please don't freak out," he adds before he sends an image. She opens it, not really knowing what to expect, but once her brain registers it she gapes, quite shocked. It's a news piece.

"Lovers Reunited," says the title. "Hot Israeli Drummer Oren Hason Back with His Long-Time Ex." It's followed by a pretty bold photo of Oren and Eleanor. "An accidental meetup in San Diego leads to a comeback."

"Where did you get this from?" Eleanor tries to get her erratic nerves under control as Gillie follows up with a WhatsApp video call.

"I hope you're sitting down," Gillie says, barely giving Eleanor a chance to breathe before he continues. "It's decently distributed across social media..."

"What in the world?! This is an old photo from like five years ago." She looks at her younger, bathing-suit-clad self, enjoying the sunny Tel Aviv beach in Oren's arms.

Gillie shares the link to the post so she can enjoy the whole entire story. "Right now, it's still relatively contained, so maybe your new boyfriend won's see it," is his attempt to control the extent of her rage. "Although you might want to give him a heads up…" She can barely bring herself to scroll through because this is a real fucked-up shitshow. The first comment was made by someone who calls themselves UnderDog28, "Messing around with her professor, that's what brought her to San Diego… Has to be fate," the asshole wrote. Then they followed up with additional sarcastic and degrading gems about Eleanor sleeping her way for career advancement and about Aiden and sexual harassment. And yes, names are mentioned. And of course, GERI's official Instagram account is tagged, and it seems to have sparked a whole inflammatory chain reaction, setting the tone for a long list of comments about nothing and everything that could wreak havoc on her and Aiden's careers.

"Who the hell is UnderDog28?" she shouts.

"Is that your biggest concern right now?" Gillie gives her an incredulous look.

"Yes, I need to find out where this little shit lives and shove their head into the toilet."

"Well, I think you have a point there. Looks like the original post came from this same jackass, UnderDog28, who tagged both Oren's fan page and several GERI official groups. And then also posted the same comments on their pages… Talk about toxic fans. And that's how it blew up. There's also a photo of you and Aiden—"

"Don't send it to me, I don't want to know."

"Okay, I guess ignoring is… a strategy." Gillie's worried expression fills up the screen. "But Eloosh, the way UnderDog28 presented it—it looks like a love triangle. I think Aiden might appreciate an explanation here."

"Well, Aiden and I are not really on speaking terms right now," she mumbles, trying to unsee some of the comments in the post and mostly remind herself it's still a contained blunder. Plus, as far as she knows, Aiden has no time for or interest in social media.

"I figured there was something going on when you switched so abruptly to sparse mode on text messages, right after you texted the entire family group chat that you were done with love."

"I'm just a little crazy, is all. Got mad at Aiden for taking a minute to announce us to the world. But that really pales in comparison to this... chaotic state of affairs." She grimaces as she says it. "Why would anyone do something like that? I'm nobody, this is such a useless piece of news, and a complete lie."

"Jealousy?" Gillie offers.

"That's ridiculous." It might have been the price of dating someone famous, but that celeb-fest had been long gone since she and Oren broke up a few years back. Who would have thought it would come back to bite her like this?

And what happens if these comments get to the wrong hands in GERI? They probably have already... A serious, world-class shitshow. And now she has much more to apologize for than just lashing out at her fake-boyfriend-professor during his lab meeting. Because this fake news story might cost them everything. Thanks to her, once upon a time, being Oren Hason's girlfriend. And possibly also pissing off someone who identifies themselves as UnderDog28, because this feels like a personal vendetta.

However, at this moment, more than the slut shaming and all other derogatory, career-wrecking comments, Eleanor's biggest concern is what Aiden will think when he sees that photo of her and Oren. Clearly it's an old photo from when they were still together, but for all he knows this could have been taken now.

And that apology letter she was drafting? It needs a complete revamping now. She has no idea where to start or what to say. Or even how to say it. One thing for sure—a short, abbreviated explanation jotted on a piece of paper is not going to cut it. Not anymore. This calls for something extensive... And creative. More like an entire book.

She scrolls through the long list of contacts on her phone, searching for Oren's number. It's been a while, and she only has his Israeli number, but she gives it a try.

"Please, please answer," she chants in Hebrew to herself, hoping he'll pick up. What are the chances that he still has the same number, even after moving to the US? Close to none. And is probably why no one picks up. There's an automatic voicemail, which doesn't indicate whether he still owns this number. But at her level of desperation, it's at least worth a shot.

"Oren," she says into the phone, recording her message. "It's Ellie. You probably don't have this number anymore, but if you somehow hear this message, please call me back!" Her voice sounds even more anxious than she feels.

Gillie is right, giving Aiden a heads up is probably a good idea. There's no point wondering whether he will find out, because he surely will. But that can wait till morning.

And of course, Eleanor can't sleep. She spends most of the night responding to family texts—for them it's already morning. And yes—they've all seen the post and read the comments. Even her grandparents, apparently, have started to immerse themselves in social media. And now that the whole thing between her and Aiden is sort of out in the open, it would be a relief to talk about it freely, if it weren't so twisted and generously sprinkled with juicy yet incorrect info about her and Oren.

She spends the rest of the night tossing and turning and mostly dreading the moment morning comes. Dealing with this thing head-on might be the right thing to do, but doing the right thing is typically far from being a fun option.

"Babe, you look terrible!" is Alannah's reaction to her dreadful-morning self.

"I know, I've been up all night," Eleanor mumbles, not even an ounce of energy left in her body.

"I know exactly what shake you need. Sit tight, I promise you'll feel better in under ten minutes." Alannah's optimism is usually contagious, but today calls for something stronger to lift Eleanor's spirit. There's no amount of vegetable and plant juice in the world that could undo that image and the comments from Instagram. That ridiculous post has already been shared thousands of times since yesterday, and has an unimaginable number of likes.

What is there to like about it?!

So when the fresh-green-brownish juice is ready and served, she just turns her phone to Alannah, getting her up to speed. Speedy quick.

"WHAT THE FUCK?!" is Alannah's uncharacteristic response. *Fuck* is the one word her roommate avoids using under any and all circumstances.

"My thoughts exactly," Eleanor sighs.

"Have you spoken with your ex?"

"I left him a message, but I don't think I have his current phone number. We hadn't really kept in touch. It was too painful after the breakup. And he was nice enough to not push it last week when we met in San Diego."

"You need to find a way to contact him." Alannah's eyes grow wider, emphasizing the apprehension on her face. "And you *HAVE* to warn Professor Kowalski."

"There's still a chance he won't see it. I mean, with all due respect to Oren Hason—he may be famous, but not *that* famous."

Is she backing out of the entire apology?

The thought of exposing Aiden to this whole thing, showing him this photo—despite it being an old photo—makes her stomach churn. Based on his possessive reaction to her and her ex's matching tattoos, Aiden is not going to take this too well. Fake breakup or not. Just an evidence-based assumption.

"I am no expert," Alannah says. "But it's juicy enough. He needs to know, at least about the comments he's mentioned in. I can see why, given Professor Kowalski's position, people might think he was taking advantage of you. These are serious accusations." It doesn't take a genius to notice how hard it is for Alannah to hold this conversation. Yet she seems to feel it's her responsibility to gently reflect on how the world might see this whole mess from the sidelines.

"But it's not true. I've been provoking him for months. He was trying to stop me, push me away, warn me this could be bad for our reputations and careers. But I didn't care, it was like an imaginary magnet was calling the shots. This pull between us. I can't even explain it." Eleanor looks at the post again. "Alannah, how do I fix it ?"

"Well." Alannah scratches her head gently like she's trying to make sense of a bunch of nonsensical data. "You start with drinking this juice. Then you take a shower, you get dressed—and I mean actual clothes. Not whatever it is you've been wearing. And *not* Professor Kowalski's sweater. And you go talk to him. In person." Her roommate pushes the green-brownish juice in her direction.

"Don't take this the wrong way," Eleanor pinches the tip of her nose as she brings the weird potion looking thing to her mouth, "but this smells awful."

"I know," Alannha chuckles. "But you'll feel better after you drink it."

"Better, as in get pulled over for alcohol testing? Or for consumption of illegal substances when I attempt to enter GERI?"

"Well, it's good juice, but no," Alannah laughs, "not that good."

With a lack of any better options, Eleanor drinks the thing. It doesn't taste as bad as it smells. Or maybe her mind is so preoccupied that all other sensations are only partially coming through. If at all. She showers, gets dressed, and folds the little note she started drafting yesterday. It's incomplete and doesn't really include the latest events, but it does begin to explain how she feels and it does include Eleanor's own way of apologizing. Which granted, is not your typical straightforward apology. Aiden might need to read hard between the lines here. Unless he knows her well enough by now, which she really hopes he does.

The metro ride, despite being only a few stops long, is excruciating. Eleanor hides her shaking hands in her lap, and when that doesn't help, she tries to hide them in her jeans pockets, then finally resorts to sitting on them.

And despite not usually caring what other people think, she can swear that faces are turning toward her. Is it her horrified-sleepless-tired-terrible look? Is it her imagination? That stupid post could not have made it global so quickly. That's ridiculous.

When they get to the GERI stop, Alannah takes her hand. "Breathe before you have a heart attack," she whispers, and doesn't let go until they get to the gate that only allows one person to pass at a time.

They walk silently, side by side, to the building. Eleanor feels her anxiety level picking up with every step.

"Where do I even start?" she asks her roommate in a weak voice she can barely hear herself.

"At the beginning would be nice. You were planning to apologize for snapping at him at the lab meeting, right?"

"Right, apologize," Eleanor tries to say, but she's not sure her voice actually made a sound, so she defaults to nodding her head slowly and unconvincingly.

"Okay, that's a start. And right after you do, you need to tell him how you really feel, regardless of the post."

"How do I really feel?" Eleanor asks. And not because she doesn't know how she feels. But because admitting her feelings is a brand-new territory and mostly because—she's never actually felt this way before.

"Yes! Tell him how you really feel about him. Before you bring up this whole fiasco." They enter the building and start climbing up the stairs to the third floor. "He needs to know you love him."

"I never said..." This particular word was not on the menu. Eleanor hasn't admitted it to anyone, not even to Alannah, barely to herself. "This was not part of the plan. It's not ready for prime time." She shakes her head.

"Oh, yes it is. And it's about time he knows you feel the same way about him that he feels about you."

"Dr. Ruth, where do you bring all these insights from? Has he said anything?" Eleanor asks as they step into the hallway.

"Babe, don't give me that look. Even for someone as inexperienced as me—you guys are SSSOOOOOO obvious!"

They enter the large, open space of the Kowalski lab. Eleanor slowly makes her way to his office, feeling all eyes on her. She opens the door slowly, without even knocking, stepping inside.

But despite never missing a day at work since her arrival, Aiden is not there.

29
CONFESSIONS

Eleanor walks down the hall to the one person who usually has all the answers when it comes to... hmmmm... the well-being of colleagues at GERI. The controller of all info, also known as Mrs. Tara Jones. And right now, that's exactly what Eleanor is after.

"Good morning," Eleanor says quietly as she enters the room.

"Eleanor!" Tara lifts her eyes from her computer and offers a smile. It's warm, yes, but laced with a great degree of something else. Concern? Apprehension? Pity? "How are you, darling?"

"Had better days." Eleanor tries to bend her lips upward, but it feels more like a flinch. "Do you know where Professor Kowalski is?"

"Oh," she says. "He's with HR, there's an internal investigation."

"An investigation?" This thing is spinning out of control so quickly. And Eleanor is reeling.

"There are rumors, darling. I... It's really none of my business, but there is quite some talk about you two."

"It's all my fault," is the only thing Eleanor manages to say. "Where is he now?"

"I don't think it's a good idea..."

"Where, Tara? Please."

"They're on the sixth floor, conference room," she sighs. "You didn't hear it from me, you just happened to be there—"

"Thanks!" Eleanor calls as she sprints out of the office and up the stairs, frantically running through the sixth-floor corridor, a place she's never been to before, searching for a conference room. This is an issue on its own, seeing as the sixth floor is mostly composed of conference rooms.

Eleanor is already breathless when she finally finds it. She can only see shoes, thanks to the painted glass walls that hide who's wearing them, but she is almost certain those are Aiden's shoes. She opens the door and jumps in. There are three suit-clad, serious-looking people, two women and one man, all sitting on one side of the long mahogany table. Aiden is sitting across from them, looking... resigned. Like he's lost all sense of hope. Every single ounce of it.

All eyes turn to her, surprised. "It's all my fault," she says, almost wheezing, keeling over, hands on her knees, trying to reorganize that complex inhale-exhale process. She should really go back to exercising regularly. Although at the moment she suspects it's not just the frantic running up the stairs and through the hallways. It's seeing Aiden like this. It sucks all the air out of her. It crushes her heart, and she can't breathe.

"Who are you?" the man asks in a not-very-patient tone.

"Eleanor, Eleanor Benjamin," she says. One of the women looks down into her notes, a sign of recognition briefly crossing her face. "Please hear me out before you—"

"Dr. Benjamin." The woman holds out a hand, stopping her mid-sentence. "We are planning to hear all sides. Please, if you could wait outside for your scheduled time." And when she notices what must be a confused look on Eleanor's face she adds, "Please take a look in your email, it's all there."

Email? Who has time for emails in the middle of—

"Now, if you could please step outside." She gestures toward the door.

Eleanor's eyes turn to Aiden, but he won't even look at her. Slumped, she turns and steps outside the room, closing the door behind her. She takes a sit on one of the chairs in the hallway and opens the Outlook app on her phone.

And yes, it's all there. The poker face woman was not lying. Her eyes skim through the never-ending document. Her vision blurred. Investigation. Possible misconduct. Position of power. Suspected sexual harassment in the workplace.

Fucking hell.

"We will see you now, Dr. Benjamin." The woman from earlier appears beside her, clutching a notepad. Aiden walks out of the room. Their eyes meet for a brief second. He looks... broken. Hurt. Hopeless. And she's the one to blame for it all.

"Aiden." She jumps to her feet, trying to reach out to him, but is blocked by that notepad-clutching woman.

"Professor Kowalski was advised against making any contact with you until the investigation is complete," she explains in a firm tone. "And we expect that you do the same. It's all in the email," she says, pointing at the little cellular device in Eleanor's hand. Yes, the one that still has her and Aiden's selfie on its lock screen. And home screen.

This is ridiculous, it will take her a whole week to read this long email.

"Now if you could follow me, please," she says once Aiden is out of sight. She ushers Eleanor into the conference room and to the same seat Aiden was just occupying. It still has some of his body heat.

They introduce themselves briefly; they're GERI employees, from somewhere in the depths of HR, but Eleanor is too shaken to register any information at this point.

"Please state your name and your GERI ID number," the man says, and Eleanor does as asked.

"I just want to make it clear," he says. "You are not under investigation, but it would be helpful if you could share as much information as you can with us, as honestly and objectively as possible, to help us make our assessment." He pauses to make sure she follows. "And we will try to keep it confidential, but depending on the information, there may be parts we would need to act on or report. However, we will do our best to keep your name confidential."

"Okay." Eleanor takes a deep breath. "I'll tell you everything, just please, you have to understand, Aiden... er... Professor Kowalski didn't do anything wrong."

"Let's go about it in a more organized fashion, shall we?" the woman from earlier says. Eleanor nods.

"Could you please tell us about the nature of your relationship with Professor Kowalski?" The man asks.

Wow, jumping straight into the deep. Where would she even start?

"Starting with how you two met," the other woman says, as if reading her mind.

"We actually met at an airport in Spain. I was on my way here for the first time. He was coming back from a scientific conference, but at the time I didn't know who he was. I was running to catch the last charging station because my laptop was dying. And I tripped, almost landed flat on my face and he caught me."

"He?"

"Aiden. Professor Kowalski. And my nose started bleeding, and he helped stop the bleeding and gave me a band-aid for a cut on my knee. And made sure I was okay." She stops for a breather, realizing she's talking way too fast. Hebrew words are mixing into her sentences. She's in some sort of an unfamiliar anxiety mode. "And then he let me text my mom from his phone because I lost my phone. Our flight was being delayed and I didn't want her to worry." A small smile creeps up into her face as she recalls those moments. The look on Aiden's face when she asked him to download WhatsApp and a Hebrew keyboard. "And then we ended up sitting next to each other on the plane to the US. I was cold, and he gave me his hoodie, and he let me cuddle into him when I wanted to sleep. And he let me hold him close when we said goodbye because I really needed a welcome hug."

"And at that point, you knew who he was?"

"I still had no idea. I didn't even know he was a scientist; I thought he was a drummer. And he didn't know who I was either. I never told him my last name, not even my full first name, I just said Ellie—only my closest friends and family call me that. And he introduced himself as Aiden, which is actually his middle name, but the people who are closest to him call him that."

"I'm sure you'd done extensive research about GERI and your future mentors and collaborators before you came here, had interviews, but you didn't recognize him?" the second woman asks.

"Well, GERI had 'no visitor' policy then, so a face-to-face interview and a prep visit were not approved. Professor Harrington—my sponsor—he's great, but he's kind of old school. He doesn't do all those video conference stuff, so we all stuck to emails.

And I read every single one of his and Professor Kowalski's papers, but I never actually... looked up their images."

"How come?" the first woman asks, surprised.

"I was blown away by their research, their discoveries, their publications. Why would I care about how they looked?"

"Well, could have saved you some trouble," the second woman says quietly and receives an admonishing look from the one with the notepad.

"Perhaps," Eleanor says because this is probably true and would have been the responsible thing to do. But she doubts it would have changed the way she feels about Aiden. This thing—it's strong enough to overcome any mindset. Heck, it's stronger than anything she's ever felt before.

"And when did you find out he's your boss?"

"He's not really my boss, he's my collaborator. My boss is Professor Harrington."

"Yes, yes," the woman with the notepad says. "But you do partly work in his lab and report results to him."

"I work in his lab when I need the instrumentation he has, and discuss the results with him, but it's part of our collaboration," Eleanor tries to clarify. Gosh, they're making it sound bad. "And as I said, I didn't even know he was a scientist. I came here around Christmas and couldn't get into GERI until after New Year's. So, I had a whole week to find something to do and get settled. And Aiden was the only person I knew in the area. Actually, in the entire country. And I was kind of leaning on him for help. And we got close."

"How close?"

"Emotionally and physically."

"Did he press you to do anything you didn't want to?" the second woman asks.

"Gosh, no! If anything, I was the one pressing him. He was

looking for a serious relationship and I wasn't, yet I couldn't keep my hands off him."

The man clears his throat. "So how did you finally find out who he was?"

"On my first day at GERI, I came to meet Professor Kowalski in his office, and that's when we both found out. We were both shocked. And then Aiden made rules—he wanted to keep our relationship on a professional level. Even though there isn't any rule at GERI that would not allow us to get romantically involved."

"That's correct, since you are a postdoc, and technically he's not your sponsor or mentor," the woman says.

"Exactly. So why is there even an investigation?"

"It's more about the optics," the woman says. "The perception. I'm sure you are aware of the information that has been very publicly spread through social media. Therefore, we have to investigate."

Uh-oh…

"So, from that point on, you both decided to keep it strictly professional?"

"Well, *he* did. And that's why I said it was all my fault. If you are considering blaming anyone for sexual harassment, I would be the one to blame."

"It's very often that victims feel guilt—" the second woman starts to say.

"No," Eleanor interrupts. "You have it all wrong. I kept pushing him and provoking him. Rubbing against him at any chance I got, making sexual comments, trying to kiss him. He was really putting up a good fight, tried to resist."

The three people in front of her exchange looks. The woman with the notepad is battling a smile. The man scratches his head and clears his throat again.

"So, would you say, whatever happened between you was consensual?"

"Very consensual, very much desired."

"Does that include this scene as well?" The woman picks up a printed paper and hands it over to Eleanor.

It's a photo of her and Aiden, dancing, passionately kissing. She's wearing Alannah's black dress, arms wrapped around Aiden's neck, fingers digging into his hair, their bodies tight together—exactly the way she likes it. This could easily be any occasion during that party Oren and Tiffany talked them into during their heated San Diego fake-relationship adventure. And despite still being mad at Aiden, Eleanor has to fan herself—because this is some HOT stuff.

"Where did you get this from?" is what she needs to know. Because she doesn't recall being photographed, and Aiden clearly looks as busy as she does.

"From the same post. Please answer the question," the woman says. "Was this consensual?"

So that's the second photo Gillie was mentioning...

"Very much so." This makes her blush. "Although we have more appropriate photos than this one." She takes out her phone and flashes their airplane selfie at them. "But this," she points back to the photo on the table, "this was a private moment. An intimate thing that shouldn't have been photographed. You can't use this against him."

"It looks like a night club, not very private," says the first woman, "but we also have an entire footage of the GERI surveillance camera, starring the two of you—" She clears her throat. "Playing in the snow after hours. On GERI grounds."

Eleanor has to challenge that. "Is playing in the snow against the GERI rules?" Questioning everything is an important quality in a scientist.

"This is not the kind of activity we wish our professors would engage in," she responds.

"Friendly snow fight team building activity?" Eleanor tries.

"Friendly might not be the most accurate description." The woman clears her throat again. "Would you like to watch the footage, Dr. Benjamin?"

Coming to think of it, she does recall some close proximity snow rolling and limb tangling. "I'm good," she answers. "But just so you know, the snow fight was totally on me. And the fact that rumors about us went out into the dark world of social media, that's my fault too. My ex-boyfriend is kind of famous and we ran into him."

"This guy?" The woman pulls out another photo. The one of her and Oren.

Shit. They have that one too. What are the chances they skipped the opportunity to show it to Aiden? Probably close to none. Is it legal to use torture in HR investigations?

"Yes, his name is Oren Hason, but this is a very old photo. I am not seeing him anymore, not since we broke up five years ago. And I certainly have not engaged in kissing him or doing anything else with him since. And I am sure he would corroborate the story if I knew how to contact him..."

"That wouldn't be necessary," the man says. "At least not for our investigation. But maybe would be helpful information for Professor Kowalski."

"Did he say something about it? How did he react when he saw it? Was he okay?" Eleanor can't help the questions coming out of her mouth. The three HR members exchange looks again.

"We are not allowed to discuss these kinds of details with you. The same way we would not discuss anything you say with Professor Kowalski," the woman says as she puts the photos back into a folder.

"Would you say your behavior around Professor Kowalski has

granted you any special treatment, any benefits or favoritism in his lab or with anything that involves your professional life?"

"My behavior?"

"Sexual favors." The man coughs.

"Oh, come on, these were not sexual favors, it's a two-sided relationship. A relationship that involved lust and love, like any good relationship should." Eleanor is a bit surprised hearing the 'L' and 'R' words coming out of her mouth, and both in one sentence. She's even more surprised that it feels so natural to just come out and say it. "But to answer your question—no, it did not grant me any special treatment, or benefits or favoritism outside of our personal life. When it came to science, he judged my work as harshly as he did anyone else's. He takes these things very seriously. He's a good mentor, a touch too serious sometimes, but cares a lot about his students' success."

"We need to understand if it was a pattern," the second woman says.

"A pattern? Are you suggesting there were others?"

'There's no one, just you. You're everything.' Drunk Aiden's words flood Eleanor's memory.

"A pattern? No, no way." There's not a doubt in her mind, of that she's sure.

"A one-off then?" the woman asks.

"No, not a one-off either," Eleanor responds with certainty. All of their moments together all come barging into her mind like a hurricane. "More like a once in a lifetime."

Why has it taken her so long to understand?

"Would you say it made your life here at GERI harder?" the second woman asks.

"That's leading, Dr. Benjamin, please disregard the question," the man jumps in.

Eleanor considers it for a moment. "I'd like to answer that," she says. "These past few months since coming to GERI, since meeting Aiden—I've actually had the best time of my life." Saying it out loud makes so many things click into place at once. It feels exhilarating. "My only remorse is that it's gotten him into trouble. It was never my intention."

The HR crew nods in unison, finally done with their line of questions. They do, however, walk her through some excruciating guidance on how to interact with the press, with social media comments and questions from colleagues, before they lead her out of the room and let her go back to her life. And despite numerous reminders to avoid making contact with Aiden until things are settled, she runs back into the lab and into his office. But he's not there. Again. And a quick check with Tara Jones drains the last bit of hope and courage out of her.

"Professor Kowalski was asked to go on leave for a while," Tara says gently, resting a hand on Eleanor's shoulder. "Until this whole jumble clears up."

30
Surprises

Grandma: "Ellie, how are you doing honey? Make a sound."

Eleanor: "Hi Savta, I'm okay. How are you?"

Grandma: "Been alive long enough to know you're bullshitting over text."

Har'el: "She's exercising advanced concepts in positive thinking."

Orly: "Honey, don't let any of these nonsense comments on social media get you down."

Eleanor: "I can't believe you all saw it. Please don't believe anything on social media, none of it is true."

Grandpa: "I still don't understand why you'd take that boy Oren back."

Har'el: "No, Saba, she's not with Oren again. It's an old photo. She's dating her professor now."

Grandpa: "Oh, thank goodness, this wild boy Oren was not for her. Never made her happy."

Orly: "Couldn't agree more."

Eleanor: "He's not my professor and I am not dating him. And his name is Aiden. And I didn't go back to Oren, that's for sure."

Grandma: "I don't want Oren's name mentioned in this chat again. Orly, honey, would you add this to the group rule page?"

Eleanor spends the rest of the day at the Harrington lab, tucked in her little dungeon, trying again, quite unsuccessfully, to avoid everyone.

"May I just say," Mano stops by, shoving his head through the partly opened door, "this picture of you and that drummer, man! That's hot! I think you've made a smart choice taking him back. Although the second photo with Professor Kowalski is no less—"

"Mano, I don't think that's helpful." Antoine jumps in right behind him, trying to herd him back into his lab.

"Antoine, I know that you're more into same-sex kind of thing," Mano grins, "but for heterosexuals—this is some steamy shit!" He zooms in on the photo on his phone screen. "I never want to unsee it."

"Same-sex kind of thing, Mano?" Antoine snorts, clearly not taking Mano's comment to heart. "But Eleanor is our colleague," he says with a heavy French accent. "Our friend. So we're here to support, not make comments about these posts, and no zooming in." He snatches the phone out of Mano's hand and deletes the photo.

"So were you cheating on your rock star with Professor Kowalski or the other way around? I'm confused." Mano can't help himself. "And who's a better kisser?"

"Mano!" Antoine scolds.

"No, Mano. This guy in the photo is my ex. That's an old photo, from like five years ago when we were still together." For some reason, she still feels like she has to explain. "And Aiden... Professor Kowalski and I, for the past few months we were friends. I wanted more but he kept turning me down," she admits, even though the HR gang made it pretty clear that this whole thing should be under embargo.

"It didn't look like he was turning you down in San Diego," Mano says, a sly smile on his face. "Man, the way you were devouring him at the dance party... No wonder you had unlimited reagent budget."

"Eleanor, please ignore him. That's enough big guy." Antoine pulls Mano by his shirt and turns back to Eleanor. "I apologize on my colleague's behalf. And if there's anything I can do to help, or if you need someone to talk to, or just get you some of the good coffee, I'm here for you." He gives her a heartwarming wink.

"Dance party? You were there?" She can feel blood rushing to her ears.

"Uh-huh," Mano nods haughtily.

"UnderDog28... is you," she mumbles. She debates between the thousand options for revenge one can choose to take in a lab full of hazardous chemicals. But Antoine beats her to it, landing his clenched left fist in Mano's face. It doesn't knock the villain down, but should at least leave him with a nasty black eye for a while.

Being far away from home, far away from her family and most established support system, somehow makes everything feel like a dream. A bad dream. Or more like a nightmare. Her brain seems to be under the impression that if she got on a plane and flew back home, she'd wake up, and things would immediately fall back into place. Her issues would be resolved and life would go back to normal, the normal she once knew. It might not be very rational, but she has a strong urge to just pick up her stuff, shove it in her suitcase, book the first flight she can find, and go back home. As if her troubles are bound to a specific location, and being home would magically reverse and erase everything.

Would she want to erase everything though? Being with Aiden is the one thing that made her feel like she belonged. The one person who made her feel home again. But if she could take the mess in Aiden's life away, reverse that sad-broken, forlorn look on his face—she would.

On her way back to the apartment, after working way too many hours—her go-to activity any day, but especially on such a terrible one—a plan quickly forms in her head. She's already looking at flight options while jiggling her keys into the lock. She wants to go home. She *needs* to be home. There, even if not fully resolved, things will surely feel better. She had wanted to be alone, and had traveled thousands of miles away from home to achieve it, only to realize that being alone wasn't really what she needed. Quite the opposite actually.

She walks in, kicking her shoes off by the door, hanging her rain jacket, dropping her backpack to the floor, her usual post-work routine. A shower would be next.

She wants to go home so bad that she can almost smell her mom's cooking.

"Ellie!"

Or even hear her dad's voice.

Her mind has gone to the incredible length of willing itself to imagine her parents standing in front of her.

She blinks several times. That's pretty wild, even for her imagination.

"Ima? Aba?" she says in disbelief.

The two people she would most like to see in the entire world right now pull her in to their famous family hug. She really needed this hug. And just like her five-year old self who bruised her knee at kindergarten, staying brave and composed until she was reunited with her parents—that's when she finally allows herself to let go and break down. Tears start flooding her eyes, wetting her face. She's overwhelmed by emotions she had no idea she was bottling up. "I'm so glad you're here," she says in Hebrew.

Her mom pulls her by the sleeve and sits her down on the pink sofa, taking her right side, and her dad takes the left. The three of them are huddled closely, like they used to when she was a kid.

"We figured, since you're so far away from home, we'll bring home over to you," her mom says in Hebrew, then tries to repeat it in English for Alannah, who's been standing in the kitchen, shedding some empathetic tears of her own.

"How did you know I wanted to go home?"

"Well, your very brief texts lately gave it away. Then Aiden called your mom," her dad says.

"Aiden? Why would he...? He's mad at me, he wouldn't even look me in the eyes. It must have been someone else," Eleanor blabbers. "Did he have a French accent? Probably, that would be Antoine, he's my friend—"

"No, honey. It was Aiden," her mom says with certainty.

"Are you sure?"

"I am very sure. It was a WhatsApp video call. The same guy from the selfie, from the airport. Your man."

Her man... Ima knows everything. Except that he's no longer her man, thanks to Eleanor's relentless efforts to get into his pants. And her fear of relationships.

"That doesn't make sense Ima... What did he say?"

"He cares about you. A great deal. He said you're going to need our support. It was shortly after that post and comments started popping up. I don't know this gentleman too well, but he looked so worried, and sad."

Only her mom could still call the guy a gentleman after reading those comments and seeing their smutty photo together. But she focuses on the more important thing: Aiden cares about her. Even now. Even when he's neck-deep in this mess, even after thinking she's back in her ex's arms, he still makes sure she's surrounded by her support system.

But does he have anyone to support him? Eleanor doubts that he's shared any of it with his dad or Kim.

"There's no one," he told her that night, when he was too drunk for his own good. *"Just you."*

She's here, surrounded by parental affection and pieces of home. And Aiden...

He's all alone.

"Luckily there were some spots on the direct flight, so we just hopped on it, and here we are." Her mom's voice pulls her back into the room. "And don't worry, your dad and I won't be bothering you too much, our travel agent booked us rooms in this quaint hotel down the road, it's just five minutes' walk from here, so we won't be sitting on your vein," she switches back to Hebrew. "Sorry honey." She smiles to Alannah. "I'm not sure whether this expression could be translated to English word for word."

"No worries, I got the context." Alannah smiles and joins them in the living room, carrying a tray with tea and freshly made vegan cookies. "And don't be ridiculous, you're staying with us."

"Yes, you can take my room, this sofa turns into a bed," Eleanor insists. "Wait, did you just say 'rooms?' As in more than one room?"

"Yes." Her mom smiles. "You didn't think we'd share a room with Gillie, did you? I mean, we love him like our own child, but—"

"Gillie?!" Eleanor perks up. "Is he here—" she starts to say before getting swiped off her feet into a familiar Gillie-bear-hug.

"Of course I'm here! Where else would I be?" His laughter floats through the room, warming even the coldest and broken-est of hearts. "Told you I was on my way. Ask your grandma, I wrote it in the chat."

Grandma: "Ellie, honey, did the package arrive?

Eleanor: "Package?"

Grandma: "Your parents and Gillie. Did they make the trip safely?!"

Eleanor: "Oh, yes, Savta, they're sending their love."

Grandma: "And how is work treating you?"

Eleanor: "Fine, thanks."

Grandma: "Good. Now listen to your Savta, it's time to follow your heart."

Eleanor: "Savta, following my heart is a risky business."

Grandma: "Honey, *not* following your heart is the real risk. Now go take that leap of faith."

Har'el: "You people are aware that we're on this group chat too, right? This is getting cringier by the minute!"

"I have to agree with your grandma on this one," her mom says as she puts down the phone and gently squeezes Eleanor's knee. "Have you told Aiden how you feel?" She grins broadly.

"No Mom, he tried to talk to me, and I shut him down. First, I was too busy being scared of relationships, then too busy being mad at him. And now he won't talk to me. Actually, he's not allowed to talk to me because of this stupid investigation... And I really need to talk to him."

"What investigation?" Alannah asks. They've been going back

and forth between Hebrew and English, trying to keep Alannah in the loop.

"GERI are running an internal HR investigation. To make sure there wasn't sexual harassment or abuse of position of power or any other stupid terms they're able to shove between us."

"That's ridiculous. You're both adults and you can both do whatever you want on your own private time. He's not your boss, and there's no rule against romantic relationship between GERI employees and postdocs." Alannah has some hidden legal potential.

"They said it was about perception. It's a high-profile incident, thanks to the evil UnderDog28, who turned out to be Mano from the Harrington lab, who made the original post and tagged Oren's fans and GERI. They want to make sure they don't expose themselves to lawsuits or God knows what. It's all in this long email. I barely read half." Eleanor hands her phone to Alannah.

"I'm going to kill Mano," Alannah mumbles. "So you can't speak with Professor Kowalski, not even over the phone?"

"No, they said no meeting him in person, no phone calls, no emails, no text messages. And especially not to reach out to him through social media."

"Well, sounds like there's one avenue they've missed," Gillie chimes in, a big smile on his face. He takes a noisy sip from a cup of tea Alannah has just handed him, creating a dramatic sound effect. All eyes are on him now. "How about an actual letter? You know, old-fashioned pen and paper? Have they mentioned anything about that?"

"I guess with modern technology they forgot about that. I actually started drafting what I was going to say to him. Maybe I could turn it into a letter." Eleanor feels a renewed spark of energy. "And it would be impossible to track if I hand deliver. Gillie, you're a genius!"

"Thank you, I get that a lot," he chuckles.

"But babe," Alannah jumps in. "You can't be spotted by his house. And he's not going to show up at work, Yan said he's on leave."

"Yeah, on leave until this whole thing clears. But I have a work around."

31
The Plan

After some tea and Alannah's vegan—but nonetheless delicious—cookies, and equipped with over sixty years of relationship experience combined (contributed by Eleanor's parents), and three tired scientists, including one who does not believe in pre-marital relationships (Alannah), one who's still waiting to find his special someone (Gillie) and one with mostly some failed relationship attempts (Eleanor), they all brainstorm a plan. It's a multifaceted, multi-step plan, and it includes:

1. The letter, that lame letter Eleanor started writing last night. Yeah... the one that could really use some work. She'll polish it up and drop it off at Aiden's dad's house on one of the days Aiden is not expected to be there. Then Eleanor needs to cross her fingers and hope his dad will remember to deliver it. Gillie and Alannah tried to volunteer for the delivery but there's no way Eleanor would drag them into this mess.

2. A more creative route for contacting Oren: crashing his gig in New York City. Oren is probably the only one who can get the media off their backs and put an end to this getting-back-together-with-her-ex stupidity. And also clarify the year that photo was taken. Oren hasn't returned her message—he's probably, unsurprisingly not checking messages on his old Israeli number. But Alannah found out his band is performing in New York city tomorrow! It's a smallish event, only about four hours away. And so they're going. And by 'they' she means Alannah and Gillie are coming with her. And they're taking Antoine, who without even blinking, jumped on the opportunity when Eleanor called.

3. This one builds on the rave success of the two previous steps. It also requires a great degree of helplessly naive positive thinking, and some TBD items. But it mostly involves getting the grumpy professor Kowalski back into her life ASAP, because frankly, not having him in it is unacceptable. And is just not compatible with... anything really.

So yeah... the letter. Filled with her dreadful writing. But hey, being the worst love-letter-writer this universe has possibly ever encountered is part of who she is. And definitely shouldn't stop her from getting what—ahem, who—she wants. Despite being able to write an entire scientific paper in English, completing a whole letter—be it in English or any other language—would be an impressive achievement of its own. Pen still in hand, Eleanor re-reads her masterpiece one more time.

Dear Aiden,

First, full disclosure. Please accept my condolences for subjecting you to what might be an awful imitation of an apology letter. Nonetheless, it's an accurate representation of my creative writing skills. As you are probably able to tell, it's probably not my strong suit; you can ask my high school Hebrew literature or grammar teachers, even my English teacher, they'd all be able to corroborate. They all advised me to stick to what I was good at (not writing, thankfully—science). I know you're going to say that I am capable of writing reasonable scientific papers. Science is different, but putting romance aside for a second, once I get my own lab, I'll probably have to hire a full-time medical writer.

Just putting it out there.

So now that we've got that out of the way... There are a few things I really wanted to tell you. Which sucks because now that I finally have the courage to say them out loud, we're not supposed to talk to each other. Consequently (my English teacher would surely be proud), I figured, with a little help from my best friend Gillie, that an old-fashioned letter might help me out here. I've underlined for you for better reading experience.

<u>So first things first</u>, I'm sorry about the way things came about. The situation you're now in—it's all my fault. Hurting you was never my intention. And if I could take it all away, I would. Although what we had between us—that unbelievable pull, our kisses, the amazing night we had together (mind blowing!)—I'd never want to take those away. I might be contradicting myself here, sorry about this too. What I'm really trying to say, is the last few months since falling into your lap at the airport have been the best of my life.

<u>My despicable lack of self-control</u>—I usually have better self-control, but with you it was impossible. Sorry I couldn't keep my hands to myself and constantly challenged you. Also for jumping you constantly in the darkroom, in your office, and pretty much everywhere (except when I was sick and totally wiped out), which leads me to that steamy photo of us together that somehow made it into the hands of those three no-fun GERI people. You had tried to warn me that this could end badly for us. Had I listened—something I don't do often, especially not when it involves you coupled with delayed gratification—you would have been spared from this social media shitshow and this stupid investigation. I'm so sorry for getting you in trouble, and I'm planning to fix it.

<u>Being your fake girlfriend</u>—This was, sadly, the best romantic relationship I've ever been in. And even though it was pretend, you were the most amazing boyfriend I've ever had. And I say 'sadly' because it made me realize how I wished it was real. How I wished we were real. To the point that I thought you wanted that too. Maybe I even imagined you said it, but granted, I was too delirious from high fever and dehydration, so I'm sorry for being mad at you for reverting back to our pre-fake relationship and for fake-breaking up with me upon our return to GERI.

<u>Which leads me to your lab meeting</u>. Rationally speaking, I had no right to be mad at you, especially since I was the one who kept telling you I wasn't looking for a serious relationship. It was a clear case of disconnect between my mouth and my... well, every-thing else in me. Lashing out at you during your lab meeting was inappropriate and out of place, and I'm sorry for what I said back there. I think you are a great mentor, despite your grumpiness and broodi-ness around other people. Your students look up to you and are grateful for everything you do for them. I know because they told me. And because I've wit-nessed it first-hand. And even though you weren't my formal mentor, I've learned a lot from you. I do, however, stand behind what I said about the 7:30 a.m. meeting time and the fact that it's painfully, excruciatingly early.

<u>My (not anymore) mythological ex</u>—And before you get yourself all worked up—he IS still my ex but certainly NOT mythological anymore. You were right. There was no such thing. Not for me, at least. But until I met you, I just didn't know better. I do now. The way I feel about you is so much stronger than I've ever felt before, toward anyone. It took me a while to realize and to admit it, even to myself, because it scared the shit out of me. It doesn't anymore. And I'm sorry I never got the chance to tell you. Or maybe I did, there's a blank blob in my memory from the fever adventure. And I'm sorry this whole thing got out of control and blew up on social media. That's what I get for dating someone famous five years ago. I am working on fixing that too.

<u>My very creative collection of symptoms</u>—The crazy fast heartbeats that are incompatible with breathing, the butterflies, the lack of self control, and I suspect even the nosebleeds are all part of the same diagnosis. My Aiden-induced symptoms—in case you're having trouble reading between the lines here.

<u>And back to the fever adventure</u>—Like I said, there's an entire Swiss cheese block of holes in my memory. But what I do remember is you being there for me, taking care of me, as if nothing else in the world mattered. And it breaks my heart that you're going

through this whole mess now, entirely alone, and I'm not allowed to be there for you. So I'm sorry for that too. This is probably where I should add my giant thank you for, despite how much you probably hate me right now, putting it all aside and asking my parents to come be with me. It's all part of how incredible you are, and selfless, and is one of the reasons I love you.

I love you—There, I said it. Well—wrote it (to be precise). I love you, have been in love with you from like the first moment I saw you. Right after thinking I should have brushed my teeth before falling into your lap. I'm sorry it took me so long to admit it, to myself and to you. And sorry for going out of order—I know I talked about my feelings earlier in the letter, but I wasn't brave enough to write it a few paragraphs ago. I am now.

This letter—I hope it wasn't too tortuous to read, I am sure it would have made my English teacher pull out some hairs and maybe even revoke my high school diploma (English is part of the high school graduation requirements in Israel), but hey—it would have taken a while to get through professional editing services (if that's even a thing for personal letters) and I wanted to get it to you ASAP. I also hope you didn't find this letter too annoyingly long, but I figured—compared to all the emails, scientific papers and reviews you read every day, you should be fine.

I love you with all my heart.

And I miss you like crazy.

And I need you.

And the fact that I can't see you or hear your voice is driving me insane.

Which is why I couldn't decide on a single note to end this letter with—so there are four.

And I counted 11 sorries in this letter, in case you've lost count, to show that I really mean it.

Ellie

Eleanor puts down her pen, rethinking her closing sentences. She doesn't like how final all the endings she can possibly come up with sound. And something like *'I look forward to hearing from you'* would sound more like a follow-up communication for a job interview. So she leaves in the multiple closing remarks. Then she folds the letter and gently seals it into an envelope, mustering her best efforts when writing 'Aiden' on top.

Having her parents and Gillie around, and her feelings out on paper, helps get her nervous-wreck of a brain and aching heart a reasonable night's sleep. The smell of her mom's homemade burekas is the first thing to greet her senses when she wakes up. And she's amazed by how relieved she feels to know they are there and the sense of comfort they've brought with them. And then she's amazed by how her mom managed to make vegan burekas taste almost like the real thing, so that Alannah could enjoy them too. Her family is all about inclusion.

"How did you sleep, honey?" her mom asks as Eleanor finishes devouring her breakfast and clears up the table.

"With you, Aba and Gillie around? So much better!" Eleanor says, smooching a noisy kiss to her mom's forehead, melting into her loving embrace. "Thank you!" Her parents were right, having them there, despite not being physically back to the place she grew up in, brings so much of home to her, instilling that sense of security and confidence, which is exactly what she needed. But there's a startling ache in her chest that comes along with it, as she thinks of Aiden and his lack of lifeline to fall back on right now, in these moments when everything is just too tough to deal with alone.

"I'm glad to see you starting to believe in fairytales, Ellie," her mom chuckles.

"What?" What makes her mom think that?

"Your bed covers." Her dad's rolling laugh sounds from the other room.

"Oh, the princess bed covers? I wish they had superhero covers at the store, but it was either this or not using covers at all," Eleanor says, hearing Gillie's infectious laugh.

"Now go get dressed." Her mom hands her a plastic box filled with more burekas. "You have a letter to deliver. And give the poor boy some breakfast."

"That's really sweet but I'm not allowed to see him, remember? I'm going at the exact time that he's *not* there."

"Fine, just leave it on the kitchen table. You should never go anywhere empty handed." Her mom winks. Yes, that's her mom, always making sure people around her are well-fed. Time to pay Professor Gordon Kowalski a visit.

Eleanor gets off at the bus stop closest to Gordon's house. She walks down the little road leading to his small street, checking that Aiden's car is not in sight. Aiden doesn't normally break his habits, so it was easy to pick out a day he wouldn't be visiting his dad. But then again, Eleanor is not looking for any surprises, so double-checking is always a good idea.

After a few moments of vigilant inspection, Eleanor climbs up the few steps leading to the front porch, taking in the scent of mint leaves.

With a shaky hand, she knocks on the door lightly. Then a little harder.

"I'm coming!" She hears a cheerful female voice.

Shit...

She was so busy double checking for traces of Aiden that she forgot to account for the possibility that Kim might be there. She considers running.

Yeah, go ahead, real mature.

So she stays put, her hand clutching the envelope and box with her mom's made burekas.

"Ellie, what a nice surprise, come on in!" Kim's friendly smile doesn't leave many options. "Good to see you!" she says warmly.

"Good to see you too, Kim," Eleanor says, holding out the box to her. "My mom's homemade burekas, still warm."

"Kimmie, who is it?" She can hear Gordon's voice from the Livingroom.

"It's Aiden's girl!" Kim says loudly and jovially.

Aiden's girl. How Eleanor wishes it were true.

"How nice to see you, Ellie," Gordon says when she walks in, gesturing for her to take the seat next to him on the couch.

He's having a good day today, even remembered her name!

Her heart squeezes, recalling how Aiden said the count of good days was diminishing quickly. He should be here with his dad, right now. These moments are just too precious to waste.

"Can I make you anything to drink?" Kim asks, getting up to the kitchen. "Coffee? Tea?"

"No, thanks," Eleanor refuses in her most polite tone. She can't stay long. Can't risk coming face to face with the man who steals her breath away. "It's just a short visit," she says, and once Kim is out of sight, she hands Gordon the little envelope with her letter.

"Could you please give it to Aiden when you see him?" she asks quietly while Kim is in the kitchen.

Gordon slips the letter under his book and gives Eleanor a nod and a knowing smile.

Please please let him remember this one...

"What are you guys hiding there?" Kim's playful voice sounds behind them. Apparently, she's no longer in the kitchen.

Busted.

"For Aiden."

"Modern technology is not your cup of tea?" Her eyebrow pinches, the same look her brother has, just a female version of it.

"Aiden didn't tell you?"

"Told me what?" Kim's voice takes on a seed of concern. "I haven't seen him in a few days," she admits. "Too many night shifts at the hospital lately."

"Modern technology hasn't been on our side, and I should leave it at that." Eleanor squirms in her seat next to Gordon. "Better talk to him directly. I think he could really use someone in his corner right now."

Kim nods quietly before she says, "From the way I've seen him look at you, the way he talks about you, I don't think there's anyone in this world he'd want in his corner more than you."

"I would love for it to be me," Eleanor tries to blink away the tears welling up in her eyes, "but I doubt he'd want to talk to me right now."

"I may be speaking out of turn here," Kim says, very aware—or completely unaware—of the fact that she has no insight into the backstory to this pitiful situation. "My brother is a brilliant scientist and I love him dearly, but when it comes to you... he can't tell his left from his right. Please don't judge him too harshly."

"Well, I'm no picnic either," Eleanor sighs. "This one is on me."

32
SHOW MUST GO ON

The visit to Aiden's dad clearly didn't go as planned. Eleanor expected to be in and out without being spotted by anyone else but Gordon. Hopefully step two will work out better.

After a long drive to New York in Antoine's small Fiat—which miraculously was able to fit them all relatively comfortably—they've finally arrived to the city and found a parking spot at an outrageous location.

As they get closer to that small venue in the heart of Manhattan, arms linked like the perfect entourage, Antoine to her left, Gillie to her right, Alannah leading the way, Eleanor's doubts start overflowing, but she tries to keep her spirit under control. Gillie rubs her shoulder from his side, and Antoine does the exact same from the other side, like his long-lost match.

It's a small-scale show, nothing like the ones she used to accompany Oren to back home, but she still feels uneasy. Being in the spotlight was never comfortable, and now with the latest social media craziness, uncomfortable would be a welcome feeling compared to the war going on inside of her.

They walk into the club, waving their overpriced tickets. This is probably the first time she's actually needed to pay money to watch her drummer ex perform.

"I need to speak with Oren Hason," she tells the beastly large security guard blocking the back of stage passageway.

"Sweetheart, you can stand in line," the guy smirks.

"No, he actually knows me."

"Sure he does," he says without even looking in her direction.

Nice...

Eleanor looks around, trying to find familiar faces, someone who could confirm she knows Oren. Or at least an Israeli bodyguard she could speak Hebrew to—her conviction somehow gets lost in translation.

But before she knows it, the show starts, and they're forced to sit through it. Or more like—dance through it. Because Oren's new band is actually pretty good, and Alannah pulls Eleanor up and won't let her sit back down.

"Since we're already here," Alannha shouts in her ear, "we should at the very least have fun!" Her eyes carry to Gillie and Antoine nodding enthusiastically.

So they dance, and they sing out loud, and it feels good to let the music wash over her, after holding it together for so long, avoiding music, avoiding everything that reminded her of Oren Hason. Looks like that part of her life has already healed, or at least been put to rest. Because everything she felt before, it all pales in comparison to the past few months, since that moment at the airport. Her heart, her mind, her soul are all rooting for one person, for one broody professor, and there's nothing she can do about it. It's non-reversible. Done deal.

"You've got to let me in, I have to speak with Oren, please!" Eleanor urges the same unimpressed security guy from earlier once the show ends.

"Babe, you need to use the situation to your advantage," Alannah reprimands. "Here." She shoves her phone in the guy's face. "You see this sexy-looking girl?" she asks, waving that old photo of Eleanor with Oren making out at the beach.

"Right," he says, crossing his arms on his chest.

"Look carefully," Antoine says and turns Eleanor's head to the side, to match the angle in the photo.

The guy shakes his head and turns away, speaking into his earpiece.

"You think he believed us?" Alannah loud-whispers to Antoine above Eleanor's head.

"I doubt it. Let's go with plan B," Antoine whisper-calls back.

"What's plan B?" Eleanor shouts, forgetting the security guard is watching. "I'm not looking to get thrown out of a night club or get arres—"

"Watch and learn," Gillie says. "Antoine and I will create a distraction. Once Bulldog here turns his head," he gestures toward the security guard, "you make a run for it."

"I'm in." Antoine gives him a conspiratorial smile.

"Sounds like they've actually thought it through," Alannah laughs.

"Now," Gillie says as he pushes Antoine toward the guard, blocking his view of Eleanor. She can see Gillie's hands reaching for Antoine's face. He cups his cheeks and pulls him in for a scandalous kiss, gaining Bulldog's full attention. That's her cue. She starts running but it doesn't take too long for Bulldog to notice and chase after her, speaking into his earpiece. Eleanor speeds up, still looking back, crashing into something. Or rather, someone...

"Ellie?" Her mind registers the Hebrew accent—the true pronunciation of her name and the familiar voice. Then comes the familiar touch. She looks up, relieved to see Oren's face attached to the body she's just slammed into. "She's with me Serge, thank you," he says to Bulldog.

Thank goodness.

Oren knows better than to hug her in public, so he takes a step back and leads her through a long corridor. But when they're finally out of press or fans reach, he pulls her into his arms again. "Never thought you'd voluntarily come to watch me play." His laugh fills the air. His familiar voice and feel and scent somehow make her miss Aiden even more.

"You guys are pretty good, it wasn't all torture," Eleanor chuckles.

"Still stingy on the compliments," he smirks. "Next time let me know you're coming, I'll make sure to leave your name at the door or send you some tickets."

"I tried to call you but apparently you don't use your old phone number anymore." Eleanor points to the little device in her hand.

"Oh, right! Sorry about that, had to ditch the old number once it got public," Oren says, taking her phone out of her hand and stumbling on that selfie of her and Aiden. Yes, it's still her home screen. And lock screen. "You guys are something else," he says, putting in her password and unlocking her phone without a blink. Of course, she's still using the same password she has for ages. And of course, Oren knows that. He's the one who had told her she should change it from time to time, and she'd made a point to not listen. And of course, he knows that too. Some things, apparently, don't change.

"Here." Oren saves his new number and gives her back the phone, gesturing for her to sit. He grabs a bottle of water and chugs it within seconds. "Man, I was thirsty. Something to drink?" he asks, Eleanor shakes her head, so he takes the seat next to her. "Where's your professor boyfriend?"

"Not really speaking to me right now, thanks to mostly me pissing him off and also some social media shitshow."

"Ah," Oren says noncommittally.

"And full disclosure," Eleanor is in confession mode, "we were kind of fake-dating, Aiden couldn't bear the fact that you still thought of yourself as my mythological ex."

"Could have fooled me." Oren runs a hand through his hair, then chugs another water bottle. Performing always made him thirsty. "You guys looked desperately in love with each other. Except for the fact that the poor guy had no idea about the ass tattoo... Which kind of gave it away." *Well, he knows about it now.* "But I played along, seemed like you needed a little push."

"I needed a little push?" Eleanor tries, unsuccessfully, to appear shocked.

Oren just gives her a wink.

"Anyway," she sighs. "Have you heard the latest gossip?"

"Are you talking about that hot old photo of us? We look good in it, don't you think?"

"You've seen it?!" Eleanor gives him an incredulous look, although she can't really say she's surprised. "Why didn't you deny the rumors about us getting back together?"

"You never gave a shit about social media rumors."

"Yeah, when we were together, but after we broke up, they kind of made my life a living hell, even though you were the one who broke up with me. And now... These rumors are hurting the people I love. The person I... love."

"I'm sorry," Oren says, pulling on the curls in the back of his head.

"I can't imagine how Tiffany must have felt seeing that photo."

"Well, we might have kind of fake-dated as well," he admits, shoulders a little slumped, eyes trained on a stain on the floor."

"You? Fake-dated? Why?" Eleanor can't hide her surprise.

"Well, we did go on one actual date, but I still get a rash just thinking of a full-blown relationship. Maybe I'll get there eventually. Hopefully when I'm still young and handsome. When I saw you with Mr. Professor Bigshot it kind of caught me off guard," he sighs. "But I'm happy for you, I really am. You deserve being with someone who is crazy about you like this guy is, who makes you happy."

"Thanks, but with all the comments going around—"

"What comments?"

"Pretty degrading stuff, spiraling out of control." She pulls out her phone and shows him some. The long list of comments has grown exponentially overnight. "Put aside the love triangle shit for a minute. There's a whole bunch of bullshit that got Aiden in a whole lot of trouble at work. Now he's under investigation for sexual harassment in the workplace. This is so fucked up."

"Hell." Oren pulls on his curls again. "The collateral damage for hanging out with me. I'm sorry, Ellie."

"And that's not even the worst part. Thanks to this photo, Aiden probably thinks I ran straight back into your arms, and I'm not even allowed to talk to him."

"I would have loved for that to happen, but something tells me you'd much rather run into Aiden's arms," Oren chuckles.

"I would, if he ever agrees to speak with me again. Because now he probably thinks that I was pretending the whole time."

"But you were pretending."

"Pretending to be in a relationship, yes. But finally allowing my true feelings show. So in essence you could say—I was finally *not* pretending."

"Well," Oren says with an optimistic tone, turning her chair to face him. "How can I help?"

33
RETURN LETTER

The first thing Eleanor does once they're back from NYC is go visit Gordon. Antoine brings his mighty little Fiat to a stop as he drops her off, promising to shuttle Gillie and Alannah back to the apartment. He also promises to stick around for dinner, because Eleanor's mom wouldn't have it any other way.

Eleanor walks down the quiet street and takes the three front stairs to the house. Gordon is sitting on a rocking chair at the front porch, staring into space.

"Hello Gordon," Eleanor tries a few times without success. She comes closer and pats him on the shoulder. He turns his head toward her but his eyes don't show any sign of recognition.

"Gordon, it's me, Ellie," she says, bending over so their eyes are level. "I'm a friend of Aiden, your son." He seems lost somewhere far away. "Let's get you inside," she offers, not sure whether he should be alone outside in his current state. It's actually the first time since they've met that she's seen him like this. Absent.

She holds out her hand to him and he takes it, stepping inside with her, still holding her hand as she gets him situated in the living room.

"Can I get you anything to drink? Eat?" she asks and he shakes his head. His gaze fixes itself on the blank TV screen, so she turns it on.

What are the chances he remembered to give Aiden her letter? Probably close to none—maybe involving Kim wouldn't have been such a bad idea. Her heart squeezes at the thought of Aiden seeing his dad like this.

She takes a sit next to Gordon, determined to stick around until someone shows up. Then she picks up the pile of books and papers, checking to see if her letter is still there. A little envelope comes into view; it has her name written on top with Aiden's slanted handwriting. Hands trembling, heart shuddering, she opens it slowly and unfolds the paper.

Dear Ellie,

Thank you for the letter. It was actually a very good letter, and if I get a chance I'll be sure to let your English teacher know.

I am not mad at you, and there's really nothing for you to apologize for. I am the one to blame here. I am the one who should be apologizing. I am infuriated with myself for giving in to my feelings. For giving in to this unbelievable pull between us, for losing control and losing myself in you. I would not regret any of our moments together if it weren't for the consequences that you now have to face.

You see, being with you was the best thing that has ever happened to me. I don't care about the investigation, or about what people say or think about me. I don't give a shit about any of it. What I do care about are these horrible comments about you on social media and what this may do to your career. And for that I am deeply sorry.

I'm glad you decided to deal with the culprit for your symptoms. Thank you for walking me through your logic there. I might not have experienced nosebleeds, but I have been experiencing my fair share of Ellie-induced symptoms.

You were honest with me from the beginning. Honesty was the one thing you had asked for. Your one single rule. You had warned me you weren't interested in a serious relationship but I kept hoping that with time you'd be willing to give us a try. Being your fake boyfriend was my way of showing you how good we could be together.

For me, none of it was fake. Everything I said about my feelings, about how I fell in love with you—it was all true. Ellie, from the second you fell into my lap at the airport I wanted you to be mine.

I am sorry for not coming out about us publicly after San Diego. I'm sorry for hesitating. For putting that distance between us. I thought making us public would scare you away. But I guess I was the one who scared you away. Scared you all the way back to your ex's arms. And I'll fucking regret my hesitation for the rest of my life.

I just can't see how. How, despite everything you wrote in that letter, how you can just go back to being with him as if nothing ever happened between us. So, there is one more thing I'm mad about—that asshat of a drummer named Oren Hason.

Was it just me thinking that what we had for each other was this once in a lifetime kind of thing? Heck, I bet most people live their entire lives without ever experiencing something like that even once, so I guess at the very least—I should be grateful.

Ellie, I hope you can forgive me for letting my heart come between our science. And at the very least, I hope you'll come back to the lab to finish our collaboration, your discoveries are too goddamn important to throw away. And just so you know—I do not accept your resignation.

Yours and only yours, always and forever,

Aiden

"Gordon," Eleanor says, eyes welling up, still focused on those words that are getting more and more blurry by the second, "Where do you keep your papers? I need to write another letter." She lifts her head, but all she can see is him. The man who's been hunting her thoughts and her dreams.

Aiden is leaning against the kitchen doorframe, staring at her with his favorite-shade-of-blue eyes. His hair is disheveled, and a week-long stubble decorates his beautiful jaw. He looks sad, so sad. And tired, and hopeless. And lonely. And it breaks her heart.

Has he been there the whole time?

"No more letters," he says and his voice awakens this entire volcano inside of her.

"It wasn't just you," she says when she finally gets her voice back and her ability to speak with actual words. "It *is* a once in a lifetime thing. But you see—" She gets up and takes a step toward him. She feels lightheaded, as if her legs will give out if she doesn't get closer. "I don't believe in regret. Life's too short for that. And I think that due to my lack of literary talent, I failed to include an important detail in my letter. That photo with Oren? It's a total mishap. It was taken about five years ago when we were still dating. If you look carefully you'll see, it was taken at a beach in Tel Aviv. Which, by the way, I probably haven't been too since."

"Right." Aiden gives her an incredulous look and pulls her by the arm into the kitchen. The touch of his hand brands her skin. "It looks pretty new to me," he says, irritated. "Even the bathing suit you're wearing in the photo is the same one you brought with you to San Diego... I'd recognize this cheeky thing—" He pulls out his phone and shoves the image in her face.

"Well, it's been a while since I've gone bathing suit shopping. Although got to look at the bright side—it still fits."

"I'm serious Ellie, seeing you like this with *him*, it makes me so unbelievably jealous."

"Wait, show me that again." She grabs the phone off his hand as details of the image register, zooming in on that cheeky bikini bottom. "Looks like I have a built-in proof. Not that I need to prove myself to you," she says and hands him back the phone.

"Don't provoke me," he warns in his commanding tone.

She looks around, making sure his dad is out of sight before she pulls on the side of her sweatpants, revealing just enough to show that little hideous butt tattoo. "If you don't believe me—"

"What are you doing?" His eyes darken and the temperature in the room climbs to a dangerous zone all at once.

"Tell me what you see," she demands.

"Ellie, stop it, my dad is in the next room for fuck's sake." He struggles to keep his eyes above her waist line.

"So you better look quickly, then. Let's see if you can spot the difference." She aligns his phone with her side. Tell me what you see."

He clears his throat. "You're wearing the same watch," he says. *Seriously? Is that the first thing he notices?*

"Okay," she goes with it. "Which confirms this is my left side in this image, right? I know some people like to wear their watch on their right wrist, but nope, not me. What else?"

"Your butt tattoo is missing."

"Correct!" she says victoriously. "Because it's from before—before I got that stupid tattoo. Who thought this would actually serve as evidence one day! So here is your proof Professor Kowalski, this picture is at least five years old, if not more. But you know, I'm kind of mad that you even needed proof and wouldn't take my word for it."

Aiden looks distant and cold. Not the reaction she was hoping for. And since her heart won't survive being on the breakup receiving end—not when it comes to Aiden—she offers him an easy out. "We aren't supposed to speak to each other anyway according to the GERI lawyers' stupid guidelines, so I'm gonna go. I appreciate your willingness to take me back into your lab, but I don't think I can..." *Be around him again without thinking what could have been.* She pulls her waistband back up and leaves this shocked, sad, handsome man standing in the kitchen.

"It was good to see you Gordon." She steps into the living room and kisses Aiden's dad on the forehead. "I'll come visit soon," she promises. Gordon gives her an empty look and turns his gaze back to the TV.

She closes the front door behind her gently, so as not to alarm Gordon, despite the urge to slam it. It feels like a goodbye, although there's nothing positive in it to justify the first part of this word. There must be a more suitable expression for situations like this—maybe *badbye* would be a more accurate depiction.

She hopes Aiden will come after her. Call her name. Grab her by the hand and pull her into him. Because that would make this entire world right again. She even stalls for a few minutes at the front steps leading back to the street.

But unlike any of the romantic movies Alannah has made her watch for the past few months, Aiden doesn't come after her, doesn't call her name. Guess it would take more than a badly written love letter and her tattoo evidence to get him back.

She walks down the steps and into the quiet street, not so much into sampling Gordon's impressive mint crop anymore, mumbling some incoherent words to herself, because this whole thing really didn't go as planned. Like most of her attempts to fix what she breaks.

A metallic taste in her mouth draws her already distraught attention as she reaches for her nose to realize it's bleeding again.

That's just great. Superb timing.

With one hand still against her nose, she quickly searches her bag for a tissue—which of course she doesn't have at the moment when it's needed the most.

Ugh...

This always happens at the worst possible time. At the airport—right when she fell into Aiden's lap. In his office—when she found out who he was. Probably a few other times she can't quite recall, mostly when Aiden was around. And now—when she's so desperately trying to put a distance between them. As if her body decided to put its foot down. Or in this case—her nose.

A stupid symptom of love.

Blood starts gushing down her chin, staining her shirt. Attempting to get to the bus stop like this might alarm innocent passersby. And she could really use a tissue right now. So with the lack of any other sophisticated options, Eleanor turns around, takes those three stairs again and opens the front door.

"I'm not back to beg for forgiveness or any other terrible out-of-character ideas. Just need a tissue and I'll be out of your hair," she says without looking up.

But it doesn't take more than a second before she feels his hands helping her into a chair. A tissue presses to her nose, like all the other times when her nose decided to bleed around this man. Aiden gently smooths the bangs off her forehead before bringing an ice pack to that same spot. He's still angry, she can tell, but concern has now taken over his handsome face.

He's taking care of her, again. Whatever words they've said or haven't, whatever distance they've put between themselves, their bodies demand otherwise.

They sit in silence, waiting for the unwarranted situation to end.

"Looks like the bleeding stopped." Aiden determines eventually. He removes the obstructions and hands her a glass of cold water. "Dehydration?" he half-asks, half-knows. "Did you drink enough today?"

"Possibly not." She takes the cup and chugs it. Although really, drinking water right now is the last thing on her mind. "It's been a long day. A long weekend. I just came back from New York. Went to see Oren."

"I see." Aiden tenses. The disappointment and disdain in his voice are unmistakable.

"No, it's not what you think," she says quickly.

"How do you know what I think?" he asks, as usual for him. Only this time he sounds impatient.

"I just do," she says. Jealous-Aiden is kind of endearing. And since she has his full attention now, she continues with her confession. "It's ridiculous, but I didn't even have his current phone number. Alannah got us tickets to his concert in NYC—would you believe I actually paid money for that after years of free—" She trails off but the sight of his tortured stare snaps her back to the main story. "Sorry, as I was beginning to say—I went there to ask him to fix this social media mess. And he promised he would. So... he doesn't always keep his promises, obviously," she points to herself. "But this time he will, I know he will. He felt really bad about it all. Just so you know, he had nothing to do with it."

Aiden's tense features relax just a tad. Jaw still clenched as he asks, "Why did you leave?"

"Leave?"

"Why did you just leave? And why did you quit?"

"Ah, that," she stalls.

Yeah, why did she leave?

"Yes, that," he says, still upset.

"It's like a long list of things," she starts, but for the life of her she can't come up with a single good reason now. "First of all, we're not supposed to communicate with each other while this goddamn investigation is ongoing." She tries for a technical excuse that only partially aligns with the current schedule of events. "And also, because you wouldn't take my word when I told you there was nothing going on between me and Oren. That was over a long time ago. You should have trusted me." She stops for a breather. "You were so mad. Still mad. Like you've changed your mind. And mostly because you didn't stop me."

"You wanted me to stop you?" he asks, surprised.

"Duh," Eleanor says, nodding her head.

"I'm allowed to be angry," he sighs, but something in his expression shifts as understanding and relief cross his features. "It doesn't mean I love you any less." His voice softens. "It's not easy to see your girl in someone else's arms. I got so fucking jealous when I saw that photo, I could barely breath. What was I supposed to think?"

His girl... How can two little words make her shattered heart whole again?

"You of all people, Professor Kowalski, jumping to conclusions based on partial data?" Eleanor means to sound serious, but she can feel the corners of her mouth starting to pull up. She tries to will her lips to attention without much success.

"Ellie, when it comes to you, I'm at a complete loss," he admits, taking her hand, bringing their interlaced fingers close to his heart.

"Oh," is the only thing she can muster at the moment.

Good to know that she's not the only one suffering from uncontrollable heart palpitations when the two of them are in the same room.

"Now, what's the second part?" he asks.

"What second part?"

"You said *'first of all,'* which would normally imply there's a second part to your speech."

"Oh, the second part was that I freaked out. I... I wasn't looking for a serious relationship and all of a sudden, I found myself falling. Deep. Too deep, and that scared the shit out of me. And you were hiding us, like not wanting people to know you're with me. And I get that. I mean—I am weird."

"You're not weird," he objects but she continues at full speed.

"I'm always late, forget myself when I'm focused, my head is always somewhere in the clouds, I always run and bump into stuff—so irresponsible. A real astronaut. Do you use that term in English too, outside of the obvious job assignment, or is it just in Hebrew? And there's a lot more weird stuff you still don't know about me. Like, I color outside the lines, possibly even outside the paper... Read books from the end, put together puzzles in the wrong order. Oh, actually you do know that already—"

"Are you kidding me? I love everything about you! Those things are definitely on the list." He chuckles, smoothing a stray hair off her face. "You are perfect."

"I am far, far—as in light years away—from being perfect."

"You are perfect to me. Please don't ever change. Well, maybe just be there in time for my lab meetings. And make sure to walk me through your complex thought process next time you get mad." He smirks, taking her other hand now too. "Ellie, I know you said Oren had stopped choosing you. And he's an asshole for breaking your heart. But I'm not Oren. I may play the drums sometimes, but I have no intention of running off with my rock band or choosing any other scenario without you in it, Ellie. I promise to choose you every single day of my life."

"How can you promise something like that?"

"I already told you, the way I feel about you is irreversible. Permanent. There are no off-switches."

"And I argued against it."

"You did. But remember your sandwich philosophy? Just trust the magic," he chuckles.

Go ahead, turn her own words back at her...

"And that still doesn't resolve the issue that you didn't want anyone at GERI—except Alannah—to know about me. I hate that you want to hide us. I mean so long as HR will keep their investigation confidential... And I hope people will forget about that stupid post."

"Ellie, I want everyone to know about us. I want to shout it from the rooftops. I had asked you to be my real girlfriend. But you never said yes."

"I thought my brain was hallucinating that. Let me remind you, I was still half passed-out from the fever and dehydration."

"You weren't hallucinating." Aiden smiles, lowering his gaze to the floor in that special way of his rarely smiling self. As if embarrassed to let this glorious true feeling shine through.

"You're just saying it now, to make a point."

"Now who's not taking whose word?" Aiden teases. And when she insists, he says, "Alright, but this is the last time we're asking each other for proof." He rolls up his sleeve, exposing his attractive left forearm. And a little tattoo. Identical to the one she has.

And it doesn't look hideous anymore, not on Aiden. When did this ink-hating man get a tattoo?

"This tattoo," Aiden continues, resting his palm on the left side of her sweatpants, where her own matching tattoo is. "This aleph initial, does not belong to Oren anymore." He pulls her into his lap in one swift motion. "It belongs to me."

34
At the Principal's Office

"Still waiting on that answer," is Aiden's whisper as they sit outside the HR office on the sixth floor of their GERI building.

How can this man even focus on *them* right now when his entire career is on the line?

Granted, when HR called them both, asking for their presence, together, it was a big enough hint that things are looking up. But now, sitting outside the closed door to the conference room—Eleanor feels anxious. And nervous. What if they don't let him go back to work? What if they decide to shut down his lab?

"Seriously? That's what you want to know? Right now?" she teases. "It feels like we've been called to the principal's office after being caught smoking weed and making out in the bathroom."

"I hope you're not speaking from personal experience." Aiden raises a berating eyebrow at her. "And yes, that's what I want to know."

"Can you repeat the question?" she asks playfully. Not because the hair-pulling wait for HR's verdict has messed with her memory. Just because she wants to hear him say it again. She *needs* to hear him say it. Again.

Aiden smirks, and before Eleanor has a chance to blink or just take another breath, he rises from his seat and kneels before her. His new tattoo, the one matching hers, comes into view as he holds out his arms and takes her hands in his. Seriously handsome, ink-hater Professor Aiden Kowalski got a tattoo. For her.

Who would have thought?

"Eleanor Benjamin," Aiden says in a formal tone. His beautiful blue eyes staring deep into her soul. "Would you do me the honor of being my *real* girlfriend?"

"Why Professor Kowalski, I thought you'd never ask. Again." She grins at him.

"Would it scare you away if I told you that I love you?" he asks, a boyish smile on his lips.

"I think I'd quite like that," she says, smiling back. "Quite a lot, actually."

"Good!" he says, pulling her up as he stands. "Because you're going to have to hear it a lot." A small smile is pulling up on his face but his gaze still a bit apprehensive. Eleanor can't really blame him, she's been quite a flight risk.

"No objection here," she says, surprised by how right it feels.

That apprehensive look on Aiden's face turns into a relief, then is taken over by a sort of blissful happiness she hasn't seen on him before. Not until this moment, as he pulls her into his embrace. And as she lets her muscles relax and gives her whole body to the moment, she hopes the HR people inside the conference room will take their time, because she doesn't want this hug to end. She never wants to let go.

"Professor Kowalski?" Of course, they'd come to get them at

that very moment she was hoping they wouldn't. "Dr. Benjamin?" The woman from that last interrogation, still clutching a notepad, gives them an interesting look. Somewhere between get-a-room and this-confirms-what-we-already-knew, but interestingly enough—in a good way. "Please follow me," she instructs, and they do as she says. Only this time, Aiden holds Eleanor's hand, only breaking the contact to pull out a chair for her. And once they're seated, side by side, facing the HR team, he takes her hand again, giving her an incredibly comforting *everything will be okay*' squeeze.

"Do you know why we've asked you both to be here today?" the woman asks. There are several scenarios going through Eleanor's head right now, but something tells her she'd better not share them in this specific forum.

Since neither of them answers, the woman continues. "The first and foremost reason is that we wanted to apologize. We've completed our investigation and concluded beyond doubt that there was no basis for concern. There had also been a complaint against Professor Kowalski, made in conjunction to the social media fest. But this was withdrawn by the individual, who said it came out of jealousy and spite. He apologized deeply and expressed much regret. He also admitted he was responsible for the original post and that the details he had provided were falsified, made up. We are truly sorry for the inconvenience this may have caused."

Inconvenience? This woman has her way with understatements for sure.

"But I'm sure you understand that we had to investigate," she continues, turning her gaze to Aiden. "Your records will be wiped clean and a formal statement clearing your name beyond doubt, along with an official apology will be publicly released immediately, and signed by our team and GERI officials. I truly am sorry for what happened. I hope you understand. Until all details became clear we had to take this investigation seriously. And keep you two apart. Which, I see, did not last long."

"Effective immediately," the second woman says, "both of you can return to work. And I can clearly tell you two are very much happy together. There is no rule at GERI that stops you from proceeding, as I see you already have." She gives them a genuine smile.

"Thank you," Eleanor says, trying to sound professional. But really, she is holding back as much as she can, because right now she would happily jump up and down, and into the lap of her new, now officially not-fake boyfriend.

"And you." The first woman focuses her attention on Eleanor. "Dr. Benjamin, would you please tell your mother that things are sorted out now? She can stop calling us."

"Calling you?"

"Ah, yes. She made sure we knew this was love at first sight," she splits a stare between Aiden and Eleanor, "and that we should get off your backs."

"Reiterated every day for the past week." The man jumps in. "We also heard from someone who claimed to be this drummer." He looks down to his notes. "Oren Hason. He felt compelled to give us an additional perspective on the story, including how tagging his fan page on social media contributed to the noise."

"And finally," the first woman jumps in, "you may also want to thank Professor Harrington for doing the same, albeit not as persistently as your mother. And Dr. Finn Anderson, and pretty much all of your past and current students and postdocs for their unwavering support, Professor Kowalski."

Once they're out of the conference room and into the staircase corridor, away from everyone else—because, really, nobody ever takes the staircase in this building—Eleanor leaps into Aiden's arms and hugs him tight, looping her legs around his waist and kissing all the air out of him, and then some more. This is the best possible outcome for this crazy blunder. Now they can finally put it behind them. And go back to work. Together.

Eleanor's phone buzzes in her pocket. She tries to ignore it, but it seems persistent.

"Sorry," she says, pulling it out. "It might be my mom texting me."

But it's a message from Gillie. "Eloosh, you have to watch this," he writes in Hebrew, along with a link to a video on Oren Hason's official Instagram page. She presses it and turns the phone so Aiden can watch too, hoping it's not something too embarrassing.

"Guys, I wanted to comment about some rumors that have been going around in the media lately," Oren says in Hebrew. "About Ellie and me getting back together." He pauses. "As much as I would have loved for that to be true, this information is fabricated. The photo of Ellie and me that was recently posted is an old photo, taken more than five years ago, when Ellie and I were still an item. Ellie has since moved on, she is very much in love with her boyfriend, Aiden, which you may have seen in the other photo. And I wish the two of them a very happy ending. And Aiden," Oren switches to English, bringing his face closer to the camera as if on a personal note that only the two of them share, "you're a lucky man. In the three years Ellie and I were together, Ellie never even once looked at me the way she constantly looks at you." Then he smiles to the camera and translates the gist of his little speech. "Both Ellie and Aiden are extremely talented and hard-working scientists with outstanding scientific discoveries in their past and their future. A combination that could attract haters and jealousy, I'm sure this is not a new concept for any of you, but I hope we can all come together and show them some love. Now please put your supportive comments down below."

"Well, looks like the trip to New York was worth the trouble," Eleanor says. And from the content look on Aiden's face, he appears to agree.

They continue their way down the stairs, still holding hands.

"Aiden," she says quietly as they reach the third floor, about to open the door to the corridor leading to his lab. "We can take it slow with the GERI crowd. I'll understand if you want to take your time making us... public. That is, outside of the social media realm."

"Do you want me to take my time?" He arches an eyebrow.

"Not really," she admits. "But I'll understand if you do."

"I don't," he says, pulling her into him for another kiss. "I want everyone to know you're mine."

35
Epilogue

It's perfectly fitting that she finds herself in Aiden's lap. He's not a stranger anymore, yet they're at an international airport again, on their way back from Spain, together, where they presented the results of their shared work—their groundbreaking findings on the role of epigenetics in the development of autoimmune diseases, which received raging success and even a tenure-track position offer for Eleanor to start her own lab at GERI.

Their next destination is to visit her family back home, together. Because the entire Benjamin and Friedman clans have been dying to meet the man who rocked Eleanor's world, *her* man. Especially now that they're engaged, something that Aiden kicked off one day when they were both standing at the top of the GERI staircase. It started with:

"I changed my mind. This boyfriend-girlfriend thing, it's not going to work for me."

Followed by Eleanor's shocked and aggravated, *"WHAT?"*

And Aiden's, *"A husband-wife thing, now that's a little better."*

"Andrew Aiden Kowalski! Are you attempting a marriage pro-

posal in GERI's stairwell?!" was Eleanor's dumbfounded reaction. *"Because if you are, I think it's totally awesome."*

"I'm not. This was foreshadowing. I'm planning to shout it from the rooftops."

Yes, he did mean that literally...

Because he had to make a point out of it and do the whole thing in front of the entire Kowalski and Harrington labs, on the roof terrace of their GERI building, just to make sure Eleanor had absolutely no doubt, that he wanted everyone to know about them.

So, here they are. At an airport. Again. Her bare thighs—yes, she's wearing shorts again, well-prepared for the Israeli weather—are resting perfectly on his jean-clad thighs, her side leaning against his wall-of-a-chest, basking in his scent, in his warm embrace.

She wasn't running this time, just fast-walking to an outlet to charge her phone when Aiden pulled her into his lap despite the vast number of empty seats at the terminal.

"Going to keep you right here," he whispers fondly and pulls out a portable charger from his back pocket. "Here," he says. "But I think GERI would survive if you took some time off from emails," he says, making a point with his lips on hers, breathing her in.

"I was actually planning to text my mom," she chuckles, "to let her know our flight is planned to leave on time for a change. And that thanks to you, we're in the right terminal, also for a change."

"Already texted her." Aiden flashes his phone.

"Always one step ahead, Professor Kowalski." She steals another kiss.

His phone buzzes and he takes a quick glance. "Why is your mom asking what food to bring to the airport? Aren't we meeting them at home? Or is that code for something?"

"Uh, no, not a code. And not waiting for us at the airport would go against tradition," Eleanor laughs. "And that tradition typically includes food, even though their house is less than thirty minutes away." He's in for the full family airport surprise.

"Noted," Aiden's lips curve up, looking gorgeous as ever. "Now, smile," he says, leaning in, "your mom wants a selfie."

So back to the epic rooftop proposal—of course Eleanor said yes. Even before Aiden finished his heart-swelling, sexy little speech, because this man has completely transformed the meaning of love for her, and there's nothing she wants more than to spend her life with him by her side. Professor Harrington's new hypothesis may have been correct. Aiden and her together—inside the lab and out – they're unstoppable.

And speaking of hypotheses, there's one Aiden-driven hypothesis Eleanor now abides by: This love between them is irreversible. Permanent. So not choosing each other is NOT an option. And those symptoms? Just her own Aiden-specific *symptoms of love*.

Acknowledgements

Writing the story of Eleanor and Aiden was an incredible experience! Eleanor speaks her mind and spreads positive energy everywhere she goes. She takes making the grumpy Professor Aiden Kowalski smile as her own personal challenge. That, and also testing his self-control when it comes to ... her. While getting into Eleanor's head and writing her character, Eleanor's mood was so contagious! And since I am not known at work as Emma Aiseman the Romance author, I had a hard time explaining the constant smile etched on my face. For Eleanor, nothing—except maybe love—was impossible. Transforming her and Aiden's lives on the pages of this book kept me laughing constantly. I'd like to thank everyone who's made crossing the finish line possible:

First and foremost I would like to thank you – my readers. The love you've given my debut novel – LET IT LOVE; the reviews, comments, shoutouts, likes – they mean the world to me!

To my family - the loves of my life – my husband and our three children – for your love, smiles, support, encouragement, inspiration, and for letting me blow your ears off about fictional characters as if these were real people we see on a regular basis. I promise to keep on doing it! This is where I should also mention our family dog who's made my mouse pad his favorite pillow (and inserting random letters into my manuscript his personal hobby).

To my parents, grandparents, sisters, uncles, aunts, extended family, and close friends, for your love and support, and for learning social media just so you could follow Emma Aiseman!

To my story development team – Isaac, Lia, Anat, Ori, Jonathan, and Arik for the constant brainstorming and your incredible sense of humor.

To my beta readers, especially Inbal, for letting me experience this book through your eyes, it was the closest thing to bringing it to life.

To Julie, my editor – for your encouragement, suggestions, and clever remarks. For improving the flow and readability without changing my voice. I will keep coming back!

To Mitxeran – for the illustration and cover design, you are so incredibly talented and I can't wait to work with you again on the next cover.

Coming into this project, I had no idea that the story of Eleanor and Aiden would become part of a series, but as I was writing the last chapter I realized I just couldn't let this world go. Thus, a series was born. Each book is a standalone, featuring different fictional characters from GERI Labs. Some you've already gotten to know, some you haven't met. Book 2, the story of Claire and Christian is being unfurled as we speak. Christian is a GERI scientist and Aiden's new best friend, thanks to Eleanor—who decided to play matchmaker. Claire is the woman of Christian's dreams, only she doesn't know it yet. Follow me on Instagram @emmaaiseman-writes or TikTok @emmaromanceauthor for updates.

Don't Miss: Let it Love

By Emma Aiseman

Continue on for an excerpt from LET IT LOVE

Chapter 1

Chloe

"Okay, ladies, one more stretch for the day." Chloe walks around the room, adjusting her mic and switching to "Wonderful Tonight" by Eric Clapton to lower the pace. She stops mid-room and drops to the floor to demonstrate a minimized version of a cobra stretch. "Stretching your abs is going to feel amazing after all the ab work you ladies worked so hard on today." She exhales vocally, reminding them to breathe. "You should stop where it still feels good. Rest on your elbows if you need to lower the intensity of the stretch," Chloe jumps back up to standing to make sure no one is doing more than they should. "Now back to child's pose." Chloe counts a few beats to let them recharge. "Great job, everyone." She claps cheerfully as they all rise up to standing.

"That was incredible," Louise says, rubbing Chloe's shoulder. "I love your evening classes so much, Chloe," she says.

"Thank you, Louise." Chloe smiles, taking her mic off and fixing her ponytail.

Thank you, Chloe. Voices, smiles, and hugs appear and disappear as the ladies make their way to leave. There's nothing like teaching an evening Pilates class to get a smile back on her face. Helping these ladies feel better and stronger makes her day brighter every time.

It's not very often that she wakes up with a smile, probably close to never, but this morning was different. A blow to the concrete walls she's worked so hard building around herself, yet it made her lips want to curl up all the way to her ears, and she had no idea why. Thankfully, she didn't need to spend too much time figuring it out because Jimmy was able to undo the warm and fuzzy feeling in under ten minutes. By the time she was done getting ready and out the door, a familiar drained sensation had already been snapped back into place. Who said despondency wasn't comfortable? Walls and fences are much-needed mental contraptions to allow one to go about their daily life peacefully and unpainfully. Why would she want to take them down?

Chloe shakes away the thought and packs her backpack. She turns off the lights, locks up the studio, and runs to her usual stop, barely making it to the 5 p.m. bus. Georgia Allentown's 60th birthday party is today, and Chloe promised to be there on time.

"Hey C." The bus driver smiles at her as he opens the doors. Kendrick Lamar is blasting on the radio.

"Hey Al." Chloe smiles back and plops into the seat behind him. You can trust Al to lift up your mood any day.

"Classes canceled again?" He looks at her worriedly through the mirror.

"No, big party today, Al. Had to leave early." She checks her cell phone. "On my way," she texts Jimmy, who doesn't seem to be online.

"Go dazzle them," Al says as he stops at her station.

"You're too nice to me, Al." Her laugh rolls in a trail behind her as she jumps off the bus and sprints to her old condominium complex, up the stairs to the third floor. They need to leave by 5:30

at the latest, which means she has a generous fifteen-minute window to shower, do her hair, put some makeup on, and get dressed. She jiggles her keys through the old peeling lock and storms inside. Jimmy is sitting on the couch in his boxers, feet stretched on the coffee table, watching one of his favorite TV shows that Chloe has already lost count of.

"Jimmy!" she scolds. "We need to leave in fifteen minutes! I texted you when I left work." She undresses as she runs into the shower.

"I know, I know ... stupid party," he grunts and gets up to put some clothes on. He smells like soap, his hair tousled and still damp. Chloe turns around for a small kiss before stepping in the shower, but his mind seems to be somewhere else, not unusual for Jimmy—God forbid he has to turn off the TV for a few hours. She reappears ten minutes later, dressed and ready in record time, breaking her most recent record of twelve minutes. Jimmy is now wearing his black, and only, suit and tie, looking handsome but a little out of place.

"Is this what you're wearing tonight?" he asks, looking critically at Chloe's black dress.

"Yes, you said you liked this dress," she says tentatively.

"I *liked* this dress. It was true when I said it," Jimmy says, emphasizing the past tense of his statement, "but that was last year. You gained like two pounds since." He looks at her belly. She may have gained a couple of pounds, but her abs are still visible, and objectively, based on the scale, she may have been underweight before. These two additional pounds make her breasts look a little fuller, and she's actually been pretty happy getting some curves. But seeing his disappointed eyes has a crushing effect on her confidence right now.

"Should I change to something else?" she asks, despite it being the only cocktail dress she owns that could look fancy enough for tonight.

"I don't know... Maybe stretch the top part down a bit, show more cleavage. And put on some more makeup, maybe red lipstick," he says. She knows Jimmy loves red lipstick, or anything a bit more provocative, for that matter. Seeing other men turn their heads after his girlfriend somehow makes him feel proud. But she hates how it looks on her, hates how it makes her feel. She looks at her watch. Five-thirty...

"Jimmy, we need to leave now, or we'll be late."

Jimmy grunts again and picks up his car keys from the kitchen table. "I don't understand why we always have to do everything last minute. You knew about this party like a month ago," he says, annoyed. "You should have left an hour earlier to give yourself enough time to get ready and put some effort into the way you look. Your makeup is too minimal. It makes *me* look bad."

"I went for a classy look." She tries to smile teasingly, which doesn't seem to be working for her, not tonight, not ever. "You know how much I dislike makeup on my face, plus sometimes less is more."

"Not in your case, honey." His face has gone sour.

"I was teaching a class, Jimmy," she says calmly, trying to keep her composure. "You know we need the money."

"If you spent less time at that worth-nothing college of yours, you would have more time to work and more time to spend with your boyfriend, like a normal person."

As if spending time with her has ever been on his wish list...

"Well, I am sorry I also have dreams." Her voice betrays her, not sounding as assertive as she would have liked right now. Since she re-enrolled herself in college to complete her long—but not forgotten—health science degree, she's been hearing it with increasing frequency. Why he does not consider her a normal person for trying to pursue a college degree is beyond her. "I wish you were more supportive. You know how important it is to me." She should be able to control her tone by now, having responded to this clause pretty damn often. But she can't, apparently. Her voice breaks mid-sentence, and she takes a deep breath, trying to battle that too-familiar lump in her throat.

"Dreams are okay, as long as you don't lose touch with reality," Jimmy says, also not a new phrase of his, but this one hurts the most every time. Maybe because sometimes, when things get rough, she actually believes he's right.

CHAPTER 2

A Birthday Party

Mrs. Georgia Allentown lives in one of those enormous mansion-looking houses on the way to Sugarloaf Mountain. The huge front grassy area that has been turned into extra parking space for the event is now almost full. Jimmy parks his old sedan next to a red car.

"Look at this Ferrari!" is Jimmy's admiring reaction to the car as he turns the wheel. Chloe takes a quick look in the mirror. Despite the emotional ride, her makeup still looks intact.

"Do I look okay?" she asks Jimmy, winning herself a scoff of disapproval.

"I told you, Chloe, don't ask a question if you can't deal with the answer."

That bad?

She picks up the wrapped box for Georgia from the back seat and nervously shuts the door behind her. This last hour has been so draining, she just wants to turn around, go home, curl into her side of the bed, and go to sleep. But she promised Georgia she'd be there. Georgia has been nothing but supportive ever since she walked through those glass doors of the studio for the first time a little over a year ago, asking if they had room for one more without an ounce of cynicism, even though the room was completely empty. Class had been canceled that day due to snow, but Chloe showed up anyway, hoping someone would come. She really needed the money and the company. Georgia had arrived with her driver, who was waiting outside by the door, making sure his employer made it safely through the unplowed sidewalk.

"I'm Georgia," she said warmly as she approached to shake Chloe's hand.

"Pleased to meet you, Georgia. I'm Chloe. Come on in," she said as she took her hand. Georgia's strong handshake was almost a contradiction to her soft skin, her eyes earnest and kind. *"Class got canceled due to snow, but I'm here and happy to teach a class!"* Chloe said with a smile.

"I read you have the best Pilates class in town, I had to give it a try," Georgia had said, and the rest was history. Georgia became her favorite and most loyal client, taking every possible class combination Chloe would teach; reformer classes, TRX, jump board, yoga classes, private classes, group classes, bringing her positive spirit and attitude with her every time, making Chloe forget about the world outside and think ... even if just for an hour at a time ... that maybe life had more in store for her somewhere on the horizon.

Jimmy takes Chloe's hand, shaking her off her journey down memory lane and slapping on his public smirk. They walk slowly to the front entrance, then ring the doorbell. A man dressed in all black holding a tray of champagne flutes opens the massive door and welcomes them politely.

"Welcome! Welcome!" Georgia's voice appears quickly behind him. "My dear Chloe, you look glorious!" she says, pulling her into her arms for a hug.

"Oh, Georgia, you are too kind." She smiles, feeling her insecurities slowly melting away. "Please meet Jimmy Miller, my boyfriend. Jimmy, this is Mrs. Georgia Allentown, my favorite customer."

Jimmy shakes Georgia's hand politely. "Pleased to finally meet you, Mrs. Allentown," he says, gathering all his charms. He definitely knows how to be that Prince Charming when he wants.

"Oh, please, call me Georgia." She smiles and leads them to a gigantic room decorated with flowers and candles and multiple tables covered in soft golden fabrics, all perfectly placed. The center of the space has been designed as a large dance floor, giving it a fancy ballroom look, making Chloe feel somewhat out of place.

They are shown to a table with an older couple and a young woman who is introduced as the couple's daughter, draped in a bright red tube dress that reveals generous cleavage, the kind that Jimmy can never get enough of.

"I'm Jennifer." She smiles politely, giving Jimmy a quick once-over. Jimmy, of course, takes that as an invitation, introducing himself eagerly and positioning himself on the seat closest to her. Jennifer seems pleased with the attention, and the two of them carry the conversation away from Chloe, who scans the place around, desperately looking for familiar faces.

"Please, let me introduce you to my closest friends." Georgia reappears to her rescue. She links her arm with Chloe's and steals her away, an understanding look on her face. They walk together from table to table. Georgia introduces her as "the amazing Chloe," and "the most talented trainer on the planet." They each get up to greet her politely and respectfully, then go back to their conversations. "One more," Georgia squeals with excitement. "You haven't met my nephew William, have you?" She pulls Chloe excitedly across the room, making a beeline to one of the more central tables, stopping by a young man who may have been following Chloe with his eyes since she walked in – or perhaps it was her wishful imaginative self.

The man rises immediately as their steps become committed enough to show their direction, looking handsome and approachable.

"Chloe, I'd like you to meet William Allentown, my favorite nephew," Georgia says in a celebratory voice. "William, this is Chloe Barrett, the amazing," she announces, and as her nephew takes Chloe's hand, Georgia disappears, leaving them on their own.

"Pleased to meet you, Ms. Barrett," he says formally, his baritone voice wrapping itself around her. His hand is strong and warm, and the touch of it does something to the tiny hairs on her skin.

"Pleased to meet you too, Mr. Allentown," she plays along, his formality makes her smile – or maybe it's just her being shy. "Please, call me Chloe." Something in his composure and bearing makes it hard to look away.

"Please, call me Will." He smiles back, holding her gaze. His eyes are dark and captivating, his black hair carefully cut. He looks slightly too handsome to be real. His charcoal suit is tailored perfectly to his build. This guy definitely knows how to rock a suit... "Georgia talks about you all the time," Will says, and Chloe realizes he's still holding her hand. She pulls it back gently, along with her eyes, stealing a quick glimpse at her table. Jimmy is still in deep conversation with that girl. Chloe looks back at Will, who seems to follow the trail of her eyes. An understanding look appears on his face. "There's a spare seat next to me if you'd like to join our table," he offers, pulling a chair for her.

"Oh, I ... am here with my boyfriend," Chloe responds in the most polite manner she can gather, gesturing toward her table, where Jimmy clearly has his eyes fixed on Jennifer's cleavage again. The thought of returning to her spot near Jimmy for a close-up presentation of him drooling all over Jennifer makes her queasy, but she can't see any other way around it.

"I'm sorry," Will says, and from his gaze, she's not sure whether he is sorry that she has a boyfriend, sorry for assuming she didn't, or sorry for *her* that *this* is her boyfriend. *Perhaps all of the above?* She's not sure how to respond to it either. "Please don't take this the wrong way," he frowns lightly, "and it's probably none of my business ... but you deserve more than that," he says, earnest eyes looking at her carefully. "This is ... not how one should treat their—"

"Girlfriend." The word escapes her mouth before Will has a chance to finish his sentence. As if hearing it from someone else would make it any worse. Her eyes fall to the floor.

"I made you uncomfortable... I'm sorry," he says quickly, although his voice is still filled with intention. But it's Jimmy who's making her uncomfortable. The way he strips this Jennifer girl with his eyes does not leave much room for guessing.

"Can you blame him? Look how beautiful she is."

Is she actually trying to defend Jimmy, or is it the last bit of her remaining self-dignity she's guarding?

Will's lips curve up to a dimpled smile. He's about to say something, but their attention shifts when the music changes, and everyone is called into the dance floor for some slow dancing. Her eyes bounce back to her table, where Jimmy gets up and pulls Jennifer behind him. "Seriously?!" she hears herself blurt.

Oh gosh, did she just say it out loud?

"I do, in fact." Will's deep baritone voice brings her back.

"You do, in fact, what?" Her eyes meet Will's again, puzzled, tilting her head in response to him still bearing that smile.

"Blame him," he says. "He's here with you. And he is totally messing it up."

"You have to admit, she *is* beautiful," Chloe can't take her eyes off them dancing with each other, Jimmy's hands on the small of Jennifer's back. And it's true, Jennifer is beautiful, with her long-nurtured blond just-spent-hundreds-of-dollars-at-a-torturing-hair-place hair, her turquoise blue eyes, looking like a supermodel in that dress... She's probably also the proud owner of numerous sets of fancy lingerie. In fact, Chloe wouldn't be surprised if she's wearing one of those uncomfortable sets right now, a dream come true for Jimmy. Jennifer is everything Chloe is not.

"*You* are beautiful," Will says, making her snort. This brings a puzzled look to his face, as if he's surprised by Chloe's lack of awareness of her own looks.

That's what a few years with Jimmy will do to you.

"Dance with me." Will offers a rebuttal, and somehow getting back at Jimmy feels like a good idea. She takes his hand and finds herself in the spotlight as they make their way to the dance floor. Heads turn, all eyes are on them, probably wondering what a breathtaking guy like him has to do with an ordinary gal like her, but Georgia... She's there too, and her eyes look encouraging, pleased. Will stops to face Chloe. She reaches for his shoulders, noticing how broad and tall he is. His suit jacket feels nice, a sort of fabric her fingers haven't felt before.

"This okay?" he asks softly as his hands come to touch her hips, warm and reassuring. She nods, smiling to herself. No one has ever cared whether she was comfortable during a dance. She moves a tad closer to him almost reflexively. His scent wraps around her, a mix of fresh soap and some alluring bergamot cologne she can't quite recognize. She's pretty good with guessing cologne brands, but this one is probably above the Macy's price range. She takes in the scent with her inhale, relishing it secretly. He must notice that little hitch in her breath, because his smile curves upward a little more, revealing his adorable dimples and perfect teeth. His eyes are focused on her as if she's the only person in this entire huge ballroom. She must be imagining things because that's impossible with so many beautiful women surrounding them, dressed in their fancy gowns ... yet it feels like they are alone.

Something flutters in her lower belly.

Gosh! What has gotten into her?

Is it the wine? No, she hasn't even had a chance to take a single sip.

It must be hunger; she hasn't had anything to eat since lunch.

"I need to free you up, I'm sure," she offers. "There's already a line." She gestures with her head toward the bar where two meticulously groomed blondes in glamorous designer dresses are staring Will up and down from a distance, and Chloe is clearly not a worthy competition.

Not that she's trying...

"There's no one in this room I'd rather dance with," Will says simply, still holding her gaze.

Wow...

Her mind escapes for a second before she catches a glimpse of Jimmy, who is enjoying the proximity to his dance partner a tad too much. The pace of the music changes to salsa, and the scene heats up. It's her favorite kind of dancing, which Jimmy usually refuses to take part in. Will, however, seems quite well-versed with the moves – twisting and turning her, her hips swaying with the music, and she can't help the big smile that makes its way across her face.

She's actually having fun. At a rich people's party.

What. Is. Up. With. Her?

But existing in a bubble can't possibly last long for her... Chloe feels a tap on her shoulder, and it's Jimmy, claiming her back, stretching his neck, and inflating his chest to look larger ... but to no avail. Next to Will, Jimmy looks ... well ... small. Will just nods politely and lets Chloe go, leaving an imaginary imprint where he touched her. She pulls herself away from him into Jimmy's arms, and to her disappointment, they return to the table, skipping the last part of the dance. Jimmy brings his face closer to whisper something in her ear.

"You need to move your hips more when you dance," is all he has to say.

CHAPTER 3

S'mores

The music fades, and the guests are called back to their tables for dinner. Food and wine are flowing; glasses, plates, and silverware clank softly around. Jimmy is back to his spot next to Jennifer, enjoying an extreme surface-level conversation about the weather that lasts way too long.

"So what do you guys do?" Jennifer gets bored and tries to change the topic. Jimmy assumes she's talking business and brags about his last insurance sales position, which he recently lost for not being able to get to work on time on more than one occasion within the same week – but he fails to mention that minor detail. "And Chloe is a Pilates instructor," he jumps in before she has a chance to speak for herself.

"I am also studying health science at—" she tries to squeeze in, but Jimmy beats her to it.

"Yeah, that's her side gig," he says apologetically and nudges Chloe's knee under the table. *Whatever.* "How about you?" He turns his head, along with his body, to Jennifer.

"I'm studying law at Johns Hopkins. I'll be graduating next

year," she says proudly. Jimmy makes sounds of being way too impressed. "Where do you go to school, Chloe?" Thankfully Jennifer's social etiquettes pull her back into the conversation.

"It's a community college," Chloe responds. Seeing how Jimmy's chest deflates, she decides to skip additional information. Why Jimmy can't be proud of her is beyond her. College is college, she goes where she can afford, and she works damn hard to pay for it. And yes, it's been an extremely long and winding journey with a lot of bumps along the road that mostly had to do with life and money, but Chloe has finally been able to move forward at a steady, albeit slow, pace. And now she's determined to get her bachelor's degree in health science, get an internship in nutrition, and sit for the accreditation exam to get her license as a nutritionist, whether Jimmy thinks she can or not. She's been secretly saving for it.

"Excuse me," Chloe says and gets up to search for the ladies' room. It takes a while to find, since Georgia Allentown's mansion is enormous. On the way back, she wanders around a bit, her chest feeling heavy. Opting for some fresh air, she steps out into the garden. Hundreds of soft little lights decorate the terrace, somehow perfectly merging into the star-dotted sky above, giving off gorgeous fairytale vibes. A few people are there, enjoying their wine, chatting away, some standing in small groups, some sitting under the lights or next to scattered cobblestone firepits, each with cushioned outdoor furniture surrounding it. Chloe walks down to one of the unattended sets and sits down with a sigh. The pleasant heat and soft light of the flames help clear her head. She isn't hungry anymore, and actually feels a little sick. Watching Jimmy interact with other women has this effect on her.

She wishes Jimmy was a tad more attuned to her feelings. The sweet atmosphere in the garden must have gone to her head, letting in all those unrealistic thoughts. In this fairytale world, Jimmy would be more in touch with his girlfriend, he would follow her outside, ask what's wrong, spend some time with her, alone. Heck, he wouldn't be ogling Jennifer to begin with. He would pay attention to Chloe, and he would definitely notice if she walked away. But as Jimmy so frequently reminds her, no one is perfect, maybe she should take his advice and stop focusing on what he can't offer. Fairytales are just not what life has in store for her, so why fight it?

"Is this seat taken?" She hears a male voice, not Jimmy's.

"Obviously not," she says, then hearing the bite in her voice, she looks up to assess the damage. Apparently, Will Allentown was the one to notice she'd walked away.

"Ouch," he says, eyebrows colliding softly. "Is everything okay?"

"Sorry, that wasn't aimed at you," she says. "Please sit down. I could use some company right now."

"Yes ma'am." He obeys and sits down next to her. They sit quietly for a while, taking in the night sky, the clean countryside air, and the slow, quiet whispers of the flames as they burn into the wood. "This is my favorite spot," Will finally says. "When I was a kid, I would come here a lot, stay with my aunt and uncle every summer. We used to make s'mores every single night."

"S'mores?!" She feels the edges of her mouth starting to curve. "That's my very favorite dessert! I haven't had it in like ... forever!" Thinking about it somehow manages to lift her spirits up a notch.

"Really?" His head turns toward her, looking pleasantly surprised.

That she likes s'mores? Or that such a simple thing can stave off her frustration?

His eyes bright, portraying the little flames' reflections dancing all around. Chloe has to force herself from staring. He smiles at that. "Wait here," he says and gets up suddenly, disappearing back into the grand brick mansion, taking away the positive air with him. Guests are going in and out, but the garden is mostly quiet, almost surreal. Chloe wonders what Jimmy is up to right now, but she doubts he's even noticed her absence. Her throat feels tight, that lump reappearing, making it harder to breathe or think properly. This has been happening too often lately, understandable given the provocation, but she hasn't had much time to prepare.

C'mon, not now ... not when there are so many people around.

She takes a deep breath, trying to control it. She blinks a few treacherous tears away, and then Will is back by her side, handing her a long wooden stick and marshmallows, brightening up the grayness with every move.

"We're making s'mores?" She looks up to face him.

"We certainly are." He smiles cheerfully. "Making your very favorite dessert and reliving a childhood memory of mine. It's been a while for me too." He slides a marshmallow onto his stick and pushes it into the flames for a few seconds. Chloe follows along. His lips arrange themselves into a childish smile, and she can't help but smile back. He pulls back his stick and deftly slides the marshmallow between two large pieces of graham cracker and chocolate. She follows his moves with her own marshmallow, which comes out of the fire looking way too burnt for human consumption. "I see you like yours well-done," he chuckles, but then breaks his into two pieces and hands her the larger half.

"Thanks," she says quietly, "I need to brush up on my s'more skills. I'm a little rusty." Jimmy resents any mention of marshmallows or sweets in general, especially if it involves her eating them. But at this very moment, thinking of Jimmy does not bring back the familiar lump in her throat, and that feels like a major relief. "Georgia was probably a fun aunt to grow up around," she says, taking a small bite of the hot marshmallow, trying to clean up the chocolate melting away on the sides of her lips.

"Yes, very much!" he says, and his eyes light up even more as he pulls up his memories. "I used to wish she and Uncle Benjamin were my parents. Being around happy, positive people is contagious. I don't think I've ever heard my parents laugh out loud. They are complete opposites."

"I love how accepting and warm Georgia is, and I have to agree, her laugh is contagious."

"She adores you, Chloe!" She likes how her name sounds when he says it. His eyes look straight into hers, saying so many things without using any words at all. "You've changed her life, you know?"

"Me?!" She can't help the surprised and somewhat humbled look that has probably lodged itself onto her face.

"Yes, you," Will says with certainty. "She suffered all kinds of pain before she started taking classes with you. I'm sure she had mentioned that." He studies her intently. "Back pain, joint pain, nothing that conventional medicine could put its finger on, no matter how much money one might throw at it. She used to say that her age had finally caught up with her."

"Yes, I remember hearing her say that, but she was determined to take the lead on that race, and when Georgia sets her mind on something ... she has an amazing attitude."

"You know my aunt well." He smiles, and those dimples appear again. "And then she met you. It was almost like she was shedding layers of pain with every class."

"Nah, it's not me. Pilates and yoga can do that, you know? And Georgia has certainly been taking her training seriously. She's also completely transformed her nutrition from comfort food to a Mediterranean diet. I'm so proud of her."

"Under your guidance."

"I'm no expert. I just make suggestions based on established and proven scientific research." Talking about nutrition makes her excited. "The Mediterranean diet is rich in antioxidants, fresh produce, and healthy fats. It helps reduce inflammation and is good for the heart. I figured if it didn't help, it surely wouldn't hurt, right?" She could go hours on this topic. If Jimmy were here, he'd have said she was babbling again. But Will seems interested – tilting his head to the side, studying her, watching what must be her face lighting up.

"What made you go into teaching Pilates?"

"It's my favorite sport, and I needed a job. The studio offered a trainer certificate, and Tania, my boss, was willing to let me take the training for free if I committed to teaching there for a full year." She notices how Will's eyes follow her with enthusiasm as she speaks, encouraging her to continue. "Helping others feel more comfortable in their own skin has always been a passion of mine." As the words leave her mouth, it dawns on Chloe that she voluntarily lets Jimmy do the exact opposite to her on a daily basis. "I'm also working on getting my health science degree," she dares. Jimmy's voice jumps into her head, reminding her how she shouldn't start a conversation about her no-good college and the forever-taking degree. "I hope to one day get my license in nutrition and open my own business for Pilates, yoga, and nutrition consultation, all in one place. The information out there is so confusing. I want to make it simple for people to take their health into their own hands. And I've seen what incredible impact nutrition and exercise can have on people's health and well-being. I want to help make a difference, even if it's a small one."

"I like your idea! And you already have Georgia's health transformation as testimony," he says, not an ounce of skepticism or criticism in his voice. It feels ... refreshing. "Where do you go to school?" Of course, that's always the follow-up question.

"It's a local community college," she answers reflexively, not bothering with the details of her probably anonymous community college, hearing Jimmy's voice in her head. "The only place I can afford right now, and it's close to where I live ... and they let you take classes at your own pace so I can keep my day jobs," she blurts out, expecting a disappointing or degrading look, like the one Jimmy always has when she brings her schoolwork up. But that look does not appear, not with Will.

"Wow! I'm impressed," he says supportively.

Is he for real?

"Thanks," she says, genuinely surprised. She's just poured some of her heart on an almost complete stranger, and he didn't try to break her or shatter her dreams. Her eyes look up, admiring all those stars one can spot in the countryside. She can never see that many under the city lights. "But I'm starting to doubt whether this dream will ever..."

"Dreams can come true, you know, if you dream hard enough." His childish smile still hasn't gone away since the s'mores. "And there are scholarships and grants." He puts two more marshmallows into the flames.

"Maybe, one day." She allows herself to get carried away with what if, but really just for a second.

"So, you said day jobs ... as in more than one? That's tough. Where?"

Chloe nods. "A Pilates studio and a restaurant called Claudia's," she huffs. "They're very flexible with my shifts, so I can juggle Pilates teaching, school work, and ... life."

"That's a lot." This somehow makes him look even more impressed.

"It's not too bad, and it pays the bills."

"I think being a waiter is the hardest job I've ever done," he says suddenly.

"You ... worked as a waiter?" She doesn't mean the prejudiced voice, but she just can't help wondering how someone coming from a wealthy family like him would end up as a waiter.

"Yes, I tried to make a point." He laughs at the sound of her surprise. "My parents wanted me to take over the family business after college, and real estate is not ... *was* not what my young, bold self wanted to do."

"You still look young and bold to me."

"Thank you. Maybe, but I've wanted to become a writer ever since I can remember. My parents weren't very supportive of this idea, to put it gently." He halts for a second to examine her face, she gives him an encouraging smile to proceed. "They said writing was not profitable. Obviously, they were not familiar with Stephen King or J. K. Rowling. Not that I had any thought of measuring up... So, I took a job as a waiter and kept at it for a year to show them I could make a living *and* write books. My parents hated this experiment. Making a living is definitely not enough for them. But believe it or not, this has been my proudest accomplishment, and I didn't even finish the book." Will slides the marshmallows off the stick and into the graham crackers and hands her another s'more. Their fingers touch lightly, sending a gentle current into her.

Did he feel it too?

"Why did you stop?" she asks, her fingers still lingering on that brief touch.

"I realized that, as their son, there are certain expectations of me... I could see why they'd want me to continue their legacy, and I respect that. We settled on me going into business school for my graduate degree." His eyes have a shade of sadness to them as he says it.

"What do you like to write?"

"*Liked* to write," he says wistfully. "Fiction mostly, suspense, sometimes romance."

"*Liked?* As in you're not writing anymore?" she says. "Because I would love to read." Will's eyes beam at the sound of that.

"Inspiration, I guess... Lost it along the way." He shifts in his seat like he's trying to shove that thought away and, with that, changes the subject. "Would it be too daring if I joined one of your classes?"

She laughs, planning to explain that it might be an issue in a women-only studio. Something from this morning's unfamiliar warmth and fuzziness reemerges for a brief second. But the moment dissipates, and her smile turns serious as Jimmy makes his appearance at the front of the terrace, signaling with a sullen expression and a nervous motion of his head that it's time to leave.

***

"What the fuck was that all about?" Jimmy scolds as he slams the car door behind him, starting his car.

"What was *what* all about?" Chloe asks, struggling to get into the passenger seat with her dress. She should be the one asking him.

"Spending the entire evening with this guy? Didn't know you were into rich boys now."

"Seriously? You were ogling that Jennifer girl the entire night." She buckles her seatbelt and crosses her arms.

"You see how important it is to put some effort into the way you look? When a woman looks hot and sexy, you can't really blame me for wanting to be around her," he says admonishingly. As if openly displaying his lust toward other women in social events, whether or not his girlfriend is around, is a perfectly acceptable thing to do.

"That's not the point, Jimmy!"

"So, what exactly *is* the point, Chloe?" He says it slowly, as if she has issues understanding social cues.

"The point is that you were there with *me*, yet you made me feel like I was the last person in there you wanted to be around. You didn't even let me get a single word out in the conversation."

"All you want to talk about is your failed college studies and your unrealistic dreams. You keep embarrassing me over and over again."

"It's not unrealistic, and you can't say I've failed if I haven't stopped trying." Okay, so it's taking her longer than typical to graduate, but that doesn't make it a failed attempt. She's still pursuing it, still attending those classes, submitting her assignments, studying for her exams, and not failing them. "Slow and steady wins the race, no?"

"Fuck Chloe, you're so naive. Winning races is not up your alley. The sooner you understand it, the better." His mansplaining tone makes her stomach churn.

Who died and made him the tyrant king?

"So, what were you doing outside anyway?"

"Making s'mores," she says simply. Trying to control a sudden urge to smile despite Jimmy's toxic propaganda. "I needed some fresh air, went to sit outside. You could have followed me if your eyes weren't so attached to Jennifer's cleavage."

"Maybe I didn't want to."

About Me

Emma Aiseman is my pen name, devoted to romance writing.

I live in New Jersey with the loves of my life – my husband and our three amazing children (and our tiny yet mighty puppy).

I am a scientist by day – working in the biotech industry. Not because I have to keep my day job, but because I love science, and I truly believe that science and art have a special, synergistic relationship.

I have a PhD in biochemistry, postdoctoral fellowships in the fields of epigenetics and human disease, and have been fortunate to work with quite a few outstanding mentors who have guided me along the way. I am passionate about research and new discoveries, especially when it involves questioning central dogmas.

I am a writer by night – writing is part of who I am. I write because it makes me happy and because I just can't – not write. I've been writing fiction since learning the alphabet, in different languages. During high school, I worked as a teen journalist at one of the top teen magazines in Israel. I also wrote and published a children's book in Hebrew as a young adult.

The first time I picked up a romantic comedy novel (well, one might argue it picked me), that book kept me up all night, put a big smile on my face, made me blush, made me laugh, and made me wish I could read it for the first time all over again. And before I knew it, I was transported back to my bookworm phase, and feel-good romance became my favorite genre. Then came the uncontrollable itch to write something new again! So here I am.

If you enjoyed A SYMPTOM OF LOVE, please spread the word! Your reviews on Goodreads, Amazon, TikTok, Instagram (or anywhere else really)- go a long way and are incredibly appreciated!

And if you miss Eleanor and Aiden already, ONE HUNDRED PERCENT MINE (Book 2 in the GERI Labs series) is coming soon and they'll be making an appearance! Follow me on Instagram @emmaaisemanwrites or TikTok @emmaromanceauthor for upcoming release dates.

Yours,

Emma

emmaaiseman.com

More by Emma Aiseman

<u>Let it Love</u>
A Contemporary Romance Novel
Available on Amazon

<u>One Hundred Percent Mine (GERI Labs Book 2)</u>
A Romantic Comedy Standalone Series
Book 2 Coming Soon